Also by Sharon Sala

The Next Best Day

Don't Back Down

Last Rites

BLESSINGS, GEORGIA
Count Your Blessings (novella)
You and Only You
I'll Stand by You
Saving Jake
A Piece of My Heart
The Color of Love
Come Back to Me
Forever My Hero
A Rainbow Above Us
The Way Back to You
Once in a Blue Moon
Somebody to Love
The Christmas Wish
The Best of Me

HEART BEAT

SHARON SALA

Published by Sourcebooks Casablanca, an imprint of Sourcebooks
P.O. Box 4410, Naperville, Illinois 60567-4410
(630) 961-3900
sourcebooks.com

Printed and bound in the United States of America.
OPM 10 9 8 7 6 5 4 3 2 1

Chapter 1

The day was new, and the sun was in Amalie Lincoln's eyes.

She was driving eastbound on the Tulsa Crosstown Expressway, coming up on a pretzel loop of rebar and concrete, also known as the Interstate 244 and Highway 169 junction, when her very normal day turned into chaos.

Suddenly, the car a few yards in front of her swerved, overcorrected, spun sideways, then overcorrected again, and broadsided Amalie's car. It sent her into a spin before hitting her again, then slamming her car into a concrete abutment. When everything finally came to a stop, the ensuing pileup had traffic at a standstill.

Amalie was dazed, bleeding, and trying to unbuckle her seat belt when her car suddenly burst into flames.

"No, no, no,!" she cried, then began screaming for help, still trying to unbuckle her seat belt as smoke rolled up around her.

She kept screaming and screaming, trying to open the door even as the first fingers of fire were licking at the legs of her slacks, then the arm of her jacket, when all of a sudden, the door came open! She could hear voices shouting, and the whoosh and hiss of fire extinguishers, and then some man's voice in her ear, telling her, "I got you, lady. I got you," and a voice whispering inside her head... *You're going to be okay.*

Then everything went black.

The time afterward was a blur. Amalie went from an emergency room to a burn unit in Hillcrest Medical Center and ensuing days and nights of living hell. Time was measured by recurring debridement, the administration of pain meds, and wrapping and unwrapping the burns, and complete isolation.

It was a week before Dan Worthy, her across-the-hall neighbor in her apartment building learned what had happened to her.

He was an accident lawyer. He knew she had no family and called the burn unit, asked a nurse to deliver a message to her, and said he'd wait for the answer.

The nurse listened, wrote down what Dan Worthy said, and headed for Amalie's room, gowned up, then moved to the side of Amalie's bed.

"Amalie, can you hear me?"

Amalie moaned, opened her eyes, and then nodded.

"Do you know a man named Dan Worthy?"

"Neighbor," Amalie said.

"He says he's an accident lawyer. Is this so?"

Amalie blinked. "Yes."

"He says he just heard about what happened to you, and if you say the word, then he's going to sue the pants off the drunk who hit you."

Amalie chuckled, but tears were rolling.

"Tell him yes and thank you."

"Consider it done," the nurse said. "Oh, and by the way, your next round of pain meds are on the way."

Tears were still rolling when Amalie closed her eyes.

The nurse went back to the phone. "Mr. Worthy, are you still there?"

"Yes, ma'am. What's the verdict?"

"She says, 'Yes and thank you.'"

"Awesome," Dan said and disconnected.

After that phone call, Dan went into action. He had the accident report. The man's blood alcohol level was off the charts when he was arrested, and it wasn't his first DUI. Dan filed a lawsuit on Amalie's behalf against the man and his insurance company for all they were worth, suing for loss of wages, emotional distress, criminal intent, all medical costs, legal fees, and the list went on. He was fighting for Amalie as she was fighting for her life.

The first wave of condolences from her colleagues at the CPA firm where she worked came in the midst of her worst days, and then as she began to heal, they dwindled to no contact at all.

In the months she spent healing, her job had been filled, her so-called friends had moved on, and then ones she happened to see either couldn't stop staring or looked away. She didn't look like she had before. There was a white streak in her hair that had never been there before. From shock, the doctors said. She had pink healing scars and grafts on the left side of her neck, shoulder, arm, and hand, and down the left side of her lower leg.

There was a healing scar on her lower jaw from being cut from broken glass. She didn't like to look at herself in the mirror, but she felt selfish for caring because so many people had worked hard to save her life.

The upside to it all was when Dan won the case on her behalf, to the tune of millions. A year to the day of her accident, he knocked on her door to tell her the only good news Amalie had had in months. When she opened the door, Dan was standing on her doorstep with a bouquet of flowers and a box of chocolates.

Amalie smiled. "It's not Christmas. What's up?" she asked, as she let him in, then led him into the living room.

He handed her the flowers and put the candy on the table between them. "We did it, Amalie. The courts awarded you everything I asked for on your behalf."

Amalie gasped. That had to mean millions.

"Everything?"

"Yes, ma'am. Everything."

Amalie leaned back in her chair, holding the bouquet like a talisman. "You are a rare man, Dan Worthy. We've traded cookies and wine at Christmas for four years, and barely said more than hello in passing. I don't know what prompted you to take all this on for me, but I will be grateful for the rest of my life."

Dan shrugged. "I get paid, too, but I chose this job because I've witnessed the system shafting people who needed help most, and seen the ones with the most money and power get away with murder. The bastard who hit you had already been let off twice for driving drunk with little more than a hand slap, and look what he did to you. They don't change. And the only options left to the victims is to, literally, make them pay. As we discussed, it was deposited directly into your bank account. You are good to go."

"Thank you. The trucker who pulled me out of the burning car saved my life, and now you've just saved my future. I owe both of you more than I can ever repay."

"Just pay it forward, and we're even," he said. "Gotta go or I'll be late to court. Take care, neighbor. I'll let myself out."

November-One Year Later

Amalie Lincoln had come a long way since her accident two years ago and was tired of being overlooked. No matter how many résumés she submitted after her accident, she'd never gotten past the first interview. The moment they saw the pink scars, their expressions froze in the smiles they'd been wearing, and they never looked her in the eyes again.

That's when she decided the only way to get work was to be her own boss. But she was done with Oklahoma. She needed a fresh start, and since she'd never been farther east than Arkansas and Missouri, she started looking for other options, which was not unusual, because Amalie had been looking for answers most of her life.

The day she turned eighteen, she sent off for a DNA test kit from Ancestry.com. By the time it arrived, she was having second thoughts about submitting it. Whoever had abandoned her didn't want her to begin with. Why was she doing this? Then rationale won out. If for no other reason, knowing medical history of your people was valid, so she took the test and sent it.

The results came back weeks later. Like most Americans, she had ancestors in different countries, obviously on the move from one place, looking for something better in another. She saw the irony. That was her to a T.

But she never got a hit from the website, and was never contacted by anyone claiming to be related. Nobody wanted her when she was born, and obviously nobody wanted her now, so she forgot about it. However, Amalie had dreams and a life yet to be lived. It was time to get out of Tulsa, and out of this rut.

Now the holidays were upon her, and with no office parties to go to, and no friends left to invite her over for Thanksgiving or Christmas, she decided to spend the time on her own, and in a new place. Somewhere she'd never been before.

After a little research, she found a tourist attraction she'd never heard of, in a place called Jubilee, in the state of Kentucky. She scanned the website, admiring the shops and the little valley in the Cumberland Mountains where it was nestled, and decided this was it! She loved country music and mountains, and the draw of stepping into a place that not only held onto their past, but had found a way to share it with tourists, seemed delightful. She made a reservation at a hotel called the Serenity Inn for two weeks, arriving the week of Thanksgiving.

Once she arrived, she knew she'd made the right choice. The changing color of fall leaves visible from her hotel window covered the mountains like a patchwork quilt. The days were sunny but brisk, and every day she lost herself within the hustle and bustle of tourists and shops, and the friendly faces of the storekeepers.

She ate Thanksgiving dinner in the hotel dining room along with dozens of other diners. Every day she became the tourist going in and out of shops, watching fudge being made and quilt makers at work. She watched the blacksmith at the forge, and wandered into a store with Native American jewelry and bought a handmade ring made of silver with a turquoise setting. She walked the streets eating funnel cake and listening to fiddlers playing bluegrass music in the square. She went to a Reagan Bullard concert at one of the music venues and caught a matinee performance of a different musician at another.

When she learned the mountain looming above Jubilee was called Pope Mountain, she felt a connection, like being introduced to someone new.

Every day afterward as she looked toward the mountain, she felt something she'd never felt before. A connection—a longing—a sense of wanting to stay, and she began thinking about living here. It didn't take long to fall in love with the concept.

At that point, she thought of work and started scoping out options. The first thing she noticed was the lack of public accountants. There was only one small CPA firm in the whole town. But she wasn't looking for a job there. She was checking out the competition.

A couple of days before she was due to leave, she rented office space in the business complex next to the bank, with a window facing the street. Hired a sign painter to mark her presence in that place, then rented a house in the residential area of the town. On the morning she left Jubilee, it was with the knowing that she was coming back to stay. It took a while to pack up her life in Tulsa and get out of her lease, but she'd done it.

It was just the first week in January when she returned to Jubilee, and when she drove into town, her eyes went straight to the mountain. The colorful leaves were gone, but there was green from the ancient growth of evergreen and pines, and the mystery of it still called to her.

There was a new sign on the window next to the First National Bank in Jubilee, painted in gold lettering.

A. Lincoln, CPA

It was an impressive sign, in big bold letters.

Amalie had been back in Jubilee for a week, knee-deep in setting up her new home, ordering furniture and technology for the office, and when she went to make a deposit at the bank next door, she asked the teller for tech-support recommendations.

The woman gave her a name. Sean Pope.

As in Pope Mountain?

When she heard the name, a chill ran up her spine. It was as if the mountain was now aware of her presence and sending an emissary to meet her.

She contacted Sean Pope via his website, made an appointment with him to come set up the system, then woke up anxious on the day he was to arrive.

She kept telling herself to get over the nerves. She'd be dealing with clients one-on-one on a daily basis, and her appearance was immaterial. He wasn't her boss. She'd hired him to do a job.

Because of the cold weather, and because the office wasn't yet open, she wore jeans, a soft baby-blue sweat-shirt the same color as her eyes, and her favorite pair of running shoes to work.

Her hair had grown out to the length it was before the accident—still thick and straight and the color of dark chocolate, except for the addition of a white streak that had appeared just to the right of the widow's peak. She could have colored it, but she'd made peace with it, just as she had the scars. After a quick breakfast of coffee and cereal, she grabbed her coat, keys, and a tote bag, and headed out the door.

Amalie loved cold mornings, with the chill on her face and the scent of air without industry. No factories. No haze. No burning dump sites. Just the sun rising above the treetops as she drove her red SUV to the office and parked in the lot behind the building.

The back entrance into the building opened up into a long hallway, accessing the other businesses on the bottom floor. The walk up the hall to where her office was located was a distance, but it was well lit and warm, and she counted off the doors as she went.

The first on her right was an insurance company, then a Realtor's office on her left, a travel agency on the left next to that, and her office, the last one on the right, but the first office for people coming in from the street.

The simple act of unlocking the door was empowering. She knew building a new business would take time, but she was good at her job. As soon as she was up and running, she intended to put an ad in the local paper and hold an open house. Free food was always a draw, and curiosity the second.

She turned up the thermostat, took her coat and purse

to the back room, checked the bathroom to make sure the roll of paper towels and toilet paper were in place. She put a new bottle of fresh-linen-scented hand soap on the vanity, started a pot of coffee, and then checked to make sure the small, apartment-size refrigerator was working before going back to the front.

The big plate-glass window gave her a clear view of morning traffic already moving at a fast clip. The mountain loomed above it all. As time passed, she began to feel tense. It was a quarter to nine. Sean Pope would be arriving soon.

Please, God, I don't need to see "that look" again on anyone's face. Not this morning.

She sighed, mentally chastising herself for even thinking about how he'd react to her appearance. All she needed was for him to get her up and running. What he thought about her was immaterial, so she moved on to something she could control.

She turned toward the room, her hands on her hips, and began assessing the arrangement of furniture and the boxes containing her technology. She had a landline installed for business, and phone jacks in three places in case she needed to move the computers around, but something was off.

Maybe if she moved the long desk to the back wall, then moved the small desk to the front, like a reception area? Then she made herself calm down. This was just the beginning. Eventually, she'd figure it out and it would be fine.

Miami, Florida

Wolfgang Outen was a self-made man who'd hit billionaire status by never taking no for an answer and never giving up.

He was a striking man in his midfifties, with a full head of iron-gray hair. He was fit from daily workouts, accustomed now to the finer things in life. He had loved one woman in his life, and when she died giving birth to a stillborn baby girl, he left his heart with her in the grave, and her family cursing his name. He left without looking back, and went out to prove to himself that he had been worthy of her love. And over the years, he made his fortune and his bed, marrying and divorcing a second wife. Then four years earlier, he'd taken a third wife, Fiona Rangely—a hot blond in her late thirties.

But Fiona wasn't just a pretty face. She had a degree in engineering and a successful career of her own, and as far as he was concerned, they were happy. The only thing he didn't have in his life was a child, and no living kin, something he deeply regretted.

A month ago, on a whim, he'd ordered a test kit from Ancestry.com. As soon as it came, he supplied the test and mailed it back.

What he never saw coming was the uproar it caused when Fiona found the remnants of the kit in the bathroom trash.

"How could you do this to me? Why? Why? Am I not enough for you? How could you betray me like this?" and then she slapped him.

Shock rolled through Wolf in waves. Before he knew it, he had grabbed her by both wrists and was shouting. "What the hell's wrong with you? That wasn't a condom in the trash. I'm not fucking another woman. I just want to know if I have any family left in this world."

"Why? Why? Am I not enough? You don't need anyone else! You have me!" she screamed.

In that moment, he was staring at a stranger. He pulled her closer, gripping her wrists tighter, his voice barely above a whisper.

"You pull a stunt like this again, and you won't have anything. You're my wife, but you do not tell me what to do, just as I honor your career and your business and your choices! I am a grown-ass man, and if I want to look for long-lost family, then that's what I'll do. Do you understand me?"

Fiona blinked. She'd never seen this side of him before. But then, he'd never seen this side of her, either. And maybe he shouldn't have. But it was too late to take it back.

Her eyes welled.

They'd kissed and made up, and she'd said nothing about it again, but she'd given life to feelings Wolf knew nothing about, and shown a side of herself to him that he didn't like.

A few weeks later, Wolf was getting ready to leave Miami for a quick trip to Jubilee, Kentucky. It was a quarterly meeting of the board of investors for Hotel Devon, of which he was one, and Fiona had just finished packing his suitcase and travel bag for his weekend trip. He'd been watching her unobserved for a while, still remembering there was a side to her that she kept hidden, when she caught him staring.

She smiled, giving him that come-hither look.

"God, Wolf, you are such a beautiful man."

He responded in kind. "And you, my love, are a beautiful woman. If I didn't have a chopper waiting, I'd take you back to bed this second."

Fiona made a sad face, as if regretting the missed opportunity, and threw her arms around his neck.

"I'm always here for you. Rain check on the sex, and I'll see you in a couple of days." Then she kissed him square on the mouth, lingering just enough to leave him wanting.

Wolf's eyes were hooded as he swatted her backside, and then he was gone. But as soon as he slid behind the wheel, his thoughts went back to the argument they'd had weeks earlier. It was an eye-opener with regards to the woman he thought he'd married, and the urge to check up on her while he was gone was strong within him. With his usual knee-jerk reaction to conflict, he decided to attack and not retreat and, as he was driving, made a call to a private investigator he'd used countless times before. The phone rang twice before it was answered.

"Good morning, Wolf. You're calling early."

"Morning, Jack. I have a request, and it needs to be carried out with utmost secrecy."

"As always. What do you want me to do?"

"Follow my wife. Something happened recently that has led me to distrust her. Dig into her past. Find out if she's playing around. I'll contact you. You don't call me."

"Done," Jack said, and disconnected.

Fiona watched her husband leave, even waving from the upstairs window, but when he didn't look up to wave as he usually did, she shrugged it off to his need for haste and went to get dressed.

She was a biomedical engineer and had her own career and office before she met and married Wolfgang Outen and, despite his wealth, kept working in her field.

A short while later, she was on her way to her office in downtown Miami, while Wolf was on his way to Sutton Airfield on the outskirts of the city.

Forty minutes later, Wolf pulled up at the airfield office and parked. To his surprise, his personal assistant, Stuart Bien, was waiting on him.

"Stu, what's going on?" Wolf asked.

Stu was on the verge of frantic, which, for him, was unheard of.

"The refinery in Sao Paulo is on fire. At least ten workers died in the initial explosion, and several others are in the hospital, and there is talk of some paramilitary group trying to take control of the tank farm. They need you there ASAP. I brought your passport and emergency suitcase you keep packed from your suite at the office. I've asked Zander for a chopper and a pilot to take you straight to the airport. They have your jet waiting there."

Wolf groaned. "What a nightmare. I was on my way to Jubilee. I need to let Marshall Devon know I can't make it. Dammit. We're voting on a touchy issue and some of the investors are dragging their heels. It would help so much if he had my proxy."

Stu frowned. "Do you have the paperwork with you?"

Wolf patted his jacket pocket. "Yes, the agenda and the proxy they always send, in case I can't be there."

"If you can talk Zander into taking me instead, I'll take your proxy and sit in on the meetings and take notes for you, if they don't mind looking at me in the same clothes for two straight days."

"You're the best," Wolf said. "And you and I are about the same height and weight. You take my suitcase. It has a couple of days worth of clothing and toiletries, and I'll take the suitcase you brought for me."

"Perfect! Just sign the proxy and we'll be good to go," Stu said.

Wolf whipped out the papers, used the hood of his car for a desk, and signed in all the necessary places before handing it over. "There's the agenda, too. I'll be in touch once we get to Brazil."

Stu pocketed the proxy and traded bags with Wolf as Zander was coming out. Wolf hailed him.

"Zander, the flight to Jubilee is still on. Stu's going in my place, and time is short," Wolf said.

"No problem," Zander said. "I had everything ready and waiting for you. I'll just load him up instead. Borden will fly you to the airport, and I'll fly Stu to Jubilee."

"Thanks," Wolf said, and without hesitation, the switches were made.

One chopper headed north to Jubilee. The other chopper headed south to Miami International, where Wolf's private jet and his pilot, Toby West, were waiting.

Jubilee, Kentucky-Same Day

The writing was on the wall.

Sean Pope was the last of Shirley Pope's four sons still living at home, and he had no plans or reason to leave. He didn't like the idea of their mother living up on the mountain alone, and since his work was all online or traveling to locations, a home office was his best bet. Although he was an IT specialist, he had recently branched his business into tech and security installations, which kept him even busier.

His older brother, Aaron, was married and working as

an officer with the Jubilee police force, and living with his wife, Dani, in Jubilee.

His youngest brother, B.J., had graduated from the Culinary Institute of America, in New York City, and was working as a sous-chef in a major restaurant.

Wiley, the brother just younger than him, had already moved into an apartment in town, after switching jobs from a security guard at the Reagan Bullard venue in Jubilee to working alongside his brother on the police force.

Sean had long ago accepted the limits of his personal freedom. Aaron had a wife. Wiley had three girlfriends on speed dial, and at the moment, B.J. was in love with his job.

At twenty-seven, Sean had already gone through the dating circus before they moved back to Kentucky. Random dating had long since lost its magic. Sometimes he still dreamed of Molly, the first girl he ever loved. But nobody had taken the relationship seriously, except the nine-year-old boy and girl they had been. He lost her when they moved away, putting an end to what might have been.

He would have liked to have someone special, but he wasn't good at meeting new people. Too many years of working on his own had turned him into something of a loner, and after the trauma their father had caused in their lives, also leery of commitments.

Work was taking him into Jubilee this morning to meet a woman who was opening a new office. He had no idea of her age or what she looked like, and it didn't matter. He knew she was a CPA, and she needed security and a new office system set up.

She'd informed him that all of the office furniture had arrived, the technology had been delivered, and she needed it to be in working order before she could open the office. Compared to what he dealt with in tech support, this was a piece of cake. He just hoped she wasn't the hovering kind. He worked best alone, and he had dressed for work and the weather—faded Levis, a gray long-sleeved sweatshirt, and boots.

His equipment was loaded in his work van, so there was nothing left to do now but eat breakfast before he headed down the mountain, and he followed the aroma of fresh coffee all the way to the kitchen.

His mother, Shirley Pope, was taking a pan of hot biscuits from the oven when he entered the kitchen.

"Mornin', Mom. Something smells good," he said.

"I know you're in a hurry, but everything is done," Shirley said.

"I'm never in too big a hurry to miss your biscuits," he said, grabbed a plate from the cabinet and filled his plate from the pans on the stove.

Shirley poured herself a cup of coffee and sat down with him. "Oh, FYI, Aaron and Dani will be here for supper tonight. Not sure about Wiley. He probably has a date, but he was invited."

"Okay," Sean said, as he buttered a couple of biscuits, then dug into the scrambled eggs and bacon on his plate.

Shirley eyed the faraway look on his face and knew

there was something on his mind. Sean was her second born and looked the most like her father, who'd been Pope to the core. Black hair, a slight olive cast to his skin, eyes so dark it was hard to see the pupils, and like all of her sons, well over six feet tall.

"Where's the job at this morning?" she asked.

"A new CPA is opening an office in the business center next to the bank. I'm setting up security and her network of computers and printers. I'm supposed to meet her at nine a.m."

'What's she like?" Shirley asked.

He shrugged. "I have no idea. Never met her. So far, my only contact with her has been by phone and online."

Shirley pushed the jar of strawberry preserves a little closer to his plate, and watched as he put some on half of a biscuit and ate it in two bites.

"Are you going to be okay here on your own today? I have no idea how long I'll be gone," he said.

Shirley sighed. *So that's what was bothering him.*

She laughed. "Of course, I'll be okay. I'm not old yet, buddy boy. Remember, I started having babies while I was still in my teens."

He just nodded and let it slide, but he still had nightmares of finding her unconscious and bleeding on their kitchen floor, and his father nowhere in sight. Then the long frightening hours that ensued afterward, not knowing if she would live, and months of the public humiliation that came afterward when their father went to prison for murder. Leaving Arkansas and coming home to the

Cumberland Mountains had been their saving grace. Sean and his brothers were overprotective of her now, but with good reason. Her life had not been easy, but she'd kept them safe, and their allegiance to her was strong.

Sean swallowed his last bite, washed it down with another sip of coffee, and then looked up.

"Do you need me to pick up anything in town before I come home this evening?"

"There's a list on the counter if you want to mess with it, but nothing urgent. I can take myself there anytime I want," she said.

"I'll take the list," he said, and winked.

Shirley laughed. The only times Sean willingly agreed to a supermarket run were when he came home with a sack full of snacks. "What? Is your office stash running short?"

He grinned. "Something like that, and you can always call me if you think of something to add to it."

"Since you're out of your office here all day, what are you doing about your other clients?" she asked.

"I sent a blanket email telling them to leave details about what they need, and left a voicemail on my office phone, so if it rings, ignore it." Then he got up and carried his dishes to the sink.

"Just leave them, son. I'll clean up after you're gone," Shirley said.

"Okay, and thanks for breakfast. Be careful. Love you, and if you do go anywhere, just text me to let me know, okay?"

"Absolutely," Shirley said, then watched him pocket the grocery list. She followed him to the living room, then stood in the doorway, watching as he crossed the frost-covered grass to get in the van. She shivered slightly from the chill in the air, but didn't go back inside until he was out of her sight.

Chapter 2

The drive down the mountain was uneventful, and Sean was heading toward the main drag downtown on the east side of the tourist area when he caught a glimpse of the new sign on the front window of the business center.

A. Lincoln, CPA

When they'd spoken on the phone, she'd introduced herself as Amalie. *Ah-mah-lee.* It was a beautiful name. It sounded French. He'd never heard it before. She'd sounded young, but identifying age by the sound of a voice was deceptive. He bypassed parking at the curb and headed for the parking lot behind the bank instead. It was five minutes past nine when he grabbed a large toolbox from his van and headed for the back entrance.

There was one person coming out of the insurance agency, and another entering the door from the street as he entered the hallway and kept walking all the way to the front, until he came to an office door with the same gold lettering on the glass.

The door was unlocked. He turned the knob and walked in.

She was standing in the middle of the room with her hands on her hips, obviously eyeing the layout of desks, cabinets, tables, and computers, but the only view he had of her was from the back—a tall, slender woman wearing skinny jeans and a sweatshirt hanging just below her hips, and with dark hair that fell way below her shoulders.

He cleared his throat.

"Miss Lincoln?"

Amalie jumped and turned. There was a fraction of a second when she felt a moment of recognition, and then she blinked, and the thought was gone.

Sean thought little of the white streak in her hair. He'd seen plenty of women with all kinds of color streaks, but he could have sworn they'd met before.

"I'm Sean Pope. I didn't mean to startle you."

Slightly flustered, and trying not to stare at the giant man who'd just entered her office, she began talking to offset the awkwardness she felt.

"No, no. Totally my fault. I've moved that desk three times in the last twenty minutes, and I still don't know if it's where it needs to be. It's as lost and out of order as I am," she said.

Her simple admission of trying to fit what was into what is resonated.

Sean put his toolbox aside. "Tell me what you want moved."

"Really? Thank you! I can help," she said.

"No, ma'am. I have long arms and a strong back. What needs to be moved first?"

"I want a reception area, but right now, I'll be on my own. As my business grows, I'll hire staff as the need arises," she said. "I was thinking this small desk could..."

Sean was already in organizational mode and began talking aloud, almost to himself. "You won't want your back to the window, but if you put the little reception desk there, toward the middle of the window and facing the door to your office, it gives the appearance of foyer space."

"Yes, perfect," Amalie said.

Sean nodded. "Then you'll want to be at the back of the room, like the boss you are, seeing everything before you, but with a wall at your back."

Amalie blinked and for the first time looked him square in the face.

"Like Wild Bill Hickok, who always played cards with his back to the wall?"

Lord. Her eyes are as blue as the shirt she's wearing. He grinned. "Except for the one time he didn't. Now which desk do you want for reception?"

Amalie pointed, and Sean picked it up like he was carrying a box of groceries and set it where she'd directed, and then they moved the long table to a side wall and put the ornate desk at the back of the room.

"Now for the computers. Are they all the same, or—?"

"The same, but this one has more memory. Put that one on my desk, and set up the printer on the long table. It's also a fax machine. I don't often have need of one anymore, but it depends on the clients I have and how they communicate, you know?"

Sean nodded. "Yes, ma'am, I do know. I get all kinds of tech problems dumped in my lap, and sometimes regarding communication devices that are almost as old as I am. So, if this setup suits you, I'll get to work."

"It suits, and stop calling me 'ma'am.' Amalie, please," she said.

Sean nodded, but as she turned to walk away, her hair shifted away from her face just enough that he saw a scar on her jaw and what looked like burn scars on her neck. He'd already seen the burn scars on the top of her hand, and all of a sudden, he was viewing her in a new light. She was a survivor. And, in his eyes, about as close to beautiful as a woman could get.

But this was business, and so he got down to it.

Amalie pulled one of the padded office chairs into a corner by the window and settled in to watch him work. Every so often he would pause to ask her a question about the layout, but as soon as she answered, he went quiet again. She grabbed her Kindle and began pretending to read, but when he wasn't looking, she watched, trying to figure out why he looked so familiar.

He was down on the floor halfway under a desk when his cell phone rang. She looked up as he rocked back on his heels, checked caller ID before he answered, then watched the smile spread across his face as he said, "Hello." She knew it was someone special from the sound of his voice and was suddenly lonely that she had no one like that in her life.

When Sean saw it was his mother calling, he guessed something was about to be added to the grocery list.

"Hey, what's up?"

"Oh, not much. How's it going on the job?"

Sean glanced up at Amalie. "It's going great. I won't be late coming home, if that's what's bothering you."

Shirley sighed. "Wiley's bringing a guest."

Sean chuckled. "Which one?"

"I didn't ask," Shirley said, and sighed again.

"Just as well. Then it'll be a surprise. Do you need extra stuff for the meal?" Sean asked.

"Maybe another bunch of romaine lettuce?"

"Consider it done," Sean said. "Love you. See you later."

"Love you, too, honey," Shirley said.

Sean laid his phone back on the desk.

"Sorry, that was my mom. A couple of my brothers are coming to eat supper with us tonight, and I need to pick up extra for an unexpected guest."

"You still live at home?"

Sean gave her a look. "My mother is divorced. I have three brothers. We all moved back to the old homeplace with her after our grandmother died. It's up on the mountain. Best move we ever made. I work out of the office at home. Aaron and Wiley are both officers of the Jubilee police force. Aaron is married to a schoolteacher here. Wiley has a girlfriend or three. And the baby brother is a sous-chef in New York City. Mom's had a hard life. Everyone else is gone now. I chose to stay with her. I'm the only 'man of the family' left, so to speak."

She nodded. "I didn't mean my comment to sound like it did. I was just thinking how fortunate you are to have family."

Sean frowned. "You don't?"

"Nope. I grew up in foster care, but the high school I went to with my last foster family was in a disadvantaged area, and some rich dude set up a program in my high school for every student entering their freshman year. If the kids stayed in school, kept up their grades, and graduated without being arrested, they had a free ride to a college degree. I chose to major in business with a minor in math. I like numbers. And that's how I became a CPA."

Sean kept staring at her, even after she stopped talking. He couldn't get over how familiar it felt to be with her like this.

Finally, Amalie frowned. "What? Are you debating about mentioning all my scars, or—"

"No. I keep thinking we've met before. The moment I saw your face, I thought I knew you. The whole time I've been here, I've been racking my brain, trying to remember."

Amalie's heart skipped a beat.

"That's weird, because the moment I turned and saw you, I had the same reaction. And since you didn't ask, the scars are from a wreck. A little over two years ago, I was sideswiped on an expressway in Tulsa, Oklahoma. I spun out into a concrete embankment. Between the shattering glass and the ensuing fire, I'm lucky to be alive."

"Oh my God," Sean muttered. "How did you get out?"

She shrugged. "A trucker pulled me out. It took so long to recover from the burns that the firm I was working for filled my position. I completely understood, and thought I'd just get the same job elsewhere, but it soon became apparent that getting rehired and looking like a slasher victim wasn't going to happen."

"People are shits," Sean muttered, thinking of how he'd lost his job at the IT firm in Conway. "That's why I chose to be my own boss, too. So, besides that weird *thought-I-knew-you* vibe, we've both been judged by members of the asshole society."

Amalie hadn't expected his anger on her behalf, or the bawdy humor, but it delighted her, and before she knew it, she was grinning.

"Been a member long?" she asked.

Sean managed a grimace, hoping it passed for a smile. "Long enough," he said, and then he crawled back under the desk and went to work.

Only five of the tiny cabins at Bullard's Campgrounds were occupied this week, and of the five, only one renter was still on-site. His name was Ellis Townley—Roadie to his friends. But he hadn't come to Jubilee as a tourist. He'd come to do a job. A job he was being well paid to do.

All he had to do was watch for an inbound chopper that would be arriving around noon, coming in from the south. And when he saw it, he was to make a call to a certain number, and when the call went through, say the words, "It's done," then pack up and leave.

Roadie knew there was likely something fishy about it, but a phone call was a phone call. He'd demanded the money up front. It came in cash, which he immediately deposited. A seemingly easy job for a nice chunk of change.

Due to the time of year, he had his pick of cabins, so he'd made sure to choose one with an open view to the south. He'd been outside watching all morning, and it was already past noon. He lifted the binoculars again, scanning the sky. Wherever the hell that chopper was, he wished it would hurry. It was freakin' cold.

He had the number he was meant to call pulled up on his phone. All he would have to do was press the call button and wait for someone to pick up, deliver the message, and his job was over.

Nearly twenty more minutes passed before he saw something high in the sky on the horizon. He lifted the binoculars to check, but it was still too far away to determine if it was a plane or a helicopter, so he hesitated, waiting for a better view. Then as it came closer, the sighting was confirmed.

"Finally," he muttered, and hit the call button, but nothing happened.

He glanced down at the phone, realized the signal was weak, and cursed.

"Fucking mountains," he muttered, walking a little farther out into the field.

The signal was strong. He pulled up the number again. He hit Call, then watched in horror as the chopper suddenly exploded in midair.

Roadie jumped back like he'd been jabbed, then watched in growing horror as the craft began spiraling down, down, down.

"Oh hell! Oh no! What the fuck have I done?"

He couldn't think. He couldn't move. He just kept watching it fall until it disappeared below the tree line. It was the second explosion that sent him running for his cabin. He grabbed the bag he'd already packed, tossed it in his car, and headed for the office to check out.

Roadie made it to the office and came in, stumbling, trying not to puke.

"Ready to check out? Was everything okay?" the clerk said.

Roadie blinked. It took him a second to realize the dude had asked him a question.

"What? Oh, yeah, it was fine," Roadie said, still thinking about what he'd done.

Outside, the sounds of distant sirens could be heard, and then the clerk's phone rang. The clerk glanced down and then frowned. "Sorry, I need to take this," he told Roadie, then answered. "Hello?"

Roadie was watching the man's face, and when he saw him turn pale, his panic increased.

The clerk looked up. "Something happened at the school. They said something blew up. Do you want to leave your bill on the credit card you gave me?" he asked.

Roadie nodded.

The clerk hurriedly printed out a receipt, handed it to Roadie, and then grabbed the keys to the office.

"See yourself out, sir. I got kids at that school. I gotta go."

"Yeah, right," Roadie said, and took off like the devil was at his heels. This kept getting worse. He left the campgrounds heading east, away from Jubilee. Away from the site of the crash. As if his life depended on it.

He didn't know why this was happening, but he knew he'd been set up. All he wanted to do was get back to Miami, pack up his shit, and leave. It was time to hit the road again.

Dani Pope's first grade class had just finished lunch, and were on their way through the school building to the playground behind it, with Dani leading the way.

The day was cold, but the weather was clear, and the children were bouncing with glee as they exited.

Kit Arnold and her kindergarten class were already on the playground when Dani's class came out, racing toward their favorite play areas. Some headed for swings, some for the big slide, and some began playing tag. It was a typical day.

Dani walked up to where Kit was standing, looked at her red nose and chapped lips, and grinned.

"At least it's not snowing."

Kit rolled her eyes. "No kidding. I swear, the older I get, the colder winter feels."

Dani laughed. "Girl, you're thirty-five. You're not old enough to complain about age."

Kit grinned, pulled a lip balm out of her pocket, and swiped it across her lips, then pulled the collar of her coat up around her neck.

"It's Friday. What are you and Aaron doing tonight? Going out?" Kit asked.

"Shirley is cooking for us tonight. I have the best mother-in-law ever," Dani said.

"Thank God mine lives in Virginia," Kit said.

Dani just shook her head, listening absently as Kit rambled on, because she was watching the children. As she glanced up, she saw a helicopter coming in from the east. but thought nothing of it. Choppers came and went with some regularity here, usually dropping off guests at the hotels, and occasionally a medevac coming for a patient at the hospital or bringing one home.

Then she heard a screech and turned just in time to see two little boys rolling on the ground, fighting.

"I swear to my time," Dani muttered. "It's the twins again. I have never seen brothers so at odds with each other as those two are," She took off running, leaving Kit behind.

She got to the boys, separated them, made each of them hold her hand as she began marching them back to the building. They were halfway across the playground when she heard a boom, like someone had just shot off a cannon. She looked around, and then looked up.

The chopper she'd seen a few moments earlier was ablaze and spiraling and spinning downward, leaving a trail of black smoke behind it.

Her heart stopped. From the falling trajectory of the burning chopper, the likelihood of it crashing into the school or playground was huge to likely.

She shouted at Kit and pointed upward, then shouted at the twins. "Run, boys! Run inside now!" and grabbed her walkie-talkie and keyed up the school secretary. "Justine! Ring the bell! Ring the bell to get the kids off the playground now! Start evacuating the school, and call the police. A chopper exploded in the air. It looks like it's going to crash on top of us!"

Seconds later, the bell began to ring, and Kit and Dani were outside grabbing kids off of swings and slides and screaming at them to run into the school. At that point, it became a madhouse. Children were running and falling and stopping to help their friends, and some were frozen in fear and couldn't move.

Dani was frantic, trying to get them all inside when

she saw Lili Glass curled up in a little ball on the ground, covering her head with her arms. Dani swooped down and grabbed her on the run as Kit was herding the last of the children inside the building.

"Hold tight to me, baby," Dani said, and felt Lili's arms tighten around her neck. Just as they reached the door, Dani glanced back.

The chopper was coming down faster than they could run. She slammed the door shut behind her and shot up the hall. She couldn't see her children. She couldn't see Kit, but she thought she could hear the principal over the loudspeaker, shouting something about exiting at the front of the building. She was still running and had just turned a corner into an empty hall when the chopper hit the ground. The explosion was earth-shattering. Ceiling tiles were falling down around them, and glass was flying.

Maisy Eggert, a teacher's aide, was just coming up the hall with a small group of children, running for the exit when it blew.

Dani ducked into the first classroom she came to as debris from the crash flew through the southern windows, through the open classroom doors, and out into the hall, catching Maisy and the children in the middle of the blast.

Dani heard the horrifying screams. She had to help.

"Lili, honey! Get under the teacher's desk. I'm going to help Miss Maisy get the children in here, okay?"

Lili nodded, dropped where she was put, and crawled

under the desk, ghost-white and frozen in fear, her eyes welling with tears.

Dani ran out into the smoke-filled hall, shouting, "Maisy! Maisy! In here!" and began herding the crying, bleeding children into the classroom with Lili. As soon as they were all inside, Maisy began tending to the children, while Dani pulled Lili out from under the desk and into her arms. Lili buried her face against Dani's neck and wrapped her arms tightly around her neck.

"You're okay, baby girl, you're okay. Aunt Dani won't let anything hurt you. Now sit here beside me while I help Miss Maisy, okay?" Then she grabbed her walkie-talkie and keyed it up to the office. "Is anybody there? This is Dani Pope! We need help! We need help! Do you read me? Maisy and I are in a third-grade room on the north side of the building with some children. Is it safe to get them out the front door? Are there any blocked hallways?"

The silence was frightening, and Dani knew they needed to get out now because the smoke in the hall was acrid and blinding. She couldn't lead children into a death trap. She needed to know the safest way out.

Then suddenly they heard Justine's voice.

"Dani? Is that you?"

"Yes! Maisy and I are here with thirteen children. They got caught in the blast. We have injuries."

"Take a right as you go out of the classroom. Proceed to the four-way junction in the main hall and turn right. You can't go out any of the side doors, because all of the other halls are compromised. Your exit will have some fallen ceiling tiles, but they've cut the power to the school to prevent electrical fires, and there are no fires in the building. Proceed at a safe pace."

"Got it," Dani said, and glanced at the aide. "Maisy, honey, are you okay?" Maisy Eggert was pale and shaken, bleeding from cuts on her face and neck, but it was the children they were most concerned about. Nearly all of them had been cut and a few were bleeding profusely. Some were too traumatized to talk. Others were in hysterics. It was to be expected.

"Yes, I'm okay," Maisy said. "So, it's safe to leave the room now?"

Dani nodded. "That's what she said," and then looked at the other children. "Okay, boys and girls, we need to exit the building now, but we only have one way out. Is anybody too injured to walk?"

"We can walk," Maisy said.

"Then everybody please stand up. I know you have cuts that are bleeding, but doctors will be outside waiting for you. Grab hands with a partner and follow me out the door in a line. Miss Maisy will be right behind you. Understood?"

One little girl was bleeding from a cut on her neck and sobbing quietly. "I want my mama," she whispered.

"I know, darling. But we have to get outside first, okay?"

Then another little girl slipped up beside her. "Don't cry, Pammy. I'll walk with you," and took her by the hand.

"Good job, all of you," Dani said, and then opened the door.

The constant shriek of approaching sirens was all they

could hear as they moved out of the classroom, but the moment they stepped out into the hall, the visibility level went to zero.

"My eyes are burning," Lili whispered.

"Then close them and lay your head on my shoulder," Dani said, shifted her hold on Lili, and then grabbed the hands of the two children behind her and started up the hall, with Maisy Eggert bringing up the rear.

Aaron Pope and his partner, Bob Yancy, were on patrol when they heard the explosion. But when they saw the flames and rising smoke, Aaron's heart nearly stopped.

"Is that the school?" Yancy asked.

Before Aaron could think, their police radio lit up with traffic.

"Chopper crash outside Jubilee Elementary. Proceed immediately to location for emergency evacuation."

Aaron hit the lights and siren and floored it.

Wiley was just coming out of booking when he heard the dispatch and raced to the patrol car where his partner, Doug Leedy, was waiting.

"Floor it," Wiley said. "Aaron's wife teaches there."

"Shit," Doug said, and sped out of the parking lot, running hot all the way.

Sean had just finished the security system installation in Amalie's office, and was running a check on it to make sure it was live, when the chopper crashed. The explosion was so startling that Amalie screamed.

"What was that?" she cried.

"I don't know," Sean said, and ran out of the building. Within seconds, he began hearing police and ambulance sirens, but when he saw two fire trucks flying out of town, he knew it was bad. And then he saw the location of the smoke. "Oh shit. Oh no. The school!" he said, and ran back inside.

"I think something happened at the elementary school," Sean said. "My brother's wife teaches there. I need to make sure they're okay."

"Go! Go! Do what you need to do! Your things will be safe here," Amalie said.

Sean grabbed his coat, dropped his phone in the pocket, and pulled out his keys. He took one look at Amalie and then ran.

Amalie's heart was pounding. She couldn't think about children and fire without remembering her own horror of being trapped in a burning car. Her knees were buckling as she dropped into her chair.

"Please God, please. Please don't let that school be on fire," she prayed, then covered her face and cried.

There were already officers on the scene and in the act of putting up roadblocks when Aaron and Bob Yancy arrived.

Seeing the school building still in one piece was a blessing. But the fire behind the building was obviously close, and the first thing he thought was, *what the hell happened, and how many windows blew out*? Were there injuries? Was Dani safe? Were her students safe? Aaron had to check on her first.

"Yancy, there will be parents swarming here within minutes. Looks like the principal has evacuated children to the football field across the street. The roadblocks are up. I'll join you at the field as soon as I know if Dani is out of the building."

"Got it," Yancy said. "Go. Make sure Dani's okay. We've got this."

It wasn't what he'd been ordered to do, but there was no way in hell Aaron was going to stand outside this building wondering if his wife was still alive and in one piece. He called her phone, but she didn't answer; then he saw the principal coming back across the street on the run.

"Mrs. Lowery. Is everybody out of the building?"

She immediately recognized Dani Pope's husband. "Your Dani and Maisy Eggert are still inside with thirteen children."

"I'll find them," Aaron said, and turned and ran.

The secretary was just coming out of the building when Aaron reached the front entrance.

"Where's Dani? Where are the other children?"

She was shaking so hard she could barely speak.

"I just spoke with her. They took shelter in a classroom on the north side. All of the windows on the south side blew out. There's glass everywhere, and some ceiling tiles came down. They're trying to make their way to the main hallway that leads to this entrance, but the building is full of black smoke."

"Which way do I go once I reach the place where the halls intersect?"

"Left. Go left, and watch where you walk," she said.

Aaron started inside, when he heard someone shouting and turned to look. It was Wiley and his partner, with Sean not far behind.

"Follow me," Aaron shouted, and headed into the building, then stopped.

The thick black smoke and the scent of burning chemicals were funneling into the building from the wreck. He turned around and ran back to the front entrance and propped both doors wide open.

Now that it had a place to go, the smoke came billowing out.

"Shit, Aaron. I can barely see where we're going," Wiley said, as he entered the lobby.

"I've been in the building enough with Dani to be familiar with the layout. Stay with me," Aaron said, and began walking and shouting Dani's name. "Dani! Dani! It's me, Aaron. Can you hear me?"

Dani was choking and coughing, and scared to death she was going to lose track of the children in the smoke. She stopped and turned around.

"Is everybody still with me? Maisy, are you there?"

"Yes! We're here," Maisy said.

"Okay, change of plans. We're going to form a chain. You'll hold hands with the person in front of you, and the person behind you, and whatever you do, don't turn loose. If you fall, shout out immediately. Do you understand?"

"Yes, Mrs. Pope!"

She waited, hearing their little feet shuffling as they moved into another formation.

"Is everybody ready? Is somebody holding Miss Maisy's hand?"

"Yes! We're good," Maisy said. "I have a flashlight on my phone. I can see the backs of their heads."

"Then here we go again," Dani said, as she grabbed the hand of the little boy behind her. "Okay, Sammy, we're walking now, we're walking," and started up the hall again, all but blind to where they were going. Her biggest fear was that she'd reach the junction and miss her turn, or that one of the children would succumb to the smoke and pass out.

And then all of a sudden, she heard someone shouting her name, and nearly broke down in tears. It was Aaron!

"Here! We're here! We're here!" she cried.

She heard footsteps. Multiple footsteps. He'd brought help. They were going to be okay! The relief was huge.

Then he appeared within the smoke like an angel coming into hell to lead them out, and it wasn't until he wrapped his arms around them that she gave way to tears.

“Thank God you’re okay. Give her to me, love,” Aaron said, and took Lili out of her arms, then picked up the little boy behind her.

“I’ve got these,” Sean said, and swooped in, swung one boy up on his back. “Hold on tight, son. We’re getting out of here,” then he gathered two more up in his arms.

Wiley and his partner were right behind them and began picking up children.

Dani turned and grabbed the hands of two more children, and Maisy picked up the last one in her arms.

“Do we have all thirteen?” Aaron asked.

“Yes,” Dani said. “I’ve been counting. Get us out of this smoke.”

Aaron took off walking, and the rest followed. Within moments, they’d reached the hall junction. The doors Aaron had left open were acting like a stovepipe, funneling the smoke out into the yard and upping the visibility enough for them to finally see their way.

Principal Lowery met them at the door and began touching little heads and hugging Dani and Maisy.

“We thought everyone was out! Oh my God! You’re all bleeding!”

Maisy quickly began to explain. “I don’t think any of the cuts are serious, but I can’t be sure. They’re hurt, and that’s not okay.”

“What happened? How did you get trapped?” Mrs. Lowery asked.

“I was bringing children back from music class when we heard the warning over the loudspeaker,” Maisy said.

"We were running as fast as we could up the hall to get out of the building, but the classroom doors on the south side were open, I guess from the evacuation, and when the helicopter crashed and exploded, we got caught up in flying glass and burning debris. The children were hysterical, and I was trying to get them back together, but the smoke was already pouring in, and I was afraid I'd lose one trying to get out on my own with them. Then Dani came out of a classroom where she and Lili had taken cover. She still had her walkie-talkie and was trying to radio someone to find the safest way out. Justine heard the call and told us where to go, but the smoke in the hall was so dark and thick, we couldn't see where we were going. If the officers hadn't found us, I don't know what would have happened."

Stephanie was struggling to maintain her emotions. "You and Dani have both been amazing, and this is definitely a situation we would never have thought to practice for. The ambulances are across the street in the football field. Is everybody okay to walk over there?"

Aaron shook his head. "No need, ma'am. We'll carry them."

Lili raised her head. "Uncle Aaron, is my mama there?"

"I don't know, sugar, but Aunt Dani and I will be with you until she comes, okay?"

Lili took a firmer grip around his neck, but the tears were still rolling, and the black smoke was still pouring out the front doors like dragon's breath.

The arrival of the rescuers with the injured children

set off a fresh wave of examinations. Doctors from the hospital were on scene now, and they soon had the children in need of further care in ambulances and on their way to the ER.

Chapter 3

Louis Glass was on the job at Trapper's Bar and Grill when the chopper crashed and exploded. It sent a shock wave across town, rattling windows and frightening everyone, including the locals and the tourists.

Louis was behind the bar when someone shouted, "I think something happened at the school!"

His heart stopped. "Lili," he cried, and raced outside. The dark, billowing smoke was already rising in the air. He ran back inside, yelling at his boss. "I have to leave! I have to find Lili!"

Then he grabbed his coat and his car keys, and left through the back door, calling his wife, Rachel, as he went.

Rachel was putting her last load of wet clothes into the dryer when her phone rang. She hit Start on the dryer, then answered.

"Hey, honey! Are you on your lunch break?"

"Something happened at the school. There was a big

explosion, and now a huge cloud of black smoke and fire. I'm on my way there."

Rachel staggered, then caught herself. "No! Oh my God, no," she moaned. "I'm leaving now, but call me the minute you know anything more."

"I will, honey, but drive safe. We need you to get here in one piece, understand?"

"Yes, Louis, I promise."

Similar phone calls were spreading up the mountain. Parents in a panic to get down to the school. Not knowing the status of their children. The line of cars coming down from the mountain was telling.

There was so much panic at the school that the helicopter crashing had taken a back seat. There was no plan for recovery. It was obvious from the start there would be no survivors from the plane. The immediate concern was containing the spread of flames to keep the school and a nearby neighborhood from catching fire from the burning debris.

For the time being, no one knew who'd been inbound, or how many were on board, or why the chopper had exploded in midair. That would be for the authorities to figure out.

All of the chaos was happening in the football field across the street.

Because of the roadblocks to leave the streets open

for emergency vehicles, parents began arriving on foot, some running, most all of them in hysterics.

Mrs. Lowery had sent out a blanket text from the school that every parent was now receiving, letting them know every teacher and student was accounted for but needed to be picked up. The students were huddled together on the bleachers, separated into the homeroom classes, with teachers and aides at their sides. All of them were in shock. Most of them were still crying.

The injured children were being transported to the ER, and the teachers were releasing each child to their parents as they arrived.

Both Aaron and Wiley caught up with Sean before he left.

"Thanks for showing up. You made the difference, carrying three children out," Aaron said.

Sean nodded. "I heard the explosion. I thought the school was on fire. Never been so scared. Do you know anything about the crash? Was it a chopper?"

"Yes. Dani was on playground duty. She saw it coming inbound from a distance, and then she said it exploded in midair. If she hadn't sounded an early warning, we would have had kids dead all over the place. There were two classes of children outside on the playground, and students in all the rooms on the south."

Sean paled. "Good lord!"

"Another fifty yards to the north and the chopper would have hit the building," Wiley muttered, then tapped Aaron's arm. "We've been ordered to stand guard at the roadblocks until someone gets here from the NTSB."

Aaron glanced at Sean.

"Tell Mom we need a rain check on supper. Lord only knows when we'll get home tonight."

"Will do," Sean said. "I'd better get back to the jobsite. I was working in an office in the business center when I heard the explosion."

"Get the medics to check your breathing before you leave," Aaron said. "And that's an order. We sucked in a lot of bad shit in there."

"Yeah, okay," Sean said, and headed for the makeshift triage area, calling Shirley as he went.

She answered on the second ring.

"Hello?"

"Mom. Aaron and Wiley have to take a pass on supper tonight. A chopper went down right behind the school. Caused a lot of damage and some minor injuries to a few kids. I'll fill you in on the details after I get home, okay?"

Shirley gasped. "Oh my God! Is Dani okay? Were any of the injured from our family?"

"Dani and Lili were suffering from smoke inhalation, as were a few others, but they're getting checked out. Like I said, details to follow."

"Yes, okay, honey. Thanks for letting me know."

"Sure," Sean said, and then disconnected.

After a quick exam by one of the doctors on-site, he headed for his van. He didn't know what he looked like until he got in the vehicle and realized his skin and clothes were covered in a thin layer of soot and ashes.

He sighed. There was no place to clean up, and nothing clean to put on, but as soon as he gathered up his equipment at Amalie Lincoln's office, he could go home.

Amalie was sick to her stomach from the worry of not knowing what was going on, and then Sean Pope walked in. One look and she was afraid to ask.

Thankfully, Sean started talking.

"It was a chopper crash just behind the school playground. The children are all mostly okay. A few have cuts from flying glass and some smoke inhalation."

"Your sister-in-law?"

"She and a teacher's aide wound up taking shelter in a classroom on the other side of the building. We found them as they were making their way out. They'll be okay."

Amalie shuddered. "And the people in the chopper?"

Sean shook his head. "The chopper blew up in the air. They probably never knew what hit them."

She reeled like he'd just slapped her. "Oh my God."

When Sean saw her expression go blank and her eyes fill with tears, he realized she was likely remembering being trapped in a burning car.

"Uh...I'll just get my things and leave you to—"

Amalie jerked, and then swiped at the tears on her cheeks. "No, wait! I have your check written, and everything is working beautifully. I have my programs loading, and you've already shown me how to set the security system when I leave. I'm so grateful for your help."

"Can I email you a receipt?" Sean asked.

"Yes, of course," Amalie said, and went to get the check from her desk.

She hurried back, still wiping tears, and then looked up as she handed it to him.

"One of these days I'm going to figure out why I thought I knew you."

"I'm sure our paths will cross again," he said. "But I promise to be a lot more presentable. I don't think I've been this dirty since I was a kid back in Conway."

The hair stood up on the back of Amalie's neck. "Conway, Arkansas?"

"Yes. We were born and raised there. We didn't come home to the mountain until after Grandma died. Mom inherited the family home and we all moved here with her."

Amalie's voice was trembling. "What was the name of your elementary school?"

"Uh...Ellen Smith Elementary."

Amalie just kept staring. "There was a boy in my class that you remind me of! But you have different last names, so it couldn't have been you."

Now Sean was the one having chills. "Was his name Sean Wallace?"

Amalie blinked. "Yes, but how would you—"

Sean sighed. "That was my name, before we changed it to my mother's maiden name."

"Why would you—"

"My father was a habitual abuser. All of our lives. Nearly four years ago, he beat my mother so badly we thought she would die, then he left the house in a drug-filled high and murdered two people he didn't even know. Mom divorced him, but it didn't matter. We were still the killer's family, and suffered the consequences. We changed our last name to Mom's maiden name and came back to Jubilee, where she was born. We live in the house she grew up in. Our ancestor founded this town. Pope Mountain is named for him."

Amalie was in shock. The only person who'd ever stood up for her, and eighteen years later, their paths crossed again!

"Do you remember some mean boys catching a little girl and putting gum in her hair out on a school playground?"

Sean frowned, thinking back, remembering how long he'd been trying to catch her eye, and how shy she'd been. "Yes, I remember but—"

"That was me," she said.

Sean was in shock, and then he frowned. "But they called you Molly."

"That was my foster mother's fault. She thought Amalie was too fancy for a kid nobody wanted."

Sean was beaming. "Oh my God! I would hug you hello, but I'm so filthy I can barely stand myself."

Amalie sighed. "You were my knight in shining armor. You gave two boys a black eye and the third one a bloody nose before the teacher stopped you."

Sean's breath caught. Her eyes…they were drowning in unshed tears.

"I got suspended from school for the rest of the week, and when I came back, you were gone. I was devastated." he said.

Amalie's expression went blank.

"My foster family cut off most of my hair to get rid of the gum and then turned me back to the state. Said I was causing trouble for them. The next foster family I wound up with lived in Eureka Springs, and the one after that was in Bentonville. My last foster family was in Little Rock. I graduated high school there."

Sean was a little bit in shock.

"Fate is a trickster. We rarely see what's coming, and it's almost always something we didn't expect. Today has been a day of shock and of surprises, and you might be the biggest one of all." Then he looked down at himself. "I'm something of a mess, but I would love to see you again when we have time to catch up. If you don't, then I totally understand, but I—"

"I would love that. Call me," Amalie said.

Sean smiled. "Yes, ma'am. It will be my pleasure. I always thought you were pretty, but you grew up beautiful, and I'm sorry I missed that." He grabbed his toolbox and walked out the door.

Amalie didn't know whether to laugh from the joy of

this unexpected reunion, or cry because he'd just called her beautiful. But she went home with a bounce in her step and joy in her heart. Something she hadn't had in a long, long time.

Shirley nearly fainted when she saw Sean walk into the house.

"Sean! Son! What on earth?"

"I'm not hurt, Mom. It's just smoke, soot, and ashes from the crash site. It funneled into the school through the broken windows. It was nearly impossible to see how to get out, which is how Dani and Maisy and some of the children got trapped. We went in to help lead them out."

"We, who?" Shirley asked.

"Me, Aaron, Wiley, and his partner. The rest of the officers were dealing with traffic, emergency vehicles, and roadblocks. Everybody got out okay. A few kids were cut by flying glass from the explosion that happened when the chopper hit the ground, and all of them had some degree of smoke inhalation. Lili was one of the kids taken to the hospital, but she wasn't injured. Just suffering from smoke inhalation and scared to death, as were they all, but can we save the rest of the questions until after I clean up?"

"Yes, yes, I'm sorry, darling. Go do what you need to do," she said.

"I'm going to undress in the utility room and stuff everything I'm wearing into the washer, and set my boots on the back porch to air out, so I'm coming back through the house commando. Close your eyes."

Shirley laughed. "I'll bring you a big bath towel to preserve your dignity. How's that?"

Sean grinned. "Probably the better plan. Thanks."

He went one direction, while Shirley went another. He was still taking off his clothes when she laid the bath towel on the washer and left him to it.

While Sean's homecoming was fairly calm, the same could not be said for the parents bringing their children home from the school. Even the ones who had not been injured in any way were traumatized and shaken. Some couldn't stop crying. Many didn't want to go to school again, and the ones who'd been taken to the hospital for oxygen treatments were sent home with their cuts stitched and bandaged, afraid to close their eyes.

It was understood that the elementary school would be shut down for a considerable period of time to repair and replace that which had been damaged or broken, and the crash site cleared of all debris. But the horror of the day slowly morphed into gratitude and relief.

Michael Devon, the co-owner and manager of Hotel Devon, was on his way down the hall to the conference room to meet his dad, Marshall, when the crash occurred.

He was on the fourth floor with a bird's-eye view of Jubilee when he happened to glance out the wall of windows and saw a burning chopper falling from the sky. It fell out of sight, and then seconds later, a ball of fire and smoke shot up into the air, and he knew the helicopter had hit the ground.

He knew Wolfgang Outen was due in for the meeting and had yet to arrive. Horrified, he immediately called the police chief, Sonny Warren, on his cell phone to alert him to possible identities.

Sonny saw the caller ID and answered, even as he was running out the door.

"Hello."

"Chief, I know this is a hell of a time for a phone call, but I was on the fourth floor of the hotel when I saw a chopper falling. It was on fire before it crashed. And I might know who was onboard. Wolfgang Outen is one of the hotel's investors. There's a board meeting scheduled for one o'clock today, and he's not here."

"Thanks, Michael. I'm sorry for whoever it is, but you've given us a head start on possible identification."

Sonny disconnected, and then so did Michael, but he was sick to his stomach, and after Outen failed to show, he delivered the ugly news to the waiting board members.

A tentative identification of both victims came late in the day, when a pilot and chopper were reported missing after losing contact. The chopper belonged to a Zander Sutton, a commercial pilot out of Miami. He'd filed a flight plan early the same morning, bound for Jubilee, Kentucky, with one other soul on board—a man named Wolfgang Outen.

Their identities were assumed, but authorities would have to wait for DNA results for definitive confirmation. However, coupled with the flight plan and Michael Devon's report of a missing man, it was evidence enough to notify the next of kin.

Fiona Outen left the office a little early to avoid the Friday nightmare of weekend traffic and was already home having a cocktail by the pool when the housekeeper came out of the home, flanked by two men in dark suits.

"Mrs. Outen, these gentlemen asked to speak to you."

Fiona set her drink aside and stood. "Thank you, Dee. Gentlemen, how can I help you?"

"Mrs. Outen, we're from the NTSB. We're sorry to tell you, but there was a chopper crash just outside of Jubilee, Kentucky, a short distance from an elementary school. Your husband and the pilot were listed as the sole passengers, and there were no survivors."

Fiona staggered in disbelief. "No! No, please no! This can't be happening," she cried, and then burst into tears.

"Maybe it's best if you come inside," they said, and led her back into the house, sobbing and stumbling as she went.

They got her settled in the living room, and after a few minutes of hysteria, she finally pulled herself together enough to hear them out.

"I don't know what to ask. What happened? Oh my God, I can't believe this is real," she wailed, and set off a fresh set of tears.

One of the men began to speak.

"We don't have details, but there were reports from witnesses on the ground that the plane exploded in midair. It was already burning before it hit the ground."

Fiona gasped. "You said it crashed near a school? Please tell me the children weren't hurt."

"The explosion damaged the building. Some of the children didn't get evacuated in time, but their injuries seem to be minor."

Fiona covered her face and leaned forward, rocking where she sat. "Thank God." Then she looked up at them with tear-filled eyes. "Would he have suffered? Would he have been alive when it was on fire? I can't bear to think that he suffered."

"We'll have more answers after the autopsies. We're so sorry for your loss. Is there anyone we can call to come be with you at this time?"

Fiona shuddered. "I'll make the calls, and I have Miss Dee." Then another thought occurred. "How will I claim his body? I don't know what to do."

"You will be contacted in due course."

Fiona nodded...and then frowned. "Wait... You said the plane exploded in the air. Does that mean mechanical failure or...?"

"There is a team from NTSB on-site. They'll begin their investigation tomorrow. We'll know more later. Here's my card. If you have further questions, feel free to call this number."

Fiona's hand was shaking as she reached for the card, then summoned the housekeeper.

"Dee, would you show the men out? I need to make some calls."

"Yes, ma'am," Dee said, and walked the men back through the house and saw them out, then came hurrying back. "I'm so sorry, ma'am. I'm so sorry. Can I get you anything? Should I call your doctor? What can I do to help?"

"Bring me a whiskey on ice, and make it a double. This is a nightmare. A fucking nightmare. I can't believe he's gone."

As soon as Dee brought her drink, Fiona took it up to her room, downed it with a sleeping pill, then called Wolf's office, as well as Arnie Walters, the company lawyer, then took herself to bed.

The crash site investigators from the NTSB arrived in Jubilee just before dark, notified the local authorities they would be at the crash site by daybreak, and checked in at Hotel Devon.

Chief Warren, in turn, notified the officers he had assigned to guard duty that the investigators would be on scene early and to keep the school and crash site cordoned off.

As far as Amalie Lincoln was concerned, today had been a day of progress and revelations. Her office and security systems were in place. Life had brought her full circle to a childhood friend she thought she'd never see again, and he'd promised her dinner.

But by the time she locked up the office and headed to her car, she was exhausted from the emotional turmoil. She'd been neglecting her own comforts to get the office in shape, and now there weren't enough groceries in her house to have breakfast tomorrow. Instead of going straight home, she headed for the supermarket.

She pulled into the parking lot with a mental note of things she needed, and went inside. It was crowded, but it quickly became apparent that the chopper crash and the damage and trauma at the elementary school were the topics of conversation.

People were huddled in little groups down every aisle she went, talking about the disaster. Some were parents, reassuring their friends that their children were okay. Others were friends or families of teachers and firemen, or the police. And that's when Amalie realized that beneath this huge tourist attraction, there was a small-town vibe of the people who lived here. One day, she hoped to be one of those people, looked upon as a resident of Jubilee.

She maneuvered her way up and down the aisles, ignoring curious glances and the double takes when they saw the ghost streak in her hair and then the scars. All she wanted tonight was food in the house.

Cameron and Rusty Pope were unusually quiet at the supper table. Their two-year-old toddler, Eric Michael, a.k.a. Mikey, was making enough noise for all of them. He was at the *I do it myself* stage and was banging his spoon on the tray of his high chair, rhythmically beating his green beans to a pulp.

Ghost, their white oversized German shepherd, was wearing the flying pulp that hadn't fallen on the floor and giving Cameron pitiful, imploring looks. Ghost was Mikey's sidekick in all things, and food slinging was the cross the dog stoically bore.

Cameron sighed. He knew what was bothering Rusty. The same thing that had given him a kick in the gut when he heard. But for the grace of God, that chopper would have crashed into the school.

Lili Glass was his niece. Rachel was his sister. She had called them from the ER to tell them what had happened, and how Dani had sounded the warning that saved them all, and then the officers who went in to help lead out the ones who'd been trapped were his friends and his people. But for them, Lili might have died today. One day, their son would be going to school, and they would have to trust other people to keep him safe.

Rusty's years of undercover service in the FBI made her immediately suspicious when she heard the news. Planes don't just blow up in midair. Neither do helicopters. They can catch on fire. And the engines can fail, and the plane can begin to lose altitude. But in midair, when something explodes, the first thing they look for is a bomb.

She leaned over to wipe green beans off Mikey's fingers before he shoved them in his hair, and then looked up at Cameron.

"I'm going to be curious as to who was onboard that chopper," she said.

"You think it's a bomb, don't you?"

"Short of a missile shooting it down in midair, you know it was. Somebody in that chopper was the target. If there was something onboard they wanted, they wouldn't have blown it up. That was an annihilation, and it almost took the whole damn school with it."

Then Mikey wailed when the spoon slipped out of his grubby little fingers and flew across the room.

Ghost crawled beneath the dining table.

Rusty sighed.

Cameron laughed.

"I'll clean up the dog and the floor. You get the kid and the high chair."

Rusty sighed. "Thank you."

Cameron cupped the side of her face. "We made him together. We'll raise him together."

Shirley Pope's plans for a festive family evening had been sidelined, but the food wasn't going to waste. She just made less of it and did without the list of groceries Sean didn't get to fill. She also talked nonstop all the way through the meal, quizzing Sean about the events of his day. He'd already been through the school rescue twice and decided to shift the subject.

"In spite of the unexpected delay, I finished up on the job in town and, in the process, ran into an old school friend."

Shirley paused and glanced up. "Really? Here? In Jubilee? Who in the world was it?"

Sean got up to refill their iced tea glasses, talking as he worked.

"Mom, do you remember that elementary school we went to back in Conway?"

"You mean Ellen Smith Elementary? Yes, of course I remember it. All four of you went there."

"Remember that time I got a week of suspension for fighting?"

Shirley frowned. "Yes. Something about them bullying a little girl in your class, wasn't it?"

Sean nodded. "Yes. Well, the woman I did the work for today turned out to be that same little girl, all grown up. Her name is Amalie Lincoln."

"Good grief! What a small world," Shirley said. "Did she recognize you, or did you recognize her?"

"We both kind of recognized each other." He paused, forked another bite of cake, and popped it in his mouth.

Shirley waited, and when he kept eating cake, she sighed. "And?"

Sean pushed his plate aside and rocked back in his chair.

"Did you know anything about her at the time?" he asked.

"Nothing I can remember now. You tell me," Shirley said.

"I found out today that she was a foster kid. She told me her foster parents were angry about the incident, cut off all her hair, then told DHS they couldn't keep her anymore because she was causing trouble and gave her back to the state. I never saw her again and found out today it's because they took her away. She lived her whole childhood in foster homes."

Shirley's eyes welled. "Bless her heart. So, she's a CPA now?"

He went on to explain where Amalie had been living, and then the accident and the scars, and that moving here was her way of starting over and being her own boss.

"Are the scars that bad?" Shirley asked.

"I think they look worse to her than they do to other

people. By the time the day was over, I didn't even see them anymore. I just saw her. She's pretty. And really smart. And I asked her if I could take her to dinner some evening."

Shirley smiled. "That's about the best news I've heard all day. Just don't drag your feet and wait too long to ask. That kind of stuff weighs heavy on a woman's heart... being asked out and then getting...getting...spooked? Is that the right word?"

Sean grinned. "Ghosted. The word is and don't worry. After all the slap downs our family had back in Conway, I wouldn't do that to anyone."

"Okay then," Shirley said. "Have you finished eating?"

"Yes, ma'am. I'll clear the table and put up the left-overs. You can load the dishwasher. Then I'm going to bring up some more firewood in case it snows tonight. Hard to get a fire to catch when thc wood is wet."

Shirley glanced out the window. "You go do the fire-wood now. I'll do dishes. It's going to be dark before you know it."

"Okay, and thanks for supper. I won't be long," he said, and went to get his work coat and gloves.

Principal Lowery didn't leave the hospital that evening until the last child had been released, and then she went home. Her husband met her at the door. Stephanie fell into his arms, sobbing, finally free to let go of her emotions and weep for the shock and horror she'd gone through, feeling responsible for everything when, in fact, nothing had been her fault.

Chapter 4

Maisy Eggert had been treated for smoke inhalation and cuts on her face and neck, and kept thinking how blessed they'd been to come out of this alive. If it hadn't been for Dani Pope seeing the chopper explosion and realizing the trajectory of the crash, children would have died.

Her husband, Duane, was a pipe fitter and was laying pipeline two states away. She hadn't seen him in over a month. He knew nothing of what had been happening, but she was cold and couldn't quit shaking, and she needed to hear his voice.

She sat down on the sofa and called him, but the moment he answered, she came undone and started sobbing.

The utter devastation in her voice scared Duane senseless, and then she began talking, telling him everything, from the frantic message over the intercom to trying to get the kids from the music class out of the building and getting caught in the blast from the debris when the chopper finally crashed.

"Oh my God, honey! Are you okay? Were you injured?" he asked.

"A few cuts and too much smoke. I'm going to be fine."

"You said it was already on fire before it hit the ground?" Duane asked.

"Yes. Dani had seen the chopper coming in a few minutes before, then heard an explosion and looked up. The chopper blew up in the air. It was on fire before it crashed."

"Jesus, honey. That sounds suspicious."

"I know. The NTSB will be investigating. The police have guards on the site. That's all I know," she said.

"Did you go to the ER?"

"Yes, along with Dani Pope and thirteen students. They gave me oxygen for the smoke inhalation and picked the glass particles out of my face and neck. I'll sleep in and take it easy for a few days. School won't reopen until repairs have been made, and they're pretty extensive to the south side of the building and hallways. I called because I needed to hear your voice."

Duane Eggert swallowed past the lump in his throat.

"I can't get over it. I was sitting in a trailer eating lunch when you nearly died. Do you need me to come home? I'll do it in a heartbeat."

"No, no. I'm good. I just needed to tell you, that's all."

"I love you, Maisy. Forever and a day, sugar. I'll be home in about a week. Stay warm. Stay safe."

"Love you, too. Be safe. I'll see you soon," Maisy said, and ended her call.

She sat staring at the darkened TV screen, at the thin layer of dust on the tables, and then made herself get up and find something to eat. Maybe she'd heat up a can of soup. Something she didn't have to cook. She needed something warm in her belly to stop the shaking.

Aaron went off duty the moment Dani was taken to the hospital. He sat beside her in the ER while they gave her oxygen for smoke inhalation, then loaded her up in his car and took her home, and then the second the door closed behind them, Dani burst into tears.

Aaron reached for her, hugging her over and over as he kept praising her until she was able to pull herself together.

"You are a real hero. Both you and Maisy faced hell today and held it together for those kids. I'm proud of you, baby, so proud, but I've never been so scared. We all heard the explosion and saw the smoke at the same time we began getting info from the PD. I couldn't think of anything but needing you to be safe."

Dani kept sobbing. "I thought the chopper was going to hit the school. I thought we wouldn't get the kids off the playground in time. Then Lili just curled herself up into a ball on the ground and wouldn't move. I grabbed her and ran. I didn't think we'd get into the building before the chopper crash. And then Maisy and her kids got caught in the blast, and they were screaming and screaming." Her voice broke, and she buried her face against the front of Aaron's coat.

"But you did it, baby. You. Your quick reactions saved them. Saved every kid that would have been in those rooms. I have never been so scared in my life, seeing that smoke and thinking it was the school that had exploded."

"If the four of you had not come to our rescue, I don't think we would have made it out. We were choking. We couldn't breathe, and we couldn't tell where we were."

Aaron hugged her again. "Wherever you are, whatever trouble you're in, always know I will find you. I will always find you."

Dani went limp in his arms.

"I'm so tired. I look like hell. I stink to high heavens, and I want this smell off of me."

Aaron stepped back and cupped her face.

"At this moment, you are most beautiful in my eyes, and I don't smell any better. Strip, honey. I'll get you in the shower and tend to our clothes."

"I don't think washing them is going to work," Dani muttered.

"I know. I'll bag them and put them in the garage and drop them off at the cleaners on the way to work tomorrow, okay?"

She nodded, unzipped and unbuttoned, and shed everything she was wearing, then headed to their bedroom.

Aaron was right behind her. He closed the lid on the toilet, then sat her on it while he started the shower. As soon as the water was warm, he helped her into the stall.

"Are you going to be okay until I get back?"

She nodded, then walked under the spray and dropped her head, letting the water sluice over her entire body.

Aaron ran to bag up her clothes, added his to it, and then left the bag in the garage. When he got back to the bathroom, Dani hadn't moved. He grabbed a washcloth and slipped into the shower with her, poured a dollop of shampoo into his hand, and then began washing her hair.

Her shoulders were shaking. She was crying again.

"It's okay, honey. Me and you. All the way," he said.

Sean had carried a half rick of wood up to the back porch and then brought an armload into the house and left it by the fireplace.

He could hear the water running in his mother's bedroom and guessed she was settling in for one of her long soaks in the tub. He kicked off his boots and left them in the kitchen, grabbed a beer from the refrigerator, and went into the living room and turned on the TV. He was still thinking about the crash and the teachers and the kids as he took a quick sip, then hit Mute on the TV because he didn't want the noise.

They'd all been through hell today. There would be children crying in the night, unable to sleep or waking up from nightmares, and there would be parents holding each other tight in their beds, grateful for the grace that had been shown on their families.

Then Amalie's face slid through his mind.

He couldn't get over the randomness of seeing her again and knowing she was living here now. Her story was heartbreaking, and yet somehow, she'd pulled herself up and out of it, all on her own.

He and his mother and brothers had gone through hell, too. But he and his brothers had always known their mother loved them and had their backs.

Amalie was something special, and this full-circle moment they'd had today felt right, like he'd been given something he shouldn't ignore. He promised her dinner. He was calling her tomorrow.

He sent Aaron and Wiley a text, hoping they were both okay, and then put the phone aside, went to the kitchen to get a bag of pretzels, and came back eating them as he went.

He'd just sat back down when his phone rang. He saw caller ID and was smiling as he answered.

"Hey, little brother! How goes it?" Sean asked.

"I'm homesick," B.J. said. "I just wanted to hear your voice. Is everyone okay? I sent Mom a text, but she didn't answer."

"She's in the tub," Sean said.

B.J. chuckled. "Oh, right! That explains it."

"Are you okay? How do you like being a pastry chef?"

"I'm a sous-chef. It's a far cry from being head chef, but I'm absorbing everything and loving it. One thing I know I'm never going to be is an asshole chef. So far, most of them are. I don't know why, but I do not respond well to shouting."

Sean laughed. "Just don't hit him. You'll hurt him," he said, then heard B.J.'s chuckle in his ear.

"You have no idea. When I left, I guess I wasn't through growing. As of last week when I went to the gym, I am officially taller than all of you."

Sean gasped. "Are you kidding me? Are you taller than Cameron?"

"I don't know how tall Cameron is, but at the moment, I am six foot seven. I think my size is part of the reason the asshole chef never yells at me directly. Just at the whole kitchen in general."

Sean grinned. "Mom is going to be over the moon."

"Don't tell her," B.J. said. "I want to surprise her."

"Are you coming home anytime soon?"

"Easter. I've already put in the request for a week off. I haven't been home since Aaron and Dani got married, and I haven't missed one day of work since I started. They couldn't deny me the time off, because they knew I'd just quit. Finding sous-chef jobs is easy up here."

"Oh man, that's awesome, little brother. I can't wait to see you. It's just me and Mom here, now. Wiley moved into Jubilee after he quit the security guard job and went to work for the PD with Aaron."

"Yeah, I knew that much. We text now and then. Oh, one of the reasons I was calling tonight. I caught the tail end of a story on national news about a chopper crash in Jubilee. What happened?"

"Oh hell, little brother. It was pure chaos," and then Sean began to tell him the whole story. The only thing he didn't mention was meeting Amalie.

"Damn, Sean. What a nightmare. The news anchor

said there were reports that one of the men on board was Wolfgang Outen," B.J. said.

"I don't know who he is," Sean said.

"He attended a big dinner at our restaurant about a year ago. Big imposing guy. Oh...and a billionaire, to boot."

"Really? So you're rubbing shoulders with the upper class now," Sean said.

"Hardly. I'm one of the nobodies in the kitchen. So, what's happening at the school?" B.J. asked.

"Nothing yet. They were waiting for the NTSB investigators when I left the scene."

B.J.'s voice deepened, a sign of his concern. "A bad situation all around. Keep me updated, and remember...the Jolly Green Giant news is a secret. Love you, brother. See you in a few months."

"Can't wait, and my lips are sealed," Sean said.

The call ended.

Sean unmuted the sound on the TV, took another sip of his beer, and grabbed a pretzel.

The chopper crash and the probability of Wolfgang Outen's demise was stirring up the past in New Orleans, as well.

Carter Bullock was in the living room with his wife, Leigh, waiting for the late-night newscast, and when it finally came on, the leading story shocked them. The last thing they expected to hear was the name Wolfgang Outen, and when they did, they immediately stared at each other.

Carter rolled his eyes and grinned. “It couldn’t have happened to a better man.”

Leigh glanced at him and then looked away. “At least we can sleep soundly again.”

“I haven’t suffered any sleep,” Carter snapped.

Leigh gave her lap robe a little tuck. “Don’t play cute with me,” the old woman said. “You know exactly what I mean.”

They were silent again as the show shifted to weather.

“Do you believe he and Cassandra will be reunited now?” Leigh asked.

Carter frowned and got up and poured himself a shot of whiskey.

“Not if there’s a God in heaven, they won’t,” he snapped, then tossed it back, swallowing it like medicine.

“She’ll tell him what we did,” Leigh said.

Carter threw the whiskey glass against the wall.

“So what? What are they going to do, haunt us?”

Leigh sniffed. “Don’t be ridiculous. Some days you can be so crude. I’m going to bed.”

Morning brought a gray sky and snowflakes so tiny they didn’t have enough weight to fall. They just kept swirling in the air, drifting from place to place, like clouds of little white gnats. It was a hell of a day to investigate a crash site, but the team from the NTSB had seen worse. At least they weren't up on the side of a mountain, and within minutes, they began their setup.

They had permission from the school district for the use of the gymnasium. They tarped the floor to keep from damaging it, set up banquet-length tables in orderly rows, and then began the methodical process of sorting through the crash site and bagging evidence. A piece of the pilot's body was found still strapped into the pilot's seat.

So as far as they knew, Wolfgang Outen's body had either blown up in the air, or what was left of the bits had turned to ash upon impact. All they could do was bag up ashes and debris in the hopes of finding enough DNA to confirm an ID, so they put in a call for more people to search the surrounding area, because there were bound to be body parts and pieces of the chopper scattered farther away.

What was already a nightmare was turning into a scene of true horror.

Sean woke early. He could only imagine the log of emails he had waiting, and downed a bowl of cereal and two cups of coffee before carrying his third cup to the office with a saucer of buttered toast on the side.

He closed the door to make sure the clicking of his

keyboard didn't disturb his mother's sleep in the room across the hall and set to work with one eye on the clock. As soon as it was a decent hour for phone calls, Amalie Lincoln was at the top of his list.

It was nearing 8:00 a.m. when Shirley meandered into her kitchen. She saw the dirty bowl in the sink. There was still coffee in the carafe. Good enough to start her morning on. She poured a cup and then took it to the window overlooking the land behind their house and realized it was spitting snowing, which was her mother's description of minimal snowfall on bitterly cold day.

But her house was warm. Sean had already upped the thermostat and built a fire in the fireplace. She thought about making breakfast, but didn't have enough appetite to bother, so she settled for buttered toast with jelly and coffee, then sat down to text Aaron and Wiley, and noticed B.J. had texted her last night.

She sighed. "Darn it, son. I missed it," she said and quickly texted him back, then hit Send. He was already at work. She didn't expect him to answer. But at least he'd know she saw it.

What she did need was to know how the rest of her family was. She sent a text to Wiley, making sure he'd suffered no lingering effects of the smoke, and then did the same to Aaron, asking about him and Dani.

Moments later, Aaron called her.

"Mom, I saw your text. We're okay. Dani is a little beat up, but physically okay. But what happened shook her to the core. They came so close to dying. I had nightmares all night, and I can't imagine what hers were like, but she was restless."

"I'm glad you called. Is there anything I can do? I'm assuming the school is closed indefinitely and nobody will be at work for a while."

"Right. The NTSB is on scene at the crash site, and until they bag up evidence and haul off the remains of the chopper, the school administration can't address the repairs that need to be done."

"Are you going to work today?" Shirley asked.

"Yes."

"Would it be okay if I visit Dani today? I'm not asking her first, because she'd just say yes to be polite, even if she wasn't up to it. You be the judge for me."

"Yes, it would be great, probably even helpful. Dani loves you dearly, and you know that."

"Okay then. Let her know I'll be there around noon and bring lunch for the both of us. I could do with a girl chat myself."

"Awesome, Mom, and thanks. I may or may not be able to stop by and check in on her at noon, so I'll be happy to know you're there. Drive safe coming down. The roads aren't slick, but if the snow gets heavy, don't chance it."

"Oh, I won't. I promise. I'll just call and talk to her instead. Be careful today. Love you."

"Love you, too, Mom. Is Sean all right?"

"Oh yes, you know your brother. He keeps things to himself, but he was up before me. Being out of the office all day yesterday probably put him a bit behind."

"Right. Okay then. I gotta go."

Shirley heard the call disconnect, then put down her phone and bit into a piece of cold toast and jelly, while trying to decide what goodies she would bake to take down the mountain. She was going to take something for Wiley, too, and leave it at their house. She thought of B.J. and smiled. He hadn't just inherited her people's looks through DNA. She was really proud of his chosen career. Being a chef! He loved to cook as much as she did. At least he hadn't gone into law enforcement. Having two sons on the force was worry enough.

It was past noon of the next day before Roadie arrived in Miami. He hadn't cried since he was twelve, but he cried off and on most of the way.

It began with just a simple text from a person he already knew, asking if he wanted to make a cool ten thousand dollars to make a phone call, to which he had immediately agreed. Then it began to sound fishy when he found out he had to go to some hick tourist attraction in Kentucky and stay at a cabin on a campground for a few days before making the call. But ten thousand dollars just to make a phone call? It was completely worth it until the fucking phone call blew up a chopper and it crashed into a school. He'd never thought of himself as "one of the good guys," but he damn well wasn't a baby killer. Yet he'd taken the money and done the deed and now he had to live with it.

But through all of the hours driving back to Miami, he finally convinced himself he was also a victim. It wasn't the first time he'd been conned, and it was something he was going to have to live with. He wasn't about to accept the guilt. He just needed to disappear. As soon as he reached his apartment, he left his phone and bag in the car and headed inside on the run.

His apartment was a fully furnished dump. The only things he had to pack were the rest of his clothes, his TV and coffee maker, and he'd be gone.

He didn't think there was any way to tie him to the phone call that had detonated the bomb, but he wasn't certain enough to chance it. He'd get his things, buy a burner phone on the way out of the city, and toss his phone in the first river he came to.

This wasn't his first rodeo. Roadie knew how to disappear and was about to make that move. He took the elevator to the third floor, then headed down the hall and hurried inside his apartment without bothering to lock the door behind him. He was trying to remember where he'd stashed his other suitcase, when someone grabbed him from behind and gave his head a quick twist.

He was dead before he hit the floor.

Vincent Romo was a hit man. He'd been waiting in Townley's apartment since noon yesterday, eating his food, shitting in his toilet, and watching his TV. He woke up this morning, still on the job, but with a headache and what felt like fever, and had been sneezing and coughing ever since. He spent the morning wiping up every surface he'd touched. Even threw the bedsheets in the laundry and set them to wash, removing his DNA from the scene, and then gloved up and set to waiting for Townley's arrival.

Vince was a killer who used his brawn far more often than he used his brain. Silent killings were his thing. And now that his target was dead, he had one thing left to do to get the last half of his pay. Retrieve Townley's cell phone, then toss the place to make it look like a burglary.

But it wasn't working out as planned. He'd gone through all of Roadie's pockets looking for that phone, but without success. He must have left it in the car!

Vince stood, looking around for the car keys he'd heard drop, and finally found them beneath Roadie's body. He sneezed as he was reaching for them, then heard a knock at the door.

He froze, holding his breath, listening and waiting, hoping they'd just go away. But it sounded like kids, and they kept pounding and calling Roadie's name. Then to his horror, he saw the doorknob turn. At that point, he forgot the keys and bolted to the bedroom, pulling up the hood of his sweatshirt as he ran, and climbed out a window and down the fire escape before disappearing up the intersecting alley.

Paul and Dougie Deal had been sent to borrow Roadie's car and were pounding on his door without success. Roadie was friends with their dad, who was in jail for assault and battery, and their mom needed groceries. Roadie always let the teenagers borrow his car, or took them to the store himself. But he had been gone for days, and they were hurtin' for food.

They had their EBT card from their SNAP membership, but no means of transportation. But when Wynona Deal looked out her kitchen window and saw Roadie's car in the parking lot again, she was overjoyed. It was Saturday. No school today, and the timing was perfect. She made them put on their jackets, gave them the grocery list and her EBT card, and told them to go beg Roadie for the car.

Now, the boys were at the door but weren't getting any response.

They kept knocking and knocking.

"Hey, Roadie! It's me, Dougie."

Nothing.

Dougie frowned at his brother, Paul. "His car's in the parking lot, right?"

Paul nodded. "Yeah, Mama looked before she sent us over."

Dougie shoved his hand through his shaggy blond hair and knocked again, then turned the doorknob. To his shock, the door swung inward. He stepped across the threshold and shouted again.

"Roadie! Hey, Roadie! Are you home?"

"Maybe he's sick. Maybe he fell and hurt himself," Paul said. "We should at least check."

"Right," Dougie said, but they didn't get far. One glance into the living room and they saw him crumpled on the floor. "Oh shit! Oh no!"

Paul started to run toward him when Dougie held him back. "Don't touch him. Look at his head. It's turned wrong. He's dead. Call 911."

They ran out into the hall, crying as they made the 911 call, then called their mother to tell her what they'd found and sat down on the floor to wait for the cops.

By the time the police arrived, Wynona was outside the apartment with her boys. Her three-year-old daughter was sitting in Dougie's lap, and her eighteen-month-old toddler on Wynona's hip. She didn't trust cops, and she wasn't having this disaster pinned on the first two teenagers on the scene.

Once the detectives arrived, it didn't take long to realize that the boys had scared the killer off before he could take anything, because the bedroom window was open to the fire escape and the apartment didn't look like it had been touched.

When the coroner showed up, he confirmed Roadie had died within the hour, apparently from a broken neck, but would confirm further details after the autopsy. He also made mention of the fact that Roadie was over six feet tall. Neither of the boys were over five foot ten, and Roadie's neck had been broken with one twist. They couldn't have done that without Roadie putting up one hell of a fight, and there wasn't a mark on him.

His wallet was there. His car keys on the floor beside his body. The only thing missing was his phone, and the boys had been searched. All they had on them was their mother's EBT card.

After the coroner's departure with the body, the crime scene techs began dusting for prints and bagging evidence, both inside the apartment and inside Roadie's car. That's where they found the phone and a checkout receipt from Bullard's Campgrounds in Jubilee, Kentucky, with yesterday's date. This corresponded with Wynona's statement about Roadie having been gone for the past five days.

For the moment, Detective Joe Muncy, the lead detective, had all the info he needed.

"Mrs. Deal, you and your boys are free to go, but we may need to speak to you again."

"Fine, you just do that," Wynona said. "And while you're at it, if you come back, bring food. We don't have a car. I don't have money for an Uber. We always borrow Roadie's to go to the store. He'd been gone five days. Now he's dead, for which I'm sorry, but I'm pretty near outta everything and sorrier that my babies are hungry."

Joe thought of his three little ones at home, then looked at the woman and her four kids and sighed.

"I'll take the boys to the supermarket for you. And I'll bring them home."

Wynona's defiance crumpled. "You'd do that?"

"Yes, ma'am."

Wynona took a shaky breath. "Then I thank you," she said, and turned to her boys. "Douglas Edward, Paul Allen...I expect nothing but your best behavior, and for you to thank the ground this officer walks on for helping us today. Do you understand me?"

Mama had called them by their whole names, which was the signal that she meant business. And they were as hungry as Mama and the babies.

"Yes, ma'am," Dougie said. "We won't act like Daddy."

Wynona rolled her eyes, glanced at the detective, and then grabbed her little ones and went back down the hall to their apartment.

Kenny Bruner, Muncy's partner, glanced at him and then at the boys.

"I'll go with you...to help carry sacks," he offered.

"Thanks," Joe said. "You guys ready to go?"

"Yes sir," they echoed.

Vincent Romo was on the run.

His contact had been texting him for hours, but he wasn't answering because he didn't know what to say, and he wasn't going to admit he'd failed his mission. His only option was to give up the last half of his pay and disappear. The only person who knew he'd been there was the one who'd sent him, and they weren't likely to file a complaint with the cops. Since he wasn't making a claim on the balance of the money owed him, maybe they'd think that he was dead.

Detectives Muncy and Bruner had been at their desks most of the morning, following up on leads, slim though they were.

Bruner was on the phone with the lab, checking to see if they'd found any DNA on Townley's clothing other than his own, and Muncy had called the number on the receipt from Bullard's Campgrounds in Jubilee, Kentucky, and was waiting for the call to pick up.

It rang and rang to the point that he thought it was going to voicemail, when a man finally answered, and from the gasp in his voice, he was obviously out of breath.

"Bullard's Campgrounds. This is Jordan."

"Jordan, this is Detective Joe Muncy. I work in the Homicide Division of the Miami PD. We found a receipt on a murder victim that is from your campground. The checkout date was yesterday. I'm trying to confirm his whereabouts to set up a timeline. Do you have a minute?"

Jordan was startled. "Yes. Yes, sir."

"Thanks," Muncy said. "The man's name was Ellis Townley. Can you confirm the check-in and checkout dates and times for me?"

"Sure," Jordan said. "Give me a second to pull it up on reservations."

Muncy could hear keys clacking as he waited, and then Jordan was back with answers.

"Okay...I have Mr. Townley checking in this past Monday around noon. He booked a cabin for five days. He checked out at 12:55 p.m. on Friday."

"Was anyone with him during his stay?" Muncy asked.

"No, sir. He came and went alone, and stopped by the canteen at least once a day while he was here to get snacks and drinks."

"Did you see him on his last day, prior to the time he checked out?"

Jordan thought back. "Umm...yes, actually, I did. It's pretty cold here, and yet he was outside for hours, standing in the field between his cabin and the office. He kept scanning the sky with binoculars, which was weird because the songbirds migrated months ago. Nothing much left in the skies but the predators...hawks, eagles, that kind of thing."

"Did he exhibit any other behavior you thought odd?" Muncy asked.

"Um...he was on the phone looking up at the sky when I heard an explosion. He arrived shortly thereafter to check out, all in a rush and sweating. I tried to hurry him along because I had just learned a chopper had crashed outside of town and just missed our elementary school. I have two children in school there, and I nearly broke my neck getting there, only to find them safe on the bleachers across the street. One of the teachers out on playground duty saw the chopper explode in midair and gave the warning that got the building evacuated in time."

Muncy blinked. Townley was watching the skies? He made a phone call in the middle of a field? A chopper exploded in midair? Townley hoofs it within minutes of the event and then is murdered the next day within minutes of returning to his apartment? *What the hell have we stumbled into?*

Muncy cleared his throat. "Thank you for the info, Jordan, and I'm glad to know your children weren't harmed. Out of curiosity, have you cleaned the cabin he was in yet?"

"No, sir. The cleaning crew will be here today to—"

"I'd like to ask you to lock it up and don't let anyone else inside. Someone from the Jubilee Police Department will be checking it out for us. Please notify your cleaning crew to skip it."

"Yeah, sure," Jordan said. "So...you're from Homicide, so are you saying Mr. Townley is dead?"

"Yes. Under suspicious circumstances. If we have other questions, we'll be in touch."

He disconnected. Glanced up at Bruner, who was still on the phone, and then called the lab.

"This is Detective Muncy, Homicide. Have you looked at the phone we found in Ellis Townley's car yet?"

"Just a moment, sir," the tech said, and began going through lab reports before coming back to the phone. "I have the log pulled off the phone, but nothing further at the moment that I can see."

"Could you send that to me?" Muncy asked.

"Yes, sir, sending now," the tech said. "Done. Is there anything else I can help you with?"

"Have you had a chance to check Townley's clothing for DNA yet?"

"It's on the to-do list, but I'm not working on that aspect. I'll check and let you know."

"This case is turning into something more than a random murder. Put some wheels on those tests, will you?"

"Yeah, sure," the tech said.

"Thanks," Muncy said, and then heard his computer signaling incoming email and disconnected.

He opened the email, printed copies of the log for both himself and Bruner, then looked for the last number Townley had called. Finding out it was a burner phone was disappointing, but he needed to confirm something else before he jumped the gun between Townley's presence in Jubilee and a chopper crash. So, he looked up the number for the Jubilee Police Department and the name of the police chief, and then made the call.

Chapter 5

Sonny Warren was hustling. A number of his officers were still on duty at the crash site, leaving him short on manpower. This morning at roll call he'd been forced to send officers out on patrol alone, and that made him antsy. And he'd just gotten word that the midair explosion was likely caused by a bomb, which would indicate murder, and the feds were on the way. He was on his way down the hall to his office when he heard his desk phone ringing and ran the last few yards to answer.

"Chief Warren."

"Chief, I'm Detective Joe Muncy, Miami Homicide. Do you have a minute?"

Sonny sat, remembering Wolfgang Outen was from Miami and thinking the other shoe was about to fall.

"Yes. How can I help you?"

Muncy began explaining his case, mentioning the deceased's name, the details of what happened, and why he was calling.

"Here's the deal. We understand you had a helicopter crash yesterday around midday. Is that true?"

"Yes, it is," Sonny said.

"And I was given to understand that a teacher witnessed the chopper explode in midair before it came down."

"Yes, that's true, as well."

"Have you taken her statement? Do you have an exact timeline from when she saw the explosion to when it crashed?"

"We have one on file. Give me a sec to pull it up," Sonny said, and swiveled his chair to the computer on his right and found the statement. "Yes, I have it here. Why?"

"What did she say about the times?" Muncy asked.

Sonny scanned the report. "Went out on the playground with class right after lunch, which would have been around twelve thirty. They'd been out there about fifteen minutes when a couple of boys started fussing. She was out in the middle of the playground dealing with that when she saw a chopper in the air, but thought nothing of it, because they come and go here frequently. She was on her way back into the building with the boys when she heard an explosion. She looked up and saw the tail of the chopper was missing, and the cockpit was on fire and spiraling. So that would have been between twelve forty-five and one. But the school secretary took her warning. She might have an exact time. They evacuated the school immediately afterward because the teacher feared the chopper was going to fall on the school or the school ground."

"Do you have the secretary's name and contact information?" Muncy asked.

Sonny frowned. "Give me a second to make a call," he said, then grabbed his cell phone and called Principal Lowery.

Stephanie Lowery answered on the first ring.

"Hello?"

"Good morning, Stephanie, this is Chief Warren. I have a weird question. By any chance do you know the exact time that Dani Pope's warning about the chopper exploding came into the office?"

Stephanie frowned. "Actually, I do. I'd just glanced up at the clock, because I had a dental appointment after school, and I'd lost track of time. It was exactly 12:47 p.m."

"Thanks," Sonny said. "That's all I need. Talk to you later."

Sonny got back on the landline call with Muncy.

"I just spoke to the school principal. She said it was 12:47 p.m. when Dani Pope called the office to tell them to evacuate the school, that a chopper had exploded in midair and she feared it was going to hit the school."

"Perfect," Muncy said.

Sonny frowned. "Now, what the hell's going on?"

"My murder victim was seen in a clearing at the campgrounds, looking through binoculars with a phone in his hand. The clerk went on to say that Townley seemed distracted and in a panic when he came in minutes later to check out, and I needed to know if that phone call on the phone we have, in any way matches up with the time the chopper exploded. We made this connection from the campground receipt, but at this time, it's still just a theory."

Sonny was stunned. "What I know is that the NTSB is here investigating the crash, and the feds are on the way, which means to me that they already suspect foul play. If you discover that timeline fits, I suggest you contact the feds and let them know your murder victim might be the trigger man, because all of this will be way out of our league."

"Can you tell me the name of the people who were on the chopper?" Muncy asked.

"I can tell you the names of the people who were registered on the manifest, but until DNA confirms the remains, no announcements are being made."

"Fair enough. Who do they think they are?" Muncy asked.

"Zander Sutton would be the pilot. He owns a charter service out of Miami, and apparently flies people in and out of here on a regular basis, particularly a man named Wolfgang Outen, who was due to attend a board meeting at Hotel Devon, here in Jubilee. Apparently, he is an investor in the hotel, and they meet here quarterly."

The hair crawled on the back of Muncy's neck. "Wolfgang Outen? Are you serious?"

"That's the report," Sonny said. "What about him?"

"Midfifties. Midas rich. I actually own stock in one of his companies," Muncy said. "This takes things to a whole other level, and I have a favor to ask. I've already spoken to the clerk at Bullard Campgrounds. They haven't cleaned the cabin Townley rented yet, and I've asked him to lock it and keep everyone out until it's been searched. Do you have a team from your crime lab who could go out to the campgrounds and do a sweep for me? It would be highly appreciated."

"Yes, sure," Sonny said. "Was it a man named Jordan who you spoke to at the campground?"

"Yes."

"Then I'll let him know my people are on the way and have them send their findings to you. I'll need an email address."

Muncy gave him the info, and then they disconnected.

Sonny made a quick call to the lab, issued the orders, and then called the campgrounds to let them know his team was on the way.

Back in Miami, Muncy was comparing the timeline of the phone call on Townley's phone to the timeline of the explosion. When he realized that the call on Townley's phone went through within the same minute as Dani's warning to the school, his gut knotted. He'd been a detective too long to believe in coincidences. There would be no questioning Townley, but his possessions and clothing would have to talk for him.

Wolfgang's plane landed in Sao Paulo, Brazil, over eight hours after it took off from Miami. The moment he was on the ground, he called Stu, but there was no answer. He frowned. Even if Stu was in the board meeting, he would have taken the call.

He took a cab to the hotel, registered for the room Stu had already reserved, then sat down and called Julio Ruiz, the manager of the refinery. He wasn't going to drive out to that location until he knew what the threat level was at the moment, and if foul play had indeed been the cause of the fire.

Ruiz hadn't been home since the explosion. He was in a panic, tired to the bone, at a loss as to what to do until the fire was extinguished, and at the moment, they did not even have the fire contained.

He had workers who were dead. Workers who'd been injured in the explosion, and workers who'd walked off the jobsite. And while he was waiting for help to arrive, they'd received word this morning that Wolfgang Outen had died in a chopper crash. He'd tried all morning to call Outen's personal assistant, but even he wasn't answering, and then his phone rang, and when he saw the call was from Wolf's company, he sighed with relief and answered in English.

"This is Ruiz."

"Ruiz, it's me, Wolf. I just landed and—"

All of a sudden, Ruiz was screaming in his ear and speaking Portuguese so fast Wolf couldn't follow. Finally, he shouted.

"Stop! Stop! I can't understand a damn word you're saying. Please start over!"

Ruiz shuddered. "*Senhor*? This is really you?"

Wolf frowned. "Who the hell else did you expect it to be?"

"We got a call this morning. They said you died in a chopper crash. They said your chopper blew up in midair. They said you were dead."

The skin crawled on the back of Wolfgang's neck.

"Who said this?" he asked.

Ruiz took a deep breath. "I don't know. The call came in from your office. Yesterday, I tried to call you about what's happening here, but Stu took the message and said he'd let you know. Then Stu no longer answers me, either."

Wolf's head was spinning. *The chopper exploded in midair? That's sabotage. The refinery was targeted. That's sabotage. Oh God, Stu. I sent Stu to his death.* And then it hit him. If a bomb took down the chopper, then they were after him, and when they find out he didn't die, they'll come after him again.

"Listen, Ruiz. Don't tell anyone you've talked to me. Don't tell anyone I'm still alive. I think someone meant to kill me, but Stu was the one on the chopper. He was carrying my proxy to a board meeting, and obviously, there aren't enough remains to identify who died or they'd already know this. Will you do that for me?"

"Yes, Boss. Of course. But what do I do about the refinery?"

"Do you believe it was sabotage?"

Ruiz took a deep breath. "Yes, Boss, I do."

"Are you in danger?" Wolf asked.

Tears quickened when Ruiz heard true concern in the boss's voice.

"Probably."

"Then here's what I want you to do. Go home. Make sure the families of those who died know that Outen Industries will pay for the burials and full compensation for their losses and pay for the ones still in the hospital. Give every employee four months wages to tide them over while the refinery is shut down, and the same to the families of the deceased, and then leave it to the authorities to put out the fire. If there's anything left, we'll deal with it then. But I'm not putting any of you in harm's way for a damn barrel of oil."

Ruiz was so relieved he couldn't focus.

"How will I tell them this is so, if you are supposed to be dead? They'll think it is me making promises I can't keep."

Outen frowned. "Tell them it's company policy, and in the meantime, I hope to have the mess cleared up here soon, but I'll need time, and if they think I'm dead, then I'll be safer to investigate for myself."

"Yes, sir. Thank you, sir. But you can't be seen here. Where will you go?"

"Don't worry about me. I'll be in touch when I can."

"Yes, sir. Thank you, sir," Ruiz said.

The call disconnected, but for the first time since it

all began to burn, Ruiz had a plan. Wolf had nothing but questions, and the moment he ended his call to Ruiz, he called his pilot.

"Toby, it's me. Don't talk to anybody back home about where we are. I know you must be exhausted, but this is an emergency. Just get the jet serviced and be ready to get us out of here."

Toby West was used to Outen's crazy life and didn't blink an eye.

"Yes, sir. Consider it done. I'll have to file a flight plan. Do we have a destination?"

"Right now, back to Miami. But just list you coming in with no passengers onboard. Nobody's going to question where I am. They already think I'm dead."

Toby frowned. "Sir?"

"My chopper to Jubilee blew up in midair. Stu's dead. Someone mistook him for me. Say nothing."

"Jesus," Toby muttered. "Then take a taxi to this address. It's a private airport for bigwigs in Sao Paulo. I know the owner. I can land there without raising an eyebrow."

Wolf took down the address. "I owe you big time, Toby," and then as soon as he hung up, he took off the clothes he'd been wearing and put on a clean outfit from his suitcase, made sure to transfer his passport and wallet into the clean suit, and then sighed with relief when he saw the amount of cash Stu had packed. He quit counting at ten thousand, put some in his wallet and the rest back in the suitcase, and headed downstairs. He gave the desk clerk the room key, said he'd been called away on an emergency, and hailed a taxi as he exited the hotel.

Within minutes, he was gone.

Amalie was up early, already in her office checking emails, making online orders for lamps and copy paper, but she kept glancing up from her desk, watching the snow coming down from the office window. She loved snow and had never gotten over the childhood joy of snow days.

As soon as she finished answering emails, most of which were from prior clients she'd contacted about her move, she decided to hit the tourist shops to pick up some artwork and maybe a figurine or two to decorate the tables in the waiting area of her office.

Even though she was going to do business in that place, she wanted it to be comfortable for her and look inviting from the street. After the decor was complete, she could schedule her open house and put an ad in the local paper.

Amalie didn't doubt her ability to gain clients. All she needed was one, and word of mouth would follow. She was good at what she did. Damn good, and she wanted to be open for business soon.

Some people waited for hunting season.

Amalie's season was taxes, and the time was already upon her. And, if she was lucky, Sean Pope would make good on his invitation to take her to dinner. With all that in mind, she grabbed her coat and purse, locked up, and then headed for the parking lot.

She could have waited for a better weather day to hit the shops, but shopping in the snow felt like something from a Hallmark movie, and she *was* setting the stage for her new venture. She also knew fate waited for no one, and she was ready to make something of it. She remembered all of the shops from her first visit here, so she already knew where she wanted to go.

She jumped in the car, turned on the wipers to keep the windshield clear of snow, and headed to the arts and craft area on the other side of town. Her phone rang just as she was parking, so she killed the engine and answered.

"Hello?"

"Amalie, it's me, Sean.

Just hearing his voice made her smile. "Hi! Are you loving this snow? It's beautiful, isn't it?

Every tense muscle in Sean's body melted. It was the delight in her voice that did it.

"It sure is. What are you doing today?"

"I'm down in the arts and craft area, about to shop for office decor. Are you okay? I mean, no aftereffects from inhaling all that smoke?"

"Yes, I'm fine. Thanks for asking. Now I have a question for you. How do you feel about dinner tonight?"

Amalie sighed. *He'd done it! He kept his word.* "I would love it."

"Awesome," Sean said. "Is six o'clock too early for you?"

"No, it's perfect."

"Do you have food preferences?" he asked.

"No. I'm not a bit picky."

Sean had a silly grin on his face and he knew it, but he couldn't help feeling like a great big door had just opened and he was standing on the threshold looking in. All he had to do was take the first step.

"I need your address. Are you in an apartment or a house?"

"A house. Got a pen and paper?" she asked.

"Yes, ma'am."

Amalie gave him the address.

"Got it," Sean said. "I'll see you at six, then."

"See you then," Amalie said, and shivered as she dropped her phone in her handbag. "Oh my God. I have a date with my nine-year-old knight in shining armor. Now I get to know him as the man he became. Best day ever!"

She put on her gloves and pulled up the hood of her coat as she got out, and locked the car as she was walking away. The Cumberland Art Gallery was going to be her first stop.

Vincent Romo was on his way to Mexico. He'd picked up a burner phone before he left Miami, removed the SIM card from his phone, and tossed the shell. He knew he'd fucked up someone's plans, but shit happened. Those damn kids appearing at Townley's door unannounced had fucked up his. He coughed, then sneezed into his sleeve and kept driving, confident that he was in the clear and about to disappear.

Snow was impeding the recovery of evidence from the crash site. One team was working frantically, taking photos of everything from every angle and bagging everything in sight to get it out of the weather, while the other team was on foot in the woods, looking for the site of the midair explosion. They found their first piece of wreckage nearly a mile east of the crash site—remnants of one of the seats in the chopper, covered in blood and bits of human remains. Then they found part of the smaller rotor from the tail of the chopper, partially embedded in the ground, along with scattered pieces of the fuselage. Recovering all this was crucial, because what they had left at the crash site was mostly ashes.

But it was the bomb fragment connected to part of a cell phone they found embedded beneath that seat cushion that clinched the search for proof that the explosion had been intentional. It was the confirmation they needed to rule this murder, and they radioed their lead investigator to let him know. A team from the FBI was already headed to the site on foot, but with firm evidence now, the investigation went into overdrive.

Wolfgang Outen was a billionaire with his fingers in

businesses all over the world. Some would grieve his death. Others would celebrate. It was the ones with the most to gain that they were looking at first.

Shirley Pope was on her way down the mountain with a pot of vegetable beef soup and two pecan pies. One pie was for Aaron and Dani, and one for Wiley. She'd already called Dani to let her know she was on the way and could tell by the rasp in Dani's voice that she was still suffering from the smoke. She would know when she got there if Dani was up for company or not, but Shirley just needed to hug her for the blessing of still being alive. Then to her surprise, as she pulled up into the driveway, Dani came out of the house to meet her.

"Mom! I'm so glad to see you! Give me something to carry," she said, as Shirley got out.

Shirley handed her the tote with both pies and picked up the pot of soup.

"This is it," Shirley said. "Lead the way. It's freezing."

The house was warm and inviting, and Dani kicked the front door shut behind her as they headed for the kitchen.

"What wonderful things have you brought to spoil me this time?" Dani asked, as she set down the pies.

Shirley put the soup pot beside them, dropped her purse, and took off her coat, and then gave Dani a hug.

"My darling daughter, you are a wonder. I don't quite

know how you found the strength to do what you did, but I'm so grateful you are okay."

It was the gentle tone in Shirley voice and the warmth of her embrace that shattered Dani's composure. One moment she'd been smiling and the next she was sobbing on Shirley's shoulder.

"I thought we would all die. I didn't think we could get the children out in time. I didn't think I would see Aaron again. It was terrible. Worse than hiding in the closet waiting to be murdered. Worse than being stalked. Those times I knew my enemy. But I never saw this coming!"

"I know, honey, I know."

Shirley kept hugging her and rocking her where they stood until Dani had cried herself out, and then Shirley took her by the hand and settled them down by the fireplace.

The flames from the gas logs were hypnotizing as the silence wrapped around them. Finally, Dani sighed.

"Thank you for that. I cried last night, but I couldn't seem to find a way to let go. I was still in fight mode, I guess. And Aaron was so worried about me this morning, leaving me on my own that I pretended I was fine. I didn't want him to think I was coming undone because they needed him at the precinct. They're shorthanded because of guarding the crash site."

Shirley nodded, just letting her talk, but there was no hiding the dark circles beneath her eyes. When she finally stopped talking, Shirley reached for her hand.

"You're cold, honey."

Dani nodded. "I know. I feel cold all the way to my bones."

"How about a bowl of my beef vegetable soup and a piece of pecan pie?"

"Is that what you brought?" Dani cried.

"Yes. One of the pies is for Wiley. I texted him to let him know I was dropping it off here."

"Will you eat with me?" Dani asked.

"If you want the company, I'd love to," Shirley said.

"Please! I always want your company," Dani said.

They went back into the kitchen arm in arm and, minutes later, were eating soup and drinking hot tea.

Amalie was freezing. She'd been in and out of shops all day, stopping only long enough to have a cup of soup at one of the shops, but the trip was successful. Everything she'd purchased was being delivered to her office in a couple of days, and there was a little box of homemade fudge in the seat beside her. All she wanted to do was go home, take a long hot bath, and get ready for her date with Sean. The sky was clearing. The snow had stopped falling, and the streets were clear as she headed back to her neighborhood.

Normally, there would be children playing out in the yards, but today, the residential area of Jubilee was quiet. Nobody was outside, and as she passed the street parallel to the elementary school, she couldn't help but notice the number of people and vehicles still behind the school, and the black burned-out hull of what was left of the chopper.

It explained the pall in the neighborhood.

Yesterday, a whole building full of children nearly died. Families were holding their babies close today, and most likely, the children were still dealing with the shock and injuries they'd suffered.

After her wreck, it had taken her months to be able to close her eyes without seeing the car go out of control in front of her, then slamming into her again and again. Sometimes, she could still feel the car spinning and spinning until it hit the abutment and burst into flames.

Poor babies.

Poor Amalie.

Life shouldn't be this hard.

She began to slow down after she turned down her street. Her house was the third one on the left. The one with a wraparound porch and green shutters. She used the remote to open the garage door, and then drove in and killed the engine. The door was already going down as she grabbed the box of fudge, slung her purse over her shoulder, and went into the house through the utility room.

The warmth inside was welcome. She left the fudge on the kitchen island, hung her coat up in the closet in the hall, and began turning on lights as she headed to her bedroom.

Within minutes, she had water running in the tub and

a liberal sprinkling of lavender bath salts dissolving in the water. She stripped down to her skin, piled her hair up on her head to keep it dry, then eased in and slid down into its depths, sighing in delight.

Only then did she remember she hadn't checked the mailbox on the porch, and she hadn't checked her email since she'd left the office earlier this morning. Then she shrugged off the thought and sank a little deeper into the water.

The once-smooth surface of her upper body was now taut and shiny from skin grafts, or slightly puckered with weblike scarring from the fire. She didn't think about them much now, but tonight was different. She had a date with a seriously handsome man, but she didn't know what to expect. And it was just the tiniest bit scary.

Still, he'd fought a battle for her once. She wanted to believe that tenderhearted child was still in there somewhere, still willing to be the hero.

Sean shut down his office at 4:00 p.m. and began going through the house, stoking the fire, carrying in more wood, and emptying the garbage. Then he gathered up an armload of wood for the fire and was coming in the back door, bringing a blast of cold air with him, when his mother entered the kitchen.

"Ah...you're home," Sean said. "Thought I'd bring in some more wood for the fire."

Shirley followed him into the living room, talking. "Dani's okay healthwise, but emotionally, she's struggling. It was a terrible thing to experience. I'm glad I went. Wiley came by to pick up his pie as I was leaving. He sends his love."

Sean nodded. "Are you going to be okay here on your own for a while tonight?"

Shirley frowned. "For heaven's sake, Sean. Of course, I will. I'm not tired so much as cold, and you've already taken care of that. The house is nice and warm. I'm going to watch a gushy love story on TV, drink Mountain Dew and eat popcorn, and probably fall asleep before it's over."

He gave her a look. "You need to quit watching love stories and watch one of those kick-ass movies I like. You wouldn't fall asleep watching them."

She snorted. "And most likely not fall asleep after it's over, either. No thanks. I like my movies like I like desserts. Soft and sweet."

Sean burst out laughing and hugged her.

She grinned. "Okay, okay, that's enough. Go get all pretty for your date, and have a good time," Shirley said.

"Yes, ma'am," Sean said, and hustled down the hall to shave and shower.

Chapter 6

It was fifteen minutes to six when Sean drove into Jubilee. Tourists were less prevalent this time of year, but they were always present. The upside of it for locals was not having to wait for tables at their favorite restaurants and finding available parking without walking too far.

Sean was nervous, but excited. He hadn't dated anyone since before his father went to prison, but he kept reminding himself that this wasn't like meeting a stranger. He and Amalie had a past of sorts—a history from childhood. What better place to renew an acquaintance than from the beginning?

He drove straight to her house. Porch lights were on, as well as all through the house, and he wondered what she did when she went home. What she liked to do for fun. If she had any hobbies. What music she liked. Then he headed up the steps knowing it was all to be revealed before the night was over.

The moment he rang the doorbell, he began to smile. It sounded like church chimes, and then the door swung inward, and Amalie was standing before him.

"The church bells threw me. For a second, I thought I'd taken a wrong turn."

She laughed. "They were here before me. Daunting, aren't they? Maybe a prior owner chose them to make sure all their callers were in the right frame of mind before they entered this house."

"I think I'm good," Sean said.

"Then you better come in out of the cold," she said, and stepped aside.

"Church bells aside, you look beautiful," Sean said.

Amalie beamed. "Is this where I'm supposed to be coy and say, 'Oh, this old thing?'"

Sean eyed her gray slacks and her cable-knit sweater the same color as her eyes.

"You don't have to say anything. You've already made your statement without saying a word."

"Then, thank you," she said, and gestured around the room. "So, this is home. Still a couple of boxes to empty here and there, but mostly because they're full of books."

"You like to read?" Sean asked.

"I love to read. First choice is always fiction, but in a bind, I'd read the back side of a cereal box. So, where are we going?" she asked.

"The Back Porch, just off the main square. Have you been there?"

"Yes, and I love it. I spent two weeks in Jubilee last year between Thanksgiving and Christmas. I don't think I missed a shop, an eating establishment, or a music venue.

I've been the tourist, but I'm looking forward to becoming a local."

He frowned. "I can't believe we never saw each other then."

Amalie shrugged. "Maybe we did and just didn't know it."

"Then I am sorely disappointed in myself. Is this your coat?" he asked, pointing to the one on the back of the sofa.

"Yes."

"Allow me," he said, helped her into it, then waited while she grabbed her purse and keys and escorted her out of the house.

Amalie glanced at his profile as they were driving away. The little boy she'd known was definitely long gone, but the adult version of him was spectacular. When he caught her staring, she blushed, thankful he couldn't see it in the dark.

"Sorry. Didn't mean to stare, but I can't get over how tall you are."

Sean nodded. "I get a lot of that, but wait until you see the rest of the Popes on the mountain. I'm just middlin' in size compared to some of them."

Her mouth dropped. "The rest of the Popes? You mean there are more than just your mom and your brothers?"

He nodded. "It's a long story, and I won't bore you with the details, but our ancestor had a trading post in the area. He was a big Scotsman named Brendan Pope. He married a little Chickasaw woman named Cries A

Lot, but he called her Meg. The mountain is full of their descendants. Big men with long legs and broad shoulders like Brendan, and black hair like his Meg. I'm just one of them."

Amalie was entranced. When they pulled up at a stop-light, she turned sideways in the seat to talk.

"All my life I've wondered who I am. Who my people were. I don't even know for sure if my birth mother named me, or if the name I have was just pulled out of a hat. When I was eighteen, I did the Ancestry.com thing. It told me nothing except that my ancestors were from all over."

"And nobody ever contacted you thinking you might be a part of their family tree?" Sean asked.

"Nope. And that was the end of that," Amalie said. "Ooh, look, it's starting to snow again. I love this place. I love this weather. I fell in love with the mountain. It's why I came back."

A wave of emotion swept through Sean as he pulled into the parking lot.

"You fell in love with the mountain?"

She nodded. "It felt like I was being called to it. I drove up it one day and then back down again. Didn't see anything or anyone but a couple of deer, one possum, and something hiding in the shadows as I drove back to Jubilee. It gave me peace just looking at it."

"Then I have Pope Mountain to thank your presence in Jubilee?"

She smiled. "I guess. Or the fact that you lived there,

and it wasn't the mountain who was calling. Maybe it was you."

All of a sudden, the smile slid off his face. "Are you psychic?"

Amalie frowned. "Not to my knowledge. Why do you ask?"

"Because we have one in the family. Ella Pope is the oldest living family member on the mountain, and the whole family claims she's got the sight. It was the way you said that it wasn't the mountain that drew you, it was me." He grinned. "It's something she would say."

"What a gift she must be to all of you," Amalie said.

Sean gave her a look. "Gifts come in many different ways, and I'm starving. Let's get inside where it's warm, but give me a sec. The pavement might be slick."

He exited the car, took her hand as she got out, then tucked her arm beneath his elbow as they headed inside.

Sean could see Amalie was nervous, but the moment they walked in, the hustle and bustle of the waitresses and diners and the engaging aromas coming from the kitchen took precedence over how she feared people would perceive her. Then he saw the hostess coming toward them.

"Hey, Sean! Great to see you again," she said.

"Hi, Betts. Looks like a busy night. How's your dad? Mom said he had a fall."

"Still limping and griping, but he's on the mend. Two for dinner?" she asked, smiling at Amalie.

"Yes. Betts, this is my friend Amalie Lincoln. She's

the new CPA in town. Amalie, this is Betts Glass, short for Bethany. She's one of the many cousins. Her grandmother was a Pope."

"Nice to meet you, Betts. Sean's been filling me in on the size of the family. I'm impressed," Amalie said.

Betts laughed. "You either sink or swim in our bunch. There are three interconnected families. Pope, Glass, and Cauley, all original settlers, and too many of us to count. Would you like a table or a booth?"

"A table in a corner would be awesome," Sean said. "We have a lot of catching up to do."

"You've got it," she said. "This way, please."

By the time they'd shed their coats and taken their seats, they had put in their order for drinks and an appetizer, then began scanning the menu for entrées.

"What are you hungry for tonight?" Sean asked.

"Pretty much anything I don't have to cook," Amalie said. "I spent all day either at the office or in the shops. When you called, it made a good day even better." But the moment Amalie said that, she felt like she'd said too much and returned to reading the menu.

A few minutes later, the waiter brought out the appetizer.

"Are you ready to order?" he asked.

"I am," Amalie said. "I want something warm and soupy…so I think I'll have a bowl of gumbo and rice, with a side of jalapeño hush puppies."

"Sounds perfect. Make that two," Sean said.

"Then I guess we're on the same wavelength," she said.

Sean was watching the play of light off her hair and in her eyes and almost forgot to comment. "Uh...I guess we are."

The waiter went to turn in their order, leaving them with the hot baked artichoke-cheese dip and a basket of bite-size bread chunks in different flavors.

"Dig in, but be careful. This stuff comes hot out of the oven," Sean said.

"One of my foster mothers used to say, 'Hot enough to burn the hair off your tongue.' She was full of adages, but not much else."

Before Sean could answer, he heard someone say his name and looked up, then groaned.

"Oh lord."

"What?" Amalie said, and then saw a man in a police uniform heading toward them with a big grin on his face. "Whoa. He looks like you."

"With good reason," Sean said.

"Hey, bro! I came to pick up a to-go order, and saw you and a pretty girl I do not know. Introduce me, please."

The minute he called Sean "bro," Amalie leaned back in her chair and crossed her arms. "I already know who you are. You're Wiley. Third brother down, and the one who swallowed a tooth with a spoonful of mashed potatoes in the lunchroom at Ellen Smith Elementary, and then tried to throw it up so you could take it home for the tooth fairy."

The smile fell off Wiley's face. He looked at Sean, and then at the girl, and then threw up his hands.

"How can you possibly know that?" he asked.

"Because I witnessed the event. I'm Amalie Lincoln. I was in Sean's grade."

Wiley kept staring, and then a light suddenly dawned. "The bullies! The gum in your hair! Wow! Talk about a full-circle moment. He got suspended after that fight. As his brothers, we were so impressed."

Sean could see where this was going and changed the subject.

"Amalie is the CPA in the new office next door to the bank. I just set up her tech stuff and a security system for her. We sort of recognized that we knew each other, but we couldn't remember how. It was the name change that threw her," Sean said.

Wiley blinked. "Right. Anyway, sorry to interrupt your evening, and sorry my big brother saw you first, but it's really good to see you again." Then Wiley winked at Sean. "Mom made me a pecan pie. You get the girl."

"Mom said you have three girls on speed dial," Sean said.

Wiley blushed, and then grinned at Amalie. "That may or may not be true."

Amalie's eyes widened.

Sean grinned. "Go home to your pie, little brother."

Wiley was still laughing as he walked out the door.

"Oh, my word! He's still a mess, isn't he?" Amalie said.

"Yes," Sean said. He scooped up a bite of dip with a chunk of herbed butter bread and popped it in his mouth.

By the time their entrées arrived, Sean had filled her in on all of the places that catered for parties so she could get quotes for her open house and clued her in on the florist with the most high-end designs and given her the name of the woman at the newspaper office who was in charge of ads and public notices.

Amalie took a quick taste of her gumbo and then moaned in true ecstasy.

"This hits the spot."

"Good choices for sure," Sean said.

"Thank you for all the names and suggestions," she added.

"You're very welcome. And you should expect to see me there."

Amalie beamed. "Of course! You have to! Bring your mom. I'd love to see her again. I remember her from school parties. She always brought the best cookies."

"It's a deal," Sean said.

Nearly two hours and two crème brûlées later, they were on their way back to her house, with the windshield wipers making half-hearted swipes at the random flakes of falling snow.

As they turned down the street to her house, Amalie glanced over at the lights on at the tent around the crashed chopper.

"I hope they haul that thing off soon."

Sean glanced over and then back at the street. "Ugly reminder, isn't it?"

Unconsciously, she rubbed the side of her neck, feeling the pucker of scars beneath her fingertips. "Yes, I guess it is."

Sean pulled up into her drive and killed the engine, then reached for her hand in the dark.

"This was the best night ever. Please say we can do this again sometime."

Amalie turned toward him in the dark. "We can do this again sometime."

Sean laughed, then lifted her hand to his lips and kissed it.

"Another thing I now know about you."

Amalie's heart was pounding. "What's that?"

"You have this wry, cockeyed sense of humor that lights every dark corner of my soul. Stay put. I'm coming around to help you out."

Amalie's heart was pounding. *Lights every dark corner of my soul.* And then he opened the door, again insisting that she hang on to his arm until they were out of the weather.

She unlocked the door, opened it, then turned around.

Sean leaned in front of her long enough to flip off the porch light, then cupped her cheeks.

He was going to kiss her. All she had to do was not faint from pure joy.

He pulled her close, so close that she felt his breath on her face, and then his lips were on her mouth and his hands were in her hair.

She didn't even know that he'd pulled back until she heard him talking.

"Thank you for an amazing evening. I am just a call away if you need me. And I'll call you soon so we can do this again."

Amalie nodded.

Then he turned the porch light back on. "It's cold, honey. Lock the door behind me, okay?"

She nodded again, but stood in the open doorway until he was backing out of her drive before she closed the door. Then she remembered the mail, opened the door to get it out of the box, then locked it as she went back inside.

Sean drove home in a daze.

Something had happened to him tonight that had never happened before.

He'd fallen in love at first kiss.

Toby West had just landed Outen's jet at Miami International, taxied off the main runway and down a smaller strip before rolling to a stop in front of Outen's corporate hangar.

Wolf was inside the plane, dressed in a pair of Toby's coveralls, with a sock cap pulled over his hair, and holding a pair of sunglasses.

"Wait here, Boss," Toby said, then exited the plane and put a maintenance crew to work running checkups. Pretty soon there were more than a dozen men coming and going around the hangar, all wearing the same kind of coveralls.

At that point, Toby went back inside, came out carrying Wolf's suitcase as if it was his own, dumped it in his car, and then turned around just as Wolf approached. Toby passed off his car keys without making eye contact and kept moving back toward the plane. He spoke to the manager, then walked out of the back of the hangar, heading for the main building, while Wolf slipped into Toby's car and drove out of the hangar with no one the wiser.

Toby caught a cab at the terminal and went home to sleep, while Wolf left Toby's car in the parking garage next to his apartment, then caught a cab to a car rental agency. A couple of hours later, he was on his way to a property he owned on the outskirts of Savannah, Georgia. There were no caretakers, so it was empty, but he kept the utilities on, loaning it out to friends for weekend getaways now and then. The nearest neighbor was a half mile away, and if anyone saw a car parked there, they'd think nothing of it. It was the perfect place to disappear.

Wolf needed someone to trust, but his first choice had already died in his stead, and he was heartsick. The authorities needed to know he was alive, but that wouldn't stop the investigation because Zander and Stu were still dead.

The first time he stopped for gas and to get some food, he sent Jack Fielding a text. It never occurred to him that his first call should have been to Fiona, because he already distrusted her enough to put Jack on her tail.

He glanced at the time. It was getting late. Jack would contact him when he could. Right now, he just wanted to get somewhere and sleep without fearing someone would kill him in his bed.

Fiona went through the day on autopilot while receiving bouquets of flowers, calls of sympathy, and friends coming to pay their respects. She hadn't gone to work this morning, and it was costing her a lot, maybe someone else's life.

She'd been in the middle of an important project when this happened, and she needed to finish building the one-of-a-kind surgical instrument needed for a doctor in Manhattan who was waiting to perform a critical surgery. People's lives depended upon her skills and abilities. She'd already made up her mind that she was going back to work tomorrow to complete the task, and was standing on the balcony of their bedroom, looking out into the night, when she saw a shadow moving through the grounds.

Her heart quickened, thinking she recognized the silhouette, and then moments later, when her phone rang, she knew she'd been right.

"Are you mad? Get off my property before the security alarms go off," she said.

"I need to see you."

"You don't need anything. You want. You always want," she hissed.

"So do you, and you know it," he said. "You want it now. You want me. In you."

Fiona moaned.

His laugh was soft in her ear. "Come to the cabana."

She left the balcony and ran down the back stairs, turned off the security alarm, and ran out into the night. From a distance she would have appeared as a wraith in white silk, floating above the ground.

The moment she entered the cabana, the door locked behind her. Before she could turn around, her nightgown was on the floor, and he was behind her. She felt him, pushing, thrusting, and then he swept her off her feet and carried her to bed.

All of Fiona's stealth had come to nothing because Jack Fielding got it all on camera. From the moment the man entered the grounds, to seeing Fiona answer her phone, then her coming out of the house, walking across the grounds, and disappearing into the cabana.

"Damn it, Wolf. You called it," Jack muttered. "I've got the evidence you wanted. You may not be alive to use it, but I'll damn sure turn it over to the police. Maybe she had something to do with your death, and maybe not. But she's not getting away with this shit."

Now all he had to do was wait for daylight to get some clear shots of their faces and he was gold. He saw the lights go off in the cabana and knew they'd make a night of it. He was secluded enough, but uncomfortable as hell, but that's how he got the big bucks. His only prayer was, "No rain."

He peeled a wrapper down on a protein bar and took a bite. Moments later, his phone signaled a text. He glanced down at it, then nearly lost his seating.

What the hell? A message from the grave?

He opened the text, reading in disbelief.

Jack, it's me, Wolf. Not dead. Had to make a last-minute flight to Sao Paulo. Stu and I switched jobs, and it got him killed. Toby knows. He flew me home. Somebody wants me dead. It may be business related, and it may be personal. Keep an eye on Fiona, and do me a favor. Find out who's heading the investigation and show them this text. Tell them to look within my organization and at her, as well. I don't trust her anymore, and I have my reasons. You have my number. I'll be in touch.

"Holy Mother of God," Jack whispered. Now he was more intent than ever to get an ID on the cabana man.

It was nearing daybreak when Wolf reached his destination.

He took the turn from the main road and into the gateless entrance, then down a long tunnel of trees framing the old low-country house at the end of the drive, then pulled the car around to the back of the house and parked.

His eyes were burning from lack of sleep. His belly was protesting a lack of food, and his steps were dragging as he circled the car to get his bags and the sack of groceries he'd stopped to get along the way.

He went up the back steps, unlocked the door, then stepped inside and flipped the light switch and set his suitcase on the floor.

Light flooded the kitchen, revealing the well-appointed renovations within. He locked the car with the remote, then closed the kitchen door and locked it. It had been so long since he'd been here that he needed to tour the house to remember the layout.

It was just after sunrise when Fiona Outen slithered back across the grounds and into her house, and Jack Fielding was still filming when her late-night guest took his leave. He didn't know who the man was, but he looked pretty pleased with himself as he headed for the rock wall, slipped behind some bushes and then promptly climbed a tree and went over the wall.

"Gotcha," Jack muttered, then got the number on the license plate as well, as the man jumped in and drove away.

As soon as it was quiet, he came down from his perch on the other side of the wall, walked two blocks up the street to where he'd parked his Jeep, and drove away. He wanted a shower and food, but not necessarily in that order, so he went through a fast-food drive-through for breakfast and ate it on the way back to his place.

After a quick shower and a change of clothes, Jack uploaded the images from the SIM card of his camera to his laptop, then watched it all from start to finish before sending Wolf a text.

Check your email. Do you want this shared with the authorities, or do you just want me to share your text?

Then he got up to get a cup of coffee, and when he came back, he had a response from Wolf.

Well, damn. I didn't see this coming. That's Hank Kilmer. I play golf with him. Yes, show it to the authorities. If they want to talk to me, get me a number and I'll call them. And thank you! Once I can come out of hiding, I'll get the money into your account.

Jack sent back a final text.

Consider it done, and this one's on me, friend. I'll be in touch.

At that point, Jack got down to business. It took four phone calls and being put on hold for a total of forty-five minutes during those calls to get the name of the federal agent in charge of Outen's murder investigation, and then he blinked when he saw the name.

It was his stepbrother, Colin Ramsey! What were the odds?

Special Agent Colin Ramsey was at his desk when the phone rang. He hit Save on his computer and swiveled his chair around to answer.

"Ramsey speaking."

"Colin, it's me, Jack. Long time, no see."

Colin blinked. "Jack as in my brother, Jack?"

Jack chuckled. "Has it been so long you also forgot what I sound like? Hell yes, it's me."

"What's wrong? Is it Dad?"

Jack sighed. "Nope. The old man is fine, or was last week when I saw him. I'm actually calling on business. I've been given to understand you're handling the chopper explosion outside of Jubilee, Kentucky."

Colin frowned. "Yes...and?"

"I'm Wolfgang Outen's go-to man when he needs things investigated, and I have some very important info to share with you."

Colin hesitated. "Look, Jack, I know we're family but I can't discuss anything to do with the—"

"Wolf's not dead."

"What the fuck?" Colin muttered. "How do you know? Can you prove that?"

"I know because I got a text from him last night and another one this morning."

"Then who was on the chopper?" Colin asked.

"Stuart Bien, Wolf's personal assistant. Apparently, there was an emergency at Wolf's refinery in Brazil, so Stu took the chopper to Jubilee with Wolf's proxy to sit in on some board meeting, and Wolf flew to Brazil on his private jet. Wolf didn't know shit about what had happened to Stu until he landed in Sao Paulo, but he believes it's someone in his inner circle who tried to take him out. And there's another angle to this story. Before Wolf left, he hired me to tail his wife. Something happened between them that led him to lose trust in her. But here's the deal. For the time being, Wolf doesn't want anyone to know he's still alive because he thinks they'll just try it again. I'm going to send you a screenshot of the texts between us. And at Wolf's instructions, I am also going to send you a video of his wife, Fiona, and his golf buddy Hank Kilmer sneaking around in the cabana outside of the big house."

Colin shifted focus. "Okay, but I'm going to have to talk to him face-to-face before I can act on any of this. I believe you. But I need to make sure someone isn't trying to pull something on you."

"Fine, but just for the record, I've worked for Outen off and on for a good ten years, and believe me, I know the man's voice better than you know mine."

Colin groaned. "You're not gonna let that pass, are you? So how do I contact him?"

"You don't. I need a safe number where he can call you that you know for sure won't be traced, or he's not having it. He'll FaceTime with you, but he's not gonna tell you where he is. I don't even know that."

"Then give him my personal number," Colin said. "I assume you still have it?"

Jack pulled up his contact list and read off the number he had.

"Yes, that's it," Colin said, "and out of curiosity, why does he suspect his wife? I mean, wives cheat, but they don't blow up a plane to get rid of the husband when it's a hell of a lot simpler just to divorce them."

"But it's a lot more lucrative to be the sole heir when they're worth a cool billion, don't you think?" Jack said.

"Noted," Colin said. "Good to hear from you, brother. We'll talk again."

"Thanks," Jack said. "Check your email in a bit. I'm about to hit Send."

Colin hung up, then turned back to his computer, pulled up his email, and waited. A couple of minutes later, the email popped up. He saw their texts. He watched the video, and then he got up and headed for the chief's office.

A half hour later, he was back at his desk. For now, they were going to adhere to Outen's request, but only until the DNA results came back. After that, Outen would have to come forward. And they were still going to continue with the investigation as it stood. Someone had blown up an aircraft in midflight and killed two people. Nobody got a pass on that.

Colin updated his partner, Mike Brokaw, on what was happening, and then while Colin was following up on the pilot who died, Mike was checking in with the lab to see if there were any updates from debris gathered at the crash site.

Colin called Sutton Airfield and was put on hold within seconds. He was trying to get information on Zander Sutton, the man who'd piloted the chopper, when someone finally picked up the phone.

"This is Borden."

"Mr. Borden, this is Special Agent Colin Ramsey. I'm very sorry for the loss of your employer, but I'm investigating the chopper crash in which he died, and I need to ask you some questions. Is that okay?"

"Yeah, sure. We're all pretty stunned about this and have no idea how it happened. Zander was meticulous about the upkeep of his aircraft."

"Were you there the day Outen and Zander left the airfield?"

"Yeah, but it didn't exactly go down like that. Wolf's personal assistant, Stu Bien, was at the airfield, waiting for Wolf when he arrived. All I know is there was a last-minute change of plans. Something about a refinery catching on fire in Brazil. Bien brought a suitcase and Wolf's passport with him, so he could fly straight to Sao Paulo. I know this because I flew Wolf to Miami airport to catch his private jet. And Stu Bien switched places with Wolf and took the flight with Zander to Kentucky. He was Wolf's proxy for some board meeting there."

Colin was stunned that the man hadn't come forward. "So, when you all were informed of Zander's crash, you already knew Mr. Outen wasn't on that chopper?"

"Well, I didn't think he was, but what do I know, right? I didn't say nothin'. Both of the men's vehicles are still parked here at the airfield, so I didn't know what to think, and you're the first person who's asked," Borden said.

Colin sighed. There were too many spoons stirring the same pot, and after talking to his brother, Jack, he guessed it was going to get worse.

"Then, Mr. Borden, I'm going to ask you to remain quiet about this for the time being. We won't officially know anything until we get DNA results back."

"Yes, sir. I don't have a problem with that," Borden said.

"Oh, and you can expect some people from the bureau will arrive to tow away both vehicles sometime today."

"Yes sir. I'll let the girls in the office know," Borden said.

"Thank you again. If I need further verification, I'll be in touch," Colin said, and hung up.

If Outen was really alive, he had yet to call. What Colin needed to do next was interview Fiona Rangely, and part of his line of questioning had to do with shaking the tree for deadfall. He was curious to see what fell out.

Chapter 7

Amalie woke with the memory of Sean's embrace and the kiss that came after. The day's weather report was vague, but cold was definite, so she dressed for warmth—thick socks for the boots she was wearing, wool pants and a soft knit sweater as comfort for the tenderness of her new scars.

She eyed the white streak in her hair as she was brushing her hair, then put it all up in a ponytail. The scars on her neck and jaw would shine like a new penny without the fall of hair to hide them, but she couldn't be bothered. Whatever anyone else thought was their problem. Today was a workday at the office. Everything she'd purchased in Jubilee yesterday was being delivered there this morning, so she put on her coat, grabbed her purse and car keys, and headed for the garage.

She was backing down the driveway when she saw a huge crane in the rearview mirror. The NTSB must be moving the chopper wreckage from the crash site. That was progress. She wondered if the investigation was making progress, too, and then kept driving. Except for feeling empathy for the families of the deceased, and for the teachers and children traumatized by the event, none of that had anything to do with her. And since she couldn't leave the office today until all of the deliveries had been made, she drove straight to Granny Annie's Bakery to get some snacks for the day.

There was a short line at the counter when she entered. The small café tables and chairs were full of customers having coffee and sweet rolls before Sunday breakfast. The aromas wrapped around Amalie like a hug as she got in line, giving her plenty of time to check out the display case, as well as the menu on the wall above the counter. By the time she got to the register, she'd made her choices and ordered two sausage biscuits, a dozen doughnut holes, and a chocolate brownie to go.

An older woman came up front carrying a tray of cinnamon rolls and slid it in the display case as the clerk was boxing up Amalie's purchases. She glanced up at Amalie and smiled.

"Welcome to Granny Annie's."

Amalie smiled. "Thank you! This isn't my first visit in here, and it won't be my last. I think I ate my way through the display case last November."

The woman laughed. "That's good to know! I'm Annie Cauley and this is my shop. I'm happy to get repeat customers. Do you live near or visiting again?"

"I've recently moved here. I'm Amalie Lincoln. I'm opening my own place next door to the bank."

Annie's eyes widened. "The CPA! I saw the sign the other day! Welcome to Jubilee."

"Thank you," Amalie said, then paid for her purchases and waved as she left the shop.

She was still smiling when she got in her car and drove away, wasting no more time getting to the office. She didn't want to leave a delivery man waiting.

Within minutes, she was inside her office and turning on lights as she carried her goodies to the back room.

She started a pot of coffee to brewing, wrapped one of the sausage biscuits in a napkin, and plopped down at her desk to eat. Once she finished off the biscuit, she got up to pour herself a cup and took it back to her desk, then began going through the enormous backlog of emails she'd been ignoring since her move. A short while later, her first delivery arrived. After that, Amalie turned her attention to office decor.

Sean's day started off slow.

He was lingering at the breakfast table, reading the news on his iPad. His mom was somewhere in the house running the vacuum, and the washing machine was on a last spin, but something was off-balance because it was beginning to thump.

He got up to shift the load and glanced at the clock. It was after 9:00 a.m. Normally, he would be in his office, but he was caught up with his workload and looking forward to a slow day when his phone rang. He glanced at caller ID, saw Carson Veterinary Clinic on the screen, and answered.

"Hello, this is Sean."

"Sean, this is Sam Carson at the vet clinic. We have some kind of issue with the computer setup in our office, and it's slowing everything down to a crawl. Do you have time to come in to town to check it out?"

"As it happens, I do," Sean said. "I can be there in about twenty minutes or so."

"I owe you, man. When you get here, you'll see what I mean," Sam said. "See you soon."

Sean dropped the phone in his pocket and then went to look for his mom to tell her he was leaving. He found her on her knees in her bedroom, going through an old trunk, with half the contents already scattered out around her.

"Hey, Mom, is everything okay?"

Shirley looked up, smiling. "Yes. I got sidetracked. All this stuff was Mom's. I'm just visiting my past."

"Then say hi to Grandma for me," he said. "I just got a phone call from the vet's office. Their computers are down. I'm heading there now. Need anything from Jubilee before I come home?"

"I'm going to town later. I have a half-dozen errands to run, and I'm taking Dani out to lunch at Cajun Katie's. Drive safe."

"Have fun. Love to Dani," he said, then grabbed his coat and car keys and headed out the door.

The day was cold but clear, and the drive down uneventful. But when he pulled into the parking lot at the vet's office and saw at least a dozen cars, he guessed it was about to get noisy, and he was right. He could hear dogs barking from halfway across the parking lot, and chaos ensued after he entered the building.

With the computers down, Arletta, the receptionist, was red-faced and hassled by demands she couldn't meet.

Leslie Morgan, Sam's vet tech, was chasing a cat down the hall.

And then Sam appeared, saw Sean, and rolled his eyes. "I did warn you."

Sean laughed out loud. "So, besides the escape from the zoo, what's going on here?"

"Follow me," Sam said, and took Sean back to his office. "The backup of patients in the outer office is because the computers are down. I can't pull up test results or anything to do with previous care. My computer went down first, and then everything else followed. I can't figure out if it's a power problem or something wonky with our technology."

"I'm assuming you've tried turning everything off and then trying to reboot?" Sean asked.

"We've tried everything but a Ouija board," Sam muttered.

"I empathize," Sean said. "Before I begin, what exactly were you doing on the computer when it quit? Did it just go black, or flicker, or were there any warning signs?"

"Other than a clown face that looked like the Joker popping up, no."

"Oh wow," Sean said.

Sam sighed. "It's a virus, isn't it? I had just opened an email when it happened."

"Sounds like it," Sean said. "Write down your log-on and password info, then leave me to it."

"Right," Sam said. "Oh, if you need to know, the breaker box is down the hall, last door on the right."

"Got it," Sean said. "Go tend to your critters and I'll see about cleaning this up."

Sam opened the top drawer of his desk, pulled out a small red notebook, and opened it to the first page.

"Log-on. Password. IP address. If you need anything else, just yell."

Sean was already in work mode as Sam left the office.

Stu Bien's absence within his circle of friends had become an issue. They knew working for Wolfgang Outen was often a twenty-four seven job. They also knew Outen was dead, so the fact that Stu wasn't answering any of his messages was a bit odd but understandable, given that he'd been the dead man's personal assistant.

But when the next morning rolled around and he still wasn't responding, his father, Ronald Bien, went by his apartment and let himself in.

The fact that there was a bowl in the sink with a smattering of dried-up cereal and curdling milk made him anxious. It was obvious it had been there for days, and Stuart was fastidious about everything.

He called Stu's number and left yet another voicemail,

then exited the apartment and went straight to the Miami PD to report him missing.

A Detective Emerson in Missing Persons took the report and was less than convinced there was an issue until he asked Ronald where his son worked.

"He is Wolfgang Outen's personal assistant. He's often out of the country, but he's never out of reach, and we're going on four days now. This isn't like him. And then we heard on the news about Mr. Outen's chopper going down, and we don't know what to think."

"Oh, I see," Emerson said.

Finding out Bien was Wolfgang Outen's personal assistant set off a whole set of alarm bells. Outen was dead. His personal assistant missing? Something was definitely off, but he had all he needed for the report.

"Thank you for coming in, Mr. Bien, and start inquiries at once. If you learn anything new, don't hesitate to call me. You have my number."

Ronald was worried, but he'd done all he knew how to do.

"Yes, and thank you. Please keep me in the loop," he said, and then was escorted back to the lobby.

But the moment Ronald Bien left Missing Persons, Emerson picked up the phone and called his boss.

It was nearing noon by the time Sean had wiped the virus and had the vet clinic's system back up and running.

"Oh my God! Thank you, Sean! Before you moved here, we had to depend on someone coming in from Bowling Green or an IT guy like you doing it remotely. What do I owe you?" Sam asked.

"I'll invoice you," Sean said. "You've got too many furry patients waiting on you out there."

"And one parakeet on the loose," Sam said. "Don't open the front door until we get it back in its cage."

"Right," Sean said. As he was walking toward the lobby, he passed Leslie in the hall. "Hey, cousin, say hi to Wade and Rita for me."

"Or, you could tell them yourself. You live closer to Mom and Dad than I do, and are you still single? I have a girlfriend who thinks you're cute."

Sean immediately thought of Amalie. "None of your business," he said, then winked and pulled her ponytail before heading to the lobby.

The AWOL parakeet was sitting on the top of Arletta's computer monitor, and Arletta had the three-legged clinic cat held fast in her lap. The cat's eyes were fixed on the little bird, and it was digging its claws into Arletta's sleeve.

Sean could see a massacre about to happen, so he put down his tool kit, walked straight toward the counter, and snatched the little bird from its perch before it knew what was happening, then turned and faced the room.

"Where's the cage?" he asked.

"Back in Exam Room four with Mildred, the owner," Arletta said.

Sean pivoted, went back down the hall and into the exam room.

The little old lady weeping in the corner looked up and then gasped.

"You caught him! You caught Peter Pan! Thank you, dear boy! Thank you," she cried.

Sean smiled. Peter Pan? He got the connection. They both knew how to fly.

"You're welcome," he said, as he slipped the little bird back into its cage and latched the door.

"He's quite the escape artist, isn't he?" Sean said.

Mildred was already at the exam table, wiping her eyes and peering into the cage.

"I told Dr. Sam not to trust him. He got out of Dr. Sam's grasp, and then someone opened the door, and out he went. I thought Captain Hook would get him."

Sean frowned. "Who's Captain Hook?"

"That three-legged cat who lives in the clinic," she muttered. "He's a scamp. A real scamp, I tell you." Then her eyes narrowed as she looked at him closer. "You're a Pope, aren't you? I can spot them a mile away."

"Yes, ma'am," Sean said. "I'll be going now. Take care."

The wind had come up while he was inside, and it made the cold day feel colder. It was just after twelve by the time he left the parking lot. He thought of Amalie and then made a knee-jerk decision to drop by her office to say hello, so he would have a good excuse to kiss her goodbye.

Amalie's last delivery arrived.

It was a painting of Pope Mountain in all its fall splendor, which was how she first saw it when she came to Jubilee. The painting was large and heavy, but she had a big wall facing the entrance in desperate need of attention, and this painting was perfect.

She was prepared for hanging it and had seen the need for extra-large picture hangers and a stud finder to make sure she got the hanger firmly set before the painting went up. But it quickly dawned on her that she was going to need a ladder, something she didn't own.

Frustrated, she plopped down on the sofa and began going through her phone, looking to see where the nearest hardware store was located, when she caught a glimpse of movement from the corner of her eye. She looked up just as Sean walked in.

"Yay! A tall person to the rescue!" she said, and jumped up and gave him a quick hug.

Sean smiled. "I don't think I've ever been greeted like this before just for being tall."

Amalie pivoted out of his arms and pointed at the painting.

"Look! Isn't it magnificent?"

Sean blinked and then moved for a closer look. "It's Pope Mountain!"

"Yes! This is how it looked last year when I first visited Jubilee. They just delivered it, and I suddenly realized I was going to have to buy a ladder just to hang it."

"Oh, nope. No need for ladders here. We've got

this," Sean said, and took off his coat. "Do you have a hammer?"

"Yes, and picture hangers and a stud finder."

Sean turned with a total lack of expression on his face. "A stud finder, hunh? Well, here I am, so it already worked. Let's do this."

Amalie burst into laughter. "Oh my lord! It's a shame you're so lacking in confidence."

He grinned. "I assume you want it on that wall?"

"Yes…centered on the wall behind the reception desk."

Sean picked up the stud finder, ran it across the wall until he found a stud, and marked it for reference. After deciding how high on the wall the painting needed to hang, he nailed the heavy-duty hanger into the stud, then hung the painting for her, shifting it until it was level.

He stepped back. "How's that?"

Amalie was standing at the entrance into her office, her hands clasped beneath her breasts as if she was praying. There were tears in her eyes.

"Perfect," she whispered. "Thank you, Sean. Thank you."

"You're welcome, honey. Are you planning to save any of these boxes?"

"No. They're all from the things that were delivered this morning."

"Then I'll break them down and carry them to the dumpster out back, okay?"

Still locked into the painting, she just nodded.

Sean made short work of the cleanup and carried the armload of cardboard out of her office and down the hall to the back entrance. A blast of cold air hit him in the face as he exited the building, and he quickly dumped the trash into the dumpster before heading back inside.

Amalie was plumping pillows on the sofa when he returned.

"What do you think?" she asked, as she gestured around the room.

But Sean's eyes were on her. "Beautiful. Just beautiful."

She turned, realized he was looking at her and not the room, and froze.

For a second, every improper thought possible was running through their heads until Sean came to his senses and made himself focus on anything but taking her to bed.

"Have you had lunch?" he asked.

"No, but I did have breakfast from Granny Annie's Bakery, and I have been in the sack of doughnut holes I brought back from there, too."

"She's my great-aunt, one of my grandmother's sisters. They were Popes."

Amalie shook her head. "I am in continued awe of your roots in this place."

"Not growing up here, so am I, and I just spent the morning at the vet's office, cleaning up a virus on their computers, and I'm starving. Will you come eat with me?"

"I'd love it, but I need to wash up first."

"I better do that, too. I've been dodging runaway cats

and endured being barked at for two solid hours. I even caught a runaway parakeet named Peter Pan, before Captain Hook, the vet's three-legged cat, could catch it."

Amalie's eyes lit up. "You're not serious."

"As a heart attack," he said.

She grinned. "Your life is far more interesting than mine. Give me a sec to wash up and then the washroom is all yours."

"Where do you want to eat?" he asked.

"At the table with you," she said, and disappeared into the back room.

The lump in Sean's throat was there before he knew it. She was already under his skin and burrowing deeper by the minute.

By the time they left the office, the wind was playing havoc with hairdos, making Amalie glad she'd left her hair in the ponytail.

"How do you feel about Trapper's Bar and Grill?" Sean asked, as he backed away from the curb.

"Love it," Amalie said, and then frowned. "Got any relatives there?"

"A couple," Sean said. "Remember the little girl from the chopper crash who was trapped with Dani in the school? Her father, Louis Glass, works there. His wife was a Pope. Her name is Rachel."

Amalie nodded. "I only ask because I don't want to be picking my nose and embarrass myself in front of your kin."

Sean grinned.

Amalie settled back to enjoy the ride.

The best part about entering Trapper's was that it was warm and out of the wind. Music was playing. A dozen televisions mounted on walls were all tuned into different sports channels with closed captions for dialogue.

Chatter and laughter overrode the music, and waiters and waitresses were doing little dance steps as they wove their way through the tables and booths with menus and trays.

As soon as they were seated in their booth, Sean and Amalie shed their coats, gave their drink orders to their waiter, and began looking through the menu.

All of a sudden, Sean heard a little voice and then running footsteps.

"Uncle Sean! Uncle Sean!"

He turned and saw Lili running toward him, and her mother, Rachel, a few steps behind, trying to catch her. He grinned and swooped Lili up in his arms.

"Hi, baby! How's my best girl? Are you feeling all better now?"

"Yes. I don't cough so much anymore. Mama says you're a zero!"

Sean grinned.

"Lili, for God's sake!" Rachel said, when she finally caught up. "Hero. I said *hero*."

Sean laughed, and Amalie was in a state of delight.

"Oh yeah. Hero," Lili said, then gave Amalie the side-eye as the waiter returned with their drinks.

"Can you give us a few more minutes to decide on food?" Sean asked.

"Sure thing," the waiter said, and walked away.

Amalie winked at Lili.

Lili giggled. "Is she your grillfriend?"

"Girlfriend," Rachel corrected, then gave Sean an adult version of Lili's side-eye. "Introductions?"

Now Rachel and Lili were both waiting for answers.

Sean sighed. "Apparently, I was so overwhelmed by the presence of three beautiful females, I forgot my manners. Rachel, this is my friend, Amalie Lincoln. We went to school together back in Conway. I am delighted to say she's recently moved to Jubilee. You might have seen the sign in the business center next to the bank about the new CPA? Amalie, this is my cousin, Rachel Glass, who is also Lili's mother and the wife of Louis Glass, who's the bartender here. He's the one looking at us now. Maybe we can all wave."

Amalie burst out laughing. "It's a pleasure to meet you, Rachel, and you, too, Miss Lili. I also understand you were very, very brave at your school, and I know how hard that can be, so that makes you a hero, too."

Lili's eyes widened. "Am I, Mama? Am I a hero, too?"

Rachel's eyes were suddenly shimmering with unshed tears. "Yes, ma'am. You sure are! Now you've said hello to Uncle Sean and his friend Amalie. Let's go back to our booth and order lunch. We came to have lunch with Daddy, remember?"

Lili reluctantly slid out of Sean's lap and took her mother's hand.

Rachel looked down at Sean. "You're a great zero to me, Sean Pope. And it's a pleasure to meet you, Amalie. Welcome to Jubilee. I'm sure we'll see you again."

Sean was a little anxious as to how Amalie had taken all that. Big families were often overwhelming, but he need not have worried.

Amalie was enchanted. "What a little beauty."

"She's all Pope, too. Impulsive, hardheaded, and loyal to the bone," Sean said.

"I could see that. I got the side-eye," Amalie said. "I think she was checking out her competition. I mean… being Uncle Sean's best girl has to have boundaries."

Sean grinned. "Technically, we're cousins twice removed, but we're all aunts and uncles to the little ones, no matter what the connection. As for you being her competition, she's just going to have to face it. Now. What sounds good to you?"

"Chicken Caesar salad and a side of onion rings."

"Umm, your food orders are as perfect as your eye for design," he said. "If I get a cheeseburger and fries, I'll trade you a handful of fries for a couple of onion rings."

"Deal," Amalie said.

Sean waved down the waiter, gave their order, and then turned his attention back to Amalie.

"You're also the prettiest dealmaker I ever met," he said.

She sighed. "Careful. You're likely to turn my head."

His voice softened. "I won't lie. I'm doing my dead-level best."

She leaned forward. "Then, fire away, Sean Pope. I am a stationary target."

Her words became a challenge Sean took straight to the heart. She'd given him all the permission he needed. He was falling fast and hard.

"Thank you for the opportunity," he said, and reached for her hand, then slid his fingers up her wrist. "Tell me about where you used to work."

"A large CPA firm in Tulsa. I was just one of the accountants, but I loved the job. Everything about it makes sense to me."

"Are you still in touch with any of them?" he asked.

She shrugged. "No. After a month or so of commiseration, the level of my suffering was too much for them to take. Calls straggled off to nothing. Even after I finally went home, nobody came to visit because they didn't know what to say. If it hadn't been for my neighbor across the hall, my life would have come to a screeching halt."

"How so?" Sean asked.

"He was an accident attorney. He went to bat for me, took the drunk driver to court, and wiped the floor with him. It was the driver's third offense. My friend made the insurance company pay, and the driver, as well. It gave me the time and finances I needed to start over, and I was kind of over Oklahoma by then. As I told you before, I came here for the holidays last year and fell in love with the mountain, which led me to you. Imagine my joy. My first friend who became my hero. I was distraught when they took me away, not because I was being moved again, but because I lost you."

Sean slid his hand across her wrist. "The bonds we create in childhood are special. Adults don't take their children's friends that seriously because they just see kids. But we were already people when we met each other. Just little ones, right?"

"Exactly," Amalie said, and looked up. "Oh, here comes our food."

They settled into their meal with the same ease they had before, like they'd known each other forever. After the meal was over, and as they were paying, Sean realized he didn't want this to end.

"You love Pope Mountain so much. Would you like to see it from the top?"

Her eyes lit up. "Yes! I would love it! When?"

"What about now?" he asked.

"Yes, yes. Take me back to the office first so I can shut everything down. I'll take my car home and you can pick me up from there. If that's okay?"

"It's very okay."

A short while later, he followed her home, waited until she parked and dropped off some things inside the house, and was ready and waiting outside his car when she came out of the house. Watching her coming toward him with that happy look on her face was like opening a present from Santa on Christmas Day. All anticipation and excitement to see what came next.

He opened the door for her as she slid into the passenger seat.

"Buckle up," he said.

So, she did.

Chapter 8

They drove all the way through Jubilee, with Sean telling Amalie about his morning at the vet and laughing about a three-legged cat named Captain Hook. He kept thinking how easy it was to be with her, and what an upbeat attitude she had towards life when life had been so hard on her.

But when they started up the mountain, her mood shifted to one of awe.

"These trees are ancient, aren't they? They have to be. They're so tall."

He nodded. "I imagine they are. If only they could tell their stories. Are you warm enough? I can turn up the heat."

"I'm fine, thank you. I actually drove a little way up this road when I was here last fall, but the forest hides the people living here, and without knowing any of them or seeing anything but mailboxes, I felt like I was intruding. Like I needed to be invited."

Sean frowned. "Really?"

She nodded. "Since I've never belonged anywhere, I don't really know how to read a room, so to speak. The mountain is so beautiful, but it feels like... Oh, I'm going to sound silly saying this...but it feels like it holds its people close...guarding them from intruders."

Sean flashed back to the disaster a couple of years ago when a younger cousin was shot up here by a man hunting for buried treasure.

"You don't sound silly at all. I think you're just sensitive to energies, and mountains are ancient. Who knows what secrets they still hold?" And then he pointed to a driveway and mailbox on his left. "That's where Louis, Rachel, and Lili live. Cameron and Rusty Pope live further up, and then the Morgans, and the Raines, and our house, and farther up, Uncle John and Aunt Annie Cauley. She's the one with the bakery. There are at least a couple of hundred people up here who can all claim some kind of kinship with each other."

"Where are we going?" she asked.

"To the top."

"What's up there?"

Sean reached for her hand and gave it a gentle squeeze. "The Church in the Wildwood. There's something I want to show you."

"I can't wait. How much farther?" she asked.

Sean grinned. "When my brother B.J. was a kid, 'Are we there yet?' was the totality of his conversation."

Amalie was laughing as she poked his shoulder. "I get the reference, but it's obvious we *aren't* there yet because you're still driving. My question had to do with time and distance."

Sean's smile widened. "Lady, you are an absolute delight, and since you asked, and unless you want to risk a wreck on these winding mountain roads, maybe another twenty minutes."

He made it in fifteen, and the gasp from the seat beside him was worth the drive.

"Do you feel that?" she whispered.

Sean glanced at the look on her face as he pulled into the parking lot. She was awestruck.

"Feel what, honey?"

Amalie shook her head and got out on her own, then closed her eyes and took a deep breath.

"It's here! This is what I kept feeling last fall when I'd look up at the mountain. Something is here that belongs to me!" Then she frowned. "No…not belongs…something that's part of me."

Sean walked up behind her and slid his arm across her shoulder.

"That does it. You're going to have to talk to Aunt Ella."

Amalie glanced up, and as she did, the features on his face shifted just enough that she thought she was looking at someone else, and then the notion faded.

"Do people still use the church?" she asked.

"The parking lot is full every Sunday. The old preacher's name is Brother Farley. If he has a first name, I don't know it. The little house behind it is the parsonage. It's where he lives, but I don't see his car. Probably visiting someone who's sick. He's known for that."

"I didn't know places like this still existed," Amalie said. "Thank you for bringing me here."

"The church isn't why we came." He held out his hand.

She clasped it without caution, already knowing she would follow him anywhere. He led her around the church to the cemetery stretching out to the edge of the forest, then wound their way through the gravestones at the far end before he stopped.

Amalie looked down. There was a very old marker, and beside it, a little wooden structure, like an upside-down box, newer but slightly weathered.

Sean pointed to the ancient marker. "The man who founded Jubilee is buried here. I've mentioned him before. His name was Brendan Pope. He's the grandfather of us all. He died in the late 1880s. His Chickasaw wife, Cries A Lot, who he called Meg, disappeared on this mountain in 1864. Her body was never found. Then two years ago, his old journal turned up. It was the first that we knew what had happened to her. And it hurt our hearts to think our little grandmother was lost all this time. We all decided that if we used the clues from the journal and some drone technology, we might find her."

Amalie was shaking as she touched the top of the little wooden house over Meg's grave.

"And you did! Oh Sean! Nearly two centuries in the dark, and you found her."

Sean blinked. She'd done it again! How the hell would she know about that abandoned cellar where they'd found Meg's bones? He shivered, then let it go.

"Yes, we did find her, and buried her beside the man who'd lost her. They're the reason we're all here now. Me and my people. The town of Jubilee. All of it."

Tears were rolling down Amalie's face.

"What a beautiful love story that finally had its ending. I can empathize with Meg. I feel lost all the time because I was given away. I used to hope someone would come find me, but they didn't. And the only reunion I've ever had is with you, so don't you ever think that didn't matter. It meant everything to me."

Sean couldn't bear the tears. When he took her in his arms, she laid her cheek against the front of his coat.

"I don't quite know how to explain this, but I don't think you're lost anymore. I think you belong here… somehow…and you found your own way back. I'm just grateful I was here to welcome you home," he said.

She looked up, lost in the intensity of his gaze.

He wiped the tears from her face and kissed her, then again and again until her lips were no longer cold and her arms were locked around his neck, giving back as good as she got.

When he finally turned her loose, she was trembling.

He tilted her chin until their gazes locked.

"You're shaking from the cold. I'm sorry, baby. I need you get you back in the car."

"I'm nowhere near cold. I'm shaking because of the fire you just lit."

Sean blinked. "Jesus wept, woman. I cannot lay you down in a cemetery in the middle of winter, but I want to."

"Another time. Another place," Amalie whispered.

His eyes flashed. "Promise?"

"Promise," she said, and let him walk her back to the car.

Once inside, silence surrounded them. It was so quiet Amalie heard the whispers.

"Goodbye," she said softly.

Sean shook his head. "I'm still here."

"Oh...sorry. Not you. They were whispering."

Sean shook his head again as he started the car and headed back down the mountain. It was getting late. The sun was already sliding below the treetops, and in winter, sunset came early. He didn't want this day with her to end, but she was so quiet.

"Amalie, honey, are you tired?"

She sighed, then laid a hand on his knee. "No, just thoughtful. You're like sunshine. It's wonderful being with you."

Sean felt like a kid again, trying out his best tricks in hopes the little girl with the long dark hair, sitting two desks ahead of him, would ever look his way.

"Would you like to stop by our house on the way down? It's either that, or lie to my mom about having you this close without stopping to say hello."

Amalie smiled. "I would love that if you think it wouldn't be an intrusion."

"I know it won't, but if it would make you feel better, I can give her a heads-up call now," he said.

"Yes, do."

Sean made the call.

Shirley answered on the third ring.

"Hi, Sean. Are you on the way home?"

"Actually, I'm on my way down the mountain. I took Amalie on a little sightseeing trip, and I was wondering if it would be okay if we stopped by before I took her home."

"Of course, it's okay. I can't wait to see her again. All I remember is a little girl with blue eyes and a lot of dark hair. Oh…and talk her into staying for supper. I'm frying chicken."

Sean laughed. "Yes, ma'am. See you soon."

Amalie was already beaming.

"How much of that could you hear?" he asked.

"All of it, and I never turn down fried chicken. This is the best day ever!"

"It's not over yet. The best is yet to come!"

Shirley went into supermom mode, and by the time they arrived, she'd run a dust mop over the living room and kitchen floors. Peeled an extra potato for the pot, and had the chicken she'd been breading already frying in the cast-iron skillet. The house was warm, and she'd turned on all the lights. It was the mountain way of making guests feel welcome.

When she heard them drive up, she was ready. There was nothing in the world she wanted more for her sons than to find their own paths to the life and the people who made them happy, and she was hoping Amalie Lincoln was that for Sean.

Then the front door opened, and Shirley called out. "I'm in the kitchen!"

They came in moments later, with Sean walking beside Amalie, with his hand at her back. The looks on their faces said it all. Shirley smiled. *What a beautiful sight. They are falling in love.*

Shirley went to meet them, gave Sean a quick kiss on the cheek, and then turned to Amalie.

"Welcome, Amalie, and what a beautiful woman you grew up to be! Do you remember me?"

Amalie smiled. "Yes, ma'am. Sean was the only boy who was nice to me, and you were Sean's mama. You brought the best cookies to the school parties, and you always gave me a hug."

Shirley's heart broke. She'd given all of the kids a hug, but in Amalie's mind, the hug had been just for her.

"I did! I can't wait to hear all about the years in between then and now, but I better get back to the stove. I don't want the chicken to burn. Sean, honey, would you get yourselves something to drink? It's going to be another twenty minutes or so before supper is finished. Show Amalie where the powder room is, and if you want, warm up by the fire."

"I'm willing to help," Amalie said.

Shirley winked. "This time you're a guest. Next time I'll put you to work."

Amalie's heart skipped. *There was already going to be a next time!*

Sean clasped Amalie's hand. "I don't have etchings to show you. How about a tour of the house and my office instead? You have to see this house. It's housed generations of Mom's family."

"This room and the living room were the original part, right?" Amalie said.

Shirley was a little taken aback. She'd never mentioned that to her boys, so how did…?

Sean saw the look on his mom's face and shook his head slightly. Shirley regained her composure. "Yes, you're right, and every generation has added on something since. I'm the fourth. My sons are the fifth generation to sleep beneath this roof."

Amalie was smiling as Sean led her away.

Shirley sighed, then went back to frying chicken, convinced there was more to Amalie Lincoln than met the eye.

Sean gave her the whole tour, and then went to his office to invoice Sam Carson, as she went to wash up.

When Amalie came out into the hall, Sean was nowhere to be seen, so she paused a moment, lost in thought. *The voices at the church. I've heard them before. They were the same voices in my head after they pulled me out of the fire. What's happening to me?*

Then she heard footsteps and opened her eyes. Sean was standing in the hall, watching her.

She shivered. "I said something earlier that made no sense to me. I'm still trying to figure out why I said it."

Sean waited.

She kept talking. "Before last fall, I had never been to Kentucky. Before last fall, I didn't know Jubilee even existed. But from the moment I first saw Pope Mountain, it felt like home. And I have no concept of what *home* really means other than where my things are stored and where I eat and sleep, and yet that's the only word that fit what I was feeling."

Sean opened his arms. She walked into them, savoring the feeling of being enveloped.

"Something's happening to me here, Sean, and I think you're part of it. Maybe all of it. I heard the words about the original part of your house coming out of my mouth, but I don't know where they came from. I have no reason to know that," Amalie said.

Sean shook his head. "Aunt Ella says the mountain has magic. It holds ancient secrets and holds fast to the people who honor it. Maybe it's just talking to you, honey, and you're the only one who can hear it."

She sighed. "Maybe, and maybe it's just me. Maybe that accident did something to my brain."

"You should do a little online research and read about people who develop certain gifts after near-death experiences. Maybe you didn't just survive, but came back with new abilities. You wouldn't be the first," he said.

Amalie's eyes widened. "I never thought of that. My head is always full of numbers."

"And my head is always full of possibilities. I'm always looking for the back door into a problem to solve it. I think we pair well, like biscuits and gravy," and then he winked.

She grinned. "Biscuits and gravy. That's probably the most romantic thing anyone has ever said to me."

He shrugged. "I do what I can."

She laughed.

And for Sean, that sound was a high like no other.

"Not to change the subject, but I feel a chill in the house. I think it's time to put another log on the fire. I'm not all brainiac. Come watch me being all strong and stuff."

Amalie grinned, and when he reached for her hand, she clasped it.

Back in the kitchen, Shirley heard the laughter and smiled. It was good to have joy in this house, and a few minutes later, they were back with her.

"I talked briefly with B.J. today. I missed his text. He says he's coming home for Easter," Shirley said.

"That's great, Mom! Now we'll have two great chefs in the kitchen."

"Has B.J. always wanted to be a chef?" Amalie asked.

"If he did, he never said anything about it growing up," Shirley said. "All he did was eat. He was never full."

"And the last one to leave the table. Leftovers were nonexistent in our house," Sean said.

Amalie giggled. "I was always a little hungry, too, but mostly because we weren't allowed second helpings. Too many foster kids to feed, I guess. One of my foster mothers made the best chicken and dumplings. It's still my favorite comfort food, but I'm no good at making the dumplings. They're either raw on the inside or falling apart in the broth."

"We'll have to make them together one day. I'll show you a secret to that," Shirley said.

"Will you really?" Amalie asked. "I would love that."

"I'd love it, too," Sean said. "Could I be the official taste tester?"

Shirley smirked. "You're the only one left at home, for which I am daily grateful, but it also means you're the designated hitter for everything now. So, yes, you're the taste tester. But tonight, the chicken is fried, not stewed, and I just took the last piece out of the skillet."

"What can I do to help?" Sean asked.

"Get the plates and flatware out for Amalie. She can set the table and you can mash potatoes. I'm going to finish up the sides."

Amalie quickly did her part, then got out of the way. She walked to the kitchen window to look out at the land beyond, and saw pasture, and outbuildings, and trees in the distance that went on forever, being blanketed by a fresh fall of snow. Big flakes, already beginning to coat the ground.

"It's snowing!" she cried, and darted outside before they could react.

They both walked to the window to see where she'd gone. She was standing in the yard with her arms out, head tilted back, letting the snow fall on her face.

Shirley saw the expression on her son's face and sighed.

"You've fallen for her, haven't you?"

He sighed. "I loved her when I was nine. This is just a reawakening."

Shirley was stunned. "Oh, honey. Well, I'm happy for you now."

"I want Aunt Ella to meet her," Sean said.

Shirley frowned. "Okay, but why Ella, specifically?"

"Because I think they're alike. She knows stuff she shouldn't know and it's bothering her. I think it started after her wreck. I took Amalie up to the Church in the Wildwood. She's so drawn to the mountain. I was telling her about Brendan and Meg, and how she'd gone missing, and Brendan had died without knowing what happened to her, and us finding the journal and wanting to find her again."

"What did she say?" Shirley asked.

"I said nothing about the search, or where we'd found her, but the moment she touched the little house over Meg's grave, she said something to the effect of how wonderful it was that she'd been found and was no longer alone in the dark."

Shirley shivered, then looked back out the window.

"She's lost, too, isn't she?"

He shrugged. "She's been lost all her life. Even from me. I actually cried the day I went back to school and found out she was gone. I'm not losing her again."

"Oh, son...I didn't know you felt that way. You never said."

He winked. "I was a kid. Guys aren't good at sharing feelings."

And then the back door opened, and Amalie came in talking.

"This is the most beautiful place on earth. You're so blessed to be here and part of the history of the place."

"You're sparkling," Sean said, and lightly brushed snowflakes from her hair.

"Inside and out!" Amalie said.

"And you're just in time," Shirley said. "Supper's ready."

Sean seated the women before sitting down.

"Sean keeps feeding me," Amalie said, as they began filling their plates.

"It's the only excuse I could come up with for the pleasure of seeing your face," he said.

"Then you're gonna have to pull a different rabbit out of the hat next time," Shirley said. "Everybody help yourselves. If it keeps snowing, I'm not letting either of you on this mountain road before daylight tomorrow. Ever been to a slumber party, Amalie?"

Amalie poured gravy over her mashed potatoes, then passed the gravy boat to Sean. "No, but I always wanted to."

"Don't worry," Sean said. "I have four-wheel drive, and the snow just began. It's probably not even snowing down the mountain. We'll be fine."

"Shoot," Amalie said. "I was all set for ghost stories and snuggles."

Shirley smiled to herself as she scooped a spoonful of coleslaw onto her plate. This girl was going to fit into their crazy family just fine.

They left the house just after 8:00 p.m. with a sack of leftovers for Amalie and an open invitation for a lesson in making dumplings when she had the time. She could still feel Shirley's kiss on her cheek and the warm hug before they walked out the door.

The snow was still falling, swirling before the headlights like duck down and just beginning to stick on the blacktop, but Sean already had his SUV in four-wheel drive.

"Thank you for today," Amalie said.

"Thank you for sharing it with me," Sean said.

"Always," she said. "In the next few days, I'm going to hit the shops to get quotes for flowers and finger food for my open house, and I don't want to do it by phone. I want to taste stuff, not order it blind." Then she leaned her head back against the seat and glanced out the window beside her into the darkness. "It's sure dark on the mountain. No streetlights whatsoever. Just a black screen of nothing except a white line in the middle of the blacktop and the car as your cursor."

Sean was surprised by the imagery and her relating it to his work.

"So, where's the next link? What do I click on?" he asked.

"The lights of the city. And after that my street, and then my house."

He smiled. "You've played this game before, haven't you?"

"I've thought about it. But there's never been anyone before to play it with," she said, and then glanced at his profile, highlighted by the dashboard lights.

Sean took a deep breath and tightened his grip on the steering wheel.

"Why do I feel like the focus of this game just changed and is sliding downhill faster than we are?"

Amalie shrugged. "Probably because life cheated us a little, and we've learned the hard way how fast happiness can disappear. I hold on to all things dear."

The skin crawled on the back of Sean's neck.

"Am I one of those things?"

"You are my sunshine," she said softly.

"I have this overwhelming need to kiss you, and I need both hands on the wheel, and…I see lights down below!"

"I know. I've been ignoring them. I don't want this day to end."

"There will be others. And short of sounding like a stalker, I lost you once. I won't let that happen again."

There was a tightening in her chest. At any moment, she felt like she might burst into tears.

"Promise?" she asked.

"Promise," he said.

As he predicted, the farther down the mountain they went, the less it was snowing. By the time he pulled up in her driveway, it was obvious it hadn't snowed here at all.

They got out of the car in unison, with Sean carrying her bag of leftovers into the house and Amalie going ahead of him, turning on lights as she went.

"Just set the food on the counter, and thank you for bringing it in," she said, then took off her coat and wrapped her arms around his neck. "One for the road? And don't even talk about what we're both thinking. No slumber party tonight. I want to know you're home safe before the roads get bad up there, and for us, there's always tomorrow. I'm here, and I'm not going anywhere. I found where I belong."

The kiss was unavoidable. Supper had been foreplay. They had been dancing around this moment for hours.

But it went from gentle to engulfing within seconds. One moment Amalie was in his arms and the next thing she was against the wall, pinned between Sheetrock and a living, breathing wall of man and muscle.

She was at the point of coming out of her clothes when he suddenly lifted his head and stared straight into her eyes. She was still pinned against the wall, so close she could feel the jut of his erection. His breathing was shaky, and yet he hadn't made a move beyond the kiss.

"Don't want to leave you," he said.

She put her hands on his chest, feeling the blood rush of his heart. "And I don't want you to go, but you're going to because it's the sane thing to do, and right now we're both too close to insanity to make the right choice."

He nuzzled the side of her neck. "Beautiful. Sexy. And wise. I can't fight that."

"Text me when you get home, so I know you're safe?" she asked.

"Yes. Walk me to the door, and then lock it fast before I change my mind."

She sighed. "Where have you been all my life?"

"On hold, pretty girl, on hold."

He held her hand all the way to the door. "For now, and for the rest of your life, when you need something, call me. I need to be wanted, too."

Then he opened the door and got as far as the steps before he turned around.

"Lock the door, Amalie."

She closed the door between them and turned the lock.

Sean's heart was pounding, his pulse was playing ricochet from his head to his toes, and he ached to be with her, but not tonight. Instead, he got in the car and drove away.

Amalie watched his taillights until they disappeared, and then she put up the food she'd brought home and stripped and crawled into a tub of hot, steamy water. A cold shower would have been wiser, but it was the wrong weather for that, and it would take more than a cold shower to turn off the fire he'd started with a kiss.

Thirty minutes later, she was still in the tub when her cell phone rang.

"Hello?"

"I'm home. Are you in bed?"

"I'm soaking in the tub."

"Jesus wept and thank you for the image," he muttered, then heard soft laughter in his ear. "It's not funny."

"You're right. This is the saddest, most miserable moment ever."

He sighed. "Okay, point taken. I'm just having a guy moment. It will pass."

"I don't want it to go away. And I honor the intention. I mean… After all, we swore a blood oath to each other on the day of gum in the hair."

"We did?" he asked, and heard laughter in her voice again.

"You don't remember? Dang, mister. I've carried that oath with me forever. It became my lucky charm. It was the spell you put on me to bind me to you for life."

He was grinning now. "Are you teasing me now?"

"I'm insulted. No, I'm not teasing. You had the bullies already laid out on the ground. They were wailing and bawling and bleeding all over the place, and teachers were coming out of the building on the run, and you were helping me up. There was a bloody cut on the palm of my hand, and your knuckles were bloody from the fight. You frowned and said, 'You're bleeding, Molly,' and I pointed at your hand and said, 'You're bleeding, too.' Then you got this look on your face. Your eyes narrowed. Your chin jutted like it always did when you got serious, and you cried out, 'Blood oath!' Then you put your bloody knuckles in the palm of my bloody hand and said, 'Ain't nobody gonna ever hurt you again,' and then the teachers dragged us away."

"Oh man… Yes, I remember that. My brothers and I were all into playing knights and slaying dragons for the princess, and we played blood oath until Mom made us quit, because she got tired of scrubbing the blood out of our clothes. You were the only for-real princess I ever got a chance to protect."

Amalie's voice softened. "And you were the knight in shining armor I needed to appear. So, no worries about me disappearing again. You slayed my dragons. You shed blood for me. You won my heart years ago. I think in the lands of knights and dragons and rescued princesses, you already own me. Rest easy, Sir Sean. All is well with me."

Sean was still smiling long after she'd hung up, and when he finally fell asleep, he dreamed of dragons bowing down, and a sword with a wolf crest, and Amalie rising from the ashes.

Chapter 9

Snowfall ended before morning.

The sight from below had turned the mountain into a giant cupcake with icing on the top.

Everyone within the icing was hustling around, getting ready to go to work, and children were begging to go play in the snow before mothers had them fed.

Cameron Pope was already outside with his son, Mikey, making a snowman, while Ghost, who was as white as the snow, was on the porch with Rusty. As big and furry as the German shepherd was, he had come from a land of sand and heat and considered anything colder than rain an offense.

A couple of miles down the mountain, Rachel Glass was bundling her daughter, Lili, up in a coat and mittens, so she could go outside with Daddy. It was Louis's day off, and he was devoting the day to his family and the daughter they'd almost lost.

Shops were opening in Jubilee, and special shows with winter-rate prices were ongoing in the music venues to keep business booming and visitors coming and going. Beneath all the fun and entertainment, Jubilee was a well-oiled dynasty, hiding in plain sight.

Amalie was kicked back on her sofa with a cup of coffee at hand, going through emails on her laptop, when it occurred to her that she hadn't checked the spam file since her move, so she opened it to make sure something important hadn't wound up in there.

As she was going through the list, she noticed a message from Ancestry.com. Thinking it was probably an advertisement, she almost deleted it and then hesitated, reminding herself there was always hope, and opened it.

And read it.

And her heart nearly stopped.

After all these years, she had a match!

Her hands were shaking. She wasn't even sure if she remembered her password, and jumped up and ran into her home office, dug her "little black book" out of her desk, and flipped through the pages until she found it and ran back to her computer.

"Oh my God, oh my God," Amalie whispered, as she logged in to her site, then went through the links to get to the name. There was the name. Wolfgang Amadeus Outen, with a suggested parental connection. Her heart was pounding. "Is this man my father?" There was a link to contact him via email and she clicked on it.

Her fingers were flying over the keyboard as she sent a message.

Dear Mr. Outen,

My name is Amalie Ann Lincoln. I am twenty-seven years old. I am a CPA and own my own business. I grew up in foster care. I have no background or knowledge of my family or parents, or where I came from. But Ancestry.com has just notified me that we share a familial connection. If you are interested in connecting with me, please reply to this email or call me at this number.

I look forward to your response.

Amalie

Then she hit Send, leaned back, and stared out the office window at the mountain looming in the distance.

"Holy crap, did this just happen?" she muttered.

All outside noises faded into the background. She kept telling herself he would surely welcome this news, or he would never have signed up on this kind of site. Or maybe not. Maybe it had been true ancestry he'd been looking for, not a by-blow of his youthful past. All she knew was that she wouldn't get her hopes up until she heard a voice, and she knew how to hide expectations. It was back to business as usual.

If there was a miracle on her horizon, she would welcome it. But today, her reality was the business she was trying to grow, and it was time to head to town. The urge to call Sean was huge, but she wasn't talking about any of this until she knew it was a fact.

Sean was in his office early, doing a remote cleanup for a small business in Bowling Green, completely focused on how they'd been hacked. They'd already lost five thousand dollars to hackers getting into their bank account, and at the moment, they had frozen their own account until further notice.

He had been working for nearly three hours when he finally found it—malware in their online security that allowed the hackers to get into the weakened system and access the money. After that, it took Sean another hour to clean it up and reinstall the security with added antimalware.

After one last run-through and getting an all clear, he called the owners, let them know they were good to go, and sent them an invoice.

It was a good morning's work, but it was nearing noon. He could smell something cooking and headed to the kitchen.

Shirley heard him coming up the hall.

"You finally came up for air!" she said.

"I just cleaned a whole lot of bad juju out of a business

system. All that hard work made me hungry, and something smells good."

"I baked a small ham and made a corn casserole and coleslaw. Biscuits are in the oven. They'll be done in a couple of minutes. Get yourself something to drink and then we'll eat."

Sean filled a glass with ice and sweet tea, then walked to the window, admiring the overnight snowfall.

"It's beautiful out there, isn't it?" he said.

"Yes. Too bad your Amalie isn't here. She'd likely be outside tromping around in it," Shirley said.

My Amalie. It had a nice ring.

"Most likely," he said, then took a drink of his tea and set it on the table. "Be right back. I'm going to add another log to the fire."

Wolf woke up before sunrise, momentarily startled by the unfamiliar shadows of the room until he remembered where he was and why. For a man who had always had his finger on the pulse of the world and his businesses, he was, for the moment, completely disconnected with all of it.

It was both unsettling and worrisome to wonder what was happening to his holdings with Fiona at the helm, and he reached for his phone to check for messages. He had one, from Jack, and opened it immediately.

Wolf, the fed handling the murder investigation of the crash turns out to be my stepbrother, Special Agent Colin Ramsey. I've given him the details. He's willing to hold off on an official notification of your death, but only until DNA results are in. But he needs to confirm for himself that you are still alive. This is his personal phone number. You need to make it a video call so he can see that it's you. If you need me for anything else, you know what to do.

Wolf threw back the covers and went to get dressed, then headed for the kitchen, turning on lights as he went. First thing on the agenda was coffee, so he filled the well in the Keurig, popped in a coffee pod, slid a coffee mug beneath the spout, and hit the power button.

After that, he began making the rounds inside the house, looking out every window until he was satisfied that he hadn't been followed. By the time he returned, the coffee was ready and so was he. He took it to the kitchen table, then pulled out his phone and made the call.

Colin Ramsey was just getting out of the shower when his cell phone rang. He glanced at the time and then realized it was a video call coming in as Out of Area.

"Outen," he muttered, grabbed a T-shirt and pulled it over his head, wrapped the towel around his waist, and sat down on the side of his bed to answer. The moment he did, Outen's face was before him. "Son of a bitch. You *are* alive," he said.

Wolf grimaced. "Only because someone set one of my Brazilian refineries on fire. I am assuming you've seen everything I asked Jack to send to you."

"Yes, and I've spoken to my superior. But you only have until the DNA reports come back confirming the identification of those onboard the chopper. Do you really suspect your wife is capable of all this?"

"Yes. Discovering her infidelity was one thing. But she's pulled a couple of stunts the past month that made me realize how little I truly know about her. I always do background checks on people I hire. Maybe I should have done that with the women I married."

"But planting a bomb on a chopper? That doesn't fit in with known scenarios of how women kill," Colin said.

"Fiona is a biomedical engineer. She builds one-of-a-kind surgical instruments for surgeons all over the world. She has a master's degree in engineering and a very successful business of her own, and she always insists on packing for me when I travel, so if there was a bomb, and if it was on that chopper, it's because I carried it to the airport and Stu carried it onto the plane."

"What do you mean?" Colin asked.

"Stu was waiting for me when I got to Sutton Airfield. I had a scheduled board meeting in Jubilee, Kentucky. I'm one of the investors in a big hotel there. Stu learned about the bombing and fire at the refinery when it was called in at the office and, for some reason, couldn't reach me by phone, so he headed to the airfield to intercept. He was waiting for me when I arrived. After a brief discussion, he agreed to take my proxy and place at the board meeting in Jubilee, and had my pilot and private jet waiting for me at Miami International. Stu and I are...were... the same height and size. I gave him my bag packed for a couple of days' stay at Jubilee, and he brought the bigger suitcase I keep packed at the office for emergency travel, along with my passport and a decent amount of cash. So, if the bomb was in the bag, then Stuart carried it onto the chopper, just as I would have done."

"Okay then," Colin said. "We'll continue to follow all leads, but with emphasis on what we can find out about her. In the meantime, if you get any further info that would help with the investigation, you have this number. No need for further video. A text on this line will do."

"Thank you, sir, and I understand Jack Fielding is your stepbrother. You should know that he's also one of three people I trust implicitly in this world, and one of them just died on that chopper. I want someone brought to justice for that. Stuart Bien died because of me."

"Understood," Colin said. "And my sympathies for your loss."

The call ended, but the day for both of them had just begun.

Colin dressed and headed for the office with this new information, while Wolf settled in for the day with his laptop, checking the stock market, reading his newspapers online, still putting off opening email. Even if he saw pressing business, he wouldn't be able to answer it, because in the eyes of the world, he was dead.

The forensic report on Ellis Townley's clothes and apartment was on Detective Muncy's desk when he got to work. Miami Homicide now had their first lead on a suspect—a man named Vincent Romo. They went to his last known address with an arrest warrant, only to discover he was no longer in residence. Yet another snag in their case. Now they had to find out where he'd gone.

It was beginning to appear that both Townley and Romo had a part to play in the chopper exploding and Outen's subsequent death, but that case belonged to the feds, and Miami Homicide needed to offload what they had that did not pertain to their case.

When they got back to the precinct, Muncy sat down at his desk and began calling until he got the name of the FBI special agent in charge, and then made another call and waited for the agent to pick up.

It was midmorning and Special Agent Colin Ramsey was at his computer running a background check on Fiona Rangely when his desk phone rang. He picked up the receiver while still focused on the screen.

"Special Agent Ramsey."

"Agent Ramsey, I'm Detective Joe Muncy. I work in the Homicide division of the Miami PD. During our investigation of a murder here in Miami, we think we might have uncovered links to the crash that killed Wolfgang Outen in Jubilee, Kentucky. We were told you're the lead investigator on the case. Is this so?"

"Yes, but what led you to this conclusion?" Colin asked.

"We caught a homicide case in an apartment building in a lower-income area of Miami. The dead man was Ellis Townley, a.k.a. Roadie. Forensics identified DNA at the murder scene belonging to a known criminal named Vincent Romo. We have an arrest warrant out for Romo, but at the moment he's in the wind. Here's where your crash feeds into our info. If the midair explosion happened because of a bomb, and if it had been detonated by a phone call, then we have reason to believe Ellis Townley made the call and Romo was the cleanup guy."

The hair stood up on the back of Colin's neck. "I'm listening."

At that point, Muncy began to explain—from finding Ellis's phone in his car and the receipt from Bullard's Campgrounds in Jubilee, and confirming his DNA was in a cabin rented under this name—that Ellis Townley had been murdered the day after the crash and within an hour of his return to Miami.

Muncy continued. "During our forensic search at the crime scene, we discovered Ellis's phone and a receipt from the campgrounds in his car. When we called the campgrounds for verification, we spoke to a clerk named Jordan, who had additional info that added to Townley's suspicious behavior. Keep in mind it's winter in Kentucky, and cold as blazes there, and yet the Friday morning of the crash, Jordan claims he saw Townley standing out in a clearing between the office and his cabin for quite a while, continually looking up at the sky with his binoculars and holding a phone. And within minutes of the crash, Townley was in the office checking out in a state of panic. Jordan, the clerk, said a chopper had crashed just outside an elementary school causing severe damage and injuries, and Townley was ashen and shaking."

Colin frowned. "Right. Of course, we know about the school."

"The last call on Townley's phone was to a burner phone," Muncy said. "When we contacted the police, they gave us access to school employees who confirmed the timeline of the warning Mrs. Pope gave to the office to the timeline of the last call made on Townley's phone."

"And?" Colin asked.

"Mrs. Pope's warning was within a minute of the last call on Townley's phone."

Colin took a deep breath. "Okay. I see where you're going, but—"

"That's not all," Muncy said. "We pulled banking records for Townley and Romo. Both men received large lump-sum deposits into their accounts on the Monday before the explosion on Friday. Townley's was ten thousand dollars. Romo's was twenty-five thousand. But we don't know who put them there, and this is where our need-to-know ends and yours begins."

Ramsey was stunned by the developments. "Can you send me all of the files and info you have on this?"

"Yes, sir, with pleasure," Muncy said. "We're still after Romo. If we find him, we'll let you know. Unless something happens, he'll likely be charged with Townley's murder. But your team is the one to dig deeper into phone calls and bank deposits."

"Much appreciated," Muncy said. "Send your files to my email address here at headquarters. We'll take it from there."

"Happy to help," Muncy said. He wrote down the email address Colin gave him, then hung up the phone and began assembling files.

A short while later, Colin received the files, made printouts, then set Brokaw on the trail of the money deposits and gave another agent the job of issuing a request for the phone records of both men, while Colin began to dig into Fiona Rangely's background.

Fiona Rangely was fully convinced that no one knew about her fling with Hank Kilmer, and she needed to keep it that way. Since she was Wolf's widow, a perception of propriety and grief was important. There would never be a public reveal of her and Hank's relationship, because Hank's wife would have something to say about that.

She had been given to understand there were no physical remains of Wolf to recover, only bits and pieces of DNA. It was a shocking realization that a body could just disintegrate.

Now she would wait until the lab's findings officially determined the identities of the crash victims before she could proceed to the business of what to do next, but scheduling a memorial service and a reading of the will would have to wait. And that was something of a nail-biter, because she didn't know what was in Wolf's will. They'd signed a prenuptial agreement, so she already knew there were boundaries, but the rest was a mystery and that made Fiona nervous. She didn't like surprises. She sat within the silence of her home, thinking through everything she'd set in motion.

It was all Wolf's fault. That damn Ancestry test.

Once she knew he'd sent it off, she spent weeks watching his email for the results. He was off on one of his trips when it came. As usual, after going through her own personal mail, she logged into his email account from her laptop. She knew the password because she trolled the account daily, making sure he wasn't cheating with another woman on the side.

Even though she knew it was coming, the day she saw it, she clicked to open it and realized it was the test results he'd sent off. But she didn't have access to the Ancestry account, so she couldn't follow through. Angry, she just deleted it from the list.

She'd spent four years of her life on this man, grooming their relationship, being the loving, attractive, devoted wife he wanted, and it had been worth it. Wolf was handsome, sexy, and rich as sin, everything she wanted in a man. Ultimately, it would still have come to this end. They always did. But he'd forced her hand, and so she'd gone into her little bag of tricks and made calls and pulled strings, and bought off people to create what she needed to make happen, and here is where she'd landed. The rich grieving widow, awaiting a death certificate to get on with her life.

She'd stayed home from the office today and got up to make herself a drink. It was early in the day, but she could be forgiven for the need. She poured herself a shot of bourbon and carried it to the window overlooking the grounds between the house and the tennis court, then took a sip.

Liquid fire, smooth as silk, slid down the back of her throat. It always made her eyes water, but she loved the kick. Then she threw back the shot and swallowed the rest of it like medicine and closed her eyes, waiting for the fire to reach her stomach.

And in that moment, while she was still riding the burn, a horrible thought occurred. She'd put an end to Wolf Outen. But now that he was officially registered, what if he got a hit from Ancestry.com?

"Shit! Shit, shit, shit!"

Wolf was gone. His laptop reduced to shrapnel and ashes. But his fucking DNA was now on record for life in that repository. What if someone had already keyed in on his new entry?

She made a sharp pivot and went to get her laptop. Wolf was gone, but nothing about his life had been changed or deactivated. She logged back onto his personal email and began searching. When she saw another Ancestry email with the heading, You have a new connection!, and knew she couldn't open it, she wanted to throw up.

If the connection reached out to Wolf, it wouldn't go through the Ancestry website. It would come in the form of a personal email to him. All she could do now was continue to troll his email and wait.

Wolf had been on his laptop all morning. He wanted to log on to his bank accounts and check in with his lawyer, but that would open the floodgates of his resurrection, and it still wasn't the time. Instead, he finally began going through the daunting task of sorting through his business email. There were hundreds of them, and the urge to purge was strong. But he didn't have anything else to do, and it was a way to pass the time.

It was nearly midafternoon when he paused, then got up and walked away. He was thinking about home, and what he wouldn't give for the freedom to walk over to the wet bar and pour himself a drink.

"Whiskey neat," he muttered, as he popped the top on a can of Coca-Cola.

The house was quiet and isolated, and after a few moments, he walked out of the kitchen and onto the back side of the wraparound porch and sat down in one of the cane-back chairs against the wall. He took a quick sip of the cold pop as he surveyed his surroundings.

The lagoon behind the house made him wary of alligators. He frowned at the neglected landscaping, knowing he was paying someone for upkeep, and made a mental note to deal with that when he got home.

It was chilly today, even with full sun, but it was January, Georgia's coldest month of the year, and he was wishing for different clothes than what he had. Next time he left the house to get food and gas, he was going to pick up a couple of sweatshirts, denim pants, and laundry soap. No way to tell how long he would be here, and washing what he had was inevitable.

He sat sipping his drink, still in shock about Fiona. He was ninety-nine percent sure she was responsible for the bomb, and stunned by the level of her betrayal. He'd never seen this coming. Never suspected her of deceit—until that day she'd found the refuse from the testing kit he'd sent to Ancestry.com. Why would she care if he found family, unless she was planning his demise and expected to be his only heir?

It was fifteen minutes to five when he finally went back

inside. He wanted a steak, but he would be having ham and cheese on whole wheat bread and be grateful he still had choices. Stuart Bien damn sure did not. So, he made the sandwich and a cup of coffee and went back to the laptop.

Another hour later and Wolf was down to the last and most recent emails on his business account, all of them advertisements or random companies peddling their wares to a mailing list when he saw a notice from Ancestry.com. Finally, his test results! He opened it, read it, and then created his account. His family tree only had one leaf. His name. He would have to enter his mother and father's names later, but all of their info was at home.

Then he scrolled down farther through his email and saw another notice.

A Possible Ancestry Link. He frowned. How could he get a personal notice so fast? He went back and checked the date of the first notice. It wasn't recent. Then he checked this notice. It had come days after his first report, and yet he'd seen neither of them on his personal account, and they'd arrived before his supposed death.

What the hell is going on?

Still confused, he opened the second notice and had to read it twice before the info sank in. Then his heart skipped a beat.

A daughter? I might have a daughter? That is fucking impossible.

He had to take the chance and opened his personal email account. Neither of those messages where there, and they should have been because he'd used both of them as contact addresses and listed the personal one first. Why were they on the business account and not the personal one?

He hadn't opened his personal account at all for fear of someone knowing it was active, but he had to find out what was happening and went to the personal account, only to find out neither of them were there.

But what he did find was a response to the notice of having a match. He opened his ancestry page, went through the info on the possible link, and began to read, and as he did, became horrified at what was unfolding in front of him.

If this young woman's DNA was a match to his DNA, then his ex-in-laws had lied through their teeth and given his daughter away! It seemed impossible, but it was the only explanation...because after his wife and daughter's deaths, and because of what they'd told him, he'd had a vasectomy to keep from ever fathering a child again.

He read the letter again, reading between the lines to the poignancy of the post, and then he googled the woman's name. Link after link appeared, regarding her connection to a CPA firm in Tulsa and then to a horrifying car crash. And then something about winning a lawsuit against the drunk driver who nearly killed her.

Then he found an article with her photo and froze.

"Oh my God, oh my God, Shandy, my Shandy...it's you. She's you!"

In that moment, he knew this had to be his child because she was the spitting image of the woman he'd loved and lost. His voice was shaking. He felt like throwing up. "That fucking family. They gave you away because they wanted no part of me. When all of this is over, I'm going to make them wish they were the ones who'd never been born."

But now that he'd seen her letter and the photo, it didn't answer the question of why he hadn't received his own information from the test he'd sent in.

Then it hit him. Fiona! She'd already had a fit about him submitting the test. *What if she'd been watching for that email results? She could have been checking my email for days. What if she'd seen it and deleted it because she didn't want me to know?*

His thoughts were in free fall, but this worked both ways. He didn't want Fiona to know this young woman existed. It could put her in danger, too! So, he copied her letter to his work email. But his elation in learning he had a daughter came with the gut-wrenching fear that her life was now in danger because of him. If Fiona wanted him dead for his money, then she wasn't going to want to share it with a daughter she didn't know he had. Stuart Bien had already died. He'd be damned before he'd let this happen again.

He wanted to call Amalie. But his first thought was protecting her, and so he called Colin Ramsey instead.

Colin was sitting on his sofa, with a pizza on the coffee table in front of him and a beer at his elbow. Between the info they'd received from Wolf Outen, and then the call from Detective Muncy in the Miami PD, it felt like the case was beginning to come together. If the leads he'd been given came to fruition, the randomness of it all was boiling down to a greedy woman. They were still waiting on reports from the evidence gathered at the crash site, but progress was slow due to the sheer quantity of it.

He'd just chewed and swallowed his last bite and was reaching for another slice when his cell phone rang. Out of Area was all the screen showed on caller ID, but he guessed it was Wolf.

"Hello, this is Colin."

"It's me," Wolf said. "I don't suppose you have any firm evidence yet to link Fiona to this mess?"

"No, we don't, Wolf. What's wrong?"

"I just discovered something that is concerning to me, and I'm not sure how to handle it," and then he went into the whole explanation, and ended with, "What should I do? I'm afraid not to warn her. But without being certain it's Fiona at the bottom of it, I don't know who to warn her from."

"What if she's not your daughter?" Colin asked. "You'd still want to confirm it through another DNA test."

"Ancestry already did that for us, and when I saw her photo, I knew it was her. She's a mirror image of her mother, Shandy, who was my first wife."

"So how did you lose a baby, if you had a wife?"

"I was overseas working on an oil rig at the time. You know...there was big money in Saudi oil patches back then, and I was gone for months at a time. We were living with her parents and Shandy was five months pregnant when I left again. The paycheck for the job would set us up in our own place. I'd been there for months and was due to fly back in three weeks when I got a call that Shandy had gone into an early labor. It was a bad scene. I hopped the first plane out, but by the time I got there, she'd already delivered and was dying from a brain bleed, one of those unknown aneurysms people have and never know about until they blow. Her parents told me the baby had been born dead and severely malformed. They'd already had it removed to a crematorium. Shandy died in my arms less than an hour after my arrival. I was out of my mind with grief and disbelief, and the day after the funeral, they kicked me out of their lives. All I can think is that the fuckers gave away the baby because they wanted no part of me."

Colin was shocked. "That's appalling. I can't imagine how you're feeling right now, but I think we both need to sleep on this a day or two. Give me a little time to get the background check we're running on Fiona before we make any decisions, okay? We still don't have a lick of proof that any of our theories are correct."

Wolf sighed. "Yeah, okay, but only a day or two. I've lost twenty-seven years of my daughter's life. Life is short and unpredictable. I don't want to die with her thinking I didn't want her."

"Understood, and it's always your call to break the news of your resurrection anytime you see fit. Just let us know in advance before you do."

"Will do," Wolf said. "Thanks."

The call ended. Colin put his phone aside and reached for another slice. But even as he was eating it, he realized his appetite was gone. He couldn't quit thinking about the tragedy, and how Wolf's life had unfolded afterward, wondering if it was anger or grief that had driven him to become the man he was today.

After talking to Colin, Wolf went back to his personal site to reread Amalie's letter again, and to his horror, it was gone.

Fiona!

Oh God, she'd read it! Deleted it like everything else, but she knew!

This changed everything!

Chapter 10

It became a time of sit and wait for all concerned.

The Miami police were still looking for Vincent Romo.

The feds investigating the crash were still sorting through evidence, although it appeared the bomb had been triggered by a phone call, which linked the info from Miami directly to their case.

Wolf Outen made a foray into a small nearby town for a larger supply of food and some hair dye and to pick up some warmer, more casual clothing and some cheap reader eyeglasses. His heart hurt for the daughter waiting for a reply to her email that hadn't come. He could only imagine what she must be thinking, but he was about to put an end to her waiting and stop wallowing in his personal rage over what Shandy's parents had done.

Back in Jubilee, the snow had melted on the mountain, and when it did, Sean came down. He was bringing Amalie a present—two boxes with bookshelves in need of assembly for the books she had yet to unpack. He had nothing on his agenda, and his mother was visiting family.

Amalie was excited Sean was coming and had spent yesterday cleaning house and cooking. Today they would not go out to eat. This time it would be her treat.

She'd put on her favorite sweats, a pair of thick fuzzy socks, and no shoes. She had the gas fireplace going in her living room, and after the day had turned out so windy, she'd upped the thermostat to seventy-four to keep the chill off the house.

She was switching laundry from washer to dryer when her doorbell rang. The church bell chimes had become the joke between them, and she was already smiling when she opened the door.

"Welcome to the Lincoln chapel. Come in out of the cold!" she said.

Sean scooped her up in his arms and gave her a quick hug and kiss, then stepped back.

"I have gifts," he said, and pulled two large flat boxes into the house before closing the door.

"Sean! What in the world?"

"Bookshelves for your books. But they're not put together. I brought tools," Sean said, and watched her eyes light up as he hung his coat on a peg by the door, and then pulled a couple of screwdrivers, a wrench, and a pair of pliers from the coat pocket.

"I am so excited! Thank you! What a darling, thoughtful thing to do," she said, and hugged him.

Sean grinned. "I can't help it. I am a darling, thoughtful person."

Amalie shook her head. "'You're welcome' would have been sufficient. Want to do this now, or—?"

"Since it's a little trashy to walk in the door and strip you naked, let's do bookshelves and lunch, and work our way forward," he said, and began opening the first box.

A little shiver of want rolled through her as she watched him tearing into the box and removing the contents. A sheet of instructions was taped to the bottom of one shelf.

"There are the instructions," she said.

"I don't need them," Sean said, and opened the little bags with two sizes of screws and the pegs for the shelves.

Amalie rocked back on her knees. "Oh no. You're one of those!"

He grinned. "No. I've already put together four just like this for my office."

"Fair enough. Am I to sit back and admire your skill and dexterity, or am I allowed to help?" she asked.

"You can totally help if you want, but since I work alone, an audience would be awesome."

"I choose to sit and watch you, because you're so pretty."

Sean wadded up the instructions and threw them at her.

She laughed, and their day together began.

After the nonsense wore off, Amalie's thoughts wandered. She wanted to talk about the message from

Ancestry, but she didn't want the pity, or Sean trying to commiserate with her, so she stayed silent, keeping the humiliation to herself.

As soon as the first shelf was put together, Sean put it on one side of her fireplace and moved the unopened box of books beside it.

Amalie immediately plopped down and began transferring books from the box to her new shelving.

Sean paused in the act of opening the second box to watch. She was a beautiful and obviously competent woman, but in some ways, he still saw the child in her, looking for approval, wanting to belong. She'd grown up lonely. He wanted to fill her up with so much love and attention that she never felt lonely again. But there was a fine line between attention and smothering, and he never wanted to be that man. She'd come to him if and when she wanted, or not at all, and it would change nothing. In his heart, she would always be his first love.

After the second shelf was done, and the last box of books unpacked, they gathered up the packing and boxes and carried them to the trash bin, then hurried back inside.

Amalie was beaming. "Look how pretty! They balance out the room, and the dark color of the wood grain is exactly my taste. All teasing aside, thank you, Sean. The gifts in my life have been few and far between, but you are the best gift of all."

Sean walked up behind her, slid his arms beneath her breasts, and pulled her back against his chest. She leaned into his body, her head beneath his chin, and let the silence envelope them.

Then Sean's phone rang. He groaned.

"If it's work, somebody is going to have to wait," he muttered, then saw caller ID and read the text. "False alarm. Mom's just letting me know she's leaving Betty Raines's house and heading up the mountain to check on Uncle John. She checks in because I ask her to. That way I know where to go looking if she doesn't show up."

Amalie turned to face him. "Family isn't just who you love or who you're related to. Family is insurance, too. Right? I mean, you always know there's someone who'll worry if you don't show up. Someone you're accountable to. Someone who'd know you'd gone missing."

He cupped her face and brushed a kiss across her lips. "You could always check in with me. I would consider it an honor."

"Then, if I have the occasion to leave town, I will let you know when I do and where I'm going, okay?"

"Okay," he said, then followed her to the kitchen table, as she took a big pot from the refrigerator and set it on the stove to reheat.

Wind rattled the dry bushes against the house. This felt like Oklahoma weather in winter. Cold and windy, and hardly any snow. At least here, it did snow without added insult of freezing rain. The trade-off was welcome, and she was glad she'd decided on chili and jalapeño hush puppies for lunch.

She turned on the fire under the pot of chili, then

turned on the deep fryer to the correct temperature and left it to heat while she mixed up the batter.

"Sean?"

He looked up. "Yeah?"

"I'm putting jalapeños in the hush puppies. What's your heat level?"

"Wow, that sounds good. Make them like you like them and it will work for me."

She forked a bunch of pickled slices out of the jar and began chopping them up on the cutting board, then raked them into the hush puppy mix and gave it a stir.

A few minutes later, the chili was beginning to bubble, the deep fryer was at optimum temperature, and she began dropping in the batter, a spoonful at a time. By the time she'd finished, she had a shallow bowl heaping full of crunchy bites.

"Lunch is ready."

Sean got up. "Everything smells so good. Do you want the pot of chili on the table?"

"Yes, please, on that trivet," she said, pointing to the one already on the table.

He took the hot pot, and she carried the bowl of hush puppies. Then they both went back for their drinks and finally sat down to eat.

Amalie had her spoon in her bowl of chili, but she was waiting to see Sean's reaction as he took the first bite.

"Oh my God, this is good!" he mumbled, and as soon as the first bite went down, he chased it with a hush puppy and rolled his eyes. "Crunchy bite of delicious," he said, and added a handful around the bowl on his plate.

Amalie breathed a sigh of relief. He liked it!

After that, she dug into her food without hesitation.

The meal continued with her upcoming open house as the main topic, and he could tell she was a little anxious about attendance.

"I don't think you have a thing to worry about. The locals are always curious about new business. They'll all want to see it for themselves and meet you, regardless."

"Will you still be able to stop by?" she asked.

"You still planning for the end of this week?"

"Yes, Friday from 10:00 a.m. to 4:00 p.m."

"Then I'll be there."

"And Shirley, if she wants to come," Amalie added.

"Trust me. She'll be there. She's already talking about what she's going to wear," Sean said.

"I've dithered with that a bit myself," Amalie said.

"Don't even dwell on that. You'll rock the look, no matter what."

She sighed. "You make me forget about the scars."

He frowned. "What scars?"

She rolled her eyes. "Oh, please. It's the first thing people notice."

"Not me," Sean said. "The first thing I noticed was your cute butt, then your long legs. Of course, you did have your back to me, but it was a great start. And then you turned around and I saw that white streak in your hair, your beautiful face, and your eyes. They're so blue.

Blue is my favorite color, by the way. But it was that haunting familiarity that stayed with me."

His words were so endearing, but she couldn't let herself acknowledge them without crying, so she made fun of herself instead.

"So, are you suggesting I greet everyone butt first, or—"

Sean burst out laughing. "Hell if I know, but it would raise some eyebrows, and I'm all for breaking rules. If we're done with lunch, I'll help you clean up."

"Just carry the chili back to the stove and put the lid on the pot. It needs to cool off before I do anything with it."

"What about the hush puppies?" he asked.

She looked at the bowl, and then at Sean. "There are only three."

"You can't toss them in the trash," he said. "I'll just set it over here for later. When B.J. was still home, we never had leftovers. He just ate until the bowls were empty."

"Poor Shirley," Amalie said. "Just starved the lot of you, didn't she? It's obvious it stunted your growth."

Sean leaned back, rubbing his stomach. "I'm too full to argue. Can I stay and play for a while?"

Amalie grinned. "Absolutely. What do you want to do? Watch TV? I have board games. Go for a walk? I don't care. This day is for you."

At that moment, for Sean, all teasing stopped. In a house full of boys and one harried, overworked mother, there had never been a day *just for him*. Not even on his birthday, because his father had always fucked it up.

He'd never realized until now, when she said that with such innocence, how truly precious a gift she'd just given him. He wanted to say something, but he was afraid he'd choke up, and men don't cry. Especially in front of women.

He took a breath and then reached for her hand.

"I just want to be in your presence. From our first day of school, when I walked into the lunchroom and saw you sitting at the end of a table, and I wished I had the guts to sit beside you so you wouldn't be alone, to this full-circle moment, having sat at *your* table, eating food that you made for me. I have enough."

Amalie blinked. Her eyes welled. "I don't understand quite how fate brought us back into the same circle, but I'm suddenly realizing how blessed I was then, and didn't even know it. Would you be up for just going for a walk?"

"If you're involved, I'm in," Sean said. He grabbed the pot of chili, carried it to the stove, and put the lid on it. Set the bowl with three hush puppies on the counter, while Amalie rinsed their dirty dishes and put them in the dishwasher.

They turned, facing at each other at the same time.

Amalie could see the look on his face.

"You're gonna kiss me, aren't you?" she said.

"Can't help it," he said. "Just one for the road," and swooped.

Fireworks!

When they came up for air, Sean was still holding her, reluctant to let her go.

"Ready for that walk?" he asked.

Amalie's heart was pounding. "I'm ready for anything. Let me get my coat."

The cold air in Amalie's face always felt like an awakening, like a burst of adrenaline. She took a deep breath, then watched the little cloud form from the heat of her breath.

Sean reached for her hand as they set off. When they reached the end of her driveway, he paused.

"Which way do we go?"

Amalie hesitated. "That way, they said."

A little chill ran up the back of Sean's neck. *She is hearing voices again and doesn't even realize what she's saying.*

"Did they say why?" he asked.

She frowned, then looked up at him as they were walking. "What? Who's they?"

"Never mind," he said, and then saw a balloon drifting high up in the air and changed the subject. "Look at that red balloon! I wonder how far that little guy has traveled?"

She smiled. "I'll bet there's a child somewhere who cried when that happened."

"In the summers when my brothers and I were young, we used to fill balloons with water and then throw them at each other. We thought it was hysterical fun, except for having to pick up the remnants afterward."

"Having siblings has to be the best thing ever. Did you sleep together, too?"

"Oh sure. Aaron and I were the two oldest. Wiley and

B.J. the next. We paired up like that, with all the fussing over pulling covers and boy stuff until we outgrew the beds. After that, we had twin beds, but we could never tuck the sheets in at the end, because our feet and legs always hung over."

She grinned, imagining four little boys turning into the giants they were today, and Shirley trying to keep them fed and in clothes.

"What about you?" Sean asked.

Amalie rolled her eyes. "Foster kids. Always two to a bed, sometimes three. In every family I lived with, there was always one bed wetter, or one who cried themselves to sleep, or one who was mean. It was hard to sleep with all that."

Sean hurt for the matter-of-fact way that she'd accepted her lot in life. No child should ever be abandoned.

"How did you make peace with that...always having to find your place within a new environment?"

"By staying in the shadows. Being as silent and obedient as I knew how. Not making waves. At least until I grew older and wound up taller than most of them."

"Did any of them ever hurt you?"

She tightened her grip on his fingers but never looked up. "You mean, did they try to get in my pants? Yes, but it was covert, and by then, I'd learned how to fight back. I was never molested. Never raped. Just never loved."

"Shit," Sean said.

She glanced up. The rage in his eyes was startling. "Don't feel sorry for me."

"Am I allowed to be pissed off at the injustice of your life?" he asked.

"Yes."

They kept walking. Sean took a deep breath. "So now I'm asking permission to step into an obvious void in your life and love you for always."

Amalie stopped and turned to face him. "God. Here we are again, in broad daylight in front of God and everybody, and all I want to do is die a little death in your arms."

His eyes narrowed, his head lowered, then kissed her—in front of God and everybody. "*La petite mort*, Amalie. The French have such a pretty way to describe sex, do they not?"

"Maybe because sex with someone you love is such a beautiful thing?" she said.

"I would say yes to that assumption," he said. "So, what do the voices say? Do we keep walking or—"

Suddenly, they heard the sound of crashing metal and breaking trees, and then a car horn blaring without stopping, but from where they were standing, it began echoing within the valley.

Amalie grabbed Sean's arm. "She went off the road into a ravine. There's a baby! The highway! Get to the highway! We will see smoke coming up through the trees!"

They started running toward the intersection and, within seconds of getting there, saw smoke rising through the trees a couple of hundred yards to the east.

"Call 911," Sean said, and took off running.

Amalie's hands were shaking as she made the call.

"911. What is your emergency?" the dispatcher asked.

"Car wreck. East of town, on the south side of the highway. You'll see smoke."

"I'm dispatching services now," the dispatcher said. "Stay on the line with me."

Amalie heard the calm in the dispatcher's voice. Moments later, she was back on the phone. "What is your name?"

"Amalie Lincoln. Sean Pope was with me. He's already running toward the scene."

"Do you know how many are in the vehicle?"

"We didn't see it happen, but we heard it, then saw the smoke. Someone ran off the road down into a ravine."

Then she dropped the phone in her pocket and took off running. Sean was already a good fifty yards ahead of her and flying. She wasn't going to ever catch him, but she wasn't the kind to stay behind.

Jubilee PD immediately dispatched patrol cars and rescue units to the scene.

Both Pope brothers responded to the call with their partners, as did a half-dozen other officers. As they drove up on the scene, their first sight was of a woman up on the shoulder of the road holding a baby. The baby was screaming, and so was the woman. Tears were running down her face as she held the baby close, and she was screaming Sean's name.

"Hurry, Sean, hurry! I'm starting to see flames!"

Aaron's heart skipped a beat. See what? And where was Sean? He couldn't see anything. He ran to the side of the road, saw his brother at the crash site, then grabbed his fire extinguisher and headed into the ravine with his partner, Yancy, at his heels.

"Sean! Get back," Aaron shouted, and began spraying the fire. Sean ducked, turned his back to the spray as he kept trying to cut the seat belt off the woman who was trapped.

Yancy had a knife as well, and together, they finally got her freed, but she was unconscious, and no way to tell where she was hurt. Moving her could make it worse. Her face was bloody from hitting the steering wheel, but the fire was almost out, and Wiley and his partner were now down at the site with their fire extinguishers, too. By the time the fire truck and ambulance arrived, the officers had the fire out and the woman was regaining consciousness.

Once all of the emergency response teams were on scene, Sean stepped aside. He'd already made one trip up the ravine to give the baby to Amalie, and the horror on her face when he went back down again was forever etched in his mind. This time when he reached the top, he went straight into Amalie's arms.

"Where's the baby?" he asked.

"EMTs already have her," she said.

"We've got to stop meeting like this," Sean said. "First the chopper, now the car."

"Did she get burned?" Amalie asked.

Sean pulled back. "No, baby, no. I don't know what injuries she has, but she didn't get burned. How did you know?"

"Know what?" she asked.

"To walk in this direction? If you hadn't listened to the voices, we would have walked the other way. If we'd walked the other way, we wouldn't have been close enough to hear the wreck. If we hadn't heard the wreck, they would have both burned to death before anyone ever knew the car was in that ravine."

She was cold. So cold her face was numb, but the shock she was feeling came from realizing she'd been saying stuff about the voices aloud.

"I don't know. Sometimes I just hear them."

"Have you always heard them?" he asked.

"I don't think so. The first time I can remember it was when I was trapped in the burning car. My pants were already burning, and I heard a voice say, 'You're going to be okay,' and I was. Please don't freak out on me about this."

He hugged her again. "Darlin', as far as I'm concerned, you're just a shade on the light side of magic, and if you start throwing glitter, I want some fallin' on me."

She started to cry, soft tears. Tears of relief that he was safe. That the woman and child had been rescued. And that's how Aaron found them. Standing on the side of the road, wrapped in each other's arms.

He walked up behind Sean and then put a hand on his shoulder.

"You okay, brother?"

Sean nodded.

"Need a ride back somewhere?" he asked.

Sean nodded again, still holding her.

"Are we gonna go far?" Aaron asked.

Sean sighed. "No. Just three blocks from your house."

"Got it," Aaron said. "Give me a sec to let Yancy know, and I'll be back with my patrol car."

Sean gave Amalie a quick hug. "Got a tissue?"

She nodded.

"Then wipe your eyes and blow your nose. Big brother is about to give us a ride home and get you out of the cold."

"Okay," she mumbled, and dug in her coat pockets until she found a couple of wadded-up tissues and did as he suggested.

"You even blow your nose cute. It sounded a little like a mouse squeak."

Amalie shook her head. "I may die from the ardent love words that you speak."

Sean was satisfied. He'd shifted her focus from the shock.

"And here comes Aaron," he said.

"I remember him, too," she said. "The boy with the Mohawk."

Sean laughed. "That was him at the age of ten. He'd just found out we had an indigenous ancestor. And since he wasn't into growing his hair long, he opted for that cut, even with Mom standing there telling him we weren't any part Mohawk."

"Better than getting shaved bald because of gum," she said, and then Aaron was out of the car and opening the door.

When Aaron saw her, he realized this was the woman Wiley told him about. The one who knew about the lost tooth in the mashed potatoes. Instead of offering to shake her hand, he just hugged her.

"Amalie. Welcome to the family."

"The boy with the Mohawk," she said. "Thank you. I'm happy to be here."

Aaron grinned. "I was going through my indigenous phase. Hop in the car. You can sit up front with me close to the heater. You're cold as ice. Little brother won't mind the back seat."

Sean gave his brother a look. They both knew the leg room in the back seat of a cop car was next to none and he was going to have to fold all six feet five inches of himself in and like it.

But Amalie wasn't having it.

"No. Sean is not getting in the back seat. He's too tall. He just ran a marathon to get to that crash, down a ravine at full speed, and came back the same with that baby, then back down again to the woman who was trapped. Get in the front seat, Sean."

Sean looked over the top of the cruiser and grinned.

Aaron smirked. "You probably don't deserve her, but congrats anyway, bro. You've got yourself a fireball."

The drive back was quick. Amalie was listening to the brothers' patter, hearing the respect and love in their voices. When they pulled up in the driveway, she started to get out, then realized this was where people rode who got arrested, and she had to wait for one of them to open the door to let her out.

It was Sean. As soon as she was clear of the car, he shut the door, then leaned in the window.

"Thanks for the ride, Aaron."

"Sure thing. Good thing you two went for that walk," Aaron said.

Amalie watched as he backed out of the driveway and sped away. "I'm selfishly glad you chose a different career path," she muttered.

"So am I. Now let's get in where it's warm."

They shed their coats as soon as they were inside, then Amalie turned the thermostat up a notch for quick heat.

"I'm going to make coffee," she said.

He looked down at his hands. "I need to clean up."

Amalie frowned. "Is any of that blood yours?"

"No," he said, and headed for the bathroom.

She went to the kitchen to wash up at the sink, then started the coffee. The house was quiet and warm, and a far sight from the trauma they'd just witnessed. The baby's screams were still echoing in her ears when shock finally set in. Her legs went weak, and then she was sliding down the side of the island and into the floor. She hugged her knees, lowered her head, and closed her eyes, waiting for the room to stop spinning.

And that's how Sean found her.

Within seconds she was off the floor and in his arms.

"I'm okay, I'm okay," she kept saying, as he was carrying her down the hall. "I was just waiting for the room to stop spinning."

"Hush now, darlin'. You just had a whole episode of PTSD, and we both know it. You're in shock, and you're freezing cold. Let me help you."

She quit fighting the inevitable and went limp as he sat her on the side of her bed, then pulled back the covers. Before she knew it, he was kneeling at her feet, removing her shoes, then tucking her into bed, clothes and all.

"Don't go," she whispered.

"You couldn't make me," Sean said, then kicked off his boots and lay down on top of the covers, curled up around her and pulled her close.

For Amalie, it was like being engulfed within a cocoon. She'd never felt this safe. Or this loved. She closed her eyes.

Sean held her, feeling the tension in her body slowly relaxing, and the even rise and fall of her breath. And then he heard her whisper.

"Sorry I'm so screwed up."

He started to respond and then realized she was talking in her sleep.

"No more than the next guy, you're not," he muttered, and scooted closer.

Amalie was dreaming.

The car in front of her spun out, slid into the median and then back into the lane of traffic, and broadsided her. Now she was spinning and screaming, knowing when it stopped, she would either be hurt or dead.

She woke up with a gasp and rolled over, right into the front of Sean Pope's chest. He raised up on one elbow and smoothed the hair away from her face.

"You're okay, baby. You were dreaming."

Her heart thumped. They were in bed together… more or less. She didn't know whether to panic or strip.

She grimaced. "I live for the day when this memory fades."

"Constant reminders don't help, and your experience is still new. Just a little over two years, right? Give yourself a break." He leaned over and brushed a kiss across her lips. "I've got you wrapped up like a burrito. Did you finally get warm?"

She nodded. "I never did get that coffee made."

"Do you want some?" he asked.

"Not any longer. A cold shower, maybe."

He grimaced. "Our timing is a joke, isn't it? Graveyard. Snowstorm. Too full of chili. Car wreck. They all tend to ruin the moment." Then he rolled out of bed and helped her up. "It's getting late. I have chores to do up on the mountain, and your open house is on Friday."

"Yes, to both. I'll open the office Monday morning. After that, I'm at work all week and Saturday until noon."

He took her in his arms. "I'll be at your office this Friday at 10:00 a.m. I wouldn't miss it for the world."

She slid her arms around his neck. "I'm anxious but excited, and so grateful you'll be there."

"A promise is a promise," he whispered, and then pointed to her bed. "The next time I'm here, we're gonna wind up in there."

"I'll hold you to that," she said. "Be safe, and my best to Shirley."

One last kiss, and he was gone.

It was nearly sundown.

Time to put this day to rest.

Chapter 11

The next few days passed in a flurry of anxiety and busy work, but on Friday morning, Amalie was at the office by 9:00 a.m. to receive the deliveries of floral and baked goods. She had a small table set up against the wall for refreshments. The floors were shining. The pillows on her sofa were perfectly plumped. And she had an OPEN HOUSE banner outside, hanging below her name.

The flowers came first. Two bouquets. One on the reception desk, and a smaller green ivy on the coffee table in front of the sofa. But to her surprise, other florists began arriving with congratulatory arrangements. One from the bank next door where she'd opened her account, and another from PCG Inc., the company that owned this building.

The baked goods from Granny Annie's Bakery came next. By the time Sean arrived, she had everything in place and was sitting quietly in one of the chairs beneath the painting of Pope Mountain, contemplating the enormity of how far she'd come. It hadn't been an easy journey, but she'd do it all over again, just for the pleasure of being part of Sean Pope's life.

She was disappointed about her ancestry link, but she had to let it go. Whoever her parents were, they hadn't wanted her before. It made sense that they wouldn't want to know her now. Maybe it had to do with guilt—not wanting to face someone they'd given away.

Then Sean walked in carrying roses and put them on the reception desk and whistled beneath his breath as she came to meet him, wearing a fitted pantsuit and heels that made her long legs look even longer.

He groaned. "Red and black. Power colors and sexy as hell! Why do I have this sudden need to publicly stake a claim before every single guy in town sees you?"

The smile slid off her face. "Don't worry. You did that the day you beat up the bullies, and you're the first man to give me roses, so you're already doing everything right. Thank you. They're beautiful," she said, and kissed him.

As she was turning away to admire the roses, she saw Shirley pulling up to the curb. "Yay! Your mom is here!"

Sean turned. "She brought Aunt Ella!"

Amalie froze. "The one who's psychic?"

"Yes, and Aunt Ella doesn't come down the mountain for much these days. Prepare yourself."

"Oh lord," Amalie said. "Should I be worried?"

"No, but when she leaves, you will have been informed," he said, and then winked. "I'm going to help Mom get Aunt Ella out of the car. She's in her nineties."

Amalie's heart was in her throat as she watched Sean bolt. He was a giver, and a caretaker, and a provider of all things necessary, and she knew he loved her. She was a little anxious about meeting the mountain elder, but she was holding the door open as the trio entered.

The old woman was tall and thin, with a long thick braid of white hair wrapped around her head, and wearing black beneath a long gray coat. Amalie could see the Pope bloodline in her face.

"Welcome, Miss Ella. My name is Amalie Lincoln. Thank you for coming. Shirley, you are so sweet to come support my new venture."

Shirley was all smiles as Sean helped Ella out of her coat and situated her on the sofa.

"Don't fuss," Ella said, as she settled onto the sofa and then looked straight into Amalie's eyes. "Come sit with me," she said, and the moment Amalie's backside hit the cushion, Ella turned to face her. "I saw you coming in my dreams." Then she touched the white streak in Amalie's hair. "The mark of an old wound. Not in this lifetime. From before."

Amalie was transfixed. Sean was standing behind her, his hand on her shoulder for support, and she hoped to God nobody walked in before this woman had her say. It was like touching a history she'd never had.

Ella kept staring into Amalie's eyes. "You don't know your people, but one knows you. Patience. He needs patience."

Amalie shivered. *Oh my God.*

"May I?" Ella asked, and held out her hand.

Amalie clasped it and felt a warmth running all the way up her arm.

"We're connected, but you already know that, don't you?"

Amalie nodded. Her eyes were welling, but she didn't want to cry.

Ella touched the scar on Amalie's chin and then the burn scars on her neck.

"They protected you. It wasn't your time to die." She pointed at Sean. "He's been waiting for something all his life. It was you." Then Ella glanced over at the painting. "The mountain called you, didn't it?" Her voice softened. Her drawl deepened. "Be at peace here, Ah-mah-lee. This is where you belong." Ella saw the tears and knew the longing within the girl. "Don't be afraid of what you already know how to do. It is a gift given to few. Do you understand?"

Amalie was shaking. "Yes, ma'am."

Ella gave her hand a soft squeeze. "Not 'ma'am.' *Aunt Ella* will do." Then she glanced over at the table full of goodies. "By any chance, do those come from Annie's bakery?"

Amalie nodded. "Would you like some?"

"I believe I would, and I'll let you choose for me. I like surprises. Sean, I'd take a cup of coffee, if you don't mind. It's nippy outside."

Sean and Amalie headed to the table, their shoulders touching, unaware they were walking in unison, but Ella saw it.

Shirley sighed. "Was I right, Aunt Ella?"

Ella nodded. "They belong together. And she's got the sight. That wreck turned it on. Nearly dying will do that."

"This makes me happy," Shirley said. "The child has grown up alone."

Ella said nothing, but she already knew Amalie wasn't alone in the world. She had family. They were still lost to each other, but that would change in the days to come.

The whole family knew how Ella loved her coffee. Two sugars and a splash of cream. Sean was stirring it into the cup, watching Amalie choosing a tiny pecan tart, and a bar cookie filled with fruit, and three colorful meringues.

He leaned closer. "I'm sorry. I feel like Mom and Aunt Ella blindsided you. I didn't have a clue any of this was happening. Are you okay?"

Amalie's eyes were bright with unshed tears, but she was smiling.

"I am more okay than you can imagine. It was a gift to treasure. I'll fill you in later."

Sean saw the truth on her face and relaxed. If she was good with it, then so was he. After that, it wasn't long before people began arriving and Sean sat back, watching her turn into Amalie Lincoln, CPA. A woman with a mission.

She was near the door greeting new arrivals, then mingling with the gathering crowd as they admired her office and the painting of Pope Mountain, which had become the centerpiece of her decor.

Michael Devon, the manager of Hotel Devon, had been at the bank next door when he saw her Open House banner and, instead of getting in his car, went in. He recognized Sean Pope and nearly everyone else in the room and decided the young dark-haired woman shaking hands with everyone must be A. Lincoln, CPA.

"Welcome to Jubilee," Michael said. "I'm Michael Devon, of Hotel Devon. It's always great to see new businesses sprouting up."

"Thank you, Mr. Devon. I'm very excited to be here. I'm Amalie Lincoln. There's coffee and refreshments on the far table, and I see someone already trying to catch your eye," she said.

Michael smiled. "That's Liz Caldwell, my fiancée. She's the event coordinator at the Serenity Inn."

"Any relation to the owner, Ray Caldwell?" Amalie asked.

"Her father...and speaking of Ray, that's him coming in now. Hope you have a great day," Michael said, and headed across the room to where Liz was standing.

Amalie hadn't met Ray, but she knew him on sight and was completely focused on him as he came toward her, barely noticing the well-dressed blond coming in behind him.

"Mr. Caldwell! How kind of you to come. I was a guest at your hotel last fall," Amalie said.

"So I've been told. My staff saw your open house notice in the paper and recognized your name. They assured me I should meet you. You must have been a memorable guest."

Amalie laughed. "I promise I didn't have wild parties in my room, but I was there for two weeks. I think they thought I'd moved in."

Ray beamed. "Wonderful! Wonderful! Anyway, I just wanted to come by and welcome you to Jubilee."

"I am honored. Refreshments are on the table. Help yourself and visit a bit, if you'd like."

"Thank you," he said. He picked up one of her business cards from the reception desk and then moved along.

That's when Amalie noticed the blond. The moment their gazes met, the woman stepped forward and began talking to Amalie, but she wasn't looking at her. She was staring at all the scars.

It was something Amalie dealt with all the time, but it still irked her that the woman was talking to her ear and neck, and not to her.

"Nice place you have," the blond said. "I'm Mary Ingalls."

Amalie said nothing, waiting for the woman to shift her gaze.

All of a sudden, Mary realized the woman hadn't answered. She shifted her gaze to Amalie's face, then flushed when she realized the woman had just called her out on her rudeness without saying a word.

"Sorry, I was...I was distracted," she said.

Amalie nodded graciously. "I noticed."

Mary flushed. She'd been caught out and didn't like that. "Yes, but I won't interrupt your event today by talking business. I'll take a card and a brochure with your info, if you don't mind, and get in touch with you at a later date?"

Amalie didn't believe her. The woman had no interest in hiring her. She didn't know what her game was, but she wasn't going to waste time trying to woo her. Instead, she handed her a card and one of the brochures.

"Coffee and refreshments are on the back table. Please help yourself."

Mary tucked the card into her purse and smiled again. "Thank you, I will."

Amalie turned away, and within moments, a reporter and photographer arrived from the local paper to take some pictures for the Sunday edition. She paused to answer their questions for the piece, posed for pictures with several guests, and then left the photographer to snap at will.

At that point, she turned around to look for Sean and saw him watching her. When he gave her a thumbs-up, she smiled.

About an hour into the event, Aunt Ella announced she was ready to leave.

Sean left the party long enough to help get her back into the car, and as soon as she was buckled in, Ella had her last say.

"She's a keeper, Sean. Bring her to see me sometime. She's still trying to find her way."

"Yes, ma'am. You two stay out of trouble. Mom, you know how to reach me if the need arises," he said.

"We'll be fine. You go do you," Shirley said.

Sean waved them off and then headed back inside and quietly replenished goodies on the table and started a brew of fresh coffee. His job today was to stay in the background as backup.

He'd been watching people coming and going with true delight. Amalie's day was a rousing success. As best he could tell, every person who'd come to the event was a local business owner or a local resident. He didn't think there was a random tourist among them except maybe for the blond woman who'd walked in behind Ray Caldwell.

She was a stranger to him, and he assumed she'd seen the Open House sign from the street and just wandered in. He saw her talking to Amalie and realized something was off when he saw the expression on Amalie's face. After that, he kept a close eye on the woman, wondering if she and Amalie knew each other from before, because the woman had given Amalie a look he didn't like. It was somewhere between disdain and disapproval.

When she turned toward the refreshment table, he snapped a couple of pictures of her on his phone. When she reached the table, he saw her eye the food like she was judging a contest, and then turn and walk away as if she'd found it lacking. Then she turned and again stared at Amalie as if she were mud under her feet. He snapped a picture of her again and then started toward her, but before he got to her, she'd taken leave on her own.

He walked to the window to see what she was driving, but she just kept walking down the street, so he shrugged off the feeling and let it go. He'd ask Amalie about her later.

Hours later, Fiona Rangely was back at Sutton Airfield, disembarking from the helicopter she'd chartered to take her to Jubilee and heading to her car. She was still patting herself on the back for thinking to check Wolf's personal email via her own laptop. She hadn't gotten where she was today without caution and perfect planning, and seeing that email from a woman claiming to be Wolf's daughter had nearly stopped her heart.

Fucking DNA. Why didn't people leave well enough alone?

Miss Amalie Lincoln. Wolfgang Outen's daughter, throwing her name into the ring to inherit a fucking fortune. *My fortune.*

So, she'd pulled Mary Ingalls out of the mothballs and taken a visit to size up the competition.

It was no big deal. Just one more tragic death and she'd be in the clear.

She aimed the remote on her key ring to unlock the car, tossed her carryall into the back seat, then started the car to cool off. The urgency to put an end to this roadblock was upon her, but she never did "business" on this phone. She dug into the console and pulled out the phone belonging to Mary Ingalls. The battery was low, so she plugged it into a charger and began scrolling through her contacts.

She'd already used up Townley, and Romo was off the map. She kept scrolling until she saw the name Stinger and made the call.

It rang once, and then she got a one-word answer.

"What?"

"It needs to look like an accident."

"Fifty thou."

"Agreed," Fiona said.

"Name and location."

"Amalie Lincoln. Jubilee, Kentucky," and then gave out two addresses.

"The first is her home address. The second is her place of business. I'll pay when it's done."

"Wire it now. All of it. Or call someone else."

Fiona frowned. "What the hell?"

"Times are hard. Trusting people even harder. My way or the highway."

"Fine," Fiona muttered. "But I want it done in two days or I'll send someone after you."

There was a moment of silence, and then a whisper.

"I know who you are. I know where you live. Never threaten me again."

The line went dead.

Fiona frowned. Maybe she'd overplayed her hand a bit, but fifty thousand would take care of that, and she'd transfer the money as soon as she got home.

Their last open house guests were gone a few minutes after 4:00 p.m., and as soon as they left, Amalie plopped down on the sofa and kicked off her heels.

"Oh my lord. My feet are killing me."

Sean sat down beside her and slid his arm around her shoulders.

"I am so proud of you. I saw you at your finest, talking about what you know and what you do. You made some big impressions on people today."

Her eyes were alight with excitement as she turned to face him.

"I have three new clients coming in next week to get their taxes done, and two people who run businesses in their homes wanting to talk about incorporating, and one client who wants me to keep the books on their business. Next week is going to be crazy busy and I couldn't be happier."

"I know exactly how you feel. I lost all my clients after we moved here from Conway. I've been rebuilding for the past two years, and after I added security installation as part of the business, it's really grown."

"We've come a long way from Ellen Smith Elementary, haven't we?" she said, eyeing the mess left behind from the event. "And now that we've patted ourselves on the back, I need to get busy. This place isn't going to clean itself."

But he didn't budge. "I have a question. That blond woman who came in before noon. You two had a conversation. Did you know her?"

"No, why?" Amalie asked.

"I don't know. She just gave off a vibe I didn't like," he said.

"You mean because she kept talking to my scars instead of my face?"

He frowned. "Is that what she was doing? I knew something was off by the look on your face."

Amalie shrugged. "That's what some people do. It didn't bother me, but I also didn't play into it. I could tell she was put off by them."

Sean frowned. "Did she give you her name?"

"Mary Ingalls," Amalie said.

Sean frowned. "Why does that sound familiar?"

She rolled her eyes. "*Little House on the Prairie* TV series, Mary Ingalls. I guarantee that's not her name, and I won't see her again."

"You're probably right," he said, but he wasn't satisfied. He was going to do some digging on his own later. "How about I help you get this place cleaned up and then get you home?"

"I won't say no," she said.

"I'll do the heavy stuff. I'll deal with the coffee urn and trash," Sean said.

"You're the best," Amalie said. "I'll take down the banner out front, get the room put back together, and box up whatever cookies are left."

Sean held out his hand. She grabbed hold of him like the lifesaver he was. They went to work, and within the hour they were headed out the door.

Amalie was taking her roses with her and stopped to set the security system and lock the door. Sean was right beside her with the cookies. They went out the back way, got in their respective cars, and headed across town to her house.

Amalie drove into her garage as Sean pulled up behind her; then they unloaded their cars and went inside. The roses went on the coffee table, and Sean took the food into the kitchen and hung up their coats.

When he came back, Amalie was sitting on a barstool, waiting.

"I never got to tell you how very much I appreciated you staying the course with me today. It was reassuring to see you from across the room, knowing you were within shouting distance."

"A familiar face is always a plus. I'm happy it was mine," he said, and brushed a kiss across her lips.

Amalie slid her arms around his neck and felt his muscles tense beneath her hands.

"Can you stay a while, or do you—"

"I can stay if you'll have me," he said, and slid his hands around her waist.

She shivered. "All night?"

A muscle jerked at the side of his jaw. "If you'll have me."

"Yes, please," she whispered. "I'm going to change. Can't take being fancy another minute longer."

Sean's heart skipped a beat.

"Need help?"

"I need you, but I have to be honest. Getting down to all the scars in front of a man has yet to happen, so I'm also scared half to death of what you'll see."

His eyes darkened. "Bullshit, and don't ever say or think that about me again. What I see in you is way beyond skin deep. You're new to this town. We're new to each other as adults. But we have history, lady. I've been holding onto you since before bubble gum. All I see... all I will ever see...is a woman of substance who makes me weak in the knees. You're in charge. Lights on. Lights off. All I want is you in my arms."

Amalie sighed. He made it all sound so simple, and in the end, it was.

Lights on in the adjoining bath with the door partially closed. Lights on at the end of the hall. They undressed in shadows and wound up in the bed in a tangle of arms and legs.

His hands were in her hair, his mouth on her lips. The shape of her all woman, from the soft thrust of her breasts against his chest to the gentle curve of her waist and the flare of her hips. The only scars between them were from a lifetime of rejection that nobody could see.

Amalie knew before he touched her how it was going to feel, what he was going to do. He'd lit a fuse and it was smoldering. He was as hard as the muscles knotted in his back, and when he slid between her legs and into her body, she moaned. After that, they moved into another space, minute by minute chasing a climax.

Making love to Sean Pope was everything she'd ever dreamed of. *He* was everything she'd ever dreamed of, and when the blood rush finally came, the last thought that went through her mind was, *Just as I remembered.*

They collapsed in each other's arms, still connected, hearts pounding, breathing little more than short, intermittent gasps.

"Love you, baby, so much. That was...that was magic," Sean said, and held her close.

She slid her fingers through his hair, feeling the short thick strands beneath her palms. "You're the magician. I'm just the rabbit you pulled out of the shadows."

"Can we do this again?" he whispered.

She smiled. "I don't know. Can we?"

He nuzzled the spot beneath her ear and heard her groan.

He smiled, then whispered in her ear. "What are the magic words, Ah-mah-lee?"

"I've loved you forever?"

Once again, he was hard within her.

The second dance was beginning when she closed her eyes.

There was only so much joy one woman could feel without coming undone.

Three hours later, they were rummaging through the fridge for leftovers. Sean had a bath towel wrapped around his waist and was heating up cold pizza. Amalie had on an oversized T-shirt hanging halfway to her knees, no longer bothered by revealing her burn scars and completely focused on the peanut butter and jelly sandwich she was making.

"I like to put peanut butter on both slices, then put jelly in the middle, squish it, and cut it in quarters," she said.

Sean grinned. "I'll keep that in mind," he said, and sprinkled a liberal helping of red pepper flakes over the pizza before he carried it to the table. She was right behind him.

"Want a glass of milk with that?" Sean asked, as he went back to get himself a Coke.

"Yes, please," she said, waiting for him to sit down.

When they were at the table, face-to-face, Amalie put her hands in her lap.

"I have something to tell you, and it has to do with what Aunt Ella said to me this morning."

"Can I eat and listen at the same time?" he asked.

The corner of her mouth tilted in a half-assed smile. "I don't know, can you?"

He chuckled. "We're about to find out," he said and took his first bite as Amalie started talking.

"When I turned eighteen, I ordered a DNA test from Ancestry.com and sent it in. I thought maybe...just maybe...I'd find something out about who I was, you know?"

He nodded and kept eating, just letting her talk.

"And of course, nothing happened. I actually forgot about it. Then a few days ago I was at home going through a ton of old email I'd let pile up during my move and saw a notice from Ancestry.com. It was one of those *you-have-a-match* emails, and my heart stopped."

"Oh wow!" Sean said.

"I know, right? They don't tell you much. You have to log on to your site to see the name and connection." She was shaking and, without thinking, took a bite of one of the sandwich pieces and sat there chewing, then took a sip of milk to wash it down.

Sean said nothing. She would tell this in her own terms and time.

"It was a man," she said. "He had two email addresses as contacts. I used both, one as an initial contact, and copied it to the second, telling him a little about me. How old I was, what I did for a living, and that I'd grown up in the foster care system. I can't remember the details of how I ended it other than I looked forward to hearing from him, and hit Send. Then waited."

She looked up at him then. "I'm still waiting. And I'd just about given up hope when your aunt Ella said that I didn't know my people, but one knew me, and to be patient."

Sean had been eating and listening, but he stopped and pushed his plate aside.

"Oh, honey…"

Amalie looked away. "I didn't intend to say anything because I didn't want anyone feeling sorry for me. It's just easier for me that way. But I wanted to tell you the moment I got that notice, and then decided to wait a bit. I wanted to share good news, not another *pitiful-me* story."

"I understand, and it's okay. If you feel the need to hold on to a story from your life that doesn't need to be told, then no one needs to hear it. Understood?"

She nodded, finished off the piece of sandwich, and started on the second.

"He had a really strange name. I have no idea what his ethnicity or nationality is. I only know mine." She finished the second piece of sandwich, took another sip of milk. "His name is Wolfgang Amadeus Outen. That's a mouthful, isn't it?"

Sean froze. That man was suspected to be one of two men who'd died in the chopper crash. It wasn't official until all of the DNA results were in, but that was the working theory, and he couldn't believe that life would kick her in the teeth like this again.

He couldn't think what to say. What to do. How to react. So, he sat without commenting, watching her finish her PB and J. sandwich and milk, and then carried their dirty dishes to the sink.

"What do you think?" Amalie asked.

Before he could say a word, her cell phone signaled a text.

"Just a sec," she said, opened it, read it, and gasped. "I'll be right back," she said and dashed out of the room, coming back seconds later with her laptop. She sat down and logged on, then opened her email.

"It's him," she said. "Wolfgang Outen. He sent me a Zoom link. He needs to tell me something face-to-face."

Sean's thoughts were racing as he sat back down at the table. Either the feds and the NTSB were way off their mark, or this guy was a fake. Either way, he was about to listen in on their conversation.

Amalie was already on the site and unmuting her screen when his face appeared. Her first thought was how strikingly handsome he was for a man of his age. Thick gray hair and dark brows slashed over shockingly blue eyes. But he wasn't smiling. He looked serious. Even a little scary, yet when he spoke, every word reeked with twenty-seven years of apologies.

"Amalie, my daughter, your letter was both a shock and the greatest joy I have ever known. I am sorry I did not immediately respond, but I am in hiding."

Amalie gasped. Had she just inherited a criminal for a father?

Wolf read her face with dismay. "No, no, it is not what you think. You live in Jubilee, Kentucky, is that right?"

"Yes," she said. "I have recently moved here."

"Then I am sure you were aware of the recent helicopter crash near an elementary school?"

"Yes, yes, I am. My...my sweetheart... Sean Pope, was one of the men who rescued some teachers and children who were trapped inside it, but that's all I know."

Wolf nodded. "I was supposed to be on that flight. My personal assistant traded places with me at the last moment so I could attend to a crisis at one of my companies in South America. He and the pilot are the two men who died. I knew nothing about the crash until the next day."

Amalie gasped and looked over her laptop at Sean. "Did you know?"

"Who are you talking to?" Wolf asked.

"Sean. He's here, listening."

Wolf groaned. "Then please ask him to join us. It is imperative that I impress upon you both the need for secrecy."

"I'm going to get my shirt," Sean said, and bolted for the bedroom. He came back seconds later with it buttoned up enough for decency's sake and laid his cell phone on the table as he sat down. The moment he saw the man's face, he recognized him from newspaper reports and knew he was telling the truth. "Good evening, Mr. Outen. I'm Sean Pope. Just for the record, Amalie and I have known each other since third grade. I'm an IT specialist and I know how to keep my mouth shut about everybody's business."

Wolf sighed. "I thank you and regret we are meeting under these circumstances." Then his focus shifted back to Amalie. "The FBI team working the crash knows I'm alive, as do a couple of my most trusted friends, and I believe my wife is responsible for the crash."

Amalie gasped. "Oh my God. Why?"

"I think it began when she found out I had recently submitted a DNA test to Ancestry.com. She became enraged, which was both confusing and shocking, but I thought little of her reaction until after the crash. She always packs my bags for me when I travel. We believe the bag she packed for my short trip to Jubilee had a bomb in it. It was triggered by a remote device, which caused the chopper to explode in midair and crash near the school. Knowing I was supposed to be on that chopper and her irrational response to me wanting to look for family, and knowing she packed the bag that was carried onto the chopper, she has become the prime suspect."

"Are you safe now?" Amalie asked. "Is she in custody?"

"I'm safe only because everyone thinks I'm dead, and no, she's not in custody yet. They're still gathering evidence, some of which I have contributed to. I discovered she has been trolling my personal email for months and deleting things she didn't want me to see. I discovered that when I found notices on my business mail that should have also been on my personal mail, as well, like the notices from Ancestry.com that I never saw."

"Then how does that affect Amalie?" Sean asked.

"I can't be sure it does, but if my wife wanted me dead, finding out I had an heir might be further reason for her to come after Amalie, too. That's why I'm breaking my silence. After I saw Amalie's letter on my personal email, I immediately sent a copy to my business email, but when I went back to delete the message so that Fiona wouldn't see it, the message had already disappeared."

Amalie was stunned. "But why would I matter to her?"

Sean reached for Amalie's hand. "Because your father is worth a cool billion, and if she's evil enough to kill to get it, she's evil enough to want it all to herself."

Wolf nodded. "Sean nailed it. It would be nothing personal with her. Just a means to an end to remove an obstacle from what she wants."

Amalie reached for the scars on her neck without

thinking, and as she did, Wolf saw the burn scars on her arm and hand, and up the side of her neck.

"You have been injured?" Wolf said.

She nodded. "A couple of years ago. A drunk driver hit me, trapped me in my car. It caught fire." She shook her head and looked away.

Sean slid his arm around her shoulders. "She spent a long time in recovery, but now she's as good as new. Don't worry about Amalie's safety. I have two brothers on the Jubilee police force, a cousin nearby who's retired from special forces, his wife, who's an ex-undercover agent for the FBI, and a mountain full of Popes who know how to protect their own."

Wolf shook his head. "I will be indebted, but after finding out Fiona has been trolling my personal mail, I am announcing my resurrection tomorrow. It should sideline my wife from setting her sights on you. Fiona is a beautiful blond and a charmer, but you can't trust her. I did, and I believe it got one of my best friends killed."

Sean heard the words *beautiful blond,* and his gut knotted.

"With regards to blonds...today was open house at Amalie's new office. It was a huge success, but the only person who came that we didn't know was a pretty blond, probably in her late thirties, maybe early forties. I got some weird vibes from her, didn't like the way she was looking at Amalie, and took a couple of pictures so I could ask Amalie about her later."

"Show me!" Wolf demanded.

Sean pulled the photos up from the gallery on his phone, then enlarged one for a clearer view of her face before turning it to the screen.

"This is her. She said her name was Mary Ingalls."

Wolf cursed. "It's her! Damn her! It's her! Don't leave Amalie alone. I am sending bodyguards tonight! I will not have your family put in danger because of me."

"You are welcome in my home," Amalie said. "But Sean is my partner for life. We take care of each other, and that's how it works."

Wolf backed off. "I'm sorry. Of course. I have no right to take over your life, but I've lost so much time with you because of lies. I want to grow old knowing you are happy and alive in this world. The bodyguards will be there. You won't see them. But they will see you. I'll get there as soon as I can, but I need to clear it with the feds to make sure I don't blow their case. Just know that I am alive, and I am overjoyed to know you exist."

"Do you know your people?" Amalie asked.

"I knew who they were, but they have long since passed," he said.

"What about my mother and her family?" Amalie asked.

"She died the day after you were born, and her parents are the ones who gave you away. I am so sorry."

Amalie paled. "My grandparents gave me away?"

He nodded.

Her voice was shaking. "Do you know why?"

"Because you were mine and they hated me. I was working in the Saudi oil patch when Shandy, your mother, went into labor. By the time I got stateside and back to New Orleans, you'd already been born, and your mother was in a coma from a brain bleed. They told me you were born dead and disfigured and that they'd already given the body to a crematorium. Your mother died in my arms. The day after her funeral, they disposed of me."

Amalie was crying now. They'd thrown her away like trash.

"Thank you for telling me my mother's name. I always wondered who you both were, and how I came to the life I was given. I'm sorry I won't get to meet her."

"Her given name was Cassandra. Look in the mirror, child. You wear her face." Then he looked at Sean. "Keep her safe for the both of us."

"Count on it," Sean said.

The screen went dark. Wolf Outen was gone.

Amalie closed her laptop and took a deep breath. "What in the world am I going to do?"

"Open for business on Monday. I'm commandeering one of your desks, and I'll work from there until somebody is behind bars and we know that you're safe."

Her expression fell. "But your mom—"

"Is a grown-ass woman who reminds me daily she does not need babysitters. She'll be fine. And just for the record, this isn't the first time she'll be inheriting a daughter-in-law in need of shelter," he said.

"Daughter-in-law?"

Sean leaned forward until their foreheads were touching.

"Obviously, you have not thought through this relationship as thoroughly as I have, or you would not have that stunned look on your face."

She clutched her hands beneath her chin in a gesture of a prayer, and when she did, Sean felt a chill run through him. It was how they'd found Meg, with her hands clasped beneath her chin, like she'd been praying.

"Does this mean I get to live on the mountain with you and Shirley?"

Sean was surprised. "You would live with your mother-in-law?"

"I never had a mother. I'd settle for borrowing yours and be grateful for the rest of my life that I had a family to go home to at the end of every day."

Sean pulled her into his lap, cradling her like the broken child she'd been, and let her talk.

"I knew last fall I would come back here. Pope Mountain was the magnet, and you were the gift I never saw coming. Are we crazy for committing this fast? I couldn't bear it if you had regrets later," she said.

"No, baby, no. This isn't fast. It's taken eighteen years for us to come full circle. I'm happy. So happy. Please be happy for us."

"I am, but do me a favor and just let Shirley know you're here. I don't want her worrying."

Sean pulled her close. "Already done."

Amalie sighed. "What did you tell her?"

"That I'd see her in the morning."

"Good enough," she said.

Chapter 12

The moment Wolf ended his Zoom call, he went into emergency mode and dispatched a team from his security division to Jubilee. They came with photos of Amalie and Sean, her home and work address, as well as a photo of Fiona. They had their orders. He knew they wouldn't let him down.

Then he called Jack Fielding.

Jack answered on the first ring.

"Wolf?"

"Yes, it's me. Are you free to go back to tailing Fiona?"

"I can be," Jack said. "What's up?"

Wolf told him.

"Shit! This is getting crazier. Can the feds really tie your wife to the bomb?"

"They're working on it, but she's stalking my daughter now, and that makes her deadly. I have bodyguards on the way to watch my daughter's back. I just need to know where Fiona is, what she's doing, and where she goes, once she finds out I'm alive."

"So, you're going to come out?" Jack asked.

"Gotta clear it with the feds first to make sure it doesn't screw up their investigation."

"Do you know where Fiona is now?" Jack asked.

"Not really. Check the Miami residence first, then see if she's registered anywhere in Jubilee under the name Mary Ingalls."

Jack frowned. "Why does that name sound familiar?"

"*Little House on the Prairie*?" Wolf asked.

"Oh hell. Yes. If she's flinging fake names around, she may have more than one. I'll dig into it."

"Thank you, Jack, and this time you're on the clock. No more freebies for me. I don't need them, but I do need you to help me get this nightmare cleaned up," Wolf said.

"You got it," Jack said.

They disconnected, but Wolf still had calls to make.

Special Agent Colin Ramsey was still at the office. The agents on the case were in a conference room in front of their murder board, talking through updates and adding info regarding the crash as they went.

Things were falling in place too fast to waste time sleeping. The background check on Fiona Rangely had turned up some shocking facts, and Colin was sharing them with the team.

"Here's what just came in on the background check," he said, and aimed a remote at the big screen on the wall. Pictures immediately appeared. "This is Fiona Faye

Whitley at her college graduation. She has a master's in engineering and runs a company called BioMed in Miami. She makes one-of-a-kind surgical instruments for doctors, and she's buried three husbands prior to her marriage to Wolf Outen. He would have been her fourth. All of her prior husbands were anywhere from twenty-five to forty years older than her. They were all wealthy and had no living heirs. One died in his sleep. One in a car crash. And one died during a sky-diving event when his chute didn't open. That's way too many 'accidental' deaths for my comfort."

Colin paused for effect and changed the screen to a wedding photo of her and Wolf cutting the wedding cake. "Here's where her routine began to vary. She did not take Outen's name when she married. She kept Rangely. And according to Wolf, she went ballistic when she found out he'd taken an Ancestry test and put his DNA in their database. None of her prior husbands had heirs, and they were all wealthy. Each time, she inherited everything. And I just found out that Wolfgang Outen learned via Ancestry that he has a daughter. He's worried Fiona might try to take her out, so she won't be sharing the inheritance."

Before he could add further details, his cell phone rang. He glanced at it and frowned. "I need to take this," he said, and walked out of the room.

"This is Colin."

"Shit's hit the fan," Wolf said. "Fiona not only found out about my daughter, Amalie Lincoln, but she's stalking her. She showed up at an open house Amalie was holding for her new business venture, introduced herself as Mary Ingalls, and chatted briefly before wishing her well and disappearing. But they had pictures at the event, and I have seen them. It is her. I just revealed myself to my daughter via a Zoom chat, so that she's aware of what's happening. Now I need to come out of hiding so that Fiona knows I'm not dead. If I'm still alive, I'm hoping she's going to switch her focus back to me. What's that going to do to your investigation?"

Colin's head was spinning. "We are close. So close."

"Then I advise bringing her in for questioning. Searching her private quarters at our house and her office. She built that bomb somewhere. It was in my house at one time because she put in it my fucking suitcase when she packed my clothes," Wolf said.

"I'm briefing the team on updates now. We'll figure it out and get warrants tomorrow. How are you making the announcement?" Colin asked.

"I'm not. You're making it. You announce I'm alive. You tell them the whole story about the switch between me and Stuart Bien. His people need to know what's happened to him. I'll appear in public later. But first thing tomorrow, I'm contacting my lawyer, changing my will, calling banks and having her name taken off of the accounts. Then I'm going to see my daughter. I just don't need my whereabouts advertised. I'll show up when I'm ready."

"We can work around that," Colin said. "You do what

you have to do and so will we. Now I have to go back to the team and let them know what's going on."

"Sorry. Prudence and safety took precedence here," Wolf said, and hung up.

Colin sighed and went back into the briefing room.

"Game plan has changed," he said, and then began explaining what had happened.

But even as they were scrambling, other reports were coming in that kept thickening the glue they needed to make a murder charge stick, and one involved bank accounts under the name Mary Ingalls, but with Fiona as the owner of the accounts. And in those accounts, they found two specific cash withdrawals that coincided with the timing of the deposits into Ellis Townley and Vincent Romo's bank accounts.

And another investigator found records of Fiona purchasing a burner phone with a credit card in the name Mary Ingalls only five days before the chopper crash. The agent also told the team that they had received security footage from the store where she bought the phone, and it was Fiona using that card. She already had two separate cell phones with two different numbers with her carrier, so why a third with a number that couldn't be traced? If she still had it, she was going to have to produce it to clear herself, and if she didn't, was it part of the crime scene debris?

By the time the team session ended that night, they had submitted requests for search warrants at the private residence, as well as Fiona's office. They were also bringing her in for questioning at the same time as Colin Ramsey's press conference.

Humpty Dumpty's wall was coming down.

Detective Muncy's investigation into Ellis Townley's murder had just gained serious traction. Agents from the Federal Ministry of Mexico had located Vincent Romo in Guadalajara and taken him into custody at the request of the American FBI. The agencies were arranging paperwork for transfer and pickup, and Romo was in a panic. He didn't know how the hell the cops had fingered him, or how they'd found him, and for the first time in a long time, Romo was scared. He'd screwed up the job he'd been paid for. That was why he ran.

His head was spinning. If Mary Ingalls found out he'd been arrested, he'd give his chances of surviving prison as less than ten percent. He'd worked for her before. She didn't play nice, and she didn't play fair. When the transfer happened, he was ready to make a deal. He was coming back to the United States to testify in a federal murder investigation, in exchange for a life sentence for killing Townley.

Even though Romo was Miami Homicide's suspect, Special Agent Ramsey would be on hand to take his statement to seal their case.

After being gone all day, Fiona was up early the next morning. She didn't like to get behind on work.

The chef had bacon, waffles, and coffee on the breakfast buffet when she came down to eat, and Dee had all three of Wolf's newspapers on the breakfast table.

Fiona eyed them as she walked in. The *New York Times*, the *Washington Post*, and the *Miami Herald*. Visible reminders of Wolf. She picked them up and put them in the trash. When she saw the shocked expression on Dee's face, she quickly explained.

"They make me sad."

Dee's face crumpled. "Yes, ma'am. I'm sorry, ma'am. I didn't think."

"It's okay," Fiona said. "We're all having to adjust." Then she served herself a healthy portion of everything and began scanning through texts on her phone as she ate.

Wolf was up before sunrise. He'd just received confirmation that the six bodyguards were in place. Now he needed to plug the holes in the dike before Fiona found out what was happening.

His first call was to his lawyer, Arnie Walters. He called Arnie's personal phone, knowing he'd still catch him at home, and knowing Arnie was going to be immediately suspicious when he saw Wolf's name come up on his caller ID, he made a video call.

The look on Arnie's face was priceless.

"What the hell?" Arnie shouted.

"Sorry for the shock, Arnie. It's me and I'm not dead. I've been in hiding, and we have a problem."

The hair was still standing on the back of Arnie's neck. "What the hell is going on?"

Wolf began to explain, then told Arnie what he needed him to do.

"The first thing is to null and void my will and remove Fiona's name from anything to do with me. Put the name Amalie Lincoln as the sole heir and recipient of everything I own upon my death."

"Is that your daughter?"

"Yes," Wolf said.

"Don't you think you need to wait until a DNA test has confirmed that?"

"She's the spitting image of her mother, who died in my arms. Ancestry.com has already linked us. That's good enough for me."

"I can do that," Arnie said, "but you'll have to personally sign the new will before it's valid."

"Say the word when it's ready and I'll be there," Wolf said.

"This is like something out of a freaking soap opera," Arnie muttered.

"More like a nightmare," Wolf said. "She killed Stu and Zander, thinking she was killing me."

"Have the feds arrested her?"

"It's in progress and under wraps. Say nothing, and if you need anything else from me, just call."

"Will do. And Wolf...welcome back to the land of the living," Arnie said.

Wolf sighed. "Thank you. It feels good to be back."

As soon as that call ended, Wolf made a call to Dillon Quarles, his banker in Miami.

After a similar reaction and conversation with Dillon, he had their joint accounts frozen until further notice.

"Is this public knowledge? Does everyone know this?" Dillon asked.

"My resurrection will be announced sometime today by the feds. Say nothing about anything else I've told you, understand?"

"You can count on my discretion," Dillon said. "We value your business, and I'm overjoyed to see your face and hear your voice again."

"Thanks," Wolf said. "I'll be in touch."

And then the last call he made was to Ruiz in Sao Paulo. But when he made the call, it went to voicemail. He didn't want to leave a message and thought little of it, making a mental note to try later.

Once the feds had a bead on Fiona Rangely's location, the teams descended.

Ramsey's partner, Special Agent Brokaw, arrived at Fiona's office with a forensic team and a search warrant, bypassing her secretary, who followed them in protesting, and walked straight into Fiona's office. He flashed his badge and put a search warrant directly into Fiona's hands.

"Fiona Rangely, I'm Special Agent Brokaw. You are being served with a search warrant for your office, and another is being served at your home. We are taking you into custody for questioning in the crash of a helicopter on the outskirts of Jubilee, Kentucky, which resulted in the deaths of two men."

Fiona was in shock. She couldn't believe it was happening, or how they'd even keyed in on her at all.

"You can't be serious! I want my lawyer!" she screamed.

"You have the right to representation, but you're still coming with us," Brokaw said. "Special Agents Leroy and Patterson will escort you to our office."

Fiona was still sputtering and screaming as they hauled her out of the building. Brokaw dismissed the employees with instructions not to return until further notice.

It was to be expected that her walk of shame was captured on cell phones and posted all over social media before the feds even got her out of the building.

At the same time she was being taken in for questioning, a separate team was at the Outen estate. The housekeeper and the chef were also sent home, while the team began going through every room in the mansion and every outbuilding on the property, shocking the elite neighborhood with the presence of federal officers.

PI Jack Fielding had followed Fiona from the Outen estate to her office this morning and was in the parking lot in front of the building with an eye on her car and in full view of the entrance when he saw a parade of black SUVs and vans come wheeling up to the front of the building.

He grabbed his camera.

"Oh man, Wolf. You just set her world on fire, didn't you?" Jack muttered, recording dozens of agents piling out of the vehicles with their equipment. He had a front-row seat and couldn't wait to see what happened next, and it didn't take long.

He began filming again when agents emerged, this time with Fiona between them. They put her in the back seat of an SUV, flanked by two other agents. From what he could see, she was not in full cooperation with their decisions, and like before, he captured it all in living color.

The media had little warning about the scheduled news conference, and the different outlets were scrambling to get into place as Colin Ramsey appeared outside the FBI office in Miramar.

"Good morning, and thank you for coming at short notice. I'm Special Agent Colin Ramsey, lead investigator of the helicopter crash in Jubilee, Kentucky, and the deaths of two passengers onboard. As has been reported by the media countless times in the past few days, the chopper exploded in midair, which has led to rumors of a bomb. I won't comment on an ongoing case, other than to say we're still in an active investigation. Also, rumors have circulated from the beginning that Wolfgang Outen and Zander Sutton were the victims of the crash. We now have proof that Mr. Outen was not on that chopper, and that it was his personal assistant, Stuart Bien. Wolfgang Outen is alive. I have seen and spoken to him personally. He will make a statement in his own time, but for now, he is staying secluded in fear of a second attack on his life. He is devastated at the loss of Stuart Bien, who was a personal friend as well as an employee, and sends his deepest sympathies to Stuart's friends and family, as well as to the family of Zander Sutton."

The place erupted in shouts of disbelief and hands waving in the air to be recognized for questions.

Colin raised a hand to signify silence. "I'm sorry. I won't be taking questions about an ongoing case, but I am issuing a warning. Anything you might try to do to hunt Wolf Outen down just to get a scoop before it's safe to reveal his location will very likely get you in deep trouble for impeding a federal investigation and endangering a man's life. Do I make myself clear?" That caveat shut down the noise. "Thank you for coming," Colin said, and walked back into the building.

The media outlets had been live during the press

conference, and shock was spreading, both on Wall Street and in the business community at large.

Dead billionaires rarely reappeared by magic, but the boost to the shares in the companies he owned had just shot through the roof.

Carter Bullock was in the bathroom shaving when he heard a scream, and then Leigh shouting.

He turned off the water and then shouted down the hall, "What the hell's happening? Are you all right?"

She came up the stairs as fast as her aging legs would carry her—her eyes wide. Her voice shaking. "He's not dead! He's not dead!"

Carter frowned. "Who's not dead?"

"Wolf, and I have a bad feeling about this," Leigh said.

"Ridiculous," Carter snapped. "We haven't seen him since the funeral. He is not a part of our world."

"No. We're not a part of his," Leigh said. "He could buy and sell us a million times over. I don't know how to explain it, but this feels like someone took the lid off Pandora's box, and we're in the direct line of fire."

Carter glared.

"You never listen to me! Be forewarned! That's just you and your fucking conscience again. I don't want to hear another thing about this. Do you understand?"

He stomped back in the bathroom to finish shaving and slammed the door.

Sean was in the living room watching television when he heard the announcement about the impending conference. He jumped up and hurried to the bedroom where Amalie was getting dressed.

"Amalie! Honey! There's something about the crash on TV," he said, and grabbed the remote to turn it on.

She came out of the bathroom with the hairbrush still in her hand and sat down at the foot of the bed with Sean beside her.

"Did they say what it would be about?" she asked.

"No, just that the lead investigator had an announcement to make."

"I wonder if this has to do with my dad." Then she glanced at him. "Do you have any idea how weird it is to feel that word on my tongue?"

"You mean *dad*?"

She nodded.

He reached for her hand. "If he's as fierce as I think he is, he probably lit a fire under a whole bunch of people."

"And we're about to find out," Amalie said. "There's a man coming out of the building now."

Sean upped the volume. When he finished, Sean turned off the television and then looked at her.

"It has begun," he said. "Eventually, news outlets will come looking for you, too, once they learn of your existence."

She shrugged. "I don't have an issue with that, as long as no one is trying to end my life."

"You're one tough lady," he said, then cupped the back of her head and kissed her. "Mom knows we're coming. Are you okay to talk about some of this?"

She nodded. "No secrets from your mom, but I don't want her ever put in the middle of this."

"She won't be. She's tougher than you think."

Amalie frowned. "Why must the world still shelter the vicious along with the good?"

"Preacher Farley would probably have an answer for that, but I don't. So, are you ready to leave now?"

"Yes. Let me get my coat and purse."

He helped her on with her coat, then hugged her. "We've got this. One day at a time, honey," he said, and they left the house.

The day was cold but clear, but Amalie couldn't quit thinking about how fast her world had turned upside down, and it scared her. She was wishing she'd let sleeping dogs lie and never started a search to find family.

As they were leaving town, she had a thought.

"Sean, remember there are three desks in the office. I only need one, and if you link up to my printer, you won't have to bring your own. I'm sorry for the upheaval in your life, but selfishly glad to work beside you for a while."

"Thanks, darlin'. That's a good idea. I'm sorry for what's happening to you, but getting to be in the same office is a plus, okay?"

"Yes, okay," she said, then looked away.

Sean still had nightmares from the aftermath of the chopper crash, and after realizing Fiona Rangely was already stalking Amalie, he was terrified at what she might do. They were both so intent upon the situation and each other that they never noticed a dusty black Jeep a good distance behind them.

Wolf Outen's men already had their backs.

Amalie was far too quiet on the drive up, and it had Sean worried. She was shutting down. Closing ranks. Probably what she'd done all her life to protect herself.

"You know I love you," he said.

Tears welled immediately. "Yes, and I love you."

"You feel like your legs have been cut out from under you, don't you?" he said.

She shrugged. "Information overload. I thought I wanted to find out about my family, but it's just an ugly story. I should have known. It's why people like me wind up in foster care—because of ugly people."

"No, honey. Your father was as cheated as you were. He lost the love of his life and missed twenty-seven years of your life because of lies. And someone wants him dead because he's rich. What's happening now is neither your fault, nor his. You are targets, but you're not victims."

The tone of her voice shifted, revealing the anger she was feeling.

"I know you're right, but I'm sick and tired of setbacks and struggles. I tried so hard not to die from that wreck. I finally get my life back together and find you, and now this. I've been fighting to survive all my life, and I'm fed up with the war."

Sean immediately pulled over onto the side of the road and reached for her hand.

"Look at me."

She sighed, and then turned to face him.

"Amalie, sweetheart...you're not alone in this anymore. I'm not a passing fancy. I'm not just the little kid who had a crush. I know the value of who you are and treasure your acceptance of me. Whatever is happening to you is happening to me. And whatever happens to me affects no less than a couple of hundred people you have yet to meet who already have my back. You aren't alone anymore. You will never be alone again."

Amalie wanted to hide. To crawl into a closet somewhere like she used to when she was a kid, and wait until all the fighting was over, but that couldn't happen. And she wasn't going to cry and then walk into Shirley Pope's house in a defeated frame of mind, but words were only words. There was a difference between a pep talk and action, and she needed confirmation like she needed air to breathe.

"So, Sean Pope, is this a promise or a proposal?"

He grinned. "Can't it be both?"

"Only if you seal it with a kiss," she said, then leaned forward and closed her eyes.

The last glimpse he had of her face before the kiss was the flutter of her lashes. Her lips were soft and warm, yielding to his arrival, weathering the shock of energy between them, and then it was done.

"Are we good now?" he whispered.

"So good," Amalie said.

He put the car in gear and continued up the road, still unaware they were being followed.

Chapter 13

It was a little after 10:00 a.m. when they drove up to the house and got out. The shift in temperature was notable, but it was always colder at this elevation.

"Let's do this," Sean said. Then they went up the steps together.

Shirley met them at the door. "Come in, come in!" she said, and shut the door as they shed their coats. "I'm in the kitchen, of course. Come sit with me a bit while I get this cake in the oven. I want to hear all about how the open house went after we left."

They followed, then Amalie sat, her hands folded in her lap to keep them from trembling, and watched what Shirley was doing.

"What kind of cake?" Amalie asked.

"It's a Mexican sheet cake. Basically, it's a chocolate sheet cake with a good dose of cinnamon in the batter. It's one of those cakes that's even better the second day," Shirley said.

"It's killer good, regardless," Sean said. "Mom's been making this for years, but we rarely have any left the next day."

"With six mouths to feed, that was the case with everything I made," Shirley said.

"So, what are you going to do with all this cake?" Sean asked.

"Marcus is coming to supper tonight," Shirley said.

Sean heard the too-casual note in his mother's voice, but didn't acknowledge it, and explained the relationship to Amalie instead.

"Marcus Glass and Mom grew up together. He married one of your cousins, right, Mom?"

Shirley nodded, as she began pouring the batter into the sheet pan. "Yes, Gloria Pope. Gloria passed away from cancer some years back. His granddaughter, Lili, was one of the children injured from the chopper crash."

"Such a horrifying experience for all of them," Amalie said.

"It was," Shirley said, adding, "Sean, open the oven door for me, please." When he did, she slid the pan into the oven, shut the door, and set the timer, then put the batter bowl in the sink to soak. "Now we can talk. The open house! Did you continue to have visitors throughout the day?"

"Yes, a fairly steady stream of them," Amalie said. "I also gained my first clients. I have appointments with them throughout the coming week."

Shirley clapped her hands in delight. "Oh, honey! How exciting!"

Sean glanced at Amalie. "No secrets in the family," he said softly.

Amalie sighed.

"What's going on?" Shirley asked.

"Entangled revelations I'm still trying to absorb, but I'll give you the cheat-sheet answers. When I turned eighteen, I entered my DNA into Ancestry.com because I wanted to know where I came from. A few days ago, I got a notice from Ancestry that there was a hit on my family tree. Long story short, I found my father."

"Oh, honey, is this good news for you? Have you spoken to him?"

"Yes. He contacted me via Zoom last night. His name is Wolfgang Outen, but his call was also a warning. As it happens, he is one of the men reported to have died in the chopper crash. Only he's not dead, he's alive, and the crash was meant to kill him. It's a fluke he wasn't on the flight."

Shirley gasped. "What on earth?"

Sean could tell Amalie had said all that she could handle.

"It's a mess, Mom. Bottom line…they suspect his wife. The feds know Wolf Outen is alive, but he's in hiding while they continue to work the case. The wife thinks Wolf is dead but found out Amalie exists, and Wolf is worried Amalie could be his wife's next target."

Shirley's eyes widened. "Oh my God! Why?"

"Outen is a very wealthy man. He's convinced his wife tried to kill him for his money. She won't want to share with an heir."

Shirley just kept shaking her head. "How could she not know about a daughter?"

"Because he didn't know either," Amalie said. "Like Sean said, there's a world of ugly behind this story, and an answer to why I wound up in foster care to go with it. But the scary part is that his wife showed up at my open house, introduced herself under a different name, and after speaking to my father last night, we all realized her real identity. She already has me in her sights."

"You come here! We'll protect you," Shirley said.

"No, Mom. It's the same thing Aaron told you when Dani's stalker found her. We don't bring trouble to you. We're handling it. Outen is handling it. This morning the FBI announced Wolfgang Outen was still alive, and once the wife hears that, hurting Amalie will gain her nothing."

Shirley nodded. "Okay. Understood. I'm so sorry this happened but, sweetheart, you have to trust you're no longer alone in the world. We've got your back, and it sounds as if your father does as well."

Amalie's defeat was in her voice. "Thank you for understanding. I'm still struggling with all of it, and I didn't want you to be angry that Sean has been drawn into all of this through his association with me."

"*Association* is hardly the word for intending to marry you," he muttered.

Shirley's eyes widened, and then she clapped her hands.

"Best news ever!" she cried.

"Even after I tell you we're kind of hoping to live here on the mountain with you?" Sean said.

Shirley gasped. "Are you serious? You would do that?"

"But only if you didn't mind," Amalie said.

"Oh, honey! I just lied. *This* is the best news ever! Having this house come to life again, and with a new generation of Popes, is a gift!"

"I'll still work in town," Amalie said.

"And I'll still be here," Sean said. "But for now, I need to move a couple of computers down to her office so I can keep up with work and keep an eye on her at the same time. Also, everything we just told you is between the three of us for now. Not even Aaron and Wiley are aware of any facet of the chopper investigation, and it has to stay that way."

"I'll say nothing about any of this. Not even about the two of you. That's your announcement to make. Just know I'm here for you, and I'm on your side," Shirley said.

"Thanks, Mom," Sean said.

"Yes, thank you, Shirley," Amalie added.

"Call me whatever, but I'd sure settle for Mom," Shirley said.

"I never had one before. I would love to," Amalie said.

Shirley glanced at the clock. The cake was still baking, but it was already after eleven.

"If you don't have plans, I can make sandwiches," she said.

Sean glanced at Amalie. "Okay with you?"

She nodded.

Sean gave her hand a quick squeeze. "Then I'm going to start loading up equipment while sandwiches are happening, and whatever they are, I'll take two."

Fiona Rangely's world had just been rattled in a way like never before. She'd been put in an interrogation room alone and was still awaiting the arrival of their lawyer, Arnie Walters, when Colin Ramsey walked in.

"Ma'am, the lawyer you requested is unavailable. Is there another you wish us to call, or do you want a court-appointed lawyer?"

She jumped up from her chair, aghast at the news.

"What do you mean, he's unavailable? He is our lawyer! Find him!"

"I mean, he knows you're here. He's not coming," Colin said.

Fiona reeled. That sucker punch had come out of nowhere, and she didn't know what to think.

"Then call Mervin Reams. He handles my business ventures. If I had my phone, I'd give you the number, but since you took it, I—"

"We're the FBI. We'll get his number," Colin said. "Have a seat, ma'am." And he walked out.

Fiona plopped back down in the chair and closed her eyes. None of this should be happening. She'd covered her bases. Hadn't she? What could have possibly…?

The hair crawled on the back of her neck.

She never got Townley's phone back, and Romo skipped out.

What the fuck had gone wrong?

Stinger arrived in Jubilee just after 9:00 a.m. Located the target's home and saw a vehicle parked in the driveway, then went to locate the work address, noting the office was closed. But when Stinger drove back to the home address and the vehicle in the driveway was gone, frustration set in. Now nobody was at either site, and it wasn't looking good for turning this hit into an accident by sundown tomorrow.

The town was full of tourists, and cop cars were everywhere. Two days to pull this off, including travel time, was a ridiculous demand with so many people watching every move. But the money was already in the account, and Stinger didn't renege on deals, which meant the method of removing Amalie Lincoln was changing to Stinger's choice and rules, and screw Fiona Rangely. Her attitude had become a liability to work with anyway.

Time to move to plan B.

Sean and Amalie drove back to Jubilee after lunch and went straight to her office. It took Sean a couple of trips to carry everything inside, and then another hour to hook it all up and sync her printer to his system.

Amalie settled at her desk as he was working and began going through her email. A couple of the clients who'd signed up yesterday were confirming their appointments, and another had requested the questionnaire she used for tax preparations.

It felt good to be in control of something again, and by the time Sean was finished, she felt better about herself and the day.

Fiona had been in custody for over two hours before Mervin Reams arrived. He was wide-eyed and in shock to see her in an interrogation room, and immediately demanded some time with her before the agents were allowed to question her. About twenty minutes later, Reams knocked on the door and told the guard they were ready.

Ramsey and Brokaw entered carrying file folders and sat down across the table from them. Brokaw turned on a recorder, and Colin Ramsey opened his folder, sifted through a couple of pages until he found what he was looking for, and laid it on top of the pile of papers. Only then did he look up. Fiona Rangely was hard to gauge and, from what they knew about her now, good at lying.

"For the record, Special Agent Ramsey and Special Agent Brokaw are in the room, along with Ms. Rangely and her lawyer, Mervin Reams. Mrs. Rangely, please state your full name and address."

Fiona did so, with her chin up and her eyes blazing with rage, and followed it up with a question of her own.

"Why am I here?" she snapped.

"We're asking the questions," Colin said. "Where were you on the morning your husband, Wolfgang Outen, was getting ready to fly to Jubilee, Kentucky?"

"I was in the house with him," she said. "I watched him leave and then a short while later left to go to my office at BioMed Technology."

"Do you always pack your husband's suitcases when he's traveling?"

Her heart thumped. "As a rule, yes."

"We understand you and your husband had a loud argument some weeks ago when you discovered he'd sent a DNA test to Ancestry.com. There was a lot of shouting between you. What was that about?"

She frowned. "Who said that? What does that have to do with—"

"Just answer the question," Colin said.

Her lawyer just shrugged when she looked at him.

She shrugged. "It wasn't an argument as such. It was just a surprise. I felt blindsided that he had not shared those wishes with me, but that all passed."

Colin pulled a photo of Ellis Townley out of the file. "Do you know this man?"

She frowned. "No. I've never seen him."

He pulled out another photo.

"Do you know this man?" he asked.

She sighed. "No, I do not. I don't see what this—"

He pulled out another set of papers.

"How many phones do you own under your name?" Colin asked

Fiona was feeling sick. "My personal phone and my business phone."

"And no others under any names other than your own?"

Oh shit. Oh shit. "No."

"Who is Mary Ingalls?" Colin asked.

She stared him down. "I haven't a clue."

"We have you on security footage buying a burner phone and paying for it with a credit card under the name of Mary Ingalls. We have credit card records of you making purchases of items that could be used in the making of bombs and paying for them as Mary Ingalls. And we have photos of you at a recent function where you identified yourself as Mary Ingalls."

Her belly rolled. *How the hell do they know this, and why were they even looking?*

"I don't know what you're talking about," she said.

Colin laid down the photo of Fiona talking to Amalie Lincoln at her open house. "This is you yesterday, talking to a young woman in Jubilee, Kentucky. You introduced yourself as Mary Ingalls."

She blinked. *What the actual fuck?*

"It's a case of mistaken identity," she muttered.

He pushed the photo of Townley back in front of her.

"Five days before the chopper crash, this man, Ellis Townley, deposited ten thousand dollars into his bank account. And on that same day, ten thousand dollars was removed from a bank account in the name of Mary Ingalls. Townley was in Jubilee, Kentucky, the day of the chopper crash. He was seen standing in an open field with binoculars and a cell phone, watching the chopper arrive. He was on the phone when the chopper blew up in midair. He checked out within minutes of it happening, drove straight back to his apartment in Miami, and was murdered upon arrival by this man, Vincent Romo."

He pushed Romo's photo back in front of her. "Twenty-five thousand dollars had been deposited into Romo's account, and a matching twenty-five thousand dollars had been withdrawn from yet another account in Mary Ingalls's name that matches the money and time of Romo's deposit. We have just extradited Romo from Mexico, where he's been in hiding. He has already given a statement that he accepted twenty-five thousand dollars to kill Ellis Townley and recover his cell phone. The woman who solicited the hit was Mary Ingalls. But he was interrupted and did not recover the phone. The Miami police found it instead. Can you explain that?" he asked.

Fiona's jaw was set, her eyes narrowed as she turned to her lawyer. "Say something!" And before he could answer her, she looked back at Colin. "I don't know anyone named Romo, and I don't know anyone named Mary Ingalls!"

Colin gave Brokaw the nod.

Brokaw opened his file. "Ellis Townley's phone was recovered at the scene of his murder. Calls to and from a phone registered to Mary Ingalls are on it."

Fiona was drowning and she knew it.

"I told you, I don't know anything about a Mary Ingalls. Somebody made a mistake."

"I think that's unlikely," Brokaw said. "You've been sleeping with the person who identified you in the photos for over four years now."

"Hank Kilmer is lying!" she said, and then realized that she'd just revealed she'd been cheating on Wolf.

"I wasn't talking about your lover. I'm talking about your husband, who is unlikely to make that mistake."

"My husband is dead!" Fiona cried, and turned on the tears.

"No, ma'am. As it turns out, he's not. Wolfgang Outen wasn't on the chopper after all. It was his personal assistant, Stuart Bien, who'd gone to the board meeting in his place. Mr. Outen was in his private jet, on his way to Sao Paulo, Brazil, when that chopper went down."

Fiona gasped. The tears dried up within seconds. "But...but...this is wonderful!" she cried. "I mean...I'm sorry about Stu, but it wasn't Wolf. It wasn't Wolf. When can I see him?"

"I don't think he's prone to a reunion at the moment. He's still reeling from the knowledge that the bomb that blew up the chopper was in his bag...the one you packed. And that he and Stuart not only traded places, but traded luggage as well. He gave Stu his clothes for the two-day trip, and Stu gave Wolf luggage they kept packed at the office for your husband's emergency trips."

"I don't know how... I didn't... I wouldn't," she muttered.

Brokaw was pushing harder now. "You've had a run of bad luck with your choice of husbands, haven't you, Fiona? Widowed three times. Wolf would have been number four. You're a careful shopper. You make sure they have no living heirs and are up in years before you commit. And when the time is right, they suddenly die. What do you think a good medical examiner might find if we exhumed those bodies?"

She was in shock. Mute in disbelief.

"I don't believe you," she finally whispered. "You're lying to me."

"About what? All of your dead husbands, or the fact that Wolf Outen is alive?" Colin asked. "You're something of a black widow, aren't you? I can assure you that your husband is very much alive, and I held a press conference this very morning and announced his resurrection to the world. Wolf knows you had to be the one to plant the bomb in his bag because you packed his clothes on top of it, and you are fully capable of building one, due to your degree in engineering. He already knows you've been deleting things from his email. He knows you tried to conceal notices from an Ancestry match regarding his daughter. They've already met and spoken. So, if anything untoward suddenly happens to his daughter, you're screwed."

She thought of Stinger and knew she'd just nailed herself to the wall and there was no way to call off the hit.

"Oh my God," she whispered.

Brokaw saw the shock on her face and got a sick

feeling they may already be too late to stop another tragedy. He leaned forward, his voice just above a whisper.

"What have you done, Fiona? What have you done?"

Fiona's eyes rolled back in her head, and she slid out of the chair onto the floor.

"Son of a bitch," Colin muttered. "Get a doctor, revive her, then read her her rights and arrest her for the murders of Stuart Bien and Zander Sutton and ordering a hit on Ellis Townley. I need to make a call."

Wolf watched the press conference with a measure of relief. That should waylay any plans Fiona might have regarding Amalie, he thought, and then started packing. It was going to be a long drive from Savannah to Jubilee, but he needed to see his daughter face-to-face. He couldn't make up for what had happened to her, but they could start from now, building a new relationship. He wanted that. He needed it.

He was gathering up odds and ends throughout the house, making sure he wasn't leaving anything behind, getting chargers for his laptop and phone, making sure his passport was in the luggage, and dumping the extra food from the fridge into the garbage. Lord only knew if he'd ever come back here.

He was gathering up a stack of notes he'd been making when his cell phone rang. It was Ramsey.

"Hello, Colin. I caught the press conference. Many thanks."

"We have a problem," Colin said, and then began to explain. "I don't know what she's done, or who she's sent, but we have reason to believe Fiona has already sent someone after your daughter."

Wolf's heart sank. "I have six men already there keeping tabs on her and Sean. But I need to give them a heads-up, and I think we should let the local authorities know, as well. That should come from you."

"Agreed," Colin said.

"Did Fiona confess?" Wolf asked.

"Not in so many words, but she had no answers for all the questions and was stunned we knew so much. We told her you were alive, and that sort of took the wind out of her sails. She kept denying responsibility for anything until we began bringing up her dead husbands."

"What? What dead husbands?" he asked.

"Oh, she has three of them. All older, rich, and no heirs when she married them."

"Holy shit!" Wolf muttered.

"She was shocked that we knew she'd been to the open house and flustered that we knew she was paying hit men out of an account owned by a Mary Ingalls, the name she'd given to Amalie at the open house. But when we mentioned disinterring her dead husbands to check for suspicious deaths, and that anything happening to Amalie now would seal her guilt, she passed out."

"This is a nightmare," Wolf said.

"You married a black widow and nearly became number four," Colin said.

"I've got to call my men," Wolf said. "After that, I'm heading to Jubilee. I need to know when you put Fiona behind bars."

"As soon as she wakes up, that's where she's going," Colin said.

"Then I'll call off my PI. I had him tailing her."

"Yes, she's not going anywhere, and we're not through interrogating her."

"Thanks for calling," Wolf said, and hung up, then immediately called his men on the ground in Jubilee.

As soon as he gave them an update, he sent Amalie a text.

Fiona in custody, but feds have reason to suspect she has already sent someone after you. Go home and stay there. I have men in place. I'm on my way, and your local police are being notified.

Wolf hit Send, then sent Jack Fielding a text.

Send me an invoice for what I owe you. Target is in jail and isn't coming out.

Then he grabbed the last of his things and took them to the car. One last walk-through of the house, turning off lights and locking doors, and he was gone.

Jubilee Police Chief Sonny Warren was finishing up a report before heading home for the day when his desk phone rang. He hit Save, and then answered.

"Chief Warren."

"Chief Warren, this is FBI Special Agent Colin Ramsey. I'm the lead investigator on the chopper crash that happened in your jurisdiction."

Sonny frowned. "I caught your press conference this morning."

"Yes, well, then you need to know that our chief suspect in the crash is Outen's wife. She is in custody, but we have reason to believe she's already put a hit out on Outen's daughter, who's now living in Jubilee. We know for a fact that his wife paid a visit to the daughter this past Friday, introducing herself under an assumed name. There are pictures of their meeting. Outen has identified the photos as those of his wife."

"Holy shit," Sonny muttered. "We can definitely put a detail on the daughter. What's her name?"

"Amalie Lincoln. Outen informed us that he's already sent a security team to Jubilee and they've been watching her back since their arrival. But our problem has accelerated. You need to be aware of the security team's presence and that this young woman's life is in danger."

Sonny flashed on the face of the young CPA he'd visited at her open house on Friday.

"I know her. I know Sean Pope, her significant other. Two of Pope's brothers are on my police force."

"Small-town vibes, eh?" Colin said. "So, touch base with Miss Lincoln and Sean Pope to let them know you are aware. Outen has likely already notified his daughter and his team as he's upping the security."

"Yes, sir. We're on it," Sonny said.

"Much appreciated. If further info arises, I'll be in touch."

The call ended, but Sonny's day had not.

Sean and Amalie were both wrapping up work for the day. Sean had everything he needed up and running, and Amalie had gone through her email and scheduled meetings with new clients.

"Are you about ready to shut down?" Sean asked.

"I just did," Amalie said, as she stood up from her desk and stretched. "Let me check to make sure the coffee maker is off, and I'll be good to go."

She disappeared into the back room as Sean got up and walked over to the sofa to get their coats. As he did, he paused to look at her painting of Pope Mountain again.

"Home, sweet home," he said, then put on his coat and picked hers up as she came back into the room.

He was helping Amalie on with her coat when her phone signaled a text. She took it out of her purse to check.

"It's from Dad," she said, and pulled it up, then moaned. "Oh no!"

"What's wrong?" Sean asked.

Her hands were shaking as she showed him the message.

Sean felt a panic of his own, but he wasn't going to let her see it.

"Okay, okay, home is where we're going, right? Lock the office. Our car's in the back. We'll be there in no time."

She locked the office door and then grabbed his hand as they headed down the long hallway to the back parking lot.

When they reached the exit, Sean paused long enough to scan the parking lot, saw no one on foot, and no one in sight, and began weaving their way through the cars to where he'd parked.

They were a good thirty feet from his car, but he was already aiming the remote to unlock the doors when movement on the roof of the building in front of them caught his eye. He looked up, and when he did, sunlight flashed on something shiny. *Like the scope on a rifle,* he thought, and then it hit him!

He grabbed Amalie and shouted, "Get down!"

There was a pop, and then a shattering pain that blew through the back of his shoulder as he threw himself on top of her, followed by two simultaneous shots that sent glass raining down upon them—and then silence.

Amalie was screaming, and he was struggling not to pass out.

"Easy, baby, easy. Are you okay?"

Just hearing Sean's voice eased her panic. "Yes, oh my God! Are you?"

Before he could answer, a bearded man in dark clothing and a black stocking cap appeared and knelt down beside them.

"I'm Joe. Sniper's down. Are you the only one hit?" he asked.

"Yes," Sean said.

"Sorry. We weren't looking for a woman. We've called the police and ambulance. Sit tight. We've got this, and Wolf sends his regards."

Sean groaned as he rolled off of Amalie, then sat up and leaned back against the side of the car where they'd taken cover.

That's when Amalie saw the blood all over her coat, and then a wide smear of it on the car behind where Sean was leaning.

"Oh my God! Sean! You're bleeding!"

"Flesh wound. Ambulance is on the way," he said, and then saw blood running from the cuff of his coat sleeve. "Blood oath," he muttered, and then closed his eyes and took a breath.

"This isn't funny, Sean Pope! You are my life and I nearly got you killed."

"Stop talking nonsense. You didn't shoot me," he said, and then he groaned.

She was on her knees now, pulling his arm out of the sleeve.

"Shit. That hurts." Sean groaned.

"You're bleeding away from me. Shut up. I need to put pressure on it." But when she got his coat off and realized there was no exit wound, her focus shifted. "The bullet's still in your shoulder. Lean forward for me, sweetheart. I need to put pressure on this."

There was panic in her voice, but she was already folding up the sleeve of his coat and using it for a pressure pad. He winced, but didn't argue. They could hear sirens. Help was coming, and Amalie's breath was warm on his face. She was safe.

"You saved my life! How did you know?" she asked.

Pain was shooting from his shoulder to the top of his head now, but she was safe in his arms, and he was trying to focus on what she'd just said.

"I...uh... Sunlight reflected off something shiny above us. I thought, *Rifle scope,* and we ducked, but if your dad hadn't sent that warning, we'd both likely be dead."

"Is this over?"

He groaned. "I don't know... I think..." Words left him. It was taking all of his strength now to keep from passing out.

"I'm so sorry. I love you, Sean. Please stay with me," she kept saying, but her hands were shaking, and she was so scared she couldn't think. All she could do for him was keep putting pressure on the wound.

And then all of a sudden, police cars came flying into the parking lot, with an ambulance behind them.

"They're here, Sean! Help is here!" she cried.

Sean looked up, saw Chief Warren, and then Aaron and Yancy coming toward them on the run. The sky was beginning to spin. Amalie's face kept morphing into the face of a stranger.

"Cavalry's here. Don't let them cut your hair," he mumbled, and passed out.

Chapter 14

Sean woke up in the ER, calling Amalie's name.

She appeared in the doorway, covered in his blood and flanked by six men he'd never seen before.

"I'm safe, Sean. Lie still."

"Safe... Love you," he mumbled, and passed out again.

"What's happening?" Amalie asked.

"We're prepping to take him to surgery," the doctor said, eyeing her as well. "Is any of that your blood?"

"No. Please fix him. I'm not doing life without him again."

"Miss Lincoln, we need to get out of the way."

Amalie turned toward the voice and then blinked. It was the man from the parking lot.

"I'm Joe, remember?"

She nodded, vaguely remembering all six of the men conversing with the police, and it was only after she heard them talking to her father on the phone that she had let them take her to the ER. She leaned back, too shocked to cry. All she needed was to know Sean was going to be okay.

And now that she'd seen him and knew he was still alive,

she let them lead her back to the lobby. People were staring, but she looked past them without thought. She could still feel Sean's arms around her as they were falling and hear the frantic tone of his voice. *Get down!*

Once she was seated, the men posted themselves around her like sentries. She looked down at her hands and the front of her coat and felt like throwing up. She was covered in blood, and police were everywhere—outside the ER entrance and inside the lobby. And then she saw Aaron and Wiley heading straight for her.

"Sean's brothers," she said, and the men stepped back.

Aaron knelt at her feet. "Little sister," he said, and then hugged her.

Wiley didn't hide his shock at the sight of her. "What the hell, girl? Are you okay?"

It was their sympathy that broke her. She started sobbing, then couldn't stop. They just gathered her up in their arms and held her close.

"It's okay, sugar," Aaron said. "Adrenaline crash. Cry it out. Sean's going to be okay. He'll probably make a necklace out of the damn bullet they dig out of his shoulder. He's our quiet brother, and you know what they say, 'Beware of the quiet ones.'"

But she just kept sobbing, "I'm sorry. I'm so sorry," over and over and over.

"Where's Mom when we need her?" Wiley muttered, and then took Amalie by the shoulders. "Girl! Did no one ever tell you the weight of the world does not belong on your shoulders? Stop apologizing for someone else's sins."

"Not gonna say this often, but Wiley's right," Aaron said. "Sean did what he did because he loves you. If something happened to you, he would never survive the grief. Protecting someone we love is a reaction, not a thought. It's instinct. Don't deny him the choice. Okay?"

She still couldn't face them, and leaned back in the chair and closed her eyes, and as she did, Wiley looked up and let out a sigh of relief.

"Thank God. Mom's here," he said.

"Just in time, because we've got to get back on duty," Aaron said. "Sister! If you need anything, call us."

Amalie nodded, but her gut was in knots. She stood, bracing herself to face Sean's mother, but she need not have worried.

Shirley saw all the blood, and the look on Amalie's face, and knew she and Sean had been through their own level of hell.

"Sweetheart!" Shirley said, and wrapped her arms around her.

Amalie was shaking all over again, her voice barely above a whisper.

"Sean's in surgery. He took a bullet in his shoulder meant for me. He saved my life."

Shirley just held her closer. "My sons take care of their own. Are you okay?"

Amalie nodded.

"Then let's go wash off some of this blood. I swear to my time, has everyone gone blind around here? Could they not have helped you do this before?" Then she realized they were being followed and gave the security team a quick look. "Are they with you?"

Amalie nodded. "They're the security team my dad sent."

Shirley said nothing more, but as they were about to go into the ladies' room, Joe stopped them.

"Ma'am, we need to make sure there's no one else in there but the two of you," he said.

Shirley frowned. "But surely—"

Amalie intervened. "The sniper who shot Sean was a woman. That's how they initially missed her, but they didn't miss when they took her out, or Sean would have more than one bullet in him, and I wouldn't be standing here talking to you."

Shirley paled. "My apologies."

Joe just shook his head. "None needed, ma'am." He knocked on the door and then shouted, "Anyone in there? Man on the floor! Incoming!"

Nobody answered, and he pushed his way in and checked every stall.

"All clear," he said. "We'll be waiting when you exit."

Shirley got down to business as they entered the ladies' room. "Here, honey, take off your coat, and then get to the sink."

Amalie grimaced when she saw herself in the mirror, then grabbed a handful of paper towels and began washing the blood off her face, then her neck, and then pushed up the sleeves of her sweater and began scrubbing the blood from her hands and wrists.

It was only after she began scrubbing the heels of her hands that she realized she'd scraped her hands when she fell. And there was a tiny cut beneath her chin from when she hit the pavement.

Bloody water was circling the drain.

Sean's blood.

Her blood.

Mingling again, like when they were nine.

Her clothes were still bloody, but there was nothing left on her skin, and by the time they left the ladies room, there was a small line of women waiting to get in.

"Sorry. Medical emergency," Shirley said, and headed back to the lobby, only to be met by no less than twenty more family members who'd arrived while they were gone.

After that, Amalie was swept up into a conclave of family. By the time the surgeon came out to let the family know Sean was in recovery and doing well, she was on a first-name basis with all of them.

Stinger, a.k.a. Darla Rae Compton, was dead.

The feds ran her name through the system to see who they were dealing with and were not surprised.

Ex-military. Dishonorable discharge. Rap sheet with a multitude of offenses.

And because she'd just failed her last mission, she was never going to spend the fifty thousand Mary Ingalls had transferred into her account. But her failure was the last nail in Fiona Rangely's coffin.

Wolf was alive.

His daughter was alive.

And Fiona's reign of terror had come to an end.

She was arrested and charged on two counts of murder, two counts of soliciting a murder, and one count of conspiracy to murder, and she had not a leg to stand on. Her only goal now was being sentenced to life in prison and not the death penalty.

The irony? That her plan blew up in her face when the refinery blew up in Sao Paulo. But Fiona wasn't laughing. She wasn't saying much of anything. Just waiting for her new criminal attorney to arrive.

The moment Wolf got the news from his security team, his heart sank. His in-laws had cheated him of watching his daughter grow up, and his wife had come far too close to killing her. The entire span of his daughter's misfortune had come through her connection to him, and he felt sick, but there was no time to wallow in his own regret and misery. He needed to make sure Fiona was truly out of circulation before he went after the people who'd stolen his daughter.

After a phone call to Ramsey to affirm that, he contacted his team to stay on the job until he'd had a chance to confront Fiona. He wasn't a man who backed away from the enemy, and she'd become his worst.

But all of this upheaval changed his plans to go straight to Jubilee. He was no longer certain of his welcome, had no idea where Amalie was and what was happening to Sean, and didn't know if she was even in a place where she could take a call, so he sent a text instead.

My darling daughter. I have just learned of what has happened. There are no words to express how deeply sorry I am. I thought I had done enough to keep you safe until Fiona was arrested, but I...we all...underestimated her. She'd already ordered the hit before she was arrested, and her decision to hire a woman was a move we never saw coming. I have been told your Sean was sent to surgery. I pray it is successful. I cannot take away the horror and fear you both experienced. All I can say again is how sorry I am, and hope that you are still willing to meet me. I want to be a part of your life, no matter how big or how small. I never knew you existed, and now you're everything to me. I'm on my way to Miami to sign some paperwork and have a face-to-face with the devil I married. Rising from the dead is more complicated than I had imagined. Please let me know if I may come see you, as we had planned.

With so much love,
Your dad

Sean's surgery was swift. No surprises. No broken bones, and one bullet less in his body than when he went in, and pumped full of pain meds when they took him to his room.

"Where's my girl? Where's Amalie? I need to see my girl," he kept saying.

Finally, one of the nurses who was helping get him settled started laughing.

"She's with your mother, half of the population of Pope Mountain, and a bunch of men who look like soldiers. She's safe. Trust me."

"Can't trust you. Don't know your name," he mumbled.

She smiled. " Linette Elgin, but everyone calls me Linnie, at your service."

"Nurse Linnie, I wanna see my girl. Get Mom. She'll bring her."

"In a few minutes, okay?"

"That's what my mom used to say just to get rid of us," he muttered.

Linnie grinned. "Who's 'us'?" she asked, as she kept working.

Sean had to focus. Who *was* "us"? "Umm, me, my brothers."

The nurse kept checking the drip and eyeing his blood pressure reading as she talked.

"How many brothers?"

"Three and me. Two are police officers here. Baby brother...chef in New York City."

"And what do you do when you're not stopping bullets?" she asked.

"Computers...IT. I've been here before, unlocking a system failure. Can I have a drink of water?"

"Your brothers are policemen here?" she asked, as she poured some water in a cup and then aimed the straw toward his mouth. He took a few sips. "Easy," she said. "More later," and set it aside, then she checked the name on his wristband again. "Sean Pope? Pope?" And then she looked at him closer. "Are you Wiley Pope's brother?"

His eyelids were getting heavy. "Yeah."

She frowned. "Are you as hell on wheels as he is?"

Sean opened his eyes again. "Ah...you've met him."

She rolled her eyes. "Yes, but I won't hold it against you. You know how to call if you need us. Rest now."

"Not until I see my girl. Tell Mom. She'll find her for me."

She sighed. "You *are* like Wiley. He doesn't take no for an answer, either. I'll let your family know they can come in now."

"Thank you," he mumbled, and closed his eyes.

Amalie was sitting among the family, letting their voices and their prayers roll on around her.

Shirley knew Amalie was still in shock and too

overwhelmed for this gathering, but it was their way—always being there for each other—and she needed it to keep from coming undone. She'd always feared one of her sons would be shot in the line of duty, but she'd never imagined it happening to Sean. Growing up, he was the steadfast son. The quiet one. The dependable one and, when the brothers got too loud, the referee.

She glanced at Amalie again and gently patted her hand, then looked around the room and saw Charlie Raines sitting on the floor playing on his phone.

"Charlie! Can you come here a minute?" she asked.

Charlie unwound himself and immediately headed her way.

"Yes, ma'am, Aunt Shirley. What do you need?"

She handed him some money. "A couple of cold drinks for Amalie and me, and get yourself one, too."

"Yes, ma'am. What's your poison?" he asked.

"Pepsi or Coke."

"Comin' up," Charlie said, and loped across the lobby to the snack area. A couple of years ago, Charlie had been the one in this hospital, hanging on to life by a thread. Now, he was fifteen years old and towering over both of his parents.

Amalie heard the interchange, but she was staring off into space, lost in the past. Remembering Sean from their school days and the miraculous full-circle moment when he walked into her office.

She closed her eyes and saw him standing before her, a skinny, long-legged little boy with a busted lip, a torn shirt, his knuckles raw and bloody, and the fire in his eyes as he helped her up out of the dirt.

Can children fall in love? Not childish crushes, but a forever bond born when soul mates find each other again? She was still lost in thought when her phone signaled a text. She took it out of her coat pocket to look, saw it was from her dad, and immediately opened the message.

It hurt her heart to see the fear in his words. He was afraid she would reject him. That she would blame him for what had happened. She responded immediately.

> Of course, I want to see you. I would be heartbroken if you gave up on me. Sign your papers. Dispatch your demon, and let me know the time and date of your arrival. We have twenty-seven years of catching up to do.

She hit Send, and then put the phone back in her pocket.

Charlie came back with the cold drinks. "For you, Miss Amalie," he said, and handed her a Coke. "And for you, Aunt Shirley," and handed her the second Coke.

Amalie looked up and smiled. "Thank you, Charlie."

"Yes, thank you, Charlie," Shirley said.

"Welcome," he said, and went back to his corner and his phone with a cold Coke for himself in his hand.

Amalie grasped the can of soda with both hands. The cold drink was a diversion—something to do with her hands besides wring them. A few minutes later she excused herself to go to the ladies' room, with her bodyguard escorts in tow. When she went to wash up, she glanced up, then paused, staring at her reflection. Then she remembered her father's words. *Look in the mirror, child. You wear her face.*

"And I've already outlived you. I'm sorry you weren't meant to stick around. Your parents were bastards," she muttered, then washed her hands and walked out to be escorted back to the waiting room.

Within minutes of her return, a nurse entered the waiting room.

"Pope family?" she called out.

They all raised their hands.

She smiled. "Awesome. But I'm going to have to limit the visit now to Sean's girl, and someone called Mom, because Sean Pope needs to rest, and he won't settle until he sees their faces."

"That's all we need to hear," Betty Raines said. "We'll get ourselves on home now that we know he's good to go. Shirley, keep us updated."

"I will," Shirley said. "Thank all of you for coming."

"Thank you for all the kind words," Amalie said.

"You're Sean's girl, which makes you our girl," Annie Cauley said. "Give him our love."

"Mrs. Pope, Amalie, if you'll follow me, I'll take you to Sean's room."

They gathered up their coats and cold drinks and followed the nurse up a long hall, then through a set of double doors and down to the room, with the security team trailing behind. But as soon as they reached the door, Joe stepped forward and entered first, then stepped aside.

"All clear, ladies. We'll be in the hall if you need us."

Linnie Elgin didn't know anything about the men trailing them, but she did know Sean Pope had been the victim of a murder attempt, so she took it as extra security on his behalf.

"Just have a seat. Talk to each other if you want. He's still sleeping off the anesthetic, so he's in and out. I'm Linnie. I'll be his nurse on this shift. Ring the buzzer if you need anything."

"Thank you," Shirley said.

Amalie dumped her things in an empty chair and headed straight to Sean's bed. She touched his arm and then his chest, feeling the pulse of his heartbeat beneath her hands. She couldn't stop shaking. All she kept thinking was, *Thank you, Lord.*

Shirley moved to the other side of the bed, touching her son's cheek, smoothing the hair away from his forehead, patting his leg.

"Still in one piece," Shirley said. "God is good." And then she sat down in the nearest chair before her knees gave way.

Amalie kissed Sean's cheek, then whispered in his ear, "Rest, love. I'm here." She dropped into the chair nearest the bed and laid her head on the mattress near his waist. Emotionally exhausted from all that had transpired, she sighed and closed her eyes.

She was asleep when Sean roused. He saw his mother dozing in a nearby chair and then Amalie, motionless, with her head resting against his hip.

My girls, he thought, then tunneled his fingers through her hair and closed his eyes.

Fiona Rangely's new lawyer, Sheldon Ryker, had no easy answers for her. No little white rabbits to pull out of his hat. The evidence against Fiona was damning. There was no reason whatsoever for wanting her husband dead, except to inherit what was his, just as she'd done before. Her past had finally caught up with her.

"What about an insanity plea?" Fiona asked.

"It might have been an option, if you did not have three dead husbands in your past. You go down that road, and the authorities could start exhuming bodies."

Fiona frowned. "They died in accidents."

"But your word means nothing now, and trying to sell that story to a jury would be impossible, since in this instance, you hired hit men to do your dirty work, using multiple identities to hide the payoffs, and were on husband number four when you tried to kill him with a bomb they can prove you built. Did they not tell you? The search warrants at your home and office yielded trace evidence of bomb material in both places, and then there's the security footage of you purchasing supplies to build it. And for what? Money you don't need. In the public eye, that's not mental illness, that's greed. Go to trial, and they'll persecute you. Throw yourself on the mercy of the court, and either way, you're in prison for life, or until they set a date for your execution."

She started weeping. "This isn't fair," she moaned.

"Neither is murder," Ryker said. "You have left a wake of unfairness behind you."

"So do I go to trial?"

"It's your call. You can pay me tens of thousands of dollars to fight this, and I'll take it because it's my job to represent you. We can file motions and injunctions for years, and I'll get rich, but you're never going free. Can you make peace with a women's prison?"

"But I have skills! Valuable skills. I help doctors save people's lives," Fiona argued.

Ryker sighed. "Then why wasn't that enough?"

She looked away, unwilling to answer. She couldn't bring herself to admit it had all become a game. A way to prove to men that she was smarter than them. She couldn't come right out and say that because it wouldn't fit with being crazy. It would make her like the men she reviled. Mowing down the competition to become "king of the hill."

She shrugged. "Then it doesn't matter," she said. "I will not be dragged through the court of public opinion. If they'll grant me solitary confinement, I'll take the judge's decision. Otherwise, there will be bloodshed in every cell I occupy with someone else. Eventually, we all die. Some sooner than later."

Ryker gathered up his things and left.

Fiona was taken back to her cell. The cell that left nothing to the imagination. It took the meaning of *one-room flat* to a whole new level. Eat. Sleep. Wash. Shit. All in a room smaller than her walk-in closet.

She'd made her decision. Her future was settled.

Or so she thought until she got word she had a visitor and found herself face-to-face with Wolfgang Outen and, in that moment, profoundly grateful to be on the other side of the wall, looking at him through a plexiglass window.

His eyes narrowed as he pointed to the phone on the wall beside her.

It was a challenge, and she knew it. She didn't have to talk to him, but it was her last chance to poke the bear, so she picked up the phone, expecting to hear rage. Expecting accusations. Expecting anything but the soft, chilling whisper in her ear.

"You fucked with the wrong man. You put out your last hit. Make peace with the Lord. You're already dead and don't know it."

Then he hung up the phone and walked out.

Her mouth was open in a scream that never emerged. Her brain was on fire and there was nowhere to run. When her bladder gave way, she couldn't stop it. Wolf Outen had shattered her bravado with a look and a whisper.

The walk back to her cell with pee running down her legs was as humiliating as the wet spot on the back of her scrubs. When they locked the door behind her, she crawled into bed and curled up in a ball, wondering when it would happen. Who would he pay to do it? A guard? Maybe another inmate? How would she die? Knifed? Poisoned? Attacked by a gang?

The possibilities were endless, but her days were ending, and it was the most horrible feeling on earth to know that this was no longer her choice. Her death would be a murder, and the irony was not wasted.

Wolf left the prison feeling the satisfaction as if he'd just plunged the knife into her himself. Because she'd done it to others, she fully believed he would have it done to her, and that was his revenge.

The doubt he'd put in her head.

That she was no longer in charge of her own destiny.

That alone would be what killed her.

She wouldn't trust the food she was given. She wouldn't trust the inmates or the guards, and if there was any justice in the world, she'd stress herself to death.

The weight of guilt was off his shoulders. His last goal in life was making sure the rest of hers was hell.

He was on his way back to his Miami estate, wondering what was going on with the Sao Paulo disaster, and tried calling Ruiz again. It went straight to voicemail, which made him anxious. Ruiz had been afraid for his life. What if someone had gotten to him? When he got back to the office tomorrow, he would call the local authorities. They could at least update him on what had happened to the refinery.

His housekeeper, Dee, was in tears when he walked in, elated to see him alive and well, and at the same time, distraught at finding out Fiona's true nature.

"Oh, Mr. Outen…what a blessing to have you back. I am so sorry for what you've been through. You didn't deserve to be treated this way. I've removed Miss Fiona's clothing and toiletries from your bedroom. Given the circumstances, I didn't think it would be something you would want to come home to."

Wolf was surprised by her loyalty.

"Thank you, Miss Dee. What a thoughtful thing to do. I'm happy to be home."

Dee beamed. She'd been worried about overstepping her authority. "Shall I tell Chef Able you're here for dinner, or do you have plans?"

"Here for dinner, and ask him to make it steak."

"Yes, sir, right away," Dee said, and hurried off to the kitchen, while Wolf made his way upstairs.

He dumped his suitcase on the bed, then looked around the room, noting the absence of anything feminine, and it was good.

Wolf called Amalie the next morning before leaving for his office. He wanted to check on her and on Sean, and to let her know he was calling off the security team, that the danger had ended.

Her grateful tears broke his heart.

"Thank you for everything," Amalie said. "Your guards have been wonderful, patient, and thoughtful."

"I'm envious they have seen you and I have not. I can't wait to meet you in person," Wolf said. "Take care of you and your Sean. Much success on your new office. I'll see you soon."

"Thank you, Dad. Looking forward to our first hug."

But it was Wolf who was crying when the call finally ended.

He'd never been called Dad.

It felt good in his heart.

Five days later, Sean Pope was home.

At Amalie's request, his brothers had taken all of his computers back to his office, so they'd be there when he was released, and left them for him to reconnect.

While Sean was still in the hospital, he'd seen Amalie every morning and every evening, and even though they talked and planned, it was as if the light had gone out inside her. Everything he was going through now she considered her fault, and nothing he could say changed it. She needed something else upon which to focus besides his healing, so he began urging her to get back to her office, reminding her she'd promised appointments, and breaking them might cause her to lose the momentum she had gained.

The first day she went in on her own, without guards at her heels, she noticed they had begun repairs at the school. It was another sign of healing.

When she met with her first client, it was like finding herself all over again. She hadn't done this since before her accident, but she was in her element doing what she knew—what she loved to do best.

And after that first day, Sean could see she was moving past the trauma and the guilt. Now, she was his happy blue-eyed girl again, lighting up every corner of his world.

Even after Sean was released, he still wasn't allowed to drive, which meant he was going to miss their daily visits, but that too would pass.

His second day home, he'd opened his office up again and eased back into work. As long as it didn't involve lifting or driving, he could chase an online virus to the ground without breaking a sweat.

Once B.J. learned what had happened, he had called Sean every day. The shock of it had put B.J. in a whole different frame of mind. He was so far away from all the people who mattered in his life that it no longer seemed worth it. He had accomplished everything he went to New York to do—graduating from the Culinary Institute and training in big restaurants.

But thinking about how close Sean had come to dying made him refocus on his future. He wanted to come home to the mountains and find a place for himself within the tourist trade. Whether it involved opening his own place, or working in one of the hotels didn't matter to him. As long as he was in Jubilee doing what he did best, he'd be satisfied with life. He had to talk to Cameron about a new dining area in Jubilee, but he'd do that when he came home at Easter. It was enough that life was getting back to normal and his family was okay.

Jubilee Elementary School was well on the road to recovery.

Amalie watched men coming to work in the morning and saw them leaving to go home at night. It was evident that more than repairs were being made. The brick on the whole south wall was also missing, and new brick had been hauled in, along with new windows. The blast from the crash had really done a number on the school, and she couldn't help but wonder how the children would be affected once they returned. The campus where the middle school and high school were located was on the far side of the football field, and school was still in session there. The littles were the ones who were going to be traumatized going back. She knew, because she remembered what it felt like after she was finally able to drive again.

Then in the middle of the building reconstruction, she saw a truck hauling in what looked like new playground equipment, and when she came home that evening, they already had a large slide, two different sets of swings, and the bare bones of some climbing equipment going up.

Going back to school was going to be hard for them, and having new things to play on was a great way to distract them from the charred crash site beyond the fences.

It was a little over ten days after Sean's release from the hospital. It was just after 10:00 a.m. and Amalie was at her office, working on an account for a client when she got a text from Wolf.

> I'm heading your way today and checking in at Hotel Devon. Will you be free for dinner around 7:00 p.m.? I'll order it in my suite so we can talk in private, if that's okay with you. I know you must have a million questions. I hope I have the answers you need. Oh...if you are free...fish, chicken, or steak?

Her heart skipped. Finally!

> Yes! Perfect! And chicken, please.

Then she made a quick call to Sean, and shivered at the sound of his voice in her ear.

"Hey, darlin'. How's my girl?"

"Good. My dad is finally coming to Jubilee. I'm meeting him for dinner in his suite tonight at Hotel Devon. Just wanted you to know where I'll be, and I'll text you when I get home."

Sean smiled. "That's awesome, and thanks for letting me know."

"I'm still not used to having someone who cares where I am, but never assume I don't appreciate the backup," she said. "Are you having a good day today?"

"Yes, now that I've heard your voice, and just so you don't forget, I love you forever," he said.

"Love you more, and if it's not too late when I get home, I'll call to say good night," she said.

"It's never too late to call me. I'm your guy."

The words were still echoing in her heart when she disconnected, and after that, her day flew past. She locked up at six o'clock on the dot, hurried home to shower and change, and was out the door and on her way to Hotel Devon with a small photo album of her life and fifteen minutes to spare.

Chapter 15

Wolf's chopper set down in Jubilee midafternoon. His arrival at Hotel Devon was more than he'd expected, but filled him with delight. They had literally rolled out a red carpet. A bellhop took his bags, and Michael Devon was waiting to personally escort him to the suite he'd reserved.

"I'm a little late for the board meeting," Wolf said.

Michael shook his head. "I saw the explosion from the fourth-floor windows. I thought I watched you die. My deepest sympathies for the loss of your friend and your pilot. I cannot imagine what you've been going through, but your suite awaits, and your stay is on the house. Follow me."

Wolf followed as Michael led him to a separate elevator and swiped a card to open the doors.

"I have a favor to ask," Wolf said, as they entered the car.

"Anything," Michael said.

"My daughter, Amalie Lincoln, will be joining me for dinner tonight around seven. Would you please have someone meet her at the entrance and escort her up to this suite?"

"I'll do it myself, and it will be an honor. I met her at her open house. She is both beautiful and delightful," Michael said.

Wolf sighed. "Thank you. Thank you for everything."

Michael nodded. The elevator stopped. The doors opened out into a small foyer facing a door labeled Presidential Suite. He swiped the card, then opened the door for Wolf.

"Enjoy your stay, and if you need anything, all you have to do is call the concierge. They have been notified of your presence. The chef awaits your menu tonight, and there will be a bottle of our best champagne with your meal."

"Thank you," Wolf said.

"You are most welcome," Michael said, then handed Wolf the key card and left him on his own.

Wolf's luggage was on his bed. The mini fridge was stocked full of every imaginable treat. The view from his window was Pope Mountain in all of its majesty. He'd seen it countless times before, but today it held special meaning. His child lived beneath its shadows now.

"Protect her when I cannot," he whispered, then turned away and began to unpack. The carefully wrapped present he'd brought for his daughter was still intact. It was his first gift to her, and he hadn't thought twice about what it would be.

As soon as he had finished, he called the chef about the menu, thanking him profusely for his help in making this meal special.

Now all he had to do was wait for her to knock on his door. He'd only seen her face and heard her voice. He didn't know if she was short or tall, what made her laugh, and what burdens she'd borne alone. But he would before this night was over. He wanted to know all about her Sean, and what had made him so special in her eyes. Why she'd chosen him would say a lot about what she valued in life.

Amalie was her own woman, but she was all that was left of Shandy. There was nothing more precious to him in this world than this child he'd never known existed. But he was never going to get over knowing that finding her had nearly cost her life.

The night was cold, but the wind had long since laid as Amalie drove across town. She had dressed for the weather in clothing that would not irritate the scars. The dress was a favorite—soft blue wool—long sleeved and with a neckline that dipped just below her collarbone and a hem that fell just above her knees. Her stockings were sheer. Her shoes, black with silver heels.

Dark hair, highlighted by the streak of white, framed her face. High cheekbones set off a perfectly straight nose. Sooty lashes and wing-shaped brows set off eyes as blue as the dress she was wearing. A brush of lipstick was the extent of makeup. She was excited, and anxious, and had been waiting for this moment for as long as she could remember.

Her heart was pounding as she wheeled her red SUV into the hotel parking lot. She grabbed her purse as she got out, tucked the photo album under her arm, pulled the collar of her coat up around her neck, and headed for the entrance, completely unprepared for the bright-red carpet rolled out before her, and the escort service awaiting her.

"Miss Lincoln! We meet again," Michael said. "I have the honor of escorting you to your father's suite." Then he offered his elbow and walked her all the way through the lobby, then escorted her up in the elevator and all the way to the door of Wolf's suite. "Just knock. He is anxiously awaiting your arrival," Michael said, then slipped back onto the elevator and left.

Amalie knocked three times. Moments later, the door swung inward, and she was in her father's presence and immediately looking for herself in his face.

He was tall, with a head of thick iron-gray hair, a nose that had obviously been broken at least once, a strong, square jaw, and sky-blue eyes.

She smiled. "I'm tall like you, and I have your eyes!"

"And your mother's face!" Wolf said, and opened his arms.

The thunder of his heartbeat was strong against her cheek as he embraced her, and then he stepped back to take her coat and hung it on a hook by the door.

"God, you are so beautiful," Wolf said. "Come. We'll sit by the fire to talk. Food will arrive shortly, but there's so much we don't know about each other. Would you like something to drink?"

She shook her head. "I'm already light-headed from the excitement, and I don't know where we start."

"You already know how I lost you. What else can I tell you that will fill in the gaps?"

"What was my mother's full name...before you married?"

"Cassandra Leigh Bullock, but I called her Shandy. Her parents were Carter and Leigh Bullock, from New Orleans, Louisiana. Old family. Old money. Upper class. I was not. They hated me from the start. Their money came from offshore drilling. I was one of the drillers on an offshore rig. Shandy loved me. I loved her. We married."

"How long were you married before me?" Amalie asked.

"Two years before she got pregnant. Out of curiosity, what day do you celebrate as your birthday?" he asked.

"April sixth."

Wolf's head came up, and his nostrils flared in anger. "I flew into New Orleans on the sixth. They told me you'd been born dead two days earlier. God damn it! Shandy was dying and I believed them. But what if you were still there?" He buried his face in his hands, and in that moment, Amalie felt every bit of his shock and pain.

"Do they still live there? Carter and Leigh Bullock?" she asked.

He nodded.

"I wonder who they paid off to make all this happen," she said.

"God only knows," he muttered. "What's your earliest memory?"

"Sitting on the side of a bed in a room full of crying babies."

His eyes welled. "Do you have any idea how old you were?"

She shook her head.

"Did anyone ever try to adopt you?" he asked.

"I don't know. I never understood what was happening for the longest time. I was just a kid with a bag who kept being moved from place to place, sleeping three to a bed. And like I told Sean, there was always a bed wetter, or one who cried herself to sleep every night, or a mean one who pinched and pulled hair."

"What kind of a kid were you?" he asked.

"The one who never made waves. It's how I met Sean."

"Tell me."

She related the playground incident when they were nine years old, and Sean beating up the three boys who'd taken her down on the playground to put wads of bubble gum in her hair.

"Oh, Dad, you should have seen him. A skinny boy with long arms and legs and the blackest hair and eyes I've ever seen. He was quiet like me. Shy, I think, but he was my first hero. The first person who ever stood up for me. And he was so funny and so intense. There was blood all over the both of us and the teachers were coming across the playground, when Sean jumps up and yells, "Blood oath!" and squishes our hands together where they were bleeding. He was vowing he'd always take care of me, and make sure nobody ever did that again, but life proved us wrong.

"My foster family was mad that they had to come get me. They blamed me for everything. Shaved my head without even trying to get out the gum and gave me back to Social Services, marking me a troublemaker. I lost my hero, and I never saw him again until I moved here and hired a man named Sean Pope to come install security and set up my office computers. At first, we didn't recognize each other, and they'd changed their last name back to his mother's maiden name after his father went to prison. They were reviled for who they were related to, just like I was reviled for being related to no one."

Tears were running down Wolf's face. He was horrified and guilt ridden, and there was nothing to change what had happened to her.

"And now you trust him completely?" Wolf asked.

"He's a Pope. That mountain is named for their family. They are held in the highest regard here. He has two brothers on the Jubilee police force and one in New York City recently graduated from the Culinary Institute of America. He's a freaking IT genius, and this past month alone, a hero twice over before he took the bullet meant for me. He helped rescue teachers and children trapped in the elementary school after the chopper crash, and just a few days ago while we were out on a walk, he pulled a woman and baby from a wrecked car before they got burned. His mother was the sweetest thing to me when we were kids. I always got a hug when she came to class parties, and she made the best cookies. Her name is Shirley, and when Sean and I get married, I've asked if we could live up on the mountain with her. I never had family, and theirs is huge. I never had a mother, and now I will."

Wolf listened, watching the play of emotions on her face, and knew that, above all else, his girl was happy. Then there was a knock at the door.

"That will be our dinner. I need to let them in. The powder room is down the hall, first door on the left if you need it before we eat. I'll be right back."

Amalie took him up on the offer, and when she came back, he was waiting for her, and so was the waiter.

"Dinner is served, and the first of many meals I hope to share with you and yours," Wolf said, and seated her as the waiter removed the cloches from their plates of food.

"Champagne, Mr. Outen, or would you prefer another beverage?"

Wolf looked at Amalie. "I could order another wine or a nonalcoholic beverage, if you prefer."

"Champagne, of course, to celebrate this day."

He nodded at the waiter, who filled their glasses, then slid the bottle back into the ice bucket. "Will there be anything else, sir?" he asked.

"No, Travis, and thank you."

"You're welcome. Enjoy your meal," he said, and left the suite.

Wolf picked up his glass. "A toast to us, Amalie. Reunited at last."

"To us!" she said.

The *tink* of fine crystal was evident as their glasses touched, and then the traditional sip before beginning the meal.

They talked as they ate, sharing favorite foods and types of entertainment, and as they were talking, she thought to ask, "That fire at your refinery in Brazil! Did they ever put it out?"

He paused. "Odd that you would ask. I've been trying to get in touch with Ruiz, the site manager, for days now, but it just goes to voicemail. I'm calling the Sao Paulo police tomorrow to get an update on the fire and see if they've been able to find out the cause. We aren't sure whether it was terrorist related or—"

"It was him," Amalie said. "Ruiz. He's been embezzling money and was afraid you'd find out. He didn't mean for it to—" And then she saw the look on her father's face and realized what she'd said, and paled. "I'm sorry. This just begun happening to me after the wreck."

"Are you telling me that you're psychic?" Wolf asked.

"I don't know what to call it. Sometimes I just know stuff and hear voices."

Wolf reached out and ran a finger through the white streak in her hair.

"This is natural, isn't it?"

She nodded.

"Were you born with it?" he asked.

"No. It happened after the wreck. After the voices came."

"God," Wolf whispered, and touched it again. "When did you first hear the voices?"

"In the car when it was burning. My clothes were on fire. A trucker was trying to get my door open, and I was screaming. And then I heard a voice say, *It's going to be okay*. And it was."

"Did they tell you about Ruiz?" he asked.

"No. Sometimes I just see things, too, and when we started talking about him, I suddenly saw a man pouring gasoline on the floor of an office and then saw it bursting into flames and he was running. I don't know how I know that I know it was him, but he was falsifying documents to cover embezzling money and afraid he'd get caught."

"Christ Almighty," Wolf whispered. "No wonder he's not answering his phone."

She was trembling, afraid that she'd just ruined everything. "You believe me? You don't think I'm crazy?"

Wolf frowned. "No, I don't think that. Does Sean think you're crazy?"

"No. They have an elder in the family just like me. She's the one who told me the day of my open house that someone was looking for me, but to be patient. And that's after I'd already sent you the letter about our Ancestry.com match and had heard nothing back."

Wolf shook his head. "Now I know I have to meet these Popes."

Amalie was still trembling. "I have a question."

"Ask," he said.

"When Sean and I get married, I'm not going to ask

you to give me away, because I was already taken from you. But would you walk me down the aisle?"

"Daughter, it would be my honor," Wolf said.

"If we've finished eating, I have something to share with you. It doesn't amount to much, but I have a few pictures of me growing up, and since you missed seeing that happen, I thought you might like—"

"Absolutely," Wolf said, "and I have a gift for you. You get your pictures and I'll get my gift, and we'll meet by the fireplace."

She went back into the living room and got her photo album. Moments later, Wolf came back carrying a gift wrapped in shiny pink wrapping paper, tied with tendrils of silver ribbon.

"You first," Wolf said, as he plopped down beside her.

She opened the photo album and put it in his lap. "A social worker gave me a copy of this baby picture when I turned eighteen. She said it was taken when I was ten days old. This picture is from one of my first foster parents. I don't remember them at all, but I was three. This picture is when I began first grade. I don't remember the school or the people taking care of me. But this is my school picture from third grade, when I first met Sean. I was at Ellen Smith Elementary school in Conway, Arkansas. I was about two months from finishing third grade when that family gave me back to welfare and sent me somewhere else. That was Miss Willis and Mr. Willis. They were scary."

Wolf kept staring at the little face as it matured from year to year, hearing the same life story about not remembering the people and losing track of the changes. And by the time she got to her high school graduation, he was once again struggling not to cry.

"When you aged out of the system, how did you get your degree?" he asked.

Then she told him about the man in Little Rock who'd promised college educations and the program she'd signed up for her freshman year of high school.

"I got a free ride to college for having a straight-A grade point average all through high school and my choice of major at the university there. I wanted to be a CPA. After college, I went to work for a firm in Tulsa, Oklahoma, and that's where I was living when I had the wreck. So that's me to date."

"Damn, girl, but I'm so proud of you right now I could bust. You had everything against you, and you beat the system and succeeded in spite of it," he said.

"Besides Sean, you're the only other person who's said aloud that they were proud of me."

"So, this is for you from me," he said, and handed her the gift.

She tore into it without hesitation, then gasped.

"That's your mother and me on our wedding day. I'm so sorry she never lived to raise you, but she would be so very proud of the woman you grew up to be."

Amalie was in tears. She was holding her past and sitting beside her future.

"This means everything to me," she whispered. "Thank you, Dad, thank you."

"Do you see yourself?" he asked.

She nodded. "In both of you. At last, I can say I know my people."

"And I need to meet the Popes," he said.

"How long are you going to be here?" she asked.

"I'm flying out in two days to hold a press conference regarding my resurrection. I have no plans to make your presence a part of my comments, but it's possible they'll snoop around and find out anyway."

"I'm not going to start waving flags bragging about who I'm related to. But I'm so proud to be your daughter and not afraid of the connection, if that's what you're saying. If it's okay with you, I'll talk to Sean tonight and feel him out about a small family gathering at Shirley's so you can meet some of the immediate family before you leave."

"It's very okay. Just let me know when and where," Wolf said.

"Oh, I'll pick you up and take you there. It's up the mountain, and about every third mailbox has the name Pope on it."

A short while later, Amalie was gone. The food was cleared from his suite, and he took the remaining champagne back to the fireside and had a long solitary talk with Shandy about what had occurred, then lifted a glass to her memory and to the child they had made.

"I swear on my life, I will make your parents pay for what they did and spend the rest of my life making it up to our girl."

Amalie walked into her house clutching the photo of her parents and then set it on the mantel above her fireplace before getting out of her dress clothes and into her pj's and fuzzy socks to call Sean. It was well after ten o'clock. She hated to call that late, but she'd promised and he would be expecting it, and she was right.

He answered on the first ring.

"Are you home?"

"Yes," she said. "It was a wonderful evening. He wants to meet you and your family before he leaves."

"We would love it, and Mom would revel in it. When is he leaving?"

"He's here for a couple more days, and then duty calls, as he said."

"I'll run it by Mom, but I can tell you right now, she'll say yes. He won't be the only one checking out the in-law business. His money won't impress her. It'll be the man himself."

"Let me know if she's up to it. I can bring food, too, if it will help."

"I'll call you tomorrow with time and day," Sean said.

"Thank you, Sean. I believe you two are going to like each other. I felt like I'd known him forever."

"That's the soul connection," Sean said. "Like I felt the first time I saw you."

"What do you mean?" Amalie asked.

"That first day I saw you, I thought I already knew you and that I'd been waiting for the sight of your face."

The room was beginning to spin as the scene played out before her.

"In the trading post, right? Fouquet, the trapper I belonged to, had just hit me. He was always hitting me when he got drunk. I was bleeding, and you let out this roar, picked me up, and sat me on the counter beside a pile of furs and threw him out the door. You wouldn't let him take me away, and so I stayed."

Sean was in shock. He didn't know what to say. What to think, but it was just like before, and he wondered if she even knew what she'd just said. And when she segued from that into the picture Wolf had given her, he knew it hadn't sunk in.

"I can't wait for you to see it. My mom and dad. They were so young. Younger than I am now! And so beautiful! Love makes everyone beautiful, and true love lasts forever, doesn't it, Sean?"

"Yes, it does, baby. Yes, it does. Now that I know you are home, rest well. We'll talk tomorrow, okay?"

"Yes, Sean. I love you."

His vision was blurring. "I love you, too," he said, and disconnected. He needed to talk to Aunt Ella. If what he believed was happening here, then finding Meg wasn't the end they'd all believed. It was just the beginning, and he and Amalie were the closure to their family's tragic past.

Chapter 16

THE NEXT MORNING AT BREAKFAST, SEAN BROACHED the subject of a family dinner to meet Wolf, and Shirley's face lit up.

"Bring him to supper tonight. I'll make sure the rest of us are here as well, and maybe ask Ella, and John and Annie. And Cameron and Rusty? What do you think?"

Sean grinned. "It's hard to find a stopping place, isn't it? But that works for me, if it suits you. I understand Amalie met all of them at the hospital."

"Rusty wasn't there. Bringing Mikey wasn't a good idea, but Cameron was. Aaron and Wiley were up on the roof with the dead sniper, waiting for the coroner to arrive."

"They've both already met her. As for what was going on after I got shot, I know nothing," Sean said. "I never lost a whole segment of time like that before."

"And I hope you never do again," Shirley said. "Call Amalie. Ask her if seven o'clock is okay? I know she's working until six."

"I will, and thanks, Mom. She offered to bring stuff, so let her know if there's anything she can do to help. It will make her feel like she's not making too much work for you."

"We've got this," Shirley said. "I'll have Annie bring dinner rolls and desserts from the bakery and get Dani to bring a couple of salads. I can handle the rest. Clear it with Amalie and I'll start the ball rolling."

Sean picked up the phone and sent her a text.

Mom's up for bringing Wolf to supper tonight. 7:00 p.m. Clear it with him ASAP and let me know.

"Message sent, Mom. House is chilly. I'm going to add a log to the fire," he said.

"No, you're not. You're not cleared for lifting. I'll do it, and remind you I grew up doing this."

He sighed. "Then I'll load the dishwasher. That I can do."

A few minutes later, he had the kitchen cleared. Shirley had the fire going. And Amalie responded to the text.

Invitation accepted. Tell your mom thank you so much. We'll see you at seven. I miss you. Love you.

Sean sent back a text.

I miss you more. Love you more. See you tonight.

After Shirley got the message, she went into spin mode, had everyone contacted and all of the food organized within two hours, and the only person who couldn't come was Rusty because Mikey had a cold. Cameron was coming on his own with her apologies.

Sean wisely stepped out of the way and went to his office with a cup of coffee and good intentions. They lasted until his shoulder got a cramp, and then he was flat on his back in bed with the heating pad, relieved his mother was too busy with her planning to fuss over him. The cramp would pass, and he'd be fine.

Amalie opened up her office, turned up the thermostat, then went to the back room to make herself a cup of coffee. As soon as it was done, she carried it to her desk and went to work.

It was nearing noon when a man entered her office carrying a huge bouquet of pink roses.

"Delivery for Miss Lincoln."

"How beautiful!" Amalie cried, and jumped up from her chair. "You can put them there on the front desk!"

"Yes, ma'am. Have a good day," he said, and left on the run.

Amalie reached for the card, then turned it over to read.

First flowers to my darling daughter.
Thank you for dining with me last night.

See you later,
Love, Dad

Her vision blurred. "So, this is how it feels to belong," she said, and carried the card back to her desk.

Wolf was in his suite, finishing up a conference call with the staff at his Miami headquarters.

He'd just designated a private investigator to catch the first flight out to Sao Paulo, Brazil, to find out what he could about the situation at the refinery and get what info he could on Julio Ruiz. He wasn't chasing any more of his business troubles down on his own until he had his personal life straightened out here, and the next call he made was to his lawyer.

Arnie Walters was working on a brief and his third cup of coffee when his phone rang.

"Arnie Walters speaking."

"Arnie, it's me, Wolf."

"Oh hey. How's it going?" Arnie asked.

"Good. I have a legal question and a request."

"Fire away," Arnie said.

"Is there a statute of limitations on kidnapping in the United States?" Wolf asked.

"No," Arnie said, wondering what the hell Wolf was up to now.

"If I want to press charges against people for kidnapping in the state of Louisiana, do I have to have a Louisiana lawyer to represent me?" Wolf asked.

"Yes… At least…the lawyer has to be licensed in that state."

"Then I need some names," Wolf said.

"What's going on?" Arnie asked.

"I'm about to take some people to task for telling me my daughter was born dead and then giving her away."

"You're taking about Shandy's parents, right?"

"Yes. I don't know who all they paid off to make that happen, but I'm not stopping until they all go down. They stole my child, and if it hadn't been for Ancestry.com, I would never have known she existed."

"So, they're still alive? How old would they be now?" Arnie asked.

"Late seventies. They think they got away with this, but they're about to receive a rude awakening."

Arnie shuddered. The rage in Wolf's voice was palpable, and he couldn't blame him.

"I have to be in court this afternoon, but I'll put some people on it. I'll get the list to you before the end of the day, okay?" Arnie said.

"Yes, thank you, and good luck in court," Wolf added.

"Thanks, buddy. Talk to you soon."

Wolf disconnected, then thought about dinner tonight with the Popes. He needed to take a hostess gift, but he didn't know Shirley Pope. He didn't want to present something ostentatious and make them feel like he was rubbing their noses in his wealth. Just something genuine, from him to her. He wanted to make Amalie proud and had the whole day ahead of him. Maybe it was time to finally see the sights of Jubilee. Surely, he'd find something that struck his fancy.

He got his coat, wallet, and the key card to his suite and was on his way out the door when he got a text from Amalie.

The flowers are lovely! Thank you, Dad. You're the best. I'll pick you up at the hotel at 6:30.

Love, Amalie

He was still smiling when he ran into Michael in the lobby.

"Good morning," Michael said. "I see you're heading out. Do you need a ride somewhere?"

"I thought I'd see the sights," Wolf said. "I've been here countless times and never got beyond the amenities of the hotel."

"I'm on my way to the bank. I'd be happy to drop you off," Michael said.

"That would be great," Wolf said. "Much appreciated."

"They're bringing my car around now. Walk with me," Michael said.

A few minutes later, they were heading uptown.

"Was your dinner satisfactory last night?" Michael asked.

"It was perfect. Thank you for everything. Your father must be proud of how you've taken over the reins here. How's he doing?"

Michael grinned. "It's hard to please Marshall Devon, but he hasn't complained, and he's doing great. As long as there's land to buy and buildings to erect, he'll be happy."

Wolf nodded. "Speaking of land to buy, I don't suppose PCG Inc. has relented on selling anything here?"

Michael shook his head. "Their answer is not only no, but *Hell No*. It is, was, and always will be their final answer. We made peace with that when we agreed to build here."

"It's a strange way to do business," Wolf said. "This place is unique. They could explode their profits exponentially if they'd let people in."

Michael shrugged. "I've lived here nearly ten years now, and I have begun to see the wisdom of perfection in small places. Besides, look at this place. Where else would they go? Surrounded by mountains. The valley caters to tourists and, at the same time, has found a way to exist within what amounts to a very small town. The land is still pure the way it was in the beginning. No logging is allowed on the mountain, and the people who live there own their homes and land, and have for generations. Big industry makes money for some and destroys the rest," Michael said. "Oh, sure we have crime here. You can't be a part of the tourism industry without the criminal element wanting in, but our police are wiser than you would assume. We had a serious case of human trafficking trying to take hold here a few years back, and they busted it wide open."

Wolf eyed the young man with renewed respect. "Don't lose that perspective. In the long run, you will be the happier man."

Michael pointed. "We're coming up on the tourist side. Is there any place in particular you intend to go?"

"Maybe the arts and crafts area?" Wolf said.

"Then I'm going to let you out here. See the carving of the black bear beside the fountain? Take the sidewalk straight past it and it's all in front of you."

"Many thanks," Wolf said.

"If you need a ride back, call the hotel. We have courtesy cars. Someone will pick you up and bring you back."

"Thanks again," Wolf said, and got out smiling. He'd been in a lot of places and been lost countless times in the process, but he'd never received directions to "walk past the bear" before. As soon as he passed the bear, his adventure began. He prowled the stands and the shops and had hot chocolate on a bench outside a candy store, while watching a little girl feeding pieces of her cookie to birds begging in the square. Her father was standing nearby, and when the cookie was gone, he swung her up into the air and put her on his shoulders. The child's laughter went straight to Wolf's heart. His little girl had gone through hell without him, and all because of the hate in Leigh and Carter Bullocks' hearts.

Unwilling to let the past ruin the day, he tossed the last of his hot chocolate into a garbage bin and kept moving, still looking for something special for the family who'd taken Amalie to love before he even knew she existed.

It was midafternoon when he wandered into a woodcarver's shop. Seconds later, he saw a bird on a shelf and wondered if the owner knew it had flown into the building. It was only after he moved closer that he realized it was a delicate carving. A hand-painted carving of a blue-gray warbler, perched upon a delicate pine branch and nearly hidden among the needles.

At that point, a thirtysomething man with long dark hair pulled back in a ponytail approached the counter.

"Afternoon. Can I help you?" he asked.

Wolf pointed to the carving. "Did you do this?"

"Yes, sir."

"It's exquisite. I want to buy it," Wolf said.

"It's three hundred and fifty dollars."

Wolf pulled out his wallet and counted out the cash.

The young man beamed. "I'll box this right up for you."

"Very carefully. It's a gift for someone special," Wolf said.

A short while later, the man came back carrying a white oblong box.

"Here you are, and thank you," he said.

Wolf eyed the man as he picked it up from the counter. "What's your name?"

"Andrew Glass."

"Are you a local artist?" Wolf asked.

He nodded and then pointed out the window. "I live on Pope Mountain. My granny was a Pope."

Wolf nodded. "Beautiful place to live," he said, and walked out carrying his gift, thinking about what Michael Devon had said. Maybe he was right. Some things are perfect just the way they are.

It was cold, and Wolf was tired, and when he got back to the fountain and passed the black bear, he called the hotel for a ride. All he wanted now was to get warm.

Fiona Rangely was on hold.

Her lawyer was in the process of trying to work out a plea bargain with the federal prosecutor, with Fiona admitting guilt to all charges and asking for a life sentence rather than the death penalty. But she knew that even if the federal prosecutor agreed to the plea deal, the sentencing would ultimately be up to the judge.

She spent every day in the prison looking over her shoulder. Every meal felt like playing Russian roulette. Will this bite kill me? Is this the day I'm going to die? Getting jostled by other inmates during their time in the dayroom was a nightmare. Every second she expected to get shanked.

At night, she saw Wolf's face in her dreams and woke up drenched in sweat or crying. She'd spent her life accumulating wealth, but money was worthless to her now. No more rendezvous with Hank Kilmer. No more trips to the hair salon or weekly massages at the spa. No more mani-pedis. She wondered what was happening at BioMed. She was the sole owner. There was no one legally capable of taking over.

She'd played a dirty game and gotten caught.

Life as she'd known it was over, and what was left of it wasn't worth living.

Amalie was outside the hotel at six thirty sharp. Wolf emerged moments later carrying a white box. She was thinking as he approached, *That's my father,* and trying not to overwhelm herself again.

She'd told him to dress for comfort, and even though he looked like he'd just stepped away from a fashion shoot, he seemed at ease in the charcoal slacks, black and white sweater, and pewter-gray trench coat he had on.

He eyed the pink velour sweater and black slacks she was wearing, then gave her a quick wink. "You look beautiful."

"Thank you. Are you ready to do this?" she asked.

He nodded. "I've been looking forward to it all day."

She put the car in gear as he was buckling up, and then they were off.

"So, who all am I meeting tonight?" Wolf asked.

Amalie frowned. "I honestly don't know. Most likely Aaron and Dani. That's the oldest of the four brothers, and Dani is his wife. Wiley isn't married, so I'm thinking he'll be on his own, although Sean says he has three girls on speed dial."

Wolf laughed. "That's a great description. Although I've seen Sean during our Zoom meeting, I'm anxious to meet him in person. From the way you talk, their mother must be something special."

"She's really pretty, I think. She might be around your age. I know she got married very young, and to a man who turned into an abuser. Sean told me their father made their lives a living hell and nearly killed her, but their mother protected them from the worst of it. But they don't talk about that. I'm just telling you."

He nodded. "Understood," he said, but as they started up the mountain, he got quiet.

Amalie could see wonder in his eyes.

"You know, for a man who grew up in the Louisiana bayous, this place is something to see," he said.

"You've been all over the world. I'm sure you've seen many ancient wonders," she said.

He shrugged. "Yes, of course, but nothing pulls at you harder than home."

Her eyes widened, and the tone of her voice lifted. "That's how I feel about Pope Mountain. From the moment I saw it, I felt a connection, like I'd been lost and finally found home. Did you and my mother date a long time before you got married?"

"About eight months, but I fell in love with Shandy the first time I saw her." He chuckled. "Like being struck by lightning and not dying."

"I love that! What a perfect way to describe being in love!"

"Been in love once. Been married more than once. Lesson learned," he muttered. "Oh...while I'm thinking about it, when you aged out of foster care, did your caseworker give you access to your file?"

"Yes. I requested a copy, and she gave it to me. Why?"

"Because I'm going after the people who gave you away, and I want all the ammunition I can get before I go to the New Orleans police about it."

"I can make copies at my office and have a file for you before you leave," she said.

Wolf nodded. "That would be great. And, we may have to do DNA tests again for the court. I don't doubt it for a second, but I don't want anybody challenging Ancestry.com as the only proof."

"We could probably have the tests done at the hospital lab, or even the police department before you leave. They could send you the results."

"I'll call both places early tomorrow and let you know. I'm due to fly out around three. I don't want to leave you, but there are so many loose ends still dangling from people thinking I was dead. And I still have to make my own public appearance and give a statement, or I'll be hounded until I do."

She nodded, trying to imagine what it took to be who he was, and then shrugged it off. It didn't matter. All he needed to be for her was her father.

"If you wind up in court with my grandparents, will I have to be there?" she asked.

He frowned. "Most likely. Is that okay?"

A sudden anger rolled through her. "Yes. They threw me away. I don't mind a bit being the nail in their coffins."

"I second that," he said.

After that, they let the conversation slide until she began slowing down.

Wolf sat up, curious now. "So, we're almost there, hunh? I was beginning to wonder if there really were houses up in these woods."

"There are hundreds of people up here. They just treasure their privacy. Wait until you see Shirley's house. The original part was once a two-room cabin, but it's been built onto several times in the last four generations. The front porch runs the entire length of the house. It's painted white now, and the fireplace is built of natural rock. She inherited it a few years ago after her mother's passing. I love coming here."

Wolf was thinking of his three-story mansion on his Miami estate, and the villa he had in Italy, and the chateau he owned in France, and realized he only owned them for the cachet. Not because he loved being there. His daughter was teaching him something, and he needed to sit up and take notice.

And then she turned up into the driveway and headed toward the house. As soon as she came around the curve and saw all of the other cars, she laughed.

"Okay, maybe a couple more people than just Shirley and the boys."

"I think I can handle it," Wolf said. The front door opened, and people began spilling out onto the porch, and when they did, for the first time in more years than Wolf could count, he was shocked. "They're giants. And they all look alike."

Amalie smiled. "You are officially in the land of Popes."

"Which one is yours?" Wolf asked.

"The one coming down the steps to meet us."

Sean hugged and kissed her as she got out. "I've been missing you. You look beautiful," he said, and then extended his hand to Wolf. "Mr. Outen, welcome to our home."

"Thank you for having me," Wolf said, taking the measure of Sean Pope's firm grip. "It's a pleasure to finally meet you in person," he said, then looked toward the porch. "The family resemblance is amazing."

"Come meet them," Sean said, and led Amalie up the steps. "Everyone, this is Amalie's father, Wolf Outen. Introduce yourselves."

"I'm Aaron Pope, Sean's oldest brother, and this is my wife, Dani."

"I'm Wiley Pope, just younger than Sean, but better looking."

"I'm Cameron Pope, one of about a hundred cousins. My wife, Rusty, is sorry she couldn't be here to meet you. Our son isn't feeling well, but Rusty sends her best wishes."

And then the eldest man stepped forward. "I'm John Cauley. My wife, Annie, is inside. She's Shirley's aunt."

"It's a pleasure," Wolf said.

Then Sean opened the door. "Let's get out of the cold. There are more of us inside."

Shirley came out of the kitchen as they walked in and

immediately gave Amalie a big hug. "There's my busy girl."

"Thank you for this. You have no idea how much this means to me," Amalie whispered.

"We're excited to meet your father," Shirley said.

Amalie turned. "Dad, this is Sean's mother, Shirley. Shirley, this is my dad, Wolf Outen."

Wolf had just removed his coat and quickly turned to greet her.

"Mrs. Pope, this is a pleasure. I've heard nothing but high praise about you since the moment Amalie and I met. I am so very grateful you and your family were kind to a lonely little girl when so many were not. You have my undying appreciation."

Shirley's heart broke for him. "Please, call me Shirley. I can't imagine how you must feel, but we're all so happy you two have found each other."

Wolf handed her the box he'd been carrying. "This is for you. A little hostess gift for organizing all this at such short notice."

Shirley beamed. "Oh my! You didn't have to do that."

"But she loves that you did," Wiley piped up, and made everyone laugh.

Wolf grinned. The one with three women on speed dial was a caution.

"Sit down and open it, Mom," Sean said.

Shirley sat, opened the lid, and then gasped.

"Oh my lord! This is the most beautiful thing I've ever seen." She lifted it out with both hands. "It's a warbler!

A mountain warbler. It was my mother's favorite bird! It looks so real. Thank you, Wolf, thank you. I will treasure this!"

"I'm happy you like it," he said.

"Did you get it in the village?" Sean asked.

Wolf nodded.

"Andrew's work," Cameron said. "He's kind of famous in the wood-carving world. He won Wood-Carver of the Year a few years back. It's really broadened his sales and craft."

"I am impressed," Wolf said. "Everything he had in the shop was outstanding, but I honestly thought the bird was real when I first walked in. After that, my decision was made."

While they were admiring the carving, two more women came out of the kitchen. Wolf was trying not to stare, but even at their ages, the Pope resemblance was striking. And then Sean saw them and began introductions again.

"Oh, Wolf, this is my aunt Annie Cauley, John's wife. She runs the bakery in Jubilee, and this is Aunt Ella, the elder of our family. Ladies, Amalie's father, Wolf Outen."

"My only claim to fame is outliving all my peers," Ella said.

Wolf smiled. "There's much to be said about persistence."

Ella arched a brow. "I like that... I am old because I persisted!"

"And we're glad you did," Annie said.

Shirley got up and carried the carving to the mantel and moved things around until it was set in the forefront in a place of honor, and then stood back admiring it.

"Isn't this the most beautiful thing," she murmured, then turned around and waved her hands toward the dining room. "I came in here to tell you supper was ready and got sidetracked, didn't I?"

"And I'm ready for it. I miss my mama's cooking," Wiley said.

"It's what you get for moving into Jubilee to chase women," Aaron said.

They laughed all the way to the table, and as they were taking their seats, Wolf couldn't help but think about the unity within this family—something he'd been missing all his life. He kept watching his daughter, and the man who loved her, and saw their future in this place. He was at peace knowing no matter where his life took him, she would always be safe and loved here.

By the time they got down to dessert, Wolf felt like he'd known these people all his life. Cameron Pope was the dark horse. He was smart, and witty, and belittled his own talents, which, when told around the table, were obviously many. The man had secrets, but he liked him.

Wolf had been an only child and was seriously envious of the camaraderie between Shirley's sons. The women were like hens in a henhouse, all talking at once and still hearing everything else going on at the same time, and Amalie was in the middle of it.

John and Annie Cauley anchored the others by age and experience and took the job of family elders seriously, but it was Ella Pope, the nonagenarian, who had him stumped. She was quick-witted and didn't mind a laugh at herself, but he'd caught her watching him more than once with those dark eyes flashing, and then she'd look away. She reminded him of an old woman from the bayou where he grew up. People had gone to her for potions and curses because that was their way. Ella didn't come across quite like that. Amalie said the family claimed she had "the sight," and if she did, he wondered what she thought of him. And then when Shirley and Dani got up to serve dessert, he found out what Ella was all about.

Ella leaned over, took his hand, and whispered in his ear.

"They paid someone to take your baby girl across state lines and abandon her in an alley in Hot Springs, Arkansas. The cops thought she'd been born there. They left a note wrapped up inside her blanket. It said crazy ran in the family so that no one would want her. Go after them. They will turn on each other."

Wolf saw his reflection in her eyes and felt like he was drowning.

"I'm not going to ask you how you know this. All I'm going to do is say thank you, because I'm already after them. They just don't know it, and this is more ammunition for the hell I am going to rain down on their heads."

Ella nodded. "I would have expected no less. You didn't get where you are without a fight," she said, and let go of his hand.

"Dad, would you rather have a slice of apple tart or Italian cream cake?" Amalie asked.

Wolf jumped like he'd been slapped. "Uh... Oh... Yes," he said.

They laughed as Shirley put a slice of each on his plate.

"I'll have the cake," Ella said. "I don't bake anymore. Too much trouble for just me."

Sean kept an eye on Wolf all the way through the meal, wanting to make certain that he was at ease so Amalie could enjoy herself as well. He knew how much this meant to her, but sitting side by side with her at a family gathering meant a lot to him, too.

However, they were coming up on well over an hour at the table, dessert was just beginning, and the muscles in his shoulders had begun to knot.

Amalie saw the pain on his face and leaned over.

"Where are your pain pills?" she whispered.

"On my nightstand, but it's okay," he said.

"No, it's not okay. I'll be right back," she said. "Excuse me a moment," she told everyone, and left the table, returning shortly and taking her seat before dropping the pills in his palm.

Sean downed them. "Thank you, baby."

Shirley was too busy cutting cake and tarts to see the

byplay, and no one else was paying attention. Satisfied that she hadn't usurped Shirley's place, Amalie took a bite of the tart and then rolled her eyes.

"Aunt Annie, you did yourself proud. This tart is delicious."

Annie beamed. "Thank you, sugar."

Amalie sighed. "Shirley's promised to teach me how to make dumplings that don't fall apart, and now this amazing bite! I have a long way to go to get to Pope-level cooking."

Sean slid his arm around her. "You can serve frozen dinners and feed me from cans for the rest of our lives, and I'll be happy."

Amalie shook her head. "You say that, knowing full well we're moving in with Shirley because I wanted a mama, and you offered me yours." Her chin trembled. "And she agreed, so I'm going to be learning from the best."

Shirley had tears in her eyes, but she was beaming.

"Well, I never had daughters. I had to wait until my boys gave me some. I have my darling Dani, and now you're on the horizon. I am a happy woman."

Wiley frowned. "Don't be waitin' on me for a third daughter. I'm nowhere ready for all that."

"And if and when it ever happens, we know it won't be Linnie Elgin, don't we?" Sean said.

Wiley's smirk faded. "What about Linnie Elgin?"

"She was my nurse off and on while I was in the hospital. When she found out you were my brother, she frowned, then she said she wouldn't hold it against me."

Wiley flushed.

Shirley frowned. "I am going to assume whatever asinine thing you did was forgivable."

"Mostly," Wiley said.

Wolf laughed out loud. "Sorry, Shirley, but I want you to know this has been, without a doubt, the most enjoyable meal I have ever had, with the most delightful people I've ever met. Does anyone here want to adopt me, too?"

"You're already in, or you wouldn't be sitting here," Sean said.

Shirley sighed. "I promise, I raised them better than this. Anybody want coffee?"

Ella held up her hand. "You know how I like it," she said.

"Two sugars with a splash of cream," they all echoed.

Wolf grinned. "Wanna know how I like my coffee?"

"Black, with a splash of whiskey," Amalie said.

He blinked. "How did you know that?"

She looked startled. "Know what?"

"How I like my coffee?" Wolf said.

Amalie felt the room tilt, then looked at Sean in sudden panic. "Crap. Did I do it again?"

He slid his arm around her shoulder and kissed her forehead. "You're just teaching me early to never lie to you," he said, then made a joke of it for her benefit. "Pay her no mind, everybody. She's slowly turning into Aunt Ella and still doesn't have a feel for her brakes. After her wreck, Mother Nature gave her this wild streak," he said, running his finger down the white streak in her hair, "and then opened up a little window in her brain that started showing her past, present, and future. That makes her special. I got shot and woke up as confused about life as ever."

Now everyone was looking at Amalie with renewed respect, including Wolf. One family member with "the sight" was special. Two might just put them on the map.

"Then coffee with a splash of whiskey, coming up," Shirley said, and pointed at Wiley. "Son, would you please go get the bottle of Jim Beam, and don't pretend you don't know where it is because I know you do. It hasn't been touched since you moved out."

Wiley got up from the table and came back moments later with the whiskey she'd asked for and set it on the counter.

Shirley winked. "Thank you."

Wiley took the cake server out of her hand, swung her into his arms, and began dancing her around the kitchen, with Shirley pink-cheeked and giggling, telling him to stop. He danced her back to the counter and returned to the table, grinning.

"What? She's my mama and she's pretty," he said, and sat down.

Ella clapped her hands in delight. "Lord, Shirley, that boy is just like your daddy."

"Thank God," Wiley muttered. "Way better than being like mine."

The blow landed straight in Shirley's heart. She walked to where he was sitting and put her arms around his neck.

"You are my sunshine, Wiley Pope, and don't you ever forget it."

The dark shadows passed, and Wiley was all smiles and laughter again. "So, what does that make Aaron?" he asked.

Shirley moved around the table, placing her hand on each son as she passed. "By order of birth alone, Aaron became our rock. The one I knew who would always pick up the pieces. Sean is the guardian—protecting us, standing between us and trouble."

"What does that make B.J.?" Wiley asked.

"He is the bottomless pit with a tender heart," she said.

"And you were always the captain," Aaron said.

Shirley turned away. "Of a sinking ship. Sorry for the dark turn, everyone."

"Hush now, Shirley," Annie said. "We're fine."

"Every time I shipped out, I knew you were going to write and send books and cookies. Mom was sick, and you, and Aunt Annie, and Aunt Ella stepped into the gap," Cameron said. "I'll never forget it… All of you. Everybody always talks about how big Pope men are, but we know it's the women in our family who are the anchors."

Amalie raised her hand, as if asking permission to speak, and then did anyway.

"I knew nothing of your life at home, but you were the face I looked for at every school party. Sean Pope's mama. The one with the pretty smile and big hugs. The one who made the best cookies. Sometimes when you're drowning and you don't know how to swim, you look for anything that will float. You were that for me, Shirley. In the one year of my life when I was fostered in Conway, you made me believe I mattered."

Wolf's heart was breaking for his girl, and for them, without knowing all the whys.

But it was Sean who ended it. "No, ma'am. You do not apologize for anything. You didn't sink the ship. You saved us before it went down by bringing us back to this family, for which we will be forever thankful. You're our hero, and if B.J. were here, he'd second that…and then ask if he could have that last piece of apple tart."

The small touch of humor shifted the moment, and once again, all was well. When the meal finally ended, it was with grateful hearts and full bellies.

Amalie took Wolf back to his hotel, confident that they'd both passed the Pope test.

But Wolf was still locked into the look on Shirley Pope's face when Wiley danced her around the kitchen, and her sons' admiration and devotion to her. After what Ella Pope told him, he was even more determined to get justice for what he and his daughter had lost.

Chapter 17

Amalie picked Wolf up the next morning at 8:00 a.m. and drove straight to the hospital lab.

After DNA swabs were taken, Wolf left info on where the results should be sent. It was serious business, and they had little to say as they left the hospital, arm in arm.

"What's your schedule like today?" Wolf asked, as they got back in her car.

Amalie started it and drove out of the parking lot.

"One appointment at ten this morning, then just working on accounts for the rest of the day. Why?"

"Now that we've just found each other, I guess I am reluctant to part company. If I brought lunch to your office, would you be free to stop and eat with me before I fly out?" he asked.

Her face lit up. "I would love that."

"Good! Do you have a preference of food?" he asked.

"No. Surprise me."

"Between eleven thirty and noon okay with you?"

"Yes! Perfect!" she said. "Oh...I have the files from my caseworker with me. I'll have them copied for you by then."

"Thank you," Wolf said.

He didn't tell her what Ella said to him yesterday, and wasn't going to, but he'd been unable to sleep last night because of it. It was unlikely he'd find proof, but it explained how a baby who'd been born in New Orleans would be abandoned in Arkansas and end up in the social services system there. And if that note had been included in her case files, it could explain why she'd never been chosen for adoption. At any rate, he'd find out when he read the files if she even knew that.

A few minutes later, she pulled up into the breezeway of Hotel Devon to let him out. He leaned over and kissed her on the cheek.

"Have a good day, sweetheart. Love you, and I'll see you later."

"Bye, Dad. Love you, too."

Amalie had just ended her appointment and walked her client to the door. She was on her way back to the desk when her cell phone rang. When she saw it was Sean, she started smiling.

"Hello, love. How's it going?"

"Good. Mom's bringing me into town this afternoon for a checkup and hopefully to get staples out. I was wondering if it would be okay if she dropped me off at the office with you while she hits the supermarket."

"Yes! Absolutely," Amalie said. "I can't wait. I miss you

so much. Dad's bringing lunch here around noon. It'll be our last visit for a while. He's flying out at three."

"Give him my best and wish him safe travels from me."

"I will," she said.

"You sure I'm not going to bother your work?" Sean asked.

"You can bother me all you want. I can always lock the door and pull the shades."

He chuckled. "You don't have shades in the front window."

"Well, yes, there's that...and I need you one hundred percent well first, too. See you later. Love you."

"Love you more," he said, and disconnected.

A short while later, she began hearing sirens and then saw a patrol car go flying past her window with lights flashing. Then people were running out of buildings, and she panicked, thinking of the plane crash from before and ran outside.

It took a few moments for her to realize there was a pileup at a stoplight, and all three drivers were in the street now, fighting with each other as another police car rolled up.

She recognized Wiley bailing out of the cruiser, with his partner on the run beside him, and before the men knew what was happening, the fight had ended. Wiley had one man on the ground and handcuffed and a second one face down on the back of his cruiser, while his partner dealt with the third.

Amalie shook her head and went back into the office.

Disaster averted. Nothing had fallen from the sky, and all three men were fit enough to fight and probably heading to jail. If she'd been a betting woman, she would have bet all three of them had been on their cell phones when it happened, and she was glad it wasn't her.

They were still working the scene when Wolf arrived with their lunch.

"Hey, sweetheart. What's going on down the street?"

"Three-car fender bender. You should have seen the drivers. They were all out in the street having a free-for-all when the police arrived. Wiley Pope was involved in their arrests."

Wolf smiled. "Sorry I missed that. Are you at a stopping point?"

"Yes! I brought folding chairs to the long table and cleared some space so we could eat."

He set the bag on the table and then looked around, admiring the efficiency of the setup and the style of the decor. And then he saw the painting. "Is that Pope Mountain?"

"Yes. Isn't it magnificent?"

"You have a good eye for style," he said, and then began pulling containers from the sack. "Chicken salad sandwiches, a little potato au gratin, and macaroons. What do you think?"

"Yum! Do we have forks?"

He pulled them out of the bag. "And bottles of soda, napkins, salt and pepper, and the chef's best wishes. Bon appétit."

As they sat, Wolf began talking as they ate, asking her about her clients and the range of her services. When there was finally a lull in the conversation, Amalie remembered the file and jumped up to get it.

"All of these are copies. You can keep them. I even made copies of the photos in my case file."

Wolf wiped his hands and opened the file, casually leafing through eighteen years of his daughter's life.

"Have you read it?"

"Sort of… Years ago. But honestly, I asked for it because all of my immunization records and school records are in it. Even a birth certificate that says Amalie Lincoln."

"Where did they get the Lincoln?" Wolf asked.

She sighed. "It's the name of the street where I was found."

He cupped her cheek. "Where did you get your given name?"

She shrugged. "I was told it was from a nun who was a nurse at CHI St. Vincent's in Little Rock. I looked it up once. It has different meanings in different languages, but I liked the Arabic root word of Amal best. It means *hope*."

"It's a beautiful name. It suits you," he said.

"What are you looking for in the records?" she asked.

"Everything and anything. I'm kind of curious how you wound up in Arkansas when you were born in New Orleans."

"Who knows? I was born and dumped. I have no idea how any of this happened beyond what you've told me."

"I'll be reading this thoroughly. I want to know everything before I take it to the police."

"Thank you for fighting for me," she said.

"I could do no less. You are my child." He glanced down at his watch and sighed. "And I should say goodbye for now. I haven't packed, and the chopper is coming early. Something about a weather change."

"I'm going to miss you so much. But we can FaceTime at will. Keep me abreast of what's happening, and let me know when you're going to hold your press conference. Maybe I can watch it."

"Absolutely, I will," Wolf said, and began gathering up their trash when she stopped him. "I'll get this. Grab your coat. I don't have set appointments this afternoon. I can lock up long enough to give you a ride back."

He put on his coat and picked up the file she'd given him, while she bagged up their trash, and then they were out the door and heading down the hall to the back to the parking lot. She tossed the trash in a dumpster and aimed the remote to unlock her car. As they were walking toward it, she pointed to the building in front of them.

"The sniper who shot Sean was on that roof." And then she pointed to a dark stain on the pavement. "That's his blood. I think of his sacrifice every time I pass it."

"God," he whispered, and then by-stepped the stain and got in her car. "You have a good man. Never doubt him."

"Oh, I know. He's been my guy since the bubble gum in my hair, and nothing is ever going to change that."

Then she drove him to the hotel and let him out, blew him a kiss, and drove away.

Wolf watched until she was out of sight before he went inside, and then he was running. There was no time left to waste.

After Amalie got back to the office, she finished cleaning up, then sat down to work, but all the while thinking about Sean at his checkup. If he was okay and healing well, would they remove the staples today? Then she saw him coming in the door and went to meet him.

"There's my girl," he said, and wrapped his arms around her. They stood within the silence, waiting for the world to reset around them.

"Are you okay? Did they remove the staples?"

"Yes, and it's a big relief to have them gone. I'm also cleared to drive when necessary, but still no lifting."

She pulled him down onto the sofa beside her, then turned to face him.

"I would not be alive now, but for you."

"Sweetheart, you don't need to—"

She immediately interrupted. "No. Let me finish. Gratitude is a pitiful word for that act, but you will have mine for the rest of our lives. When you passed out, I thought you died, and I nearly lost my mind. Then they took you away and wouldn't let me go. I was so ashamed to face your family. It felt like my fault. I just want you to know this, and then we'll never speak of it again. You have to know... You have to understand. I never mattered to anyone. Ever. Until you. I will never, ever take your presence in my life for granted. You are my hero. You are my heart. Love you forever."

She didn't know she was crying until Sean began wiping away her tears.

"Love you more," he said.

She reached for a tissue and, without missing a beat, looked up at him and smiled. "When you were Brendan, that's what you always said, 'Chickie, my little Chickasaw... Love you more.'"

The hair stood up on the back of Sean's neck. He couldn't think, wouldn't move, afraid to take a breath and break the spell.

And then she blinked. "Sean, honey, do you want something to drink? I have coffee and Pepsi. And there might be some snickerdoodles from the bakery."

"Pepsi and cookies would be great," he said.

She gave him a quick kiss on the lips. "For being a good boy when they took out your staples," she said, and jumped up.

He watched her disappear into the back room and thought, *Was this how fast Brendan lost Meg? She just walked out of sight?* A sudden wave of sadness washed through him, as if *they'd* just shown him what that loss felt like.

Then Amalie came back smiling, carrying a handful of cookies in a napkin and a bottle of Pepsi in the other.

"Are you warm enough sitting by the window? I can turn up the thermostat."

"It's all good," he said, and then her phone rang.

"Duty calls," she said, and hurried back to her desk to take the call.

He opened his drink, put half a cookie in his mouth, and kicked back to watch her in action, while coming to the realization that none of their meetings had been by chance. Brendan and Meg lost each other. She died, waiting to be found, and he died without ever knowing where she'd gone.

Until now.

About an hour and a half later, Shirley called to let Sean know she was on the way.

"Okay, I'll be watching for you," he said, and began logging out of Amalie's extra computer.

"Was that your mom?" she asked.

"Yes. Thanks for letting me use your stuff. I got caught up on email and saved one seventeen-year-old gamer from a total meltdown," he said. "And you know what he said? The best part ever was me saving his score when I got his program unlocked!"

She wiggled her brows. "You are the man."

"Thanks for the reminder, not that it was needed. The next time I see you, my mommy will not be picking me up, and I will most likely be taking you to bed," he told her, and then she was in his arms.

The room tilted again, and Amalie felt the rough brush of a beard against her face and a deep chuckle in her ear.

I said you would be okay.

Her heart skipped, and then the feeling was gone, and it was Sean, and he was telling her goodbye, and all she could think to do was keep nodding and smiling.

As soon as the door closed behind him, she dropped to the sofa.

"Oh my god, oh my god. What's happening to me?" she whispered.

You just came home, Chickie. You just came home.

The file on Ellis Townley's murder was closed.

Detectives Muncy and Bruner had solved the case, and whatever happened to Vincent Romo now was up to the courts. They had commendations in their files from the FBI for their quick observance of facts adhering to a federal case and sharing their information.

It should have all felt over, but it didn't. Because they kept remembering how Townley's death had made the life of that single mother who lived down the hall that much harder.

Muncy still thought of taking the two boys to get food and wondered how the hell they would manage now that they had lost access to a car. Trying to find a way to get one for them wouldn't work, because they obviously would not have been able to afford the gas or insurance if they had one. He kept trying to forget it—that it wasn't his job to fix the world—but he couldn't let it go.

On their next day off, he and Bruner drove by the apartment building to make a welfare check on Wynona Deal and her four kids.

Bruner sighed as they drove up and parked.

"Tell me again… Why the hell are we doing this?"

"You didn't have to come," Muncy said, as he got out and went inside the building.

"Dammit," Bruner muttered, but he was right behind him.

When they got to the apartment, Muncy expected to hear noise. Granted the boys would be in school, but with two little kids under school age, it shouldn't be quiet. But he knocked and got no answer. He knocked again and was still waiting for someone to answer when a door opened behind them.

An old man was standing in the doorway with a cigarette hanging from his lip, and holding a bottle of beer.

"They're gone," he said.

Muncy's heart skipped. "Oh yeah? Do you know where they went?"

"Her old man got shanked in prison. Her people from Virginia come and moved her and the kids back to where she grew up."

"Oh… Okay, thanks," Muncy said, and was turning to walk away when the old man called out. "Hey! Are you them cops who was here when Roadie got killed?"

They nodded.

"Did you catch who done it?" he asked.

"Yeah, yeah, we did," Bruner said.

The old man took the cigarette out of his mouth and flipped the ashes. “Good. Roadie had a hard life, but he was a decent man. He didn’t deserve to die like that,” he said, then stepped back inside and shut the door.

Muncy glanced at his partner, then headed for the stairs. It wasn’t until they got back in the car that Bruner spoke.

“Okay, I’m glad I came. This is a feel-good moment I never saw coming.”

Muncy grinned, then started the car and drove away.

Fiona’s lawyer, Sheldon Ryker, was at the Tallahassee prison where Fiona had been sent, waiting in visitation to speak with her. He had news and more news, none of which she was going to like.

When they finally brought her in, he was shocked at her transformation. She was gaunt, hollow-eyed, and looked like utter hell. Her hair was dry and stringy, and the dark roots were growing out. She shuffled when she walked and didn’t blink when the guard handcuffed her to the table where Ryker was sitting.

She looked up at him, blinked, and then frowned. “What are you doing here?”

“To give you updates,” he said. “The families of Stuart Bien and Zander Sutton have filed civil lawsuits against you. They’re asking five million dollars each for loss and suffering. And the board of education in Jubilee, Kentucky, has filed a lawsuit against you for the sum of four million dollars for the damage to the school and playgrounds from the chopper crash, for which you have claimed guilt, and to pay the medical bills of the two teachers and thirteen students who were injured during the second explosion."

A ripple of shock went through her as he continued.

"Your assets have been frozen. That includes your bank accounts and property registered under the name Mary Ingalls and BioMed, your company under your own name. Whatever monies are decided after the lawsuits are settled will come from those assets, minus my fees, of course."

Her eyes welled. "What about me? What's my fate?"

"The feds have agreed to the plea bargain…up to a point. You have no leverage, so there's no point in arguing. They have agreed to leave your sentencing up to the judge without requesting one way or the other. Either you'll be a lifer, or you'll lose your life."

She lowered her head, like a bull deciding whether to bluff or charge, then glanced up from beneath hooded eyes. "What about my single cell?"

"If you're in for life, you share. If you're awaiting a death sentence, you get a single cell to await execution," Ryker said.

"And who's the judge signing my dance card?" she asked.

"I don't know yet, and it doesn't matter. Either way, we have no say."

She grimaced. "In my high school yearbook, I was

voted most likely to succeed. When I graduated college, I was magna cum laude. Oh, how the mighty have fallen."

Ryker sighed. He didn't like her. He had no sympathy for her. She was the most narcissistic, heartless, selfish, vicious woman he'd ever met, and he was ready to be rid of her drama.

"It was the murders, Fiona. You skipped the part about all the murders. That's why you're where you are. When I get more information, you will be informed," he said, then nodded at the guard. "We're through here."

The guard took her away with her head down, shuffling as they went.

Ryker's skin was still crawling as he waited to be escorted out.

The sky was dark and threatening by the time Wolf landed in Miami. He grabbed his luggage and caught an Uber, but the rain beat him home.

He walked in dripping water and was shedding his shoes and coat when his housekeeper came running to his aid.

"Mr. Wolf! I didn't hear you come in! Welcome back," she said. "I'll take your luggage up to your room. Chef is wondering if you'll want dinner here."

"Yes, but nothing fancy. Whatever we have on hand is fine with me. I'm too tired to make the decision."

"Yes, sir," Dee said, and took off upstairs with his

suitcase, as Wolf hung up his coat and went to the library in his sock feet to pour himself a drink.

He poured a double shot of whiskey, then carried it to the French doors overlooking the back grounds, watching raindrops splashing on the veranda. He took a sip of his drink and then turned around, eyeing the ornate furnishings and elaborate woodwork, and knew in that moment he'd trade everything he had for the kind of family he'd just left.

Losing Shandy and their baby had burned him from ever wanting to be that close to a woman again. Finding Amalie had changed him. The pursuit of money had lost its spark, but his need for justice was turning into a burning rage. He downed the rest of his whiskey, went upstairs to shower and change, and then he was going to sit down and read the files from her caseworker. By the time he went to bed tonight, he would know what had happened to his child.

He sent Amalie a text to let her know he was home and sent his love. The miles between them now were long, but she was no longer lost to him.

Wolf put his phone on Mute and read files all the way through his dinner. He passed up dessert and took a coffee into the library and settled into his favorite chair to continue reading, making notes as he went. When he was finally through, two things completely shocked him.

The original note that had been found within her blanket was in the file.

Be forewarned. This child's family has a long history of mental illness.

When Wolf recognized the writing and Carter Bullock's favorite phrase, *be forewarned,* a chill ran through him. Suspecting a person of such malevolence was one thing. Seeing the proof of it was yet another.

"God is good," Wolf muttered.

The Bullocks' desire to destroy Wolf was about to blow up in their faces.

The next morning, he went to the safe-deposit box at his bank to get his and Shandy's marriage license, her death certificate, and the death certificate they'd given him for the baby he thought was dead, and added them to the file. All he needed now were the DNA reports from their tests at the Jubilee hospital, and then he was headed to New Orleans.

Satisfied he was as prepared as he could possibly be, he turned his attention to the refinery disaster and Julio Ruiz and found an email waiting in his inbox from the investigator he'd sent to Sao Paulo.

Mr. Outen,

The refinery fire is out. The damage is vast. It is a total write-off. I'm including info I received from the Brazilian government about rebuilding or, if you so choose, cleaning up and selling off. I'm forwarding you their comments and the laws they cited.

As for your manager, Julio Ruiz, he is no longer in Sao Paulo. I don't think you have other avenues to pursue there, unless you want us to track Ruiz down and question him ourselves to see if he knows more or will admit to any wrongdoing.

I await your decisions.

J. Langley

Wolf sighed. He could do nothing with what Amalie told him about Ruiz. Without actual proof of wrongdoing, Ruiz was gone, and so was the refinery. It was insured to the hilt, so Wolf wasn't going to suffer a loss, but he was heartsick about the deaths, the job losses, and facing a huge on-site cleanup before he was done there.

He thought about it for a few minutes and then sent Langley a note.

Come home. I'll send a site manager down to begin organizing and overseeing cleanup. I may have a way to smoke Ruiz out of hiding, but that's for later.

Wolf

There was nothing left for Wolf to do but go back to his Miami office and get back to work. There was no way to know what hell had gone on at his other holdings after his reported death, but he was about to find out.

And since Special Agent Ramsey had already alerted

the media that Wolf would hold his own press conference when the time was right, and now was as right as it was going to get, he called his public relations office. The phone rang twice.

"Emily Sheets. Outen Public Relations. How can I help you?"

"Emily, this is Wolf. I need you to schedule a press conference. I want it in our conference room sometime this week."

"Mr. Outen! How wonderful to hear your voice! Yes, sir! I'll get right on that and let you know."

"Thank you, Emily. Good to be back. I await your call," he said, and hung up.

Chapter 18

By noon the next day, the press release from Outen Industries was the lead story on every media outlet.

Wolfgang Outen was about to make his first public appearance since before the chopper crash. The media already knew his wife had been arrested and charged with multiple murders, as well as the attempt on his life, and they were anxiously awaiting his comments. The conference would be inside his office building. No outside guests were allowed. Media only, and questions would be taken. Wolf was braced for whatever they asked, but hoping the existence of his daughter had not been leaked. Coming at the Bullocks unannounced was his goal. After that, he wanted to tell the world of their miraculous reunion.

Wolf wasn't the only one making plans for Amalie. Sean had plans for her, too. All the time he'd been healing, he'd thought of little else but Amalie. In his heart, she was already his, but he wanted the world to know it, too. She just needed to be properly asked before he put a ring on it.

He'd been online for days, looking at engagement rings in every size and shape, in every setting imaginable, and while they were all beautiful, he hadn't found one that spoke to him.

Shirley had gone up the mountain to Ray and Betty Raines's place this morning to help Betty with housework and laundry. Betty had taken a bad fall, and cousins were bringing food daily to help out. Ray was at work every day, and Charlie was in school, which left Betty on her own, so Sean was on his own.

He'd been working since before daylight and had just finished up a remote fix for a client when his cell phone rang. He glanced down, surprised at the caller, but quickly answered.

"Hello...Aunt Ella?"

"Yes, it's me. You bought that ring yet?"

He was long past the need to ask her how she knew he was even looking. "Uh...not yet, but I've been looking."

"I have my granny's wedding rings. I wondered if you might like to take a look at them. If they don't suit what you want, that's fine. I never felt called to offer them to any of the kin before, but you and her...well... Full circle, son. Full circle."

Sean was stunned. "I don't know what to say, but I'd sure love to see them."

"Then come on up," Ella said. "This is just between you and me, and nobody else will know. The only people who know I have them are dead and gone now."

"Is now okay?" Sean asked.

"If you're feeling up to driving, now is fine with me."

His heart skipped. "I'm up to it. I'll see you soon." He grabbed his coat and keys, left a note on the kitchen island, and was out the door.

He hadn't been behind the wheel of a car in weeks, but it felt good to be in control of his life again. He'd lost track of time when he was in the hospital, and then ten more days of recuperating at home after that. Basically, the last half of January and a few days into February now. Once he reached the blacktop, he turned right and headed up the mountain.

Ella's place was just below John and Annie Cauley's. It was the house she'd been born in, and the house she would die in. There were stories about a man she'd once loved and lost, but there were just stories. Ella never confirmed or denied any of them, other than she'd made peace with the single life.

He couldn't wait to see the rings. Something told him she already knew they would suit, or she would never have called. When he reached the turnoff to her house, he stopped to see if the mail carrier had run, and when he saw mail in the box, pulled it out and took it with him, and then carried it up the porch upon his arrival.

He knocked, then heard her call out… "Door's open! Come on in!"

"Brought your mail, Aunt Ella," he said.

"Thank you, Sean! Saved me a trip down the road later!" she said, and took it out of his hands and laid it aside. "Come to the kitchen where the light's better. I haven't looked at Granny's rings for a good fifty years, but after I met your girl, I took 'em out and cleaned them up a bit."

Sean followed. "Which grandmother is this? Your dad or your mother's mother?"

"My papa's mam. Her name was Annabelle, but they called her Belle. I don't know how Papa's daddy came to have that ring to even give to his wife. Nobody had money back then. Maybe it came from the old country. Maybe he won it in a poker game. Who knows? People didn't dwell much on family history back then. Mostly because if their lives were bad enough to leave their homeland, they didn't like to be reminded of it."

"I can understand that," Sean said. "Sometimes I almost forget we were ever anywhere but here, and Arkansas is someone else's story."

Ella patted his shoulder. "Yes, boy...like that. Now sit yourself down here and open up the box. Be honest. It won't hurt my feelings none at all."

Sean sat and picked up a small black box with a tiny hinge on one side. He could see it had once been covered in some kind of fabric, but there was little left to it but a few pieces of fuzz. But then he lifted the lid, and as he did, sunlight coming through the window caught in the facets, and for a heartbeat, it was like holding fire.

The stone was a rosette-cut sapphire, the same color

as Amalie's eyes, with tiny diamonds set around it like a halo. The setting was silver, as was the single engraved wedding band beside it.

"There's a word engraved inside the band," Ella said.

He turned the band toward the light and saw one word. *Forever.*

His heart stopped.

"Jesus wept, Aunt Ella. This is the prettiest thing I've ever seen. It's her, a thousand times over, and you knew it, didn't you? But what if it doesn't fit?"

Ella patted his hand. "I already asked Spirit before I called you. It'll do just fine. So, you want it?"

He stood, put his arms around her thin bony shoulders, and just held her.

Ella was chuckling as she patted him on the back. "I'll take that as a yes."

He took a slow, shaky breath and let her go. "I don't know how to navigate the waters common to you and my girl, but I'm trusting she'll figure it out the same way you have. I know I love her so much it hurts, and sometimes I have an overwhelming fear of losing her."

"That's just soul memory, son, from when you lost her before. That won't happen to you again, but I'm not talking about losing her in this life. Understand me?"

He nodded. "She keeps slipping into that time and sliding back into this one without even knowing it. She refers to herself as 'Chickie' when talking about Brendan. Her memories of him and her memories of me are all mixed up together right now."

Ella nodded. "Because it's all so new. That streak in her hair? Don't tell her because she doesn't need to know... but that's where Meg suffered the injury that killed her. One of the soldiers hit her with the butt of his rifle. They thought she was dead when they threw her in that cellar. Suffering a second blow to her head in this life, and in the very same place, was where Spirit healed her so she wouldn't die again."

Sean shivered. Spirits and angels and reincarnated souls were so far out of his normal zone he could hardly bear it, and yet he knew it was so, and felt blessed by the journey with her.

"I will tell Amalie where this ring came from. She deserves to know your generous heart, but she'll hold the secret, too. We're both good at that. Is that okay?"

"Always," Ella said. "Now get yourself on home before Shirley knows you're gone. You don't wanna have to lie to your mama. All anyone needs to know is that you chose one that was antique because it was the color of Amalie's eyes, and let it be."

"Yes, ma'am," Sean said. He put on his coat again, put the box in an inner pocket, and zipped the pocket.

Ella walked him to the door, then watched him going down the steps. So tall and handsome—those broad shoulders and that black hair. So young, with a soul so old. She sighed. This one would do just fine.

Sean drove home in a daze, put the ring in his safe, tore up the note he'd left for his mother, then glanced at the clock. Almost noon. Amalie would be taking a break for lunch about now, so he sat down at the kitchen table and called. Just to hear her voice.

Amalie was in the back room getting her sandwich and a bottle of Pepsi out of the refrigerator. She intended to kick back on the sofa to eat her lunch. Her eyes were tired from staring at a screen all morning, and admiring her painting of Pope Mountain as she ate was the best way she knew to rest them.

She had just taken the cap off of her Pepsi when her cell phone rang, and when she saw it was Sean, she abandoned all thoughts of food and quickly answered.

"Hello, my favorite person! What do you have to say for yourself this fine day?"

"Hope I'm not interrupting. If I am, just say so. All I wanted was to hear your voice," he said.

"As always, your timing is perfect. I just stopped for lunch."

"Eating in or eating out?" he asked.

"In. Peanut butter and jelly sandwich and a Pepsi."

"I might echo that here," he said. "Mom's at Betty Raines's house for the day."

"Is Betty sick or something?" Amalie asked.

"She fell a few days ago. Really messed up her shoulder and whacked her head. Everyone's been bringing them food, so Mom went to help her catch up with laundry and cleaning."

"Sounds like the Shirley we know and love."

"Have you heard from Wolf since he left?" he asked.

"Only that he got home okay, and then a text this morning about the upcoming press conference. Apparently, it's in the morning, 10:00 a.m. Eastern Standard Time."

"I'll make a note to watch," Sean said. There was a moment of silence, and then he added, "I miss you. When can I come see you?"

"Are we talking about looking at each other's faces or spending the night?"

"I'm talking about all of that," he said.

"The answer is anytime you want, whenever you want. Always."

He sighed. "You're my drug of choice and I am in need."

"You need a key to my house is what you need," she said. "I'll get one made before I go home this evening. It'll be here for you whenever you can get free."

"Tomorrow after six?"

She laughed. "That'll work. I'll bring home barbecue."

"I'll bring dessert," he said.

"You're the only sweet thing I want," she said. "Love you. See you tomorrow."

"Love you more," he said.

The call ended. Amalie sighed, then reached for her Pepsi and took a drink before digging into her PB and J.

Wolf was as prepared for this press conference as he was ever going to be. He'd talked to Arnie, his lawyer, about what issues to skirt and what to ignore, depending on what they asked. His goal at this moment in time was to reassure stockholders he was hale and hearty.

He'd purposefully dressed for the media. Black suit, white shirt open at the collar, his thick gray hair combed away from his face with the length just brushing the collar of his suit. Black brows, hooded ice-blue eyes. He was lean and fit and did not look his age. It was his habit to never smile in public. He played tough and looked the part. Wolf Outen looked like a biker in a business suit, and today he needed that persona to maintain emotional distance because he was royally pissed about what had happened on his watch.

There was a tap on his door and then his secretary walked in. There was a moment when the thought went through him that it should have been Stu, and then he let it go.

"They're ready for you, sir. Security is waiting for you in the hall."

He nodded, straightened the cuff links on his shirt one last time, then strode past her and out the door.

Three men from his security team were waiting. One led the way. The other two flanked him as they proceeded to the conference room, and then they took him in the back door and straight up onto the stage. There was no prior announcement, just Wolf emerging without fanfare.

At least a dozen media outlets were represented, live

and on camera, and more than thirty journalists from stations all across the state were sitting in the audience.

He walked straight to the bank of microphones and looked up.

"Thank you for coming. As you can see, the rumors of my demise have been exaggerated, although the reasoning was sound. I am first going to acknowledge the depths of my grief and despair for the two good men who died because someone wanted me dead. My deepest sympathies to the families of Stuart Bien, who was my personal assistant for the last thirteen years, and Zander Sutton, the owner-operator of the helicopter that crashed. I will take some questions, but I am limited in what I can talk about, since final sentencing has yet to take place for Fiona Rangely, who has confessed to and is incarcerated for the deaths just mentioned, after she learned I did not die. I'll take the first question now."

Hands went up. Journalists were calling out to be recognized. Wolf began acknowledging them and answering.

"Mr. Outen, why did your wife want you dead?"

"We're assuming it was my money, since the first three men she'd married and buried left everything to her. I was to be number four."

"Mr. Outen, when did you learn about the crash?"

"After I landed in Brazil."

"Mr. Outen, do you think you'll ever marry again?"

He frowned. "I have to divorce this one first, and I do not speculate about the future."

"Why were you in Brazil?"

"A refinery I own was ablaze. We suspected terrorists at first, but I now suspect it was an inside job. The employee has fled the area, but I'll find him. Ten men died, and even more were injured because of him. I'll say no more about that."

"Mr. Outen, your face is so well known. How were you able to hide so successfully, and where did you go?"

"A few good friends, and I'm not going to tell you where I went. I might need that hidey-hole again one day."

And then he ended the press conference on that bit of humor by thanking them for coming and strode off the stage with his head up and his well-known swagger.

Amalie and Sean were on the phone together, watching the press conference. She was at her office, and he watched from home. When it was over, he asked, "Do you feel better now, knowing you weren't mentioned?"

"Yes! I'm satisfied the media is unaware that I even exist," she said.

"Is it still on for tonight?" he asked.

She smiled. "It's always going to be on with us. I'm locking up the office at noon and getting that key made. I'll close early if I can, but if not, I'll be home right after I pick up the barbecue. Love you, and drive safe coming down."

"I always drive safe. Love you more," but as he was

disconnecting Amalie heard an echo. *My little Chickie, love you more.*

She put her hands over her ears and closed her eyes.

"Who are you?"

But the whispers were gone. She sighed, then turned off the television and went back to work. Tonight, she would sleep in Sean Pope's arms, knowing all was right with her world.

It had been raining in Jubilee for over an hour now, cocooning the population beneath roofs and within walls. The evening meal had come and gone, leaving the faint scent of barbecue lingering in the air.

Foreplay began with conversation, teasing and flirting until the need for more moved between them. Lights dimmed as they moved from room to room until Sean was standing in Amalie's bedroom, taking off her clothes.

The silence of the act was a seduction all its own.

Every stroke of his fingers against her skin. His breath against her neck as he slid his hands beneath her hair. The weight of her breasts against the back of his hands. The scars she had been loath to reveal were nothing more to him that the topography of the woman he loved.

And then Amalie stood bare beneath his gaze, watching as he came out of his clothes without fanfare—as always, staggered by the breadth and the height of him. All man...and he was hers.

A gust of wind splattered rain against her curtained windows as she reached for him, pulling him down onto the bed beside her. They lay facing each other, her hand on his shoulder. His hand on the curve of her hip. Gazes locked, and then a whisper...*Close your eyes.*

They both heard it, thinking the other one said it, and obeyed.

But when the veil went down, the curtain lifted.

In Amalie's mind, she saw the bearded man and the tender look within his eyes.

Sean saw himself staring into the face of a young woman with brown skin and black hair so long it covered the pillow upon which she was lying. And then a whisper again.

Lost no more. It is done.

They both jumped. Their eyes flew open, and they were staring at each other in shock.

Sean cupped her cheek. "What did you just see?"

Amalie's heart was pounding. "I saw a big man... as big as you, with a dark curly beard. I think he's been talking to me. Ever since my wreck. Who is he? Why is this happening?"

"Because you came home," Sean said.

The lights flickered in the hall, acknowledging his answer.

"I don't understand. I've never been here before," she said.

"Not in this lifetime you haven't, but you were...once before. You loved a man who called you Chickie."

Amalie stilled, her eyes widening, and with everything he began saying, she was seeing it play out before her.

"When you disappeared without a trace, it broke his heart. He died never knowing what had happened to you. His name was Brendan Pope. You've been mixing him and me up in your head for weeks and I said nothing. But now, after what I just saw, what we've been shown… I think he's been trying to tell you and me…to remind us of who we were…and who we are."

"Oh my God, oh my God," Amalie said. "What do I do? What do we do?"

"What they did," he said. He rolled her over onto her back, slid between her knees, and in a single thrust, they were one, sealing a bond long since broken and healing the souls once lost.

The madness grew with every thrust, with every kiss—with every fervent whisper. The need for more was an addiction, chasing that ever-growing blood rush to the end. One minute rolled into another, into another. Rain began hammering the roof and then the windows, as if pounding to be let in.

The climax happened without warning. Jolting them out of rhythm and into a sensation of falling, falling, forever falling into each other's arms.

The shock wave passed, leaving them stunned and breathless, but so at peace in a way neither had ever known. The voices were gone now. The message had been received and accepted. Balance had been restored.

Sean rolled over and took her with him, pulling the covers up over their shoulders as he did.

"The word *love* is not enough, but it's there for you, and so am I, Amalie. Forever."

He didn't know that she was crying until he felt the tears on his chest, and then he drew back in a panic, needing to see her face.

"Are you all right? Did I hurt you? What's wrong, love?"

"I'm so good...so perfect it's hard to explain. It is a strange world for me to be accepted. To be loved without boundaries. To have been broken time and time again, shunned and shamed for things not of my doing, and then be given everything that has been missing in my life—all at once. Forever has been a long time coming, but I will always be on your side. I will always have your back."

"Amalie...sweetheart...come here to me," he whispered. "You're safe now. The war for us is over." He pulled her close, and then they slept.

Parting ways the next morning was hard for both of them, but life and work were upon them, and the future still beckoned.

"I'll call you," he said, as she was helping him on with his coat.

She nodded. "And I'll answer, and we'll talk about stuff."

"And be thinking about 'other' stuff in between," he said, and watched her eyes twinkle.

"Exactly. Be careful going home. Love you."

He kissed her square on the lips. *Love you more,* and then he was gone.

Amalie watched until he drove out of sight and then went back inside to finish getting ready.

Later, as she was leaving her house, she saw more trucks pulling up at the school. She caught a red light at the main intersection and, as she was waiting, saw a big truck roll through with the logo Winslow's Custom Windows—likely also school related.

When the light changed, she headed for the bakery. Neither she nor Sean had taken time to feed themselves this morning. He was going home to Shirley's cooking. She was taking some of Annie's to work with her, keeping it all in the family.

Julio Ruiz was on the run. He knew someone from Outen Industries had been at the refinery site since the fire was out because his brother-in-law told him. He knew Wolf would be on his tail because he hadn't answered Wolf's calls. He also knew running had been a mistake and was trying to think of a story that would fit the situation. His wife thought he had run off with another woman. His children were distraught. And all because he chose to skim a little off the top of Outen's profits. Men were dead. Men he had called friends. There were nights when he wished he had died with them and thought about ending his life. Then he'd wake up the next day and remember that in his faith, suicide was a sin. And in the end, it was the Church and a village priest that brought him to a halt.

"Forgive me, Father, for I have sinned," Julio said.

"I am listening," the old priest said, and Julio began to recount what he had done, and ended sobbing, praying for absolution, praying for his soul to be at peace.

The priest listened, and then he did and said what he always said and did for everyone sitting in his confessional, but then something moved within his heart that led him to add one thing.

"God will forgive you, my son, but will you ever forgive yourself? You cannot run away from your past. Be a man. Go home. Face and accept your truth as you have accepted God's love and forgiveness."

Julio staggered out of the church in a daze. He was afraid. He would be in prison for years. His family would suffer his shame. But then he remembered. They were already suffering for what he'd done.

He walked back down the street to the *pousada* where he'd been staying, packed up his clothes, and got in the car. If he was to make amends, they began with Wolf Outen. After that, he would let fate have its way.

Wolf was in his limo, being driven to a meeting, when his cell phone rang. He was on his laptop checking notes and almost let it go to voicemail, then remembered he had a daughter now and checked caller ID. When he saw the name, he was shocked.

"This is Wolf. Where the hell have you been?"

Julio flinched. "Running. Hiding. Hiding from you and my truth."

"I already know you started the fire," Wolf snapped. "I also know you were stealing from me. One crime led to a terrible one, didn't it, Julio?"

Julio was stunned. "I am ashamed, and I am so sorry. I am on my way home to turn myself in, *senhor*. Please forgive me for abusing your trust."

"To hell with my trust," Wolf snapped. "Men are dead. You don't need my forgiveness. You need to talk to God about that."

Julio sighed. "I already did. That is why I'm going back."

There was a long moment of silence, and then the timbre of Wolf's voice shifted.

"It is good to know your conscience is still guiding you. I trusted you completely and I have been struggling with myself, wondering how I missed this weakness in you."

Julio was crying. "I have been struggling with the weakness in myself."

"Yes, well..." Wolf let his voice trail off.

"Senhor Wolf. I have one question. How did you know?"

Wolf thought a moment and then realized that of all the people, Julio Ruiz would be someone who would believe.

"My daughter is psychic. She sees into the past. She sees into the future. She said your name. That's when I knew that it was you."

Julio gasped. "*Querido Deus! Uma psíquica!* I did not know you had a daughter."

Wolf sighed. "For a long, long time, neither did I. Thank you for calling me. Go with God, Julio. You're going to need Him."

Wolf dropped the phone back in his pocket. Chapter closed.

Julio started the car and drove away, still crying, still afraid, but going home.

Chapter 19

It was the fourteenth of February.

The dining room at the Serenity Inn was decorated for Valentine's Day and completely booked for the night. Eating establishments all over Jubilee had been running special ads all week, and Sean jumped at the Serenity Inn offer the first day it ran and reserved a table for two for 7:00 p.m.

Yesterday, he'd picked up his suit from the cleaners and polished his boots, bought gifts for Amalie and his mom.

Wiley cleared his conscience and his girls on speed dial by choosing Mom as his Valentine date, and Aaron and Dani had gifted her a trip to the hair salon and a manicure.

Shirley left the house that morning with a spring in her step, unaware.

Sean had hidden her flowers and candy in the back bedroom. After she left for her hair appointment, he got everything out and arranged it on the kitchen island so she'd see it when she came back.

From the time they were big enough to know what the

day was about, they always made mama their "favorite" Valentine and found a way to do or give her something special, because they knew the only thing their father would give her was another black eye. Even grown-up and with lives of their own, they never forgot her place in their lives.

But this year Sean had a whole new agenda. This year, Valentine's Day was most especially for his girl. All day, it felt like Christmas and the anticipation of waiting for daylight to get out of bed and open presents. Waiting for the turkey to cook. Waiting for the football game to begin. Waiting to hear Shirley call, "Go wash your hands. Dinner is ready!"

He wanted that life with Amalie. He wanted the babies and the tree and the dinner on the table and family all around it, and his mom with a grandbaby in her lap.

He'd called Amalie early that morning to wish her Happy Valentine's Day, then sent a text to Wolf.

> I'm going to ask Amalie to marry me tonight. We'll FaceTime you afterward so she can tell you herself, but I wanted you to know.

Within minutes, he had a response.

One great big HOORAH! that made him smile.

After that, he went to the office and worked through the morning, then made himself a sandwich. It was midafternoon when he heard the front door open and got up to see if his mom needed help carrying anything in, then stopped, stunned by his mother's transformation.

"Mom. Oh my God! I hope you feel as good as you look, because you look beautiful."

Shirley beamed. "I feel like a million dollars, and look at my nails! Pink with silver sparkles."

Sean pointed to the sofa. "FedEx brought you a package. It's from B.J.."

She took off her coat and sat down to open the package, then frowned. "I don't want to break a nail. Will you open it for me?" she asked.

"Sure thing," he said, pulled out his pocketknife and sat down beside her. He had the package open in seconds. "Here you go."

Shirley removed the lid, peeled back the layers of tissue paper, and then smiled. "What a beautiful scarf! Turquoise and gold. I'm wearing this to church on Sunday."

"I hope it's not the only thing you're wearing," Sean said.

Shirley swatted him on the arm. "You are so bad."

He laughed. "There's a card with it."

Shirley found the card beneath the folds and opened it.

Happy Valentine's Day, Mom.

They say absence makes the heart grow fonder, but I couldn't love you more. Hope to see you soon.

B.J.

Shirley laid the card against her heart. "Love my boys," she said, and laid everything back in the box to take to her room.

"There's more in the kitchen," Sean said.

Her eyes widened. "From you?"

He nodded.

She headed to the kitchen, then clapped her hands when she saw what was on the island.

"Oh, Sean! Pink roses! You know they're my favorites! Thank you!" Then she saw the candy. "Divinity!" she said, and immediately chose a piece and took a bite. "Ummm, every bit as good as it looks." She was still smiling as she opened the card. The smile froze, and then her chin began to quiver.

He'd signed it,

To the first woman I ever loved.

Happy Valentine's Day, Mom.

from son #2

He hugged her. "Don't cry. This is a happy day for me. I'm proposing to Amalie tonight."

Shirley looked up and, in that instant, saw him as the man he had become, and not just her son.

"Oh, honey! No more tears, I promise! I am happy for the both of you, and happy for me, too. I'm gaining a daughter for this house. You are such a dark horse. I didn't even know you'd gone ring shopping."

"I looked online for ages, and in the end, it was an antique set that won me over."

"I'm so excited! I can't wait to see it on her finger!"

"Me either," he said, and then glanced at the clock. "I'm going to bring up some wood for the fireplace, and yes, I'm using the wheelbarrow. Now go sit somewhere and be pretty until it's time to change into your fancy duds."

"Yes, okay, I will."

"When is Wiley coming to pick you up?" he asked.

"Around six thirty. He's taking me to Hotel Devon," she said.

He nodded. "I'm going to get firewood. Be right back."

She patted his cheek, then poured herself a cup of coffee and sat down at the table to finish off her piece of candy as Sean went out the door.

Amalie had a dress she'd been saving for a very special occasion, and this was the perfect time to wear it. It was the ultimate little black dress, and she hoped her black Natori lace tights had enough design to hide the burn scars running up the side of her left leg, because there sure wasn't enough dress to do it. But once she had it on, and the black lacy tights, she felt confident enough to pull off the look and was dressed and waiting when the church bells chimed.

Her heart skipped! Sean was here!

She smoothed down the fabric on the front of her dress and headed for the door, her high heels clicking on the tile in the entry as she went, wondering why he hadn't used his key.

Then she opened the door.

He had flowers in one hand, and a box of candy in the other, black suit, white dress shirt, and a devil-may-care smile on his face that stopped her heart.

Sean had thought he was ready for her and all that went with her, until he saw her in that dress. She had legs that went all the way to a hot Saturday night, in a dress that barely made it to Tuesday. It zipped all the way up the back to the mandarin-style collar, then shot demure all to hell with a heart-shaped cutout above her breasts that left nothing to the imagination.

"Holy...Lord, Amalie, you look like you just came off a runway! Beautiful, absolutely beautiful," he said, and leaned across the bouquet and kissed her.

"Thank you, darling. You look pretty smashing yourself. Come in out of the cold."

"These are for you," he said, and handed her the flowers.

"I want to put them in water before we leave," she said, taking a vase from a shelf in the living room before going to the kitchen. As soon as she had them in water, she looked up. "Look how beautiful!" she said, fingering the red roses' petals.

"I see," Sean said, but he was looking at her. "These are for you, too."

"Ooh, chocolate. I'm saving those for later." She opened the card and read the words as they blurred on the page.

My girl forever… Love you more.

Sean

"Oh, Sean, you are going to spoil me, aren't you?"

"Absolutely rotten," he said. "But I'm not done." Then he reached for her hands, took a deep breath, and dropped down on one knee. "This has been coming since the day we swore a blood oath, but I was too young to see the ending. Finding you again has been the blessing of my life. I love you, Amalie, to the depths of my soul. I can't see my life without you in it. Will you marry me? Will you be my wife?"

Amalie was trembling and crying and nodding all the way through every word he said, and the moment he paused…she started laughing.

"Yes! Yes! A thousand times, yes!"

He took the ring out of his pocket, still anxious it wouldn't fit, but then Ella was right. It slipped on as if it had been made for her.

Amalie saw the ring and gasped. "Sean! Oh my God!" She looked up at him then. "It's the most perfect thing I've ever seen! How did you know?"

He stood, touching her cheek and then the ring, and then brushing a soft kiss across her lips.

"I wasn't sure… It's an antique… The sapphire is the color of your eyes, and I—"

She closed her eyes. "Ella gave this to you. There's a band that goes with it. The word FOREVER is engraved inside." Tears were rolling.

"If it makes you sad, I can—"

"No, Sean! I'm not sad. I'm overwhelmed. I can't believe this is my life. Finding joy. Finding love. Finding you. You keep giving and giving, and all I have to give back to you is me."

"But darlin', you're all I ever wanted," he said, and kissed her. "Now, my dear fiancée, I'm starving and we're going to be late. Are you ready?"

"I just need my coat," she said.

"The gray one?" he asked, as he went to the coat closet.

She nodded.

Moments later, they were going out the door arm in arm.

Music drifted from the dining room out into the lobby as they entered the restaurant, checking their coats at the door.

People were already eyeing the striking couple. The tall man in black. The elegant woman in the little black dress standing beside him.

"Sean Pope. Table for two," he said.

The hostess looked up at him and smiled. "Yes, sir.

Right this way," she said, and led them into the dining area, winding their way to a table by the windows overlooking the night lights of Jubilee.

Special menus were already at the place settings. A single LED candlestick rested at the center of the table, and nearest the window and below it, a sprinkling of red rose petals lay on the crisp white cloth.

As he seated her, Sean leaned down and brushed a kiss against the side of her cheek, and then took the other chair across the table and reached for her hand, fingering the ring he'd just put on it.

"You are just as beautiful by candlelight as you are wearing nothing in bed."

She felt the heat of her own blush as she leaned across the table and whispered, "You are a bit scandalous, Sean Pope."

"I do what I can," he said, and then winked.

The tinkle of her laugh drifted across the dining area, turning heads and bringing smiles to strangers' faces. It was the night for love and lovers.

Every course of their meal was orchestrated to perfection, beginning with champagne. After the sommelier filled the flutes, Sean picked up his glass.

"A toast to the night and to my beautiful fiancée," he said.

"And to you, Sean Pope…the man who holds my heart," she countered.

Glasses clinked.

Bubbles tickled her nose as she took her first sip; then she glanced out the window.

"Oh, Sean! Just look at that moon. This night is magic."

He knew the moon was up there, but he couldn't take his eyes off of her.

"Love you forever," Sean whispered.

Amalie turned away from the moon to look at him, and when she did, he saw that faraway look in her eyes again. "I know you," she whispered, and then blinked. Her gaze shifted, and she was smiling. "Love you more."

He nodded and then pulled out his phone.

"What are you doing?" she asked.

"We're going to call Wolf and show him your ring. Come sit on my lap," he said.

Amalie jumped up from her seat, plopped down in Sean's lap, and then watched her father's face appearing on the screen.

"Hi, Dad!" Amalie said, and turned her hand toward the phone. "We're engaged!"

The smile on Wolf's face was nothing but pure delight. "Congratulations, sweetheart! Welcome to the family, Sean!"

"Thanks!" Sean said.

Amalie blew him a kiss, and then he was gone.

But their call had garnered attention from other diners, and when their call ended, people around them began lifting their glasses in congratulations, too.

"Just like in the movies," Amalie said, as she slipped back to her seat.

Sean smiled. "The ones with happy-ever-afters."

They made love that night in slow motion. Drawing out each moment for as long as they could bear until the walls fell down around them, they slipped into dreams that were not theirs, and woke up to a brand-new day.

It was the first week of March when Fiona Rangely learned her sentence. The good news was that she was getting that single jail cell after all. The bad news was that the single cells were reserved for death-row inmates only. She wanted to cry about it, but crying over spilled milk and dead husbands changed nothing about her fate.

The civil suits against her were still pending. The cogs of justice turned slower for some things than for others, but that didn't matter either. She wasn't fighting anything but the uncertainty of time, and how much was left with her name on it.

That night she dreamed of the estate in Miami. Dee was running a bath for her and adding the lilac-scented bath salts she always loved. Hank was waiting for her in the cabana. Then she was running down the stairs to meet him when Wolf appeared out of nowhere and opened the front door. Police swarmed into the house, dragged her out onto the lawn and cuffed her hand and foot, set the house afire, then drove away, leaving her helpless and too close to the flames.

She woke up shaking.

The analogies were clear. Karma had finally caught

up with her. She didn't want to be here anymore, but she was going out on her own terms. One last master plan, and someone else would take the blame.

It happened in the showers. Stripped and naked as the day she'd been born, Fiona started cursing the other female inmates who were in the showers, calling them names. Insulting their ethnicities, their looks, calling out their ignorance by the way they spoke, and then shoved one woman out of the way and got under the showerhead with a washrag, snatched a bar of soap from someone else, and started washing herself.

The guards went in after her to take her out, and when they did, she spit in their faces. Within seconds, every naked woman was on her, punching, kicking, pulling hair, gouging their fingers in her eyes, drawing blood.

Lots of blood. Running into a red and winding circle down in the drains.

Fiona wasn't fighting for her life; she was fighting for it to end. She heard guards sounding an alarm and never knew who threw the first punch, but it didn't matter. She kept fighting and kicking, laughing and screaming until they threw her against the wall.

Her head cracked.

Her eyes rolled back in her head.

She was dead before she hit the floor.

She had incited the riot, her last "fuck you" to the world.

Wolf was in a meeting when his new personal assistant, Mark Heinz, slipped into the room, handed him a folded note, and slipped out again. He unfolded the note, saw the words, and stood.

"Excuse me, gentlemen. I need to take a call," he said, and walked out of the conference room, back to his office, and picked up the receiver. "This is Wolf Outen."

"Mr. Outen, I'm Ken Reeves, the warden at the Tallahassee Correctional Center where your wife is—"

Wolf took a quick breath. "No need to tiptoe around the message. She tried to kill me. Say what you have to say."

The warden cleared his throat. "Er...um...she was in an altercation with some other women in the showers this morning, and I'm afraid she died during the fight. You will be notified when her body is released to—"

The rage in Wolf's voice was hovering on detonate. "You can't seriously believe I'm going to take the responsibility to bury that woman? I was already in the act of filing for divorce. Obviously, this saves me a dime. Burn her. Bury her. Choose your poison. By the law that put her there, she belonged to you. You lost her. You bury her."

He replaced the receiver, sitting within the silence until the rage had passed, then went back to his meeting.

"My apologies, gentlemen. A little housekeeping to deal with. Now, where were we?"

That evening when he went home, Wolf sat down with a glass of wine and a stack of mail and began sorting through it, discarding junk mail and separating bills from personal letters. Then he picked up an envelope from a lab in Kentucky, set everything aside, and tore into it.

As he suspected, it was the DNA results he'd been waiting for. There were no surprises. He was Amalie Lincoln's father. The Bullocks might argue she was Wolf's daughter but not their granddaughter, but they didn't know about his vasectomy after Shandy's death, and to eliminate themselves from guilt, they would have to submit DNA tests to prove otherwise. They couldn't lie their way out of that. He took the papers to his office, unlocked the safe, and put them into Amalie's file.

Today had been a collage of emotions, but this was a perfect end to the turmoil. Tomorrow would be about rearranging his schedule and contacting Toby to ready the jet, but tonight he would call Amalie. He wanted to know if she would be willing to be on standby. Just in case her physical presence would tip the scales of the Bullocks' denial.

Amalie spent all day Friday in a state of anticipation. She was going to spend the night on the mountain with Sean and Shirley so she could go to a family wiener roast with them, but by the end of the day, the location of the wiener roast had been moved from Ray and Betty Raines's place to the dining hall in the church, due to warnings of inclement weather. If they couldn't have it outside, then it had to be in the dining hall or cancel it altogether, and so the church it was.

She was beside herself with excitement. She'd never been to a wiener roast. She was going to meet a whole lot more of Sean's family. She couldn't wait for the day to be over and was closing the office until Monday.

When closing time came, she changed clothes in the back room and grabbed her coat and purse before heading out the door. She'd gone from business casual to tennis shoes and jeans, and left her good coat in the office and traded it for a lined windbreaker with a hood.

She'd locked up the office and was on her way down the hall to the back parking lot when her phone rang. She answered without looking at caller ID.

"Hello?"

"Hi, darling, it's me, Dad. Do you have a minute?"

"For you, always. I've already locked up and am on my way out. What's up?"

"Our DNA results finally came, verifying what we already knew."

"Oh, that's wonderful, Dad! Now what?" she asked.

"That's part of why I'm calling. Within the next couple of days, I'll be heading to New Orleans to file charges. I don't know how it's all going to play out, but I'm certain the Bullocks will deny everything. I have enough proof on paper to hang them, but it will all take time. Before I commit you to anything, I just need to know that, if the need arose, you would be willing to come to New Orleans and confront them, face-to-face. I'd send a chopper to get you. And if you don't want to do that on your own, absolutely bring Sean with you for moral support."

"Yes, Dad, yes. I absolutely will back you one hundred percent. I'm on my way to spend the weekend with the Popes anyway. I'll talk to Sean about it tonight. I wish you were here. I'm going to a family wiener roast! Can you believe it? I've never been to one before."

The poignancy of that remark within the joy in her voice was gutting. It was all he could do to respond without losing it.

"You are on a journey of many firsts with Sean Pope, and I am forever grateful for his presence in your life. Have so much fun and give my best to the family. I will keep you informed as this unfolds."

"Thank you, Dad. Love you. Be safe."

"You be safe, Amalie. You are all that matters to me in this world."

He disconnected.

Amalie headed for her car, blinking back tears, but by the time she left the city limits of Jubilee and started up the mountain, clouds were gathering, and she was already wondering how the evening would play out.

Sean had their car loaded except for the cookies Shirley was boxing up to take with them. He kept glancing at the time and watching for Amalie's car to show up in their drive, then missed her arrival. All of a sudden he heard footsteps on the porch and went running.

She was pulling a little suitcase in one hand and wrestling her purse with the other when he came flying out the door.

"I'll get it! I'll get it!" he said, and swooped in for a kiss. "I've been watching for you forever and then you arrive when I looked away. Come in, sugar. I'll take your bag."

He swept her into the house, shouting, "Mom! Amalie's here!"

Shirley came from the kitchen with her arms open and gave Amalie a big hug. "Here's my girl, and we're just about ready to leave. I need to box up the rest of my cookies. Everything else is in Sean's SUV."

"I'm so excited, and a little nervous," Amalie said.

Shirley laughed. "It's just a wiener roast and a bunch of kinfolks. All you have to do is eat hot dogs and fixings and meet a bunch more people who look like me and mine."

"I can do that for sure. I'm starving," Amalie said.

"Then come have an appetizer. I can't make all those cookies fit in my container, anyway."

Sean came back in time to overhear her. "Mom. What the heck? If you had overflow, all you had to do was say so. I'm good at leveling things off."

Shirley shook her head. Thunder rumbled overhead. She

made a run for the kitchen with them behind her, put the lid on her container of cookies as Sean and Amalie took a couple of extras for themselves, and they were out the door.

The first raindrops splattered on the windshield as Sean was backing up.

"Here it comes," he said.

Amalie was still chewing her bite and looked up. "Here comes what?" she asked, and then the heavens unloaded so fast it made her jump.

Sean pointed at the torrent. "Here comes that."

"Good lord," she muttered.

"Welcome to weather on the mountain. The higher we go, the harder it falls."

"Because we're closer to God," Shirley finished, and then smiled. "That's what my mother always said."

Amalie was a little apprehensive about the windshield wipers' ability to keep up, but Sean was driving. She'd already trusted him with her life, and tonight didn't feel any different. She took another bite of cookie, and by the time she'd finished hers, they were driving into the church parking lot.

Sean pulled up as close as he could get to the covered entrance and honked.

Three men came running. He popped the trunk and shouted, "Everything in here goes in there."

The men grabbed the pans and bowls, while another one helped Shirley and Amalie out and ushered them inside. It was left to Sean to find a parking place and then make a dash for the door.

He came in dripping and laughing, wiped his boots in the foyer, hung his coat on a hook beside dozens of other dripping coats, grabbed a couple of paper towels from the hall table, and wiped his face and then his boots before heading inside.

One of the Morgan boys was strumming an acoustic guitar, a cousin from the other side of the mountain was playing fiddle, and Ray Raines was playing his banjo. The music was mountain music, more bluegrass than country. It had a kick and a beat beneath the fiddler's mournful wail. The kind of music you could two-step, clog, or waltz to. The kind that spoke to their souls.

It didn't take long to find Amalie within the crowd. The women had her cornered, admiring her engagement ring and welcoming her into the fold.

He had a moment of déjà vu, remembering when Aaron first introduced Dani the same way. *The wheels of time do roll on,* he thought, then saw that faraway look on Amalie's face and went to save her from herself.

"Hey, ya'll. Don't chew her ear off before I've got her fed," Sean said, then winked at a couple of girl cousins as he swooped her out of the crowd. They were laughing as he led her away.

As soon as they were alone, he slid an arm around her shoulders.

"Amalie?"

She looked up. "Rain or no rain, I feel like I'm at my first prom, hoping my dress is okay, and when the music starts, someone asks me to dance. Thank you for bringing me to the party. Thank you for bringing me into your world."

He gave her shoulder a quick squeeze. "It's my selfish pleasure to have you, and we just got started," he said and swung her into his arms. "Can you two-step?"

"Go slow and teach me. I'm a fast learner."

So he did, and by their second turn around the room, she'd proved herself right. She was a natural!

The music shifted to a jig, and Sean paused and shook his head. "This one's beyond me," he said. "Let's go see who all's here and find something cold to drink."

The rain slowly passed, and by the time they were roasting marshmallows, the moon was visible behind passing clouds. Shirley was making s'mores as fast as they brought her the roasted marshmallows. Her fingers were sticky. There was a smear of melted chocolate on her chin.

Amalie saw her then, but not as Sean's mother. Not as the woman who'd been kind to her as a child, but as Shirley Pope, the girl who'd grown up here, and now the woman who'd returned to grow old here. Shirley was showing her what mattered most in this life, without even knowing it.

Then the band struck up a song Amalie had never heard, and Sean was suddenly at her elbow.

"Last song of the night," he said, and walked her back onto the dance floor.

"What is it called?" she asked.

"'Goodnight, Irene.' It's an old song from the thirties. It was written as a lullaby and then became popular as the way to end a dance sometime during the forties and fifties. At least, that's what I've been told."

"I love it," she said.

"Then put your head on my shoulder, darlin', and close your eyes. I've got you."

It was the last three words that resonated. The trucker who pulled her from the fire. Her father's vows, and now Sean Pope's promises. *I've got you. So, God...I'm finally getting You. Angels abound in all shapes and sizes, whenever and wherever we are in need. Thank you for my Sean. The others may come and go, but him, I'm going to keep.*

They waltzed until the last note faded, and then the task of gathering up and cleaning up and finally saying goodbye lasted the better part of another hour. By the time they started down the mountain, Amalie crawled into the back seat of her own accord and curled up in a ball. Shirley laughed, covered her with a blanket, and got in the front seat with Sean. Amalie fell asleep listening to them talk.

Sean all but carried her into bed when they got back home, helped her into her pajamas while she was muttering something about cold feet and a warm heart, then let Sean tuck her into bed. She was asleep before he even had the lights out. He was still smiling as he went through the house checking windows and locks.

Shirley was in the kitchen putting dirty dishes into the dishwasher.

"Everything okay?" she asked. "Does Amalie need anything?"

"Everything's fine, Mom, and she's already passed out. I think she had a little too much fun."

"You can't ever have too much fun," Shirley said. "Remember that. And if you do overload, just save up the good feelings for a day when you need them." Then she hung up the dish towel and kissed his cheek. "Night, son. Sleep in. We don't have anything to do tomorrow but just be together."

"My favorite way to be," he said, and went through the house turning out lights behind her.

Wolf was at the airport the next morning with two of his security guards, waiting to board his jet. Toby West, his pilot, was overseeing a refuel, and as soon as they were finished, they would be allowed to board.

Wolf eyed his security team, gauging their appearances. At first glance, they could have been business associates traveling with him. They were both in gray suits, white shirts, and black ties. But the results of daily workouts were hard to disguise beneath their tailored suits. One might even confuse the bulge of their shoulder holsters for more muscle, were it not for the aviator sunglasses and the stoic expressions on their faces.

But for Wolf, they would do nicely.

He thought of Shandy as he was waiting to board, wondering if souls knew what their people did after they were gone. Wondering if she'd cried among the angels for what was happening to her child.

He had loved her beyond words, and he was traveling to the city of her birth to destroy the people who'd given her life. Given the circumstances, it seemed like a fair fucking trade. Then the fuel truck began pulling away, and Toby came out from behind the tail of the jet and waved them on.

"That's us, men," Wolf said, and reached for his bag.

"I've got it, Boss," Joe said.

Wolf led the way as they crossed the tarmac, then climbed up the boarding ramp onto the jet.

Toby helped them stow luggage and made sure they had drinks before takeoff and were buckled in their seats.

"We have clear weather all the way. We have a tailwind, so our flying time is down to just under two hours. Any questions?" he asked.

"None," Wolf said. "Let's do this."

"Yes, sir," Toby said, then walked to the cockpit and closed the door behind him.

Moments later, the engines fired, followed by the sound of that familiar roar. After all these years and a thousand flights, Wolf still hated takeoffs and landings. He leaned against the headrest and took a quick sip of his drink, then put it in the cup holder of his chair and folded his hands in his lap, knowing they still had the usual time lapse and waiting in line for takeoff to go through, then finally, they were airborne.

At that point, Wolf glanced out the window. They

were flying through clouds. Clouds so ethereally perfect in his mind that the jet became a knife slicing through meringue. Within moments they were out of them, and it was nothing but blue sky as far as the eye could see. He wondered then, how many angels had Shandy gathered to fly with him today?

Chapter 20

They landed at Louis Armstrong New Orleans International, one hour and forty-five minutes after takeoff.

By the time they were allowed to disembark, Wolf was silent, afraid if he opened his mouth, he would be screaming. He had not set foot in this city in twenty-seven years, and he was not looking forward to spending the time here he needed to do what he'd come here to do. This place had meant nothing to him but sadness and defeat, and he wouldn't be here now if he hadn't come for war.

"I've got your bags, Boss," Joe said.

Wolf started down the ramp to the waiting limo. His guards loaded their bags in the car and then joined him.

Their driver keyed up the intercom. "Mr. Outen, are we still proceeding to the Waldorf Astoria on Roosevelt?"

"Yes, thank you," Wolf said.

The limo started moving on the tarmac, then away from the airfield, heading to the hotel on Roosevelt Way. Wolf was numb to the beauty. Lost in the past. But their arrival was duly noted as they entered the lobby.

Wolf Outen's face was known the world over, and

there was no mistaking the mane of gray hair framing it or the bodyguards flanking him as he moved toward the front desk.

Bellhops came running.

The manager came out of his office to check Wolf in, while trying not to fawn. Everybody knew of his resurrection and what had happened. Only a few knew he had reserved suites here—the presidential suite for himself and the two nearest suites for his men.

Wolf said little beyond producing a corporate credit card and picking up room keys before heading to the elevators. The guards carried all the luggage. Nothing left their sight. And nobody argued. Moments later, the flurry he'd caused in the lobby was over and he was out of sight.

But word was spreading. Wolfgang Outen was in New Orleans. What was he doing here? Who was selling? What was he buying?

As soon as the guards got Wolf in his suite and put his luggage on the rack, he began issuing orders.

"Get your things in your rooms. Do what you need to do. Order a car and meet me back here in twenty minutes. We're going straight to the PD before word gets out that I'm in the city. The element of surprise is on my side, but it won't be for long."

"Yes, sir," Joe said. "Nothing has been ordered for your suite. Don't answer your door."

Even though all of this was standard protocol for Wolf, after all that had transpired, it had amped up the reality of how fragile his safety really was. He followed them to the door, locked and chain-locked it behind them, then turned around. The luxury was obvious. And expensive. But it also meant privacy, and that was what he needed most.

He quickly hung up his suits, left his travel bag of toiletries on the bathroom counter, and then went through the file he'd brought with him one last time, making sure everything he needed was still in it. Satisfied, he slipped the file into his briefcase and set it on the sofa, then began to pace. His enemy was within this city. They were breathing the same air, and he was about to drop a bomb on their lives.

The car pulled up in front of the New Orleans Police Department long enough to let them out.

"Wait in the parking lot," Joe ordered.

"Yes, sir," the driver said, and as soon as his riders were out, he did exactly that. He wasn't about to screw up the best call he'd ever received. They'd hired him for a thousand dollars a day until their departure from the city. Sometimes he didn't make that in a week.

Wolf walked straight to the front desk.

"I need to speak to a detective in the Criminal Investigative Division."

The officer glanced up, then did a double take, thinking he recognized the man. "About what?" he asked.

"A kidnapping."

The officer blinked. "And your name?"

"Wolfgang Outen."

The officer blinked, thinking that explained the muscle Outen had with him.

"If you'll just take a seat, someone will be with you shortly."

"We'll stand," Joe said, as they moved their boss back and out of the way.

The officer picked up his phone and made a call.

Three minutes later, a linebacker of a detective came striding into the lobby, spied Outen almost instantly, and headed toward him, only to find Outen's defense a little more than he bargained for when both men blocked him, so he decided to introduce himself first.

"Mr. Outen. I'm Detective Louis Giraud. Would you please follow me?" He turned and led the way to the CID wing, and then to his desk. "Have a seat and I'll get chairs for your men."

"They'll stand," Wolf said.

Louis nodded. It was a simple mistake. He'd never had anyone bring their own security into a police station before.

"Yes, sir. Now, the desk sergeant mentioned something about a kidnapping? Who's been kidnapped and when did it happen?"

"My daughter was kidnapped. It would be twenty-eight years ago this coming April."

Louis's mouth dropped. "I'm sorry, sir. But why is this just being reported?"

"Because I didn't know until a month ago that I even had a living daughter." And then he began to explain, from being in Saudi Arabia, to trying to get home to his wife only to find her comatose and dying, and what his in-laws told him.

Louis was in shock. "You're saying your in-laws told you your daughter was born dead and deformed and had already been cremated? That your wife had been in a coma since the delivery, and she died in your arms less than an hour after your arrival?"

"Yes, and I have birth and death certificates to prove this." Then he pulled out the file and began laying out papers. "This is a picture of me and my wife on our wedding day. This is a picture taken less than two weeks ago of me and my daughter."

Louis was stunned. Except for the fact that Wolf was older, it could have been the same woman in both photos.

"These are the DNA tests proving she's my daughter. This is the note left within the blanket she was found in. A handwriting expert will tell you this handwriting matches the handwriting of my wife's father. I don't know what doctors and nurses were paid off to say my daughter died, and I don't know who they paid to take her out of Louisiana to dump her, but she was found at approximately six days old in an alley in Hot Springs, Arkansas, dirty and too weak to cry, with that note inside her blanket. Read that note, please."

Louis looked. "They mentioned a family history of mental illness."

"Yes! Except that's a lie, and I'm guessing it was meant to keep anyone from ever wanting to adopt her, thereby ensuring her a misery of foster care and orphanages. There's another birth certificate in her case file. They gave it to her after she was found. Her surname came from the street on which she'd been found, and her given name came from the nun in the hospital where she was taken. Amalie Lincoln. My daughter grew up without me and without my name. I want them dead. I will settle for the rest of their lives in prison."

Louis took a deep breath. "Sir. I can't begin to understand your emotions, but you do know we'll have to do our own investigations into the information you've given us and that will take time. Where did you get the info from her childhood?"

"From my daughter. At her request, her caseworker gave her a full copy of her own files after she aged out of the system. The caseworker's name and location are in the file. The DNA results came through tests we had done at the hospital in Jubilee, Kentucky, only a few weeks ago. At my request, the lab results came to me. Everything else in that file is either an original or a copy of the originals I have in my possession. So, investigate away, but in the meantime, I suggest you bring them in for questioning immediately, because tomorrow I'm holding a press conference stating what I've just told you, and that I have filed charges against them with the NOPD."

Louis flinched. "Are you threatening the validity of this police force?"

"I don't have to. I'm just telling you what the court of opinion is going to do to your police force if nothing is done to follow up on the information I've just given you. And, just so you know, I have already retained my own lawyers here in the city. A criminal defense lawyer and a litigation lawyer. We will be filing a civil lawsuit against my ex-in-laws, as well. Their cards are in the file, too. I understand he's one of the best attorneys in the state. I don't play games, Detective.

"Twenty-eight years ago, two residents of your city kidnapped my baby and trafficked her on the day of her birth without giving a shit about what happened to her, as long as she didn't die in Louisiana. Paid off God knows how many people to get away with it, and then sat back and watched my world coming down around me. If you have any further questions for me, I am at the Roosevelt Waldorf Astoria. Presidential suite. I will be there until they have been arrested and charged. After I am gone, you can communicate to me through my lawyer. Oh… and that file is yours. I have another one just like it, with all of the originals."

Louis was horrified by the story, and more than a little scared of Wolf Outen, but if everything Outen just told him could be proved by the info he'd given them, this would probably become the biggest scandal in recent history. He grabbed a pen.

"I assume these people still live here in New Orleans, or you wouldn't be here, so I'm going to need names and an address."

"Carter and Leigh Bullock. Pillars of old-money New Orleans. Evil to the core. I'm sure you already know where to find them. We'll see ourselves out," Wolf said.

The moment he stood, his security was right beside him. They sandwiched him between them as they walked single file out into the hall and disappeared.

"Shit, shit, shit," Louis muttered. He grabbed the file and headed for the captain's office. They couldn't stop Outen from saying whatever he wanted to say, and he was famous enough to get the media's avid attention with a single phone call. Outen hadn't threatened them. He'd just shortened their time to make decisions.

Carter was at the putting green between his wife's azalea bushes and the wisteria-wrapped pergola at the back of the property when the housekeeper came scurrying out, trying to wave him down.

"Mr. Carter! Mr. Carter! You need to come quick!"

Cursing the stroke he'd just flubbed, he jammed the putter into his golf bag and rolled it back into the house. He could hear raised voices, but when Leigh began screaming, he took off running.

The last thing he expected was to see the NOPD on his doorstep and his wife being taken out the door and put into the back of a police car.

"Stop! Stop this instant!" he roared. "I'll have your jobs for this. I demand to know what's going on!"

Detective Louis Giraud stepped forward. "We've received some serious allegations regarding you and your wife, and we need you to come down to the station for questioning."

Carter threw up his arms in disbelief. "How dare you? How fucking dare you? I'll have your jobs for this!" he said and started fighting them.

Louis didn't play games. He didn't argue; he just cuffed Carter without responding.

"I'm calling my lawyer!" Carter shouted.

"You can call him from the station," Louis said, and took Carter's elbow in a firm grip and led him to the cruiser.

When Carter realized they were putting him and Leigh in separate cars, he panicked. "I want to be with my wife!"

"No, sir. We'll be questioning you both separately. I'll see you at the station," he said, then shut the door and watched them drive away.

Louis knew this was just the beginning of a big ugly mess, but Wolf Outen's charges had to be addressed, and the proof he'd brought with him was shocking, to say the least. However, it was the captain's decision to pull the Bullocks in now, so that when Outen held his press conference, the police would already have the jump on it. At this point, nobody was being charged or arrested, but Carter and Leigh Bullock had a world of explaining to do.

Benton Warwick had been the Bullocks' family lawyer for thirty-five years and was nearing retirement when he got the call. He arrived at the police station a few minutes shy of an hour after receiving the message and came in bristling, throwing their good name and weight around like a peacock fanning its tail. But like the peacock, it was all for show. The moment he found out about the accusations that had been made, he had a clear moment of panic.

"I'm sorry, Detective Giraud, but I feel I must recuse myself."

"And your reason would be?" Louis asked.

"That I may have prior knowledge that could incriminate me."

Louis blinked. *Son of a bitch! Outen's story was true.* "Then I advise you not to leave town. If you want to give a statement regarding this now, we'll take it. Otherwise, we'll be asking you back at a later date."

"We'll make it later. I think I'd like my lawyer here when I make it."

"Fine. You're excused for now," Louis said, and went back to the interrogation room where Carter Bullock had been placed.

He walked in on a very angry man and delivered a message that turned the old man pale.

"I'm afraid Mr. Warwick has had to recuse himself from being your representative, since he claims he has prior knowledge of why you're being held. Do you have another lawyer we might call?" Louis asked.

Carter grunted like he'd been punched. "Lash Faraday. But what the hell's going on here? I have a right to know! I demand to know why we've been dragged in here like common criminals!"

"Because accusations have been made against you by Wolfgang Outen that put you in that context. He has accused you of kidnapping his daughter, trafficking her, and abandoning her in an alley to die, and he has the daughter and the paperwork to prove it."

"We did no such thing."

Louis stared. "Sit tight. I'm going to call Faraday."

"I want to talk to my wife! I demand to talk to Leigh."

"You're not in charge here, Mr. Bullock. I am," Louis said and walked out.

Carter sat staring at the door, unable to believe that this was happening.

Another hour passed before Lash Faraday's arrival. Then when he came, Louis decided to keep Carter on ice. He wanted to speak to Leigh Bullock first.

When they entered the interrogation room where she'd been placed, she was sitting with her head down, her hands motionless on the table before her.

She saw Faraday and frowned. "Where's Mr. Warwick? I need to speak to Carter! I demand to know what's happening!"

"Mr. Faraday has been informed of the accusations

against you. You have thirty minutes to discuss your options, and then I'll be in to take your statement."

Her eyes narrowed in anger. "Accusations! Who made accusations against us?"

"Wolfgang Outen," Louis said, and walked out. When he went back in, he brought his partner, Amos Cox, with him, wasted no time setting up the interview, and informed her it was being taped. After identifying everyone in the room for the tape, Louis opened up the file Outen had given him and began to question her.

The first picture on top of the file was the wedding photo.

"Leigh… You don't mind if I call you Leigh?" Louis asked.

"It's fine," she muttered.

"I'm sorry. You have to speak up for the recording," he said.

"It's fine," Leigh snapped.

He laid the picture face up in front of her.

"Can you identify these two people in this photo?"

"My daughter, Cassandra, and the man she married."

"What was that man's name?" Louis asked.

"Wolfgang Outen. He was below her status and station in life in every possible way, but she *would* have him, and there was nothing we could do," Leigh said.

"I have a copy of their wedding certificate and a copy of the marriage license. Can you please verify those for me?"

Leigh glanced at them and then shoved them away. "Yes, they belonged to them."

"I see you and your husband were witnesses on the marriage certificate. Can you verify those signatures as your own?"

"Yes, they are our signatures," Leigh said.

The next thing he laid out was the baby's birth certificate.

"Who's birth certificate is this?" he asked.

"The one given to the baby my daughter bore. It was born dead and deformed."

"There's no name on the birth certificate other than Baby Girl Outen. Why is that?"

Leigh shuddered. "It was just a lump of flesh and hair. It wasn't a person."

"But surely your daughter had a name picked out?" Louis asked.

"Our daughter suffered an aneurysm during birthing. She never saw the thing she gave birth to. She went into a coma. She was dying. We made decisions for her."

"Where was Mr. Outen during this time? Why was he not part of these decisions?"

Leigh looked him straight in the face. "He was in a foreign country working in some Saudi oil field. He wasn't there when she needed him. He arrived less than an hour before she passed."

"Where was their baby?" Louis asked.

"It had been cremated. It was the humane thing to do. Like burying roadkill."

Louis hid his shock and pulled out a death certificate. "This is the baby's death certificate. Can you please verify that for me, as well?"

Leigh glanced. "Yes. We have a copy of it, too."

Then Louis pulled out another picture. It was the first photo in Amalie Lincoln's case file. "Do you recognize this baby?" he asked.

Leigh glanced down. "No, I do not."

Louis spoke. "For the record, I just showed Mrs. Bullock a photo taken of a baby girl found abandoned in an alley in Hot Springs, Arkansas, six days after the birth and purported death of her own granddaughter." Then he pulled out the photo of Wolf and Amalie taken only weeks before.

"Do you recognize the people in this photo?" Louis asked.

Leigh barely glanced, and shrugged. "It's another photo of my daughter and her husband."

"No, ma'am, it is not. This is a photo of Wolfgang Outen and the daughter he found through Ancestry.com. Her name is Amalie Lincoln. She was found abandoned as a baby in an alley in Hot Springs, Arkansas, approximately six days after her estimated date of birth."

Leigh gasped, then slapped both hands over her mouth to keep from screaming.

Louis pulled the copy of the note found with the baby.

"Do you recognize the handwriting on this note?" he asked.

Leigh was trembling. "Uh…no. No, I do not."

"According to our handwriting expert, this note was written by the same man who signed your daughter's marriage certificate. Now I'm going to ask you again, do you know who wrote this note?"

She glanced at her lawyer in a panic, and then screamed, "No comment!"

"Did you and your husband conspire to kidnap Wolfgang Outen's baby?"

"No comment!" Leigh said.

Louis kept raising the tone of his voice. "Did you and your husband traffic Mr. Outen's daughter? Did you pay someone to abandon her to her fate in another state?"

"No comment!" Leigh said.

"How many people did you and your husband buy off to help make this happen?"

"No comment!" Leigh said.

Louis gathered up the photos and the papers and put them back in the file.

"Leigh Bullock, did you knowingly, and with malicious intent, deprive Wolfgang Outen of his rights as a father and, purposefully and with malicious intent, conspire to abandon your own grandchild to her death out of hate for the man she belonged to?"

She slapped her hands flat on the table, then screamed, "NO COMMENT!"

Louis glanced at the lawyer, waiting.

He didn't seem to have a comment, either.

"Leigh Bullock, you are being arrested and booked in a women's holding facility on suspicion of human trafficking for selling a baby, abandonment of a baby, abetting the kidnapping and fraud against the child's father, and that's for starters. You will be held for the duration of the time in which it takes to have your DNA sampled.

And if it comes back as a match to the woman we know now as Amalie Lincoln, you will be charged for the aforementioned crimes, and more if the need arises. This session is over." He turned off the recorder and pointed at the officer standing by the door.

"Officer, would you please take Mrs. Bullock to booking?"

"You can't do this to me!"

She was still screaming as the detectives turned back to the lawyer. "Mr. Faraday, do you have an issue representing both parties in this case?"

Lash Faraday was conflicted. Legally, he could do so. Technically, it would be a nightmare.

"While I'm not in favor, I don't have a personal issue with it. What I will do is assure you that I will not divulge to either client what the other has said or done during interrogations. If they object, then one or both of them may choose to replace me."

"Fair enough," Louis said. "Follow us, please. Same rules. Same routine. You'll have some time to confer with Mr. Bullock, and then we'll join you."

They walked two doors down to where Bullock was being held and let Faraday in.

Carter stood. "It's about damn time!"

Louis closed the door, then glanced at his watch. "It's late. We've missed dinner. I'll pony up for coffees if you'll get some chips or something."

"Deal," Amos said.

They returned later, refueled and ready. They'd

already faced the lesser of two evils. Now it was time to meet the monster.

"Let's do this," Amos said.

They entered the room and walked toward the table in tandem, pulled their chairs out at the same time, knowing the screeching sound they'd make on the floor, and then sat.

Carter was quiet. He was pissed Faraday refused to pass on Leigh's comments, but with Benton Warwick out of the picture, he was forced to play ball. He knew the accusations against him. He knew who'd made them. But he had no idea of the avalanche of evidence they had until they began.

He was holding it together with his usual aplomb, having an answer for everything and giving them with assurance. He didn't flinch. He didn't waver, and for a man who was contemplating murder, he was hiding it well.

And then they pulled out the marriage license and asked for verification that was his signature. Then they pulled out the pictures, and like Leigh, he fell for the one with Amalie and Wolf, and then choked on his own spit when he realized it was not his daughter's face he was looking at, but her baby fully grown—the one he threw away.

Then they pulled out the copy of the note tucked into the baby's blanket, and he felt the blood rushing from his face. His words. In his handwriting.

Jesus Lord.

"Mr. Bullock, do you recognize this note?" Louis asked.

"No, I do not."

"That's odd, because the professional handwriting expert we use has definitively identified it as the same handwriting as on your daughter's marriage certificate, which points to you as the person responsible for the kidnapping and trafficking of Wolfgang Outen's baby. It also points to you and your wife having conspired in this heinous act. You left a baby...your own granddaughter...to die. It was by the grace of God that she did not. You expected her to be lost forever. But by the grace of God and the miracle of DNA registries, your plan did not succeed. Now, I'm going to ask you, Carter Bullock, did you, with malicious intent, deprive Wolfgang Outen of his rights as a father?"

Faraday leaned over and whispered in Carter's ear.

"No comment," Carter said.

"Carter Bullock, did you, with malicious intent, conspire to have Mr. Outen's baby kidnapped and trafficked and left to die in another state?"

"No comment."

"Then I am going to inform you that you are under arrest for the aforementioned crimes. You will be taken to a men's holding facility, until which time a test of your own DNA either eliminates you as Amalie Lincoln's grandfather or confirms our suspicions that you have, in fact, committed all of the above crimes, and possibly more. I am ending this session as of 1:10 a.m. this morning."

"I will not be taken to prison," Carter said.

Louis stood and pointed at the guard at the door. "Officer, please take Mr. Bullock to booking. Papers to transfer him will be ready tomorrow. He'll spend tonight with us."

"Yes, sir," the officer said.

Carter was led away in handcuffs, wondering who, of all the people involved, would turn on him first, and then grimaced at his own stupidity. If Leigh had seen the picture of Wolf Outen and his daughter, she'd be the one to give him up. No way was he taking all the blame. She'd never wanted to lose her figure to give birth to Cassandra. The idea of raising another baby appalled her. She'd been all for the disappearing act, and if he went down, she was coming with him.

Wolf woke up to a text from Giraud.

> FYI. Both Carter and Leigh Bullock arrested on suspicion and being held in custody pending DNA confirmation before evidence goes to the DA Request details not be shared with the public at this time, but your desire to acknowledge your daughter is understood. This case is going to get ugly and she will be drawn into it, regardless of your desire to protect. It's my opinion that she would be most protected if, at this time, nothing was said. But again, it's your call.
>
> Giraud

Wolf was surprised that they'd acted this quickly, and Giraud's advice was sound. He knew his desire for revenge was driving this, and maybe he did need to step back for now. Protecting Amalie had to come first. But his distrust of the Bullocks and their presence in this city was uppermost in his mind. They'd paid off a whole lot of people to get rid of Amalie. He didn't trust they wouldn't start throwing money around to try to make paperwork disappear.

So maybe he didn't hold a public press conference. Maybe he just dropped this story to the *New York Times* and the *Washington Post*. The local papers would pick it up from the AP and run with it.

And Amalie was as mad and hurt as a woman could be at what they'd done. He'd warned her what might happen. She'd already told him to go for it. This was their fight. Him and his girl. He wasn't giving anybody a break. Not the Bullocks. Not the cops. Not the DA.

He'd let her know, and her decision would be the one he followed.

Amalie was knee-deep in tax reports. The deadline for filing was about a month away and she kept getting walk-in customers asking for appointments, which was good but definitely increasing the workload.

She had a client coming in soon to finish up an online filing. She had their copies ready to sign and an invoice waiting, and was getting up to get a cup of coffee when her phone began to ring and she ran back to her desk to grab it.

"Hello?"

"Hey, sugar, it's me. Got a second?"

"Just," she said. "I have a client due any moment. What's up?"

"The New Orleans police arrested Clark and Leigh Bullock on suspicion of a butt load of charges last night. They're both in holding, pending DNA testing. It's procedure for the cops. The Bullocks already see the writing on the wall but so far are denying everything and down to 'No comment.'"

"Oh my God! That's wonderful, Dad! Thank you. Thank you for not letting this go."

"Hell no, I'm not letting it go, and that's why I called. I told the detective I was going to hold a press conference regarding the kidnapping of my daughter and the crimes committed by the Bullocks to make it happen. They can't stop me from doing it, but they want me to wait until the DNA tests come back and they turn everything over to the DA."

She frowned. "What are your thoughts on that?"

"I think I don't trust anybody here. The Bullocks bought off a lot of people to make you disappear, and I don't trust them not to try destroying evidence to get away with it. Granted, you are the ultimate proof, but destroying the evidence trail would then be just my word against theirs as to how you disappeared."

"Then follow your gut, Dad."

"Pulling you into the public eye could become a problem for you."

"My truth won't hurt me. I've already survived it. My truth won't hurt my business. It would be the reverse. As for the media, my future brothers-in-law are cops, and Sean is over the top when it comes to protecting me."

"Then you're okay with this?"

"I'm okay with this," she said.

"Enough said. Love you. Talk to you soon."

"Love you, too."

The call ended.

Her client came in, and her morning continued.

But Wolf was on a mission. He started going through his contacts until he found a journalist at the *Miami Herald* who he knew and trusted, and gave him a call. Might as well start at home.

The phone rang a couple of times, and then the call picked up.

"Whiskey Tango Foxtrot! Wolf Outen! Is this you?"

Wolf grinned. Leave it to a wordsmith like Danvers to use International Civil Aviation Organization spellings instead of just blatantly saying, "What the fuck!"

"Yes, it's me. I have a story. Do you want the scoop?"

"Does a bear ask for Charmin in the woods? What's it about?"

"My daughter."

There was a moment of silence. "I didn't know you had a daughter."

"Neither did I, up until a month or so ago."

"Holy shit, Wolf. Where do we start?"

"At the beginning, which was nearly twenty-eight years ago. You're going to need to record this. It's a sad, long-ass story with a very happy ending."

"Give me a sec," Danvers said.

Wolf heard footsteps running away and then footsteps running back. Danvers was slightly breathless when he picked up.

"Are you giving this to anyone else?"

"Only you. Once the story runs, I'll probably give comments to other papers, but that's it."

"Thank you for this, but why me?" Danvers asked.

"Because I trust you," Wolf said.

Another moment of silence, as he heard Danvers clearing his throat.

"Thanks, man. I'm ready when you are."

Wolf started talking, and when he finished, Danvers was in disbelief.

"This is... I can't imagine how... Is she okay with all this coming out?"

"What? You mean her truth? She hasn't known who the hell she was for the past twenty-seven years of her life. We're both celebrating each other's existence right now, and honestly, she's angry, maybe even more than I am, at what happened because she's the one who was thrown away. She's the one who grew up with nobody to love her. Write the truth, Danvers. That's all I ask."

"Consider it done. Do you want to vet it before I send it in?"

"No. If you screw me over, I'll just make you sorry you were ever born, okay?"

Danvers laughed. "And that is exactly why I love you, man. You're the real deal. Are you here in Miami?"

"Not yet, but I will be by tomorrow."

"Then watch for the headline. I might even win a Pulitzer for this!"

Wolf hung up, satisfied with their joint decision, then called down to room service and ordered breakfast.

Chapter 21

The story broke the morning after Wolf's arrival back in Miami.

His phone started ringing by midmorning. He transferred all the calls to his personal assistant's office, with instructions to Mark to tell callers he had no further comments at this time.

The AP picked it up, and by evening the story was nationwide, with every news anchor trying to put a new spin on the same information they all had and then digging through the dirt to add his wife's bloody death in prison to the gore.

He guessed shit hit the fan in the New Orleans world as well, but he didn't care. More pressure on them to nail the Bullocks before they started flashing money and pulling strings.

He sent Amalie a link to the story in the *Miami Herald*, with a suggestion to not to respond to calls and, if journalists ran her down, to refuse to give them a story.

"Once the shock wears off of all this, we'll be old news in no time," Wolf said, and then he sent Sean a message.

Watch her six, son. The reporters won't hurt her, but they can be absolute assholes without trying.

Sean sent a three-word reply.

Already on it.

And he was. Every family member in Jubilee had been warned about reporters asking questions, and the police force had been forewarned about the possibility of paparazzi.

But that didn't faze them. It was business as usual in Jubilee. They'd dealt with the media before because of the entertainment world of the music venues. The minute one of the entertainers started having personal problems that hit the news, the press came looking for photos and scoops on what was going on—like being caught cheating or in the middle of a messy divorce—so the long-lost daughter of a billionaire who was now living in their midst sort of fell into the same category.

Sean had assured her that if some random reporter got in her way, he'd make them sorry. Her thoughts flashed to the bubble-gum fight of their youth and she laughed, but Sean didn't. After that, she wasn't so sure he hadn't meant it. So she accepted that if the cops didn't run the nosy media out of town, the Popes might take them up the mountain to see the sights.

Either way, their fate was out of her hands.

In the end, Amalie took it all in stride, just as she had

every other bump in her road, believing eventually it would work itself out. Problems always did.

The bigger excitement in her world was the remodeling going on up at Shirley's house. They were turning two of the now-empty bedrooms in the house into a master suite and en suite for her and Sean, and as soon as it was finished, they were setting a wedding date.

All she knew was that it was Shirley's idea, and she was having the time of her life. Sean was working through hammering and sawing and his mother's sudden appearances in his office, coming in with color swatches and paint chips. It was quite the noisy event up on their quiet mountain.

While down in the valley, Jubilee Elementary was getting ready to reopen. Teachers were preparing themselves for problems, but with the hope that all of the renovations and new desks and new playground equipment would be enough to help them get past it.

And even more helpful, thanks to a huge donation from PCG Inc., a brand-new privacy fence to go with the new playground equipment had gone up behind the school, hiding all of the burned-out area of the crash site. It was the best they could do with a bad situation.

Their first day of school would be the Monday after Easter.

But Sean wasn't just looking out for Amalie. He'd been keeping his brother's secret, and tomorrow was the big surprise.

B.J. was coming home, and as soon as Shirley left for town, he raced into B.J.'s old room to put clean sheets on the bed, then dusted and swept it.

Due to Sean's suggestion, the carpenters weren't due back for five days. Shirley thought it was because of the holiday weekend, when in truth it was the actual length of time B.J. was getting to stay.

Whatever noise happened in the house this weekend would come from making up for lost time with Shirley's baby boy.

At the same time Shirley was picking out sweet potatoes from the produce shelf, Wolf was in his Miami office opening email, when he noticed a message from Detective Giraud.

When Wolf saw the heading, BULLOCKS CHARGED, he quickly opened it. Then as he began to read, he physically sagged from the release of guilt that had been upon him.

> DNA results confirm the Bullocks are Amalie Lincoln's grandparents. They are officially under arrest, having been charged on multiple counts, and everything has been turned over to the district attorney.
>
> There's word they may try for a plea deal, but rest assured, they are not getting away with anything. They're going to prison for the rest of their

lives and, to my knowledge, have named no less than thirteen people who assisted and abetted them. They are all being processed as I write this. On behalf of the City of New Orleans, we deeply regret the injustices you and your daughter have suffered. I know it changes nothing, but I have two sons, and I cannot imagine them having to go through what happened to your child. You are a good and dutiful father for seeking justice, and I greatly appreciate your choice to come to us, rather than seeking your own level of revenge.

Detective Louis Giraud
CID/NOPD

Wolf felt weightless, thinking if he moved, he might disappear. He sat until the feeling passed, then walked to the windows overlooking the city that had become his home. He needed to let Amalie know, but he couldn't think. He just kept staring at the vista until it blurred. He tried to shake off the flood of emotions, rubbing his eyes with the heels of his hands as if that alone would stop the tears.

Help me. The thought came from his soul as he leaned his forehead against the window and took a breath, but when he exhaled, a sob came with it, and then another, and another, until he was crying too hard to stop, and the city disappeared before him. All he could see was Shandy's face, smiling up at him, like the day they wed.

I'm sorry. I'm so sorry I lost our girl. I will forever believe you led us back to each other. I swear on my life, I won't lose her again.

Shirley was home from the supermarket, and Sean was on the way to Jubilee to pick up Amalie, leaving Shirley happily on her own to begin baking for the weekend festivities.

Amalie had closed the office at noon and had been home for over an hour, watching for Sean to arrive, when it dawned on her that the same car had been driving slowly by her house. Ever since the news broke about her identity, she'd had call after call at her work, and reporters and photographers walking into her office looking for a story or to snap a few unsolicited photos.

They'd been an aggravation, but nothing more. If they didn't leave when asked, she just called the police. After the tenth one was locked up and forced to pay bond to be released, that process slammed to a halt. Word was spreading.

Then she began to notice a different kind of harassment. They were the ones who didn't want a story. They just wanted photos for the tabloids, then made up the story they wanted to go with it, but they were few and far between, and when they finally disappeared, she thought they were gone—until today.

The car had just circled the block again, and she was stewing about what to do when Sean drove up. She noticed the driver's brake lights flash, and then the car sped up to go around the block again, probably in hopes of catching pictures of the both of them. She ran to the door before Sean was even at the steps.

"Hurry, Sean, hurry. Some guy has been circling the block for a solid hour. I think he's paparazzi," she shouted.

Sean stopped in midstep and turned back toward the street.

"What make and model car?" he asked.

"Dark-blue Toyota. It has an Illinois license plate. It could just be a tourist looking for an address, but I don't think—"

Sean saw it coming. "Get back in the house and close the door."

She frowned. "Honey, please. I don't want you getting hurt again on my behalf."

"I'm not gonna hurt him," Sean said.

She groaned. "I meant you!"

He didn't look back. "Just shut the door, Amalie."

She shut the door, then ran to the window as Sean was getting something from the back of his SUV, then gasped when he walked out into the middle of the street, forcing the driver to stop to keep from hitting him.

She watched the driver get out holding a camera with a long lens attached. He was grinning and talking and in the act of aiming it for a shot when the size and height of the man before him suddenly dawned, and then he saw the look on Sean's face, and a *maybe I'm too close* look crossed his face. The hesitation was his undoing.

Sean's arm swung up. There was something in his hand! And for a second, Amalie thought he was going to shoot the man. Then he did, but with a swath of yellow spray paint that blasted the camera lens and most of the man's face.

Amalie gasped. The man was cursing a blue streak and waving his arms when Sean started toward him.

The man backed up, still shouting and cursing, before he realized Sean was now painting something on the hood of his car.

A word.

Just one word all across the hood—in letters so large Amalie could read it from the house.

It spelled RUN, in yellow, and from the look on the man's face when he saw it, he was considering the suggestion. Then Sean tossed the paint can into the open hatch of his SUV, pulled out a tire iron, and turned around.

The man jerked like he'd been slapped, leaped back in the car, and spun out so fast he fishtailed sideways, clipping a neighbor's mailbox on the way.

And Sean was still standing in the street holding the tire iron and watching the intersection until he saw the car shoot around the corner and turn toward the main highway, pausing only long enough for one car to pass before it turned east. Other than going up the mountain, it was the only way out of town. It appeared the man had chosen to heed Sean's warning.

Amalie watched in disbelief at the calm, methodical manner in which Sean replaced the tire iron, then got a rag from the back of the SUV and cleaned his hands and shut the hatch before heading back to the house.

She opened the door and burst out laughing, then threw her arms around his neck and began kissing him wildly, madly, deeply, square on the lips.

"You are my hero. Then. Now. Forever. Always. This was better than bubble gum," she said.

Sean wasn't even smiling as he cupped the side of her face. "I already made a promise to God and your daddy that you would never be afraid again, and I intend to keep it."

The smile slid off her lips. "To God *and* Daddy?"

"I'm not joking. Anybody messes with you will go through me to do it. You suffer no more on my watch."

He slid his hands beneath her hair and pulled her toward him, and this time he was the one doing the kissing, and nobody was laughing when it was over.

"You ready to go home with me, darlin'?"

She nodded.

"Then get your coat. It's still nippy up the hill."

She put on the coat as he picked up her bag. She locked the door and followed him down the drive to his car and got in as he loaded her bag into the back seat.

"Thought I'd better put your bag here, rather than the back, just in case there's yellow paint somewhere. I did kind of give it a toss."

She choked on a giggle and buckled up, but by the time he was driving away, she was laughing and bragging about the uniqueness of his wrath and the ingenuity of using yellow—the mark of a coward.

She finally had Sean grinning.

"In all honesty, the yellow part was just a fluke because I knew the white can was empty."

She started laughing all over again.

When they pulled up to the house, Sean reached for her hand.

"Let's don't mention this to anyone."

She leaned over the console and kissed him.

"Cross my heart and hope to die."

Sean stowed her bag in his room, then gave her a tour of the renovations in progress before they joined Shirley in the kitchen. Sometime later, she was sitting out on the back porch with a barn cat winding around her ankles and dreaming of the day when this would be her norm.

Sean was on tall-man duty, pulling down baking pans stored too high for Shirley to reach and putting others back up, and she could hear them talking and laughing. Being in this family was healing her in ways she'd never known were undone, when she heard a voice.

You're coming out of the dark. It is a blessed place to be.

At that moment, her phone signaled a text. She pulled it out of her pocket to see who it was from. It was Wolf.

Both Bullocks talked. They are going to prison. They will die there. Thirteen other people also being charged for abetting in various ways. Doubt there will be a trial. Looks like you're off the hook as to testifying. If you want to be in court the day they're sentenced, I will make that happen for you. Happy Easter, little girl. I wish I could have been the daddy who hid the eggs. I will settle for getting to walk you down the aisle. Your mother would be so proud of the woman you have become. I know I am.

Love, Dad

Amalie came back into the house with tears running down her face, and when they saw her, everything came to a halt.

"Honey, what's wrong?" Sean asked.

She handed him the phone. "Good news, but Daddy's sad. I feel it in my bones."

They read it, then reached for her at the same time.

"Group hug. This is how we fix all the hurts in this family."

"That and cookies," Sean said, and kissed the top of her head.

It made them laugh, but when Shirley sent them outside with pop and cookies, they didn't argue.

"Your mother is a healer, isn't she?" Amalie said. "A fixer of all kinds of aches, even the ones you can't see."

He shrugged. "We all have gifts and burdens. Some people use them to the fullest. Some people waste them. And some people never even know that they are there."

She leaned her head against his shoulder. “How did you get so smart?”

“I guess Clyde Wallace beat the stupid out of all of us. What’s left is gold.”

Sean never talked about his father. He never ever said his name. She knew their scars ran deep. And the only way she knew how to make the dark go away was to be his light. She glanced longingly at the cookie she was holding, then sighed.

“Sean…remember when you used to give me your dessert at school?”

He nodded.

“Back then, I thought you just didn’t want it, but you were giving up something you wanted to make someone else’s world better, weren’t you?”

He grinned. “Maybe.”

“So here,” she said, and handed him her cookie.

He sighed. “God, woman…you humble me on a daily basis.”

“Just eat the cookie.”

And so he did.

That night, they made love within the silence of the old house, within the walls of a room where lives had been lost, and babies had been birthed, and the passage of time had been stopped within the moment of a heartbeat, making love in the dark.

And in the morning of the next day, while grease was still warm in the skillet where she’d cooked the eggs, Shirley Pope’s last son walked in the door.

He dropped his bags, threw his coat on the sofa, and caught his mother on the run and swept her up into his arms.

"Happy Easter, Mom!"

Shirley was in shock. "What happened to you?"

"I grew. I hope I'm done. Big-man clothes are expensive."

Sean was grinning. "Damn, son, I think you're right. As of this moment, you are officially the tallest Pope on the mountain...and you're early."

"Caught a different flight last night. Stayed over in Bowling Green. Started home before daybreak. And this beautiful woman must be your girl!"

"My fiancée, Amalie Lincoln. Amalie, this is Brendan James Pope, our baby brother, but we call him B.J.. You never knew him. He wasn't old enough to go to school then."

Amalie smiled. "Finally, we meet," she said. "Your reputation in this family is epic."

He hugged his mother again, smiling. "What have you been saying about me?"

"The truth, the whole truth, and nothing but the truth," Shirley said.

And laughter filled the house.

They spent the rest of the day together, but from time to time, Amalie would make herself scarce just to let them be. Brothers with each other. Brothers with their mother. Mother with her sons.

It wasn't until supper that B.J. shared another secret. Something he'd been working on for some time.

"I've taken a job as the head pastry chef in a five-star hotel restaurant, and I'll be leaving New York City."

Shirley clapped her hands in pure delight. "Oh, son! I am so proud of you. You've worked hard to get to this. So where are you going, and when do you begin?"

He glanced up, anxious to gauge their first reactions.

"To the kitchens of the Serenity Inn here in Jubilee. I start in two months."

The cries of delight were music to his ears.

Sean shook his head. "I'm so happy for you, little brother, but I never thought you'd come back."

"I didn't think I would either until you nearly got yourself killed, and I found out you loved a woman enough to die for her, and I was missing out on everything family, and you guys are worth more than all the money and prestige the world could offer. This new job is perfect. I still get to do my thing and get paid a great salary to do it. I'm not meant for a solo life. I want what you and Amalie have. What Aaron and Dani have. Not sure about Wiley's choices, but I miss him, too."

"None of us are sure about Wiley's choices, but so far he's kept himself out of hot water," Sean said.

B.J. glanced at Shirley. "And I don't want Mom to get older without me."

He had them all blinking back tears, and Shirley wouldn't have it.

"You can't bake a cake big enough to stop me from aging, but you *can* make my life sweeter with your presence. And I'm selfish enough to say it. I'm glad you're coming home!"

Sean glanced at Amalie, then leaned back in his chair. "So, in two months, you'll be looking for a place to live, and in about the same length of time, Amalie will be moving up here."

B.J.'s eyebrows rose. "Are you leasing?"

"Yes. I signed a two-year lease. I didn't know my world would turn upside down within a month of moving in."

"What happened?" B.J. asked.

She rolled her eyes. "Oh lord, that's a whole other story and Sean can fill you in with all the uglies. However... while you're here, have Sean bring you down to check out the house. He has a key. If you want to do a sublet, I'd be happy to do that. I was going to just sell all my stuff. I don't need to bring anything here. But if you want to lease the house, then I'll leave it all furnished for you, too. None of it is personal to me."

"If it's larger than three hundred and twenty-five square feet, I want it."

Shirley frowned. "What's that got to do with anything?"

"It's the size of the apartment I've been living in for the past two and a half years," B.J. said.

Shirley reeled. "Oh my lord! I didn't know. My bedroom is larger than that."

"I know. You also do not want to know what rent goes for something like that. New York City isn't all flash and glamour, but it's a great place to be. However, I'm at the *'been there, done that'* stage. I just want to come home. I need to live close to the job and was planning to look for a place in Jubilee anyway. But it appears my new sister has just solved that problem for me." He winked at Amalie.

"Anything for family," Amalie said, then eyed him closer. "However, unless you plan to sleep with your legs hanging off the end of my bed, you're probably going to have to get a different one."

"The continuing story of our lives," B.J. said. "That, I can do. One last thing. Keep the news to yourselves for now. Ray Caldwell, my new boss, wants to make a big announcement upon my arrival, and I don't want to spoil whatever PR he's planning for the hotel."

Sean shrugged. "We're good at keeping secrets in this family, remember?" Amalie let the comment roll over her head. She had secrets of her own she would probably never share. In her world, it was how people stayed safe and sane.

When B.J. walked into church on Easter Sunday, the congregation was still arriving, gathering in little clumps to visit and sharing family news before the service began. Both of his other brothers were already there, and when they saw him walk in with their mom and Sean and Amalie, they both came running. Then all the hugging and laughing and back thumping began, and the first words out of Aaron's mouth were, "You grew!"

Wiley was wide-eyed and in disbelief. "You're bigger than Cameron."

B.J. shrugged. "Don't blame me. Blame the DNA."

Cameron appeared, grinning from ear to ear.

"Son! When did all this happen?" he asked.

"Lots of taste-testing in the kitchens of New York City?" B.J. said.

"Well, it all went to height and not weight, which is always good," Cameron said. "It's good to see you here," he added, and then lowered his voice. "And even better to have you home."

"Thanks for helping make it happen," B.J. said.

Cameron shrugged. "I didn't make it happen. I just heard the word and passed it on. Your résumé and application got you the job. When do you start?"

"Two months, but that's not being advertised," he said.

"Understood. Anyway, it's good to see you again."

"It's good to be home," B.J. said.

And then the pianist took her seat at the piano and sounded a chord, the signal services were about to begin, and everybody began scrambling for a seat.

On that Easter Sunday, Shirley Pope was as happy as a woman could be. She had all four sons and their significant others lined up in the pew beside her, a hymnal in her lap, Preacher Farley standing at the pulpit with sunlight coming through the windows onto his face, and she was feeling the timelessness of this place, with the future sitting beside her.

Epilogue

WOLFGANG OUTEN HAD ONCE ATTENDED A FUNERAL in the Cathedral of St. John the Divine in New York City, but had never felt the presence of spirit as profoundly as he did today in the Church in the Wildwood, waiting to walk his daughter down the aisle.

They hadn't issued invitations for the wedding. It was family only, because there was no room for anyone else. Family filled the pews and all the folding chairs along the walls and sat holding children in their laps to save room to witness the marriage of another Pope and the woman he was bringing to the mountain. For them all, it was acknowledgment of the continuation of their heritage and reassurance that even after they were gone, there would still be Popes on the mountain that bore their name.

The reception afterward was being held at the ballroom of the Serenity Inn, and Brendan Pope, the new pastry chef at the hotel, had received the honor of making both the groom's cake and the wedding cake. The last touches had gone onto the cakes just before midnight last night, and then the cakes had been rolled into the massive coolers to await their presentation.

B.J. had four hours of sleep before he was up and getting ready to join his brothers at the wedding. By age alone, Aaron was Sean's best man. And by order of birth, Wiley and B.J. were his groomsmen.

Amalie's choices had been the wild card.

She'd asked Ella to be matron of honor, and Dani and Shirley to be her bridesmaids. Lili Glass was her chosen flower girl, and to everyone's horror, she wanted Mikey Pope to be the ring bearer.

Even Rusty and Cameron were doubtful of the choice. It wasn't until Amalie suggested Ghost walk with Mikey to keep him in the aisle that they all threw up their hands and gave in.

"We're delighted, but on your head be it, and don't be surprised if Cameron winds up in the aisle with them riding herd," Rusty said.

"Pomp and parades are not my thing, but belonging to this family is everything. I've learned to celebrate the flat tires and ruts in my road. I don't want perfect. I just want them," Amalie said.

"And I want what she wants," Sean said, and the discussion ended, and today it was happening.

They'd tied the Forever wedding band onto the ring bearer's pillow. Ghost was on a short leash, and Cameron was riding herd.

But it was Ella who'd gone over the moon.

She had never been a bridesmaid. She had never been a bride. But today, at the age of ninety-four, she was going to walk down an aisle toward a preacher holding a bible, wearing a dress of sky-blue silk, with a bouquet in her hand. It was the closest thing to married she was ever going to be.

Her heart was full to bursting.

She would ask life for nothing more.

The Sunday-school classroom was full of women wearing gowns in different shades of blue. Shirley's wedding had been before a justice of the peace, and she was so honored to be part of Amalie's wedding party that it was all she could do not to cry. Dani and Amalie were Shirley's girls. The daughters she had never had, and she treasured their places in her heart.

Everyone was chattering and pinning curls into place and tucking flyaway ribbons back where they belonged, while Amalie stood before the full-length mirror in silence, staring at the woman looking back at her—pretending it was the mother she had never known, present with her on this day.

Wolf and Shirley had taken her dress shopping. He wanted to fly her to New York to pick something out from a couturier. She had opted for bridal shops in Frankfort and hugged his neck for the offer. Now here she was, wearing the dress. Not hiding the scars. With pearls at her throat and diamonds in her ears. She had moved her engagement ring to her right hand for the ceremony and was waiting for everything to begin.

Beautiful.

She blinked. *You're here,* she thought.

My beautiful baby...I have always been here.

Amalie's eyes widened. *Mother?*

Forever.

And then all of a sudden, she was watching the puzzle falling into place. So many souls. So many lives. Connected forever through eternity.

There was a knock at the door.

"They're ready," someone said.

The bridesmaids gathered at the door clutching their bouquets.

Amalie turned around to look for Ella, caught her watching, and smiled.

Ella winked, blew her a kiss, and then took her bouquet from the florist and got in line.

Amalie sighed. Life was good.

The music sounded, and they began walking out the door.

Sean was standing at the altar with Aaron, waiting for sight of Amalie. But when Ella appeared in the doorway on her own, with that braided crown of snow-white hair, owning the elegance of her years, one could have been forgiven for thinking an angel had entered here.

The congregation hushed as music led her down the aisle, and when she took her place at the altar, she winked at Sean.

In that moment, Sean realized the depth of the honor Amalie had given Ella. She was elated to be there.

B.J. and Shirley came next, and took their places.

Wiley and Dani followed, moving at a sedate and proper pace.

Then a ripple of voices and some whispers of delight rolled across guests when Lili Glass appeared in a miniature gown of pink chiffon, with ruffles beneath her chin and ruffles around the hem. She took hold of her basket and started down the aisle, sprinkling multicolored rose petals on the old pinewood floor before taking her place beside the women.

The pianist was still plunking at the same sonorous sedate pace when the ring bearer, Mikey Pope, appeared, wearing a little blue suit with a bow tie already cockeyed beneath his chin, his eyes dancing with delight at being the focus of their attention, clutching the ring pillow like a handbag.

His mother, Rusty, saw the look on his face and held her breath as Cameron and Ghost appeared beside him.

A single gasp rolled through the congregation as the big white dog slipped up beside his little boy and nosed his elbow.

Cameron leaned down and whispered in Mikey's ear. "Taking Ghostie for a walk now."

Mikey grabbed onto Ghost's hair with one hand, still holding onto the pillow with the other, and down the aisle they went.

Somewhere in the congregation, they heard a clear quiet voice.

"Whatever you do, don't anybody laugh."

They knew it was Rusty, and she knew her son. One laugh, and he would turn into the class clown. When the trio made it to the altar without disaster, Cameron turned the ring over to Aaron and took the ring bearer to sit in his mama's lap for the rest of the service, then sat down beside them with Ghost between his knees.

The music stopped.

Everyone turned to look back up the aisle.

Father and daughter, standing so close together they could have been one.

The music sounded again, and the notes of the traditional wedding march rolled out of the open doorway and onto the mountain.

Amalie's gaze went straight to the altar, to the man waiting for her there.

"Are you ready?" Wolf whispered.

She leaned against him. "Yes."

She had been waiting for this moment, and the man at the altar, all her life.

Sean was blinking back tears, and it was all he could do to be still and wait for her to come to him. He understood the gesture of a father giving away his daughter, but it was an unnecessary act. She had always belonged to him.

Then they were standing at the pulpit, and Preacher Farley asked, "Who gives the woman?"

Wolf's voice never wavered. "Her mother and I do,"

he said, and then he kissed Amalie's hand and took his seat.

Amalie and Sean's fingers locked as they faced the pulpit, waiting through all the ritual, waiting through all of the prose and promises... Waiting for the words...

"Do you, Sean, take thee, Amalie..."

"Do you, Amalie, take thee, Sean..."

The FOREVER ring went on her finger, and the engagement ring was moved to follow.

Brother Farley's voice was wavering. "You may now kiss your bride," he said, but the words would forever echo in their minds.

The moment they turned, a loud whoop came from somewhere in the congregation, and then everyone was smiling as they made their escape down the aisle and out into the parking lot to the waiting limo. The reception was down the mountain, and nobody wanted to miss it.

Wolf was standing in the doorway with his hands in his pockets, grinning from ear to ear when Shirley slipped up behind him and gave him a pat on the arm.

"Welcome to the family," she said.

He turned and gave her a big hug. "It's good to be here! Is Miss Ella coming to the reception?"

Shirley nodded. "She wouldn't miss it for the world, and I'm not so sure if she's ever taking that dress off again."

"If I asked her to dance, would it be a bad thing?" he asked.

"It would be the perfect end to her most perfect day.

And save a slow one for me. I may need rescuing. Wiley's on fire today."

Wolf laughed. "At his age, I was just like him."

Sean leaned over in the limo and whispered in Amalie's ear.

"So, Mrs. Pope, how am I doing so far?"

She was so full of happy she was shaking.

"You're always my home-run hitter, Mr. Pope."

"We have the honeymoon suite for the next two days, and then home to the mountain. Whatever should we do with all that time?"

"As long as it has nothing to do with bubble gum or spray paint, I'm your girl."

He chuckled, then put his arm around her and pulled her closer. The trees on the side of the road were just a blur.

Wolfgang Outen had given Liz Caldwell, the event coordinator, one directive. Turn the ballroom of the Serenity Inn into a palace, and he gave her carte blanche to make it happen. With money as no object and all of the technology of modern moviemaking at her disposal, she pulled from Camelot and castles and turned a ballroom into a night of magic.

The dance floor awaited. The room was dimmed but for the lights from the ornate candelabras, filled with hundreds upon hundreds of flameless candlesticks. The walls were draped with tapestries. The tables were adorned with silks. The cups for wine were chalices. Pewter-colored plates awaited food. And in the center of it all, the castle. A monument of cake art and sugar, a beacon as white as snow.

And then the bride and groom came through the door, and the moment they entered the room, they paused in tandem, stunned by the sight before them.

Wolf walked up behind the both of them, his hands on their shoulders.

"I never got to read you fairy stories, and you already found your prince. All I could give you was Camelot." He gestured toward the cake. "Your castle awaits."

Then they saw B.J. at the other end of the room, standing by the cake, and started toward him in total awe.

They looked at B.J. and then at the cake towering above them all—marveling at the size and exquisite detail of every facet of the design.

"Oh, Sean, look what they have given us! If this is Camelot, then B.J. has to be Merlin. This cake is magnificent! The ballroom is magic. Thank you, Dad, for everything!"

Sean was right behind her with praise.

"Wolf, I am at a loss for words. Little brother, you are a master at your craft. Thank you both for making this night so special."

"I have been blessed with a daughter, and now a son. My cup runneth over," Wolf said.

B.J. was beaming. "For me, it was a work of love. Here come the photographers. Everybody smile."

The night became a blur of faces and names, of laughter and tears. The ballroom was packed, the hot and cold buffets constantly being refilled.

Sean led his bride onto the dance floor to share the first dance—the tall man in black, the young woman in white, dipping and swaying in candlelight, head to head, cheek to cheek, heart to heart.

And then the father-daughter dance that brought everyone to tears. What was lost had now been found.

The sight of Ella Pope dancing in Wolfgang Outen's arms, the candlelight dispelling the years and age between them.

Sean dancing with his mother, before his brothers all cut in. He walked off laughing at the turmoil and went to find his bride.

They toasted each other with champagne from chalices and cut the cake with a glimmering sword, revealing yet another layer of magic waiting within.

The faint taste of highbush blackberry jam between one of the layers, and then almond and cherry between another, and then the sweet-sharp tang of lemon custard, and another of vanilla buttercream with fresh grated cinnamon in a sponge so feathery light it melted on the tongue.

The groom's cake was chocolate with a dark chocolate ganache, and the words *Sean and Amalie Forever* written across the surface.

Amalie tossed the bridal bouquet without ever seeing where it went, and in the melee, no one noticed they had disappeared.

The party went on in the ballroom, as Sean was laying Amalie down on a bed of silk.

They made love until they crashed and then rolled up in each other's arms and snuggled close.

Amalie's cheek was on Sean's chest.

She could hear his heartbeat.

The steady *thump-thump* pulse against her ear.

As she was falling asleep, she felt her pulse skip and then pick up to match his own.

Two souls.

One heartbeat.

Forever.

Read on for a sneak peek of
Sharon Sala's next thrilling romance,
LEFT BEHIND

Chapter 1

It was Linette Elgin's day off, and being a nurse, days off rarely came two in a row. This morning she was hustling, getting ready to walk out the door, get all of her errands over with so she could clean her apartment and do laundry later.

The day was already hot, but it was June in Jubilee, Kentucky, which meant if you wanted to stay cool, you either looked for shade or went where there was air conditioning. She had dressed for the weather in old jeans and a light-weight gray T-shirt with the word NO printed in blood red ink as she headed for the elevator. When the doors finally opened, she found herself face-to-face with Cecily Michaels, one of the women who'd rudely interrupted her first date with Wiley Pope.

Cecily looked startled, and then frowned. "What are you doing here?"

"I live here," Linette said, and then saw the shock spreading on Cecily's face and grinned. "Welcome to the neighborhood."

Cecily was horrified that she'd moved into the enemy's camp, and still pissed that Wiley had blocked her calls. So, being the utter bitch that she was, couldn't keep her mouth shut.

"How's Wiley?" she drawled.

Linette pivoted so fast Cecily flinched, and in the sweetest voice, put her in her place.

"Bless your heart, honey. You must be the most miserable little thing to have nothing better to do with your life than interfere in someone else's, so because I am a really nice person, this is just a friendly little warning." Then she leaned forward. "Don't fuck with me."

The elevator stopped. The door opened, and then she was gone.

Cecily was in shock and just a little bit cowed. Every woman in the south knew *bless your heart* was code for *kiss my ass*, and Linette was taller and scarier up close. By the time she gathered herself and got to the parking lot, Linette Elgin was nowhere in sight, and that was just fine with her.

Linette had already forgotten the new neighbor, and was on her way to the bank. Traffic was already getting heavy, which was par for the course in a tourist town like Jubilee, and she was grateful to find a parking place. She was thinking about making meat loaf later when she entered the lobby, and what she needed to get at the supermarket. She had personal business to attend, and sat down in one of the chairs outside the vice president's office to wait her turn. She was reaching for her phone when she heard a sudden commotion at the front entrance.

To her horror, three men came charging into the lobby, wearing surgical masks, waving guns, and shouting. A big heavyset man wearing gray coveralls and a Texas Rangers baseball cap issued the first order.

"Everybody down! Get down on the floor now!"

People started screaming and panicking, and one lady fainted where she stood.

Texas Ranger fired a shot into the ceiling. "Shut the hell up! Next one screams is dead! Belly down on the floor, and don't look up!"

There was a collective gasp, the quick shuffling of feet as people dropped down onto the floor, and then silence.

Linette was horrified. Her phone was in her pocket, but she was belly down and couldn't move. Mr. Trotter, the vice president she'd been waiting to see, wound up lying right beside her. She could hear the rapid, shallow gasps of his breathing, and knew he was as frightened as the rest of them.

Texas Ranger shouted at the two men with him. "Get the money!" Then pointed at the tellers who'd frozen in place behind the plexiglass windows. "All of you! Empty your tills into the bags and no funny business!"

The tellers began cramming the money from their drawers into the bags they'd been given as fast as they could.

One of the gunmen, a short, skinny dude, kept pulling up his pants and dancing from one foot to the other, then trading his gun from right hand to left hand, and back again.

Linette's best guess was that he was high on something, which didn't bode well for any of them.

"Hurry up, bitch!" Skinny Dancer shouted, and pounded his gun on the counter in front of the teller.

Texas Ranger shouted again. "Who's in charge?"

"That would be me," Randall Trotter said, and held up his hand.

"Then get the hell up and open the vault," Texas Ranger ordered.

"Yes sir!" Randall said.

"Be careful," Linette whispered, as they shared a brief look.

Randall was in the act of getting up when Skinny Dancer swung around, saw Randall getting to his feet and shouted, "He told you not to move!"

And shot him in the face.

Randall Trotter was dead before he hit the floor.

More screams, then moans of dismay rolled through the lobby. Linette was in a state of disbelief. Randall's body had fallen across her outstretched arms, pinning her to the floor. She was screaming inside so loud her ears felt numb, but in actuality, she was lying in frozen silence, watching the blood pooling around his head.

"Goddamnit!" Texas Ranger shouted. "What did you do that for? Now how the hell are we gonna get in the vault?"

The third man, who was standing look out at the

entrance, was distracted by the disruption of the killing, and didn't see the cop coming in the door behind him, but Linette did, and this time, her heart nearly stopped.

Jubilee police officer, Wiley Pope, was unaware of the robbery in progress, or that the silent alarm had been activated at the PD, until he entered the lobby. Within a heartbeat, his brain registered the customers in total panic, belly down on the floor with their arms stretched out before them.

The frantic expressions on the teller's faces.

And the three armed men in the act of robbing the bank.

Wiley was already drawing his weapon, when lookout man finally spotted him, yelled "Cop!" and fired off a shot.

Wiley ducked behind a pillar and fired back. Lookout man dropped, and the other two robbers were scrambling, which gave every teller in sight the opportunity to hit the floor below the counters.

The robbers were firing off shots at Wiley as they scrambled for cover, and he returned fire in rapid succession.

Skinny Dancer dropped.

Wiley and Texas Ranger were the last men standing, and a heartbeat later, both aimed and fired.

Texas Ranger's shot hit Wiley's chest and sent him

flying backward, while Wiley's shot ripped through Texas Ranger's shoulder, splattering blood all over the plexiglass window at the tellers' stations behind him.

The silence afterward was as frightening as their entry had been.

The robbers were unconscious, bleeding on the floor, and Wiley was staring up at the ceiling, reeling from the impact, and trying to catch his breath.

All of a sudden people began screaming.

Tellers came running out from behind the counters, and a teenage boy was on the phone calling 911, unaware the silent alarm had already been triggered.

Wiley was still struggling to breathe, and grabbing at his shirt when a woman ran into his line of vision.

Oh my God! Linette!

"Help..." Wiley gasped, trying to unsnap his shirt to get to the bulletproof vest beneath.

Linette was in a panic. From the moment the robbers entered the bank, to when Wiley was shot, every dream she'd ever had for a *happy ever after* life flashed before her eyes. It seemed like a lifetime but it was, in fact, mere seconds. She knew how deadly a chest wound would be, and was up and running toward him when she realized he was tearing at his shirt and struggling to breathe.

Body armor! He was wearing a bulletproof vest! Thank you, God!

Without saying a word, she grabbed at the front of his shirt, knowing the vest that just saved him was now impeding his ability to catch his breath.

Wiley was fighting her, grabbing at her hands, when she grasped his wrists.

"Wiley, don't fight me! Relax. It knocked the breath from your lungs. Relax and it will come."

Even as he was struggling to breathe, her voice, and her face splattered with blood shocked him out of his own panic. Then he realized she was mobile and talking, and he was not, so he leaned back against the pillar and tried not to pass out, as she unsnapped his shirt and began yanking at the Velcro straps to loosen the vest.

His heart was pounding, the room was spinning. It felt like he'd just been hit in the chest with a sledgehammer. And then all of a sudden, the vest was loosened, his lungs inflated, and he was finally able to inhale. The look of gratitude that passed between them was telling.

"I hear sirens," she said. "You're doing great, Wiley. My God, my God, you saved us."

"Check pulses," he mumbled.

Her voice was shaking. "I hope they're dead. All of them. They killed Randall Trotter, and were fighting among themselves when you walked in."

He grabbed her wrist. "Check...please."

She cupped his cheek, then did as he asked, moving from body to body.

"They're alive," she said.

"Shit," Wiley muttered, rolled over onto his hands

and knees, and finally staggered to his feet. His hand was splayed over the center of his chest, afraid to move it for fear he'd fall apart, while he waited for the room to stop spinning. Once he could breathe and stand up at the same time, he reached for his radio.

"Officer Pope reporting. Attempted robbery at Jubilee bank. One bank employee dead. Three perps down, but still have pulses. I took a shot in the chest. Suggest haste."

Aaron Pope was on patrol when dispatch notified them of a silent alarm at the bank. As they were responding, they also heard Wiley radio in.

"Holy shit," Officer Yancy said, giving his partner, Aaron, a quick glance.

Aaron's gut was in a knot. "At least he's alive and conscious enough to make the call."

But inside the bank, Wiley was already in containment mode, trying to get everyone away from the perps without passing out in front of them.

"What do you need? I'll do it," Linette asked.

"Move the customers to the front of the lobby."

Linette turned around and began issuing his orders, loudly and firmly.

"Can we leave?" one man asked.

"Nobody leaves," Wiley mumbled, then doubled over as a wave of pain rolled through him. He needed to get the weapons contained, but he couldn't bend over for the pain.

Linette slid her arm beneath his shoulder to steady him, and was moving him toward a chair, when the police began pouring into the lobby to contain the scene. Once they had retrieved the weapons, they gave the all clear to the EMTs. After that, Rescue moved inside in teams, and did what they did, readying the wounded for transport.

Aaron came in running, headed straight to Wiley, and then knelt beside his chair. "Damnit, brother, are you okay?"

Linette recognized him. "Your brother was our hero. He took a bullet in the chest. The body armor stopped it, but he's hurting. Steady him. He's dizzy. I'm going to get an ambulance for him." Then she passed him off to Aaron without another word and ran.

"What happened?" Aaron asked, as he slipped his arm beneath Wiley's shoulder.

"They killed Trotter before I got here," Wiley said, holding his hand against his chest. "Body armor saved me. Feel like I've been hit with a sledgehammer. Can't breathe. Sick to my stomach. Perps still have a pulse."

"Stop talking, buddy," Aaron said. "We'll figure it out," and started walking Wiley toward the door.

At that point, Linette sped back into the lobby. "The first ambulances are here. Walk him out. They're waiting to take him to ER. I'm staying here to help."

Wiley started to thank her, but she was already gone.

Aaron helped him out of the bank, and loaded him up into the back of an ambulance.

"Don't tell Mom. She'll fuss," Wiley said.

"You don't get to choose," Aaron said. "She'll kill the both of us if I don't. I'll get there as soon as I can," he said, then stepped back as they closed the doors and took off to the hospital. At that point, he called home.

Shirley was mopping the kitchen floor when her cell phone rang. She saw Aaron's name on the caller ID, leaned the mop against the wall, wiped her hands, and then answered.

"Hello, honey. You caught me in the middle of mopping. What's up?"

"There was an attempted robbery at the bank. Wiley walked in on it. He's okay, but on the way to ER. He was wearing his body armor, but took a bullet in the chest. It never penetrated, but he's hurting. Just wanted you to know."

"Oh my God," Shirley said. "What about the bank robbers?"

"He took down all three of them, but they'd killed Mr. Trotter before he got there. The perps were all still alive when we got to the bank, and in the process of being transported to ER. I've got to go."

"I'm leaving now," she said. "Thank you for calling me. He wasn't going too, was he?"

Aaron chuckled. "What do you think?"

Shirley sighed. "Right. Does B.J. know?"

"Not yet, but I'm calling him next," Aaron said, and disconnected.

At that point, Shirley dropped her phone in her pocket and took off through the house to Sean's office while Aaron was calling their youngest brother. He was the head pastry chef at the restaurant in The Serenity Inn, and most likely elbow deep in sugar and flour, but he had to let him know.

As Aaron predicted, B.J. was in the hotel kitchen when his cell phone rang. He started to let it go to voicemail, and then noticed it was from Aaron, and stepped out into a hallway to answer.

"Hey, Aaron. What's up?" he asked.

Aaron repeated everything he'd just told their mom.

B.J. was stunned. "He shot all three of them? Are they dead?"

"No. They were all still breathing when they transported them."

"Is he conscious?" B.J. asked.

"Yes, and talking once he was able to breathe again."

B.J.'s eyes welled. "All this shit was happening while I was baking bread."

"And I was sitting in a police car on patrol. And Mom was mopping the floor, and Sean is likely in his office, and that's how life works. Don't go there. We live our lives by our choices until we're done. Wiley is damn good at what he does. He saved a bunch of lives today, okay?"

B.J. took a breath. "Yes, okay. It's just overwhelming to

think about. I'm not sure if I can get away. I'll call Mom first and if he's in trouble, I'll be there. Thank you for letting me know."

"Of course. Just take a breath for Wiley, and one for yourself. I'm sure he's okay. I walked him out to the ambulance myself."

"Right," B.J. said, but the moment he disconnected, he called his mom.

Within minutes of receiving the message, Sean and Shirley were in the car and heading into Jubilee, with Sean behind the wheel, and Shirley riding shotgun. They'd barely left the driveway when her phone rang. She glanced at the caller ID, and then answered.

"Hello, honey."

B.J. was shaking inside, but trying to hold it together. "Aaron just told me what happened. I'm not sure I can get away without bringing the whole pastry line to a halt. Will you tell Wiley I'm saying prayers, and let me know if he's not okay?"

"Of course. Sean and I are already on the way into Jubilee. Wiley was wearing his bulletproof vest. He'll be bruised and hurting, but I'm sure he's going to be fine. I'll keep you updated, okay?"

"Yes, okay. Love you," B.J. said.

"We love you, too. Go back to work, and I'll call you when I know details."

"Thanks," he said, then hung up and hurried back into the kitchen, waved at three of his sous chefs, and pointed at the timer. "Get the pans ready. The rye dough is on its last proofing. And this time, remember to braid the loaves before you set them to rise. The dough for the baguettes is also ready, and for the love of God, delicate cuts, delicate cuts, on the baguettes this time. Last time they looked like they'd been run through a guillotine. I want them as perfect as that diamond in your fiancée's engagement ring, understand?"

"Yes, Chef!" they all echoed, and jumped to obey, while B.J. fretted that he was here, and not there with the rest of his family.

By the time the ER staff had Wiley's upper body devoid of clothes, the contusion on his chest was turning a deep shade of purple, and they were moving in a portable x-ray to check for broken bones, followed by a CT scan to check for internal bleeding.

Blood tests on the wounded men revealed high contents of meth, which explained the manic behavior they'd exhibited. They were all still alive as they were being taken to surgery, and if they survived, they would be moved to a prison ward for recovery, then to court to face charges of attempted bank robbery, murder, and the attempted murder of a law officer. They were going nowhere fast, and the coroner was on his way to Jubilee, while outside the bank, officers were stringing crime scene tape across the sidewalk.

Sean and Shirley Pope walked into ER and straight to Wiley's exam room. His chest was bare, revealing the dark purple contusion. They'd raised the head of the bed to make breathing easier, and police chief Sonny Warren was with him as they entered.

When Sonny saw Wiley's family walk in, he waved them over.

"Shirley. Sean. I was just commending Wiley for the body armor. He's going to be miserable for a few days and will need to rest. He'll also be off duty until the doctor releases him."

Shirley nodded, then walked straight to Wiley's bedside, kissed his cheek, then eyed the spreading bruise in the middle of his chest. But for the vest, and the grace of God, he could have died today.

Wiley patted Shirley's arm. "I'm okay, Mom. Just a cracked rib, and a bruise that hurts like hell, but as you always say, 'this too, shall pass.'"

Shirley cupped his cheek. "I honor you and the job you chose, and I'm so grateful you're okay."

"You and me both," Wiley said, then grinned at Sean. "So, I had to get shot to get you out of your cave?"

Sean grinned. "I had no idea you were yearning for company, considering all those women you have on speed dial."

Wiley frowned. "They've been blocked."

Shirley's eyes widened. Something had happened, but now was not the time to ask.

Sonny Warren decided it was time to make an exit. "They're getting his release papers ready. I am assuming you will take Wiley home. Wiley, we'll get your patrol car back to the lot and your personal car back to your house. Consider yourself clocked out until further notice, and take care of yourself, Pope. I don't want to lose you."

"Thanks, Chief," Wiley said.

Moments later, Sean's wife, Amalie, appeared, wild-eyed and breathless as she hugged Sean, then hurried to Wiley's bedside. There were tears in her eyes and her voice was trembling. The bruising on his chest was shocking and the pain in his eyes was visible.

"Wiley, honey! I heard gunshots from my office. I didn't know until then that the bank was being robbed. I didn't know you were in the middle of it. Then they wouldn't let any of us out of the building until they'd cleared it for accomplices. I'm so sorry you were hurt. What can we do to help?"

Wiley patted her hand. "I'll be okay, but thanks for caring. I am one lucky dude. I have the best family."

"Do you want to come home with us for a few days?" Shirley asked. "At least until you're a little more comfortable?"

"I'll be okay, Mom, but thank you for the invitation. However, I won't say no to receiving home cooking you care to share."

Shirley smiled. "That I will gladly do."

A short while later, Wiley was waiting for his release papers when Linette appeared in his doorway.

"Hey you! Come talk to me," he said.

She hesitated, eyeing the family around him, then slipped past them to get to his bed.

"What's the verdict?" she asked.

"Cracked rib. Big ass bruise. They're getting the paperwork ready to sign me out." Then he reached for her hand. "Thank you for everything. You are one cool lady under fire. Please tell me none of that blood is yours."

She glanced down at the gray shirt with the big red NO, and realized the word was a good statement for the hell they'd lived through.

"It's not mine. It's Mr. Trotter's."

Wiley frowned. "I'm so sorry. And this isn't how I imagined introducing you to my family, but you already know my brothers. This is my Mom, Shirley Pope. Mom, this is Linette Elgin. She was in the bank, and the first one I saw coming toward me after I was shot."

Linette smiled at Shirley. "We've met. I was Sean's nurse when he was shot."

"Oh yes! I remember," Shirley said. "And here you are again, helping another one of my sons. We are so grateful."

"We're the ones who are grateful," Linette said. "He saved our lives." Then she realized Wiley was still holding her hand, and gave it a squeeze before turning loose.

"I should go. I just wanted to make sure you were okay before I went home. Take care of yourself."

And then she was gone.

Wiley sighed. Other than the bank, this was the first time she'd even spoken to him since their disastrous first date a year ago, and with family all over the place, he couldn't say what he wanted to say.

And then a nurse came in with his release papers, followed by an orderly with a wheelchair, and he was on his way home.

About the Author

New York Times and *USA Today* bestselling author Sharon Sala has more than 135 books in print published in six different genres—romance, young adult, western, general fiction, women's fiction, and nonfiction. First published in 1991, her industry awards include the Janet Dailey Award, five Career Achievement awards, five National Readers' Choice Awards, five Colorado Romance Writers' Awards of Excellence, the Heart of Excellence Award, the Booksellers' Best Award, the Nora Roberts Lifetime Achievement Award, and the Centennial Award in recognition of her 100th published novel. She lives in Oklahoma, the state where she was born.

Website: sharonsalaauthor.com
Facebook: SharonKaySala_
Instagram: @sharonkaysala_

Also by Sharon Sala

The Next Best Day

Don't Back Down

Last Rites

Blessings, Georgia
Count Your Blessings (novella)
You and Only You
I'll Stand by You
Saving Jake
A Piece of My Heart
The Color of Love
Come Back to Me
Forever My Hero
A Rainbow above Us
The Way Back to You
Once in a Blue Moon
Somebody to Love
The Christmas Wish
The Best of Me